THE AUCTION SERIES

Formatting and Interior Design by Bella Media Management.

First Pink Zebra Publishing Paperback Edition

13 Digit ISBN: 13: 978-1480247048

THE AUCTION SERIES

JAYMIE HOLLAND

PINK ZEBRA PUBLISHING
SCOTTSDALE, ARIZONA

Contents

Sold

Chapter 1

"I found a Navy SEAL I want to bid on." Leslie held her wine glass to her lips as she looked across the room where the pre-auction wine tasting was happening. The small gold triangle pin, signifying she was one of those here with ulterior motives, sparkled in the lighting. "Watch. I'll get him."

Christy set her glass on a table as she followed Leslie's gaze to see the drop-dead gorgeous man. She'd noticed the SEAL bachelor in the charity auction's program and he was enough to make a woman's blood run hot. "He's not wearing a pin."

"Neither are you." Roni, her other close friend, elbowed her in the side. "You need to put yours on."

Christy bit the inside of her lip before continuing. "I've never done this kind of thing before." She'd wanted to, had even been excited about coming tonight. But now she was being a big chicken. Without her pin, she'd probably end up with some nice, boring, vanilla guy. So why didn't she want to put on her little circle pin?

The red corsage on the shoulder of her black sequined evening dress was to indicate that she was one of the bachelorettes. The men with red boutonnieres were the bachelors.

Everyone here who had an ornate triangle pin or a beautifully styled circle pin belonged to a special club of people who enjoyed a certain BDSM kink—K-Club, or KC as members liked to call it. A circle pin meant the wearer was a submissive, the triangle meant a Dominant.

Christy wrapped a strand of her long dark hair around her finger, a nervous habit she'd had since she was a child. It was something she still did despite being a confident, successful businesswoman. "Being auctioned off to the highest bidder…" She looked at Roni. "This is all your fault."

"I accept full responsibility." Roni looked stunning with her gorgeous red hair and her barely-there little black dress. Her own circle pin, which she wore proudly, winked in the lighting. "I see some hot buyers on the floor. The mystery, the excitement of it all… I can't wait."

Christy loved Roni. She was curvy in the all the right places and her look combined with her personality seemed to draw men in. She dressed to compliment her abundant assets. She had an "if you've got it, flaunt it" attitude and she had a confidence about her that she could get any man she wanted. She was right more often than not.

"This event fits you both perfectly." The knot in Christy's stomach grew tighter. "Me, on the other hand…I think not."

Because I'm a big fat chicken.

Leslie touched her hand to her white-blonde hair that was swept up in an elegant knot. She was stunning, sophisticated, and elegant. She wore a silver metallic evening dress that complimented her pale beauty. If she wasn't such an amazing friend, Christy might have felt overshadowed by her. But that wasn't Leslie's style.

She smiled at Christy as she said, "Relax. You're going to have fun."

"I hope you're right." Christy took in the glitter and beauty of the night. Women in evening dresses, men in expensive suits. Only the elite had been invited to this auction where the bidding would get well into the thousands since it all went for a great cause. The entire room sparkled from the crystal chandeliers to the champagne and wine glasses to the diamonds and sequins women were wearing, to the pins on about half of those in attendance.

Somehow Leslie and Roni's club had become involved with the auction with the plan to make it a high-level auction for those who were a part of a special community that enjoyed a BDSM lifestyle.

"Yes, that SEAL is mine," Leslie was saying to Roni. "I've already imagined a few things I would like to do with a man like that."

"Not all men like what you like, Leslie." Roni said with a grin. "SEALs are extremely alpha. If you do win him, I don't think it's going to be easy making him your boy toy."

"What fun is easy?" Leslie said. "I will just have to explore the possibilities. I have turned a few tough ones, you know. I have my technique." The devious smile matched her sparkling eyes, a look that Christy always found amusing. "This is a perfect venue for the start of the ideal time together. A quasi-slave auction." Yes, Leslie was beautiful, sophisticated, and wealthy...and she loved to ensnare men in her traps. Literally.

"You are over the top, Leslie. I think I'm glad that you don't like women." Christy said.

"Don't speak too soon... When the light hits you just right." Leslie had up her hands in a rectangle as if framing Christy in it.

Leslie was so fun and Christy knew her friend too well to know she wouldn't spend time with a woman.

"Funny you, Leslie," Christy said with a smile.

Leslie looked around the room. "So many hot men here tonight to bid on, but I need to meet that SEAL and see if he's a candidate for my proclivities. If he is, a weekend away with someone like that would be perfect."

"Yes." Christy's insides fluttered and she held her palm to her belly. "The weekend at the resort does actually sound nice."

A tall, almost intimidating man came up to them. He looked like he did some major working out, had a goatee, and was bald—a seriously sexy bald man—and he wore a triangle pin. "Hello, ladies."

"Well hello, Garth." Leslie went up to the man, a seductive look on her features. "Have you changed your mind? I would love to have a little time alone with you."

Garth laughed. "Only if that alone time involves you on your knees, Les."

Leslie gave him a little pout. "You know I love them strong... And at the end of a leash. You wouldn't do that for me?"

"Not for a moment." He smiled at Roni. "Good to see you here, Veronica."

"Wouldn't miss it." She smiled and touched Christy's shoulder. "This is our friend, Christy Clarkson." She turned to Garth. "And this is Garth Mason, one of our board members."

"A pleasure to meet you." The big man took her hand and his grip was firm as he greeted her. "No pin?"

Her face heated. "Not tonight."

"She's a little bashful right now," Leslie said.

"Too bad." His eyes held sensual meaning. "I think I'd be doing some bidding."

Christy's face grew hotter and he winked at her. She decided to change the subject in a hurry. "I'm a little confused on how this all came together."

"The Uptown Charity has put on this auction for the last five years," Leslie said. "Garth is on the board and he is also a part of KC."

Roni nodded. "The charity needed more participants for the auction so Garth thought it would be a great idea to quietly put the word out to the kink players to participate in a high-level auction. A number of kinksters from KC have been discreetly incorporated into the auction for charity."

"He said nothing to the charity board, of course," Leslie said. "He privately approved any participants so that he would know they would be safe. So the charity board isn't aware of our group's participation."

Roni tucked a stray lock of red hair behind her ear. "We could help a good cause while having a little fun at the same time." She touched the circle pin on her dress. "It was Garth's idea of giving these pins to club members so that we could recognize each other. Not everyone goes to all of the meetings."

"And everyone who doesn't have a pin is a vanilla." Christy nodded in understanding. "Vanilla meaning they're not into kink."

"KC members can choose to wear the pin or not," Garth said. "There are a few who are too discreet to wear them. The pins are meant to help each of us ID each other for those who choose to wear them." Garth gestured to Christy. "I am pretty good at reading people. Let me guess, you have a circle pin with you."

A hot flush swept over Christy. She hurried to avoid the question. "But people in the club can still bid on vanillas."

"As long as they understand the rules. It's all about consensual," Garth said.

"We're supposed to mingle." Leslie smiled and set her wine glass on a server's tray. "I intend to do some serious mingling."

"I bet you do," Christy said with amusement.

"Go get him, girl," Roni said.

Garth shook his head. "Be easy on the vanillas tonight, Les."

"Now what would be the fun in that?" Leslie gave a sensual smile. "See you later, ladies. Gentleman," she added before turning and moving gracefully through the crowd, in the direction of the SEAL.

Christy looked at Roni who said, "The guy won't know what hit him."

With a smile, Christy said, "So true."

Garth was still looking in the direction Leslie had disappeared in the crowd. "Someone seriously needs to give that woman a spanking."

"I'd love to see the man who could do it." Roni grinned. "I really, really would."

"I need to move on and talk with some of the other buyers and bidders." He touched his triangle pin. "Make sure everyone is ready."

Christy smiled. This guy was friendly but had such an intimidating presence about him. He would scare her to death if he bought her tonight. But she said, "It was nice to meet you."

"See you later, Garth," Roni said.

He gave each of them a nod before turning and walking into the crowd.

"Isn't he hot?" Roni pointed to Christy's purse. "You really should dig out that pin. If Garth wasn't like a big brother to me, I'd be all over him. You would get quite the introduction to our kind of fun if he bought you."

Christy swallowed at the thought of being that big man's sub. "I don't think so."

Roni gestured around the room. "There are some hi-profile bidders from K-Club who have been involved with members of The Uptown Charity and are wearing pins. A couple of congressmen, a senator, and other politicians from the D.C. area."

"They're into it—bondage?" Christy asked.

"Oh, yes or at least some form of dominance or power exchange as we call it." Roni lowered her voice. "KC is a very elite group kept highly secret. There are different levels of the group due to discretion. I would not have known about some elite parties for the members if I had not been invited into KC. That includes exclusive private dungeons, and the like."

"How did you become involved?" Christy asked, but figured she knew the answer as she added, "The congressman you dated."

"That's right." Roni rolled her eyes. "That's one thing I can thank him for. Other than that, he was just a selfish, egotistical SOB."

Christy laughed. "So even after he got booted out of office, you kept coming to the club."

Roni nodded and swept her gaze around the room. "Not long until we each go to the highest bidder."

Christy took a deep breath. "Not long at all."

"Try the pin, Christy," Roni said. "Everything is safe. Board members have screened the participants and Garth knows everyone from KC. It's a class act."

Christy looked around the room. Why stick with vanilla when she could have so much more?

Because I really am a big chicken.

"The pampering is going to be amazing. You can have a facial and massages at the resort, not to mention the wonderful dinners out." Roni gave Christy a quick hug. "You'll have fun. Promise."

"A little pampering does sound good," Christy said. And maybe some fun that didn't involve a relationship outside of playing around. After Ted had cheated on her… She wasn't ready to jump into another serious or exclusive relationship. She would really have to trust the next man she gave her heart to and know that he wouldn't hurt her.

Roni handed Christy her drink she had set on the table. "You never know what you might find out there."

Christy smiled at her always-enthusiastic friend. "I suppose you're right. We should follow Leslie's lead and do the mingling thing."

"Oooh, this is going to be fun." Roni pushed her bouncy red curls behind her ear. "I'm ready."

Christy took a deep breath. "Here we go."

Chapter 2

Christy smoothed her short black sequined dress as she looked at the crowd. Then she raised her chin and headed into the mix. She put on a smile, doing her best to look elegant and appealing to prospective bidders. Normally she sold trinkets in her boutique but this time she was selling herself.

She nodded at people she knew and she smiled, doing her best to act natural. She put her hand up to the red corsage and took a deep breath, telling herself she was ready for anything. Maybe she should put on the little circle pin. After all, wasn't that why she was here? She'd been excited, thinking of being bid on by someone who was into BDSM.

Yes, she should put on the pin, but she just couldn't bring herself to do it.

A man touched her elbow and caught her attention. He was several inches taller than her, had an adorably boyish smile and baby blue eyes, and he wore a white boutonniere, indicating he was a bidder.

No gold pin.

A dimple appeared in his cheek. "I'm Jeff."

She held out her hand and he took it. "Christy."

"I saw you in the program." He released her hand. "You're even more beautiful in person."

Pleasant warmth went through her as he paid her the compliment. He said it so genuinely that it would be difficult to not take him seriously.

"Thank you, Jeff." She started to ask him a question about himself when another man joined them. Another man with no pin.

"Larry Schmidt." He shook hands with her and then with Jeff. Larry had a little bit of a receding hairline, but he had the air of a playboy to him. He looked like he'd be fun for a weekend. Not the kind of guy to write home about, just pure fun—if you didn't mind his eyes wandering to every pretty girl who walked by. Which he was doing even as he spoke.

Amused, she said, "I'm Christy."

"I know you are." Larry held up the program. "This is my little black book for the evening. A sexy brown-eyed brunette with a cute figure—you're at the top of the list."

"Looks like there will be some competition." Jeff smiled at Christy again. "Hope to see you later."

"Not possible." Larry shook his head. "Christy will be mine."

The two men started arguing in good humor over who would win Christy. She'd never been fought over by anyone. Did this count?

The more the men talked, the more she realized she didn't want to be won by some vanilla guy. They couldn't give her what she really wanted.

She reached into her purse and pulled out the circle pin. She pinned it on her dress, beside her corsage then straightened her spine and raised her chin. Now she was ready for the real fun to begin.

A groan rose up within her and she had to fight it down as she glanced away from the two men and saw the CEO of one of her major suppliers, Henry Hawthorne. She'd had no idea he would be here tonight or she might have backed out of the whole thing. He'd been trying to get her to date him for years. And if he wanted to bid on her, he had the money to make sure he would win.

The heavyset man pushed his thick black glasses up his nose. Using his bulk, he bumped other guests out of his way as he headed in her direction.

Not Henry. Please not Henry.

She wanted to put her face in her hands and hide like a toddler who thinks that if he can't see you, you can't see him.

She looked at Jeff and Larry as if they might rescue her, but they were now embroiled in a conversation about the upcoming World Series playoffs. Baltimore was in this year, playing the Yankees, and from what she could tell by the tiny bit of conversation she overheard that Jeff was a diehard Orioles fan, and Larry a Yankees fan.

She didn't stand a chance now.

Ladies room. She searched in vain with her gaze, praying she could make her escape. Where's the ladies room?

"Christy." Henry reached her, his cologne about knocking her over. His suit stretched across his hefty form, straining at the buttons.

He was wearing a triangle pin.

And she had just put on hers. The last thing she needed was for him to know that she was with the "kink set."

Too late for that.

She tried not to be stiff as she said, "Hi, Henry."

He took her hand in his fat one. "When I heard you were going to be here tonight, I had to come." He looked at her pin. His eyes glistened with excitement. "And to find out you're a member of the club. Very exciting." He seemed to get a good look at Christy's expression. "Don't worry. The nice thing about our interests is that we don't go around telling people about them or other people we know in the lifestyle. And you a submissive, no less. We seem to be a match."

Christy felt ill but worked up a smile and tried unsuccessfully to draw her hand from his. "I'm not in the life—"

He cut her off as he squeezed her hand harder and she winced. "Looks like I'll get that date after all. You've been playing hard to get for far too long. Tonight will settle it."

She took a deep breath, trying to think of someway to politely put him off as she managed to pull her hand from his. "Henry—"

"Christy?" A masculine voice came from behind her. A familiar voice.

A thrill caused her to shiver from head to toe as she turned and faced Zach Nikas. Eight years ago she had left him… And had regretted it long after.

Their gazes met and held and she didn't think she would ever be able to breathe again. He was as magnificent as he'd been when they had dated, maybe more so. His black eyes were as intense as ever and his black hair gleamed in the light from the chandeliers. His olive complexion and the cut of his features reflected his Grecian ancestry. His suit fit perfectly on his tall, muscular form and his sexy smile made her toes curl.

Seeing him brought a wave of memories that started with the amazing times they had spent together and ended with the reason why she'd broken up with him. She'd thought about him so many times since then and a part of her had thought about what it might be like if they had a second chance. Now that she had a better feel for the part of him that she hadn't understood back then, she wondered if things would be different if they had stayed together. But they had each moved on with their lives, end of story.

Yet here he was, larger than life.

"Zach." Her throat was so dry that she barely managed to get his name out.

The magnetism that had drawn them together the first time was just as strong now as it had been then. Maybe stronger. She felt electrified just being near him. "It's so good to see you."

"I was thinking the same thing." His smile was sending her heart into overdrive.

Henry cleared his throat. "Excuse me," he said, jerking her out of her Zach-induced trance. He sounded irritated. "Ms. Clarkson and I were just speaking together. Do you mind?"

She cut her gaze to Henry. She had forgotten about him but could not believe how rude he had just been. He was glaring in Zach's direction and she turned her attention back to him.

With a slight bow of his head, Zach said to Christy, "A pleasure seeing you again." He started to turn away.

"Wait." She placed her hand on his arm. "Give me a moment. I want to talk to you."

"I'll be at the bar getting another glass of wine." He smiled but she could tell he wasn't pleased by how rude Henry had been. "Can I get you anything?"

"Yes." Christy moved her hand away. "A chardonnay, please."

He met her gaze for one long moment then and then gave Henry a nod and walked away.

When Zach left, she turned back to Henry. He looked a little put-off but then he smiled. "I suppose we'll have plenty of time together once I buy you at the auction." He bowed. "Until then."

Another sick feeling traveled through her belly as she watched him wade through the crowd and then she couldn't see him anymore. Being forced to spend an entire weekend with Henry—she couldn't imagine anything worse as an outcome to this auction.

Is it too late to back out now?

She glanced at Larry and Jeff who were oblivious to what was going on and she mentally sighed. They were vanilla, not what she truly wanted. But being with one of them was a far better prospect than being with Henry.

When she faced the direction of the bar she saw Zach talking with a couple of women with red corsages…and they each had a gold circle pin, meaning they were submissives, and their corsages told her they were up for auction.

She sucked in her breath. Zach had a triangle pin, a Dom's pin. She hadn't even noticed it before. But he wasn't wearing a white boutonniere, so he wasn't a bidder.

He smiled and laughed at something one of the women said. Then he turned his head and met Christy's gaze. Her heart seemed to stop. It was like the very first time she'd seen him, all over again.

Electrifying.

He excused himself from the other women, who looked disappointed, and he came toward her, carrying two glasses of white wine. When he reached her she caught his clean, masculine scent. Thoughts of what it had been like making love to him rushed through her mind. It had been nothing short of amazing.

What would have happened if she hadn't freaked out and bolted?

"Your friend?" Zach's gaze flickered in the direction Henry had gone.

"Not exactly." She held back another groan as Zach pulled out a chair for her at a small table. "Henry's the CEO of one of my suppliers. He's had a thing for me and he doesn't know what the word 'No' means." She sat and Zach pushed the chair in before taking his own seat.

Zach's gaze slowly traveled over her as if he wanted to memorize every curve of her body. "What man wouldn't want you that badly?"

Fire seared her through and through and her cheeks heated.

When his eyes met hers again, he studied her for a long moment and the corner of his mouth curved. "Christy Clarkson. You've changed."

More heat flooded her as he gestured to her pin. "Maybe a little," she said.

"I seem to remember something about this lifestyle…upsetting you," he said. "And now you're here."

"I came with friends." She rushed her words. "This is my first time."

He nodded, looking at her thoughtfully.

"How have you been?" she said, her words soft amidst the murmur of conversation around them.

He gave a little smile and it seemed like there was something more in his words when he spoke. "I've missed you."

"I've missed you, too." She bit her lower lip. "And I've thought about you a lot."

He smiled. "I would have welcomed a friendship at least."

"I know you would have," she said.

He looked at her with that crooked smile that she'd always loved. "You didn't want any part of even a friendship then. You thought I was some guy with a psychotic hidden life. And here you are sitting with me now. Do you feel safe since we aren't alone?"

He always loved to tease me, she thought. He hasn't changed.

She teased him back. "I am not too worried about you in a room like this."

He glanced at her pin. "Something tells me it wouldn't freak you out now."

She glanced down at her hands that were folded in her lap. "You would be surprised to know," she said, "that I've thought about being alone with you a lot since we split up and—"

"After you left me," he corrected.

"Okay, you made your point." She offered him a smile. "I was saying, I have thought about you a lot since I left. I couldn't get my thoughts off you and that part of you I ran from."

She couldn't believe she was actually telling him all of this, but she couldn't help herself. She'd regretted leaving him. His interest had caused her to research and understand him better. The more she looked into it, the more regret she'd had.

"You never called." He leaned back in his chair. "What part of you was intrigued by the bad boy side, but couldn't bring yourself to come back to me? You just didn't feel safe, did you," he stated.

"I almost called a hundred times." She gripped her wine glass. "But, you jumped into a relationship with Brittany Larson right away. I figured it would not last long, and then two years later you were engaged to her. At that point, I wasn't going to call and tell you I couldn't stop thinking about you."

"I wished I'd have known." His dark eyes had a seriousness about them. "I would have called. Brittany was nice, but she wasn't you."

Thoughts of Zach with Brittany made her heart hurt. "I imagine she was into that stuff with you."

"I think she put up with it," he said. "She loved me and knew 'that stuff' was part of the package deal. I love introducing people who haven't tried it, bringing them along slowly, and watching them get into it. With her, it never quite worked. It isn't the same when the other person doesn't share the same passion."

"So, you are still into it?" She asked, then realized it was a dumb question. While talking with him she'd fallen back in time and forgot where she was and the fact that he was wearing one of the pins.

He gave her that crooked smile again. "Probably more now than at that time. I won't change."

She moved her fingers up and down the stem of her wine glass. "It isn't something you hear about every day."

"It can make a relationship challenging." He picked up his wine glass and swirled the golden liquid. "It's hard enough to have regular every day interests match up. When you add that certain component to a relationship…well, lets just say some pretty special ladies, like yourself can get eliminated, or eliminate themselves."

She leaned forward and put meaning behind her words. "I don't want to be in the eliminated category anymore, Zach Nikas."

His intent gaze took her in. "How did you end up here?"

She settled back in her seat. "It took some time, but I got over being freaked out by what I saw—the pictures of the women you had on your computer." She swallowed, not sure she should be spilling everything like this. "I started to look at all of that stuff online."

He looked intrigued. "And?"

"The more I read and looked at it, the more I liked it and I thought about you. It gave me a better understanding of all of it and what you like and why." She glanced down then back at him. "It actually drew me more to you. By then, like I said, you were involved with Brittany and I didn't know what happened to you after that."

He continued to study her, like he was trying to figure her out. "You're here, but it doesn't sound like you've actually tried it."

"Only in my mind… Every night before I fall asleep." Warmth traveled through her at the thoughts of her fantasies. "I haven't had anyone to try it with." She shook her head. "I can't believe I am telling you this."

He leaned closer. "I had a feeling you had it in you. The way it happened was a bad introduction, finding the pictures and some of the equipment. It was too much before you were ready to know about it."

Zach studied her. "Take off the pin."

"Why—?" she started. For some reason the look in his eyes had her taking off her pin without question.

A voice came over the sound system. She looked in the direction of the podium where Garth stood with a microphone.

"Ladies and gentlemen, please join us in the ballroom," he said. "The auction is about to start. Bachelors and bachelorettes, please meet behind the stage. Everyone else find a seat and we'll get started."

"We were supposed to mingle with bidders." She returned her gaze to Zach. "I only met a couple of men. I didn't think they would start so quickly."

"I arrived early and talked with a lot of people," he said. "Interesting what you can learn about people in just a short conversation with them."

"That's true," she said before looking toward the door leading into the ballroom.

The low murmur of the crowd grew a little louder as everyone migrated.

Her stomach twisted. She had to face the fact that she might end up being with Henry at a resort for a whole forty-eight hours. Even though she would have her own room, she wouldn't be surprised if he tried to push himself on her for more than just a weekend in each other's company. It would not be pretty if he tried.

Would those other two men bid on her? Would they be willing to bid more than whatever Henry had planned?

Unless Zach would bid on her...but he didn't have on a boutonniere She would be happy to give him whatever it cost, although it could possibly break the bank.

She turned to face him with a proposition on her tongue.

He was gone.

Chapter 3

Christy's heart pounded as she waited to be called on stage, her escort at her side. She was the last one to be auctioned off and the crowd had started to thin. Habit and her nerves had her twirling a lock of hair with her finger.

Earlier, Leslie had won the bidding for the Navy SEAL and was nowhere to be seen. Roni had been snagged by a man who looked sexy in a primal way… almost dangerously so. Christy only hoped her friend wasn't getting in over her head and would be safe. But then Roni had told her that this was a safe, vetted crowd.

She peeked through the draperies and saw Henry in the first row wearing a smug expression. She did groan out loud this time.

One of the two men she'd met earlier, Jeff, sat in the third row. She had kept an eye on him and Larry, hoping one of them would outbid Henry. Larry was out of the picture now since he had already left with a stunning model-beautiful blonde. The fact that he hadn't waited for her and had chosen someone gorgeous, hadn't surprised Christy in the least.

She wished in the worst way that Zach was a bidder, but since he wasn't wearing a white boutonniere, she knew he wasn't. It was a small consolation that he hadn't had a red carnation pinned to his chest that would tell the women that he was up for auction.

But if he wasn't a bidder, and he was wearing a gold pin, what was he doing here? Maybe he *was* a bidder.

She looked around for him but couldn't see him.

Even if he wasn't a bidder, he was the one she wanted. It was a weekend only with one of these guys. She wanted more than a weekend with Zach.

Earlier Zach had been in the third row from the back. Throughout the night she had watched people in the audience and mentally notated which individuals purchased a bachelorette or a bachelor.

"Christy Clarkson!"

Her stomach pitched as she fixed a smile on her face and stepped onto the stage. Her escort led her toward center stage and she waved to the audience—what was left of it—and continued to where the MC waited.

"Christy is the owner of Baubles and Beads, a boutique in downtown Baltimore." The MC made a circle with his finger, Christy's cue to turn around. "One of you lucky men will spend a weekend with Christy at an Arizona resort."

Light applause was followed by the MC stepping back and the auctioneer saying, "Take home Christy. Let's start the bidding at fifteen hundred dollars."

Surprise almost made her drop her jaw but she managed to remain poised. He had started the bidding out higher than what he had for everyone before her, which was the minimum bid of one thousand.

It was no surprise, however, when Henry raised his hand, indicating his bid. To her relief, Jeff immediately bid against Henry.

She bit the inside of her lip as the biding went back and forth and her eyes widened the higher it went until it reached eight thousand dollars.

Henry was the highest bidder. When the auctioneer said, "Do I hear nine thousand dollars?" he looked to Jeff who shook his head.

Christy wanted to hide. Not Henry, not Henry…

"Going once, going—" The auctioneer gestured toward the back.

A familiar voice called out from the back. "Ten thousand."

Zach.

This time her jaw did drop from shock as she saw his tall form at the back of the room. She couldn't believe that he had just bid on her. He wasn't one of the bidders. And he bid such an enormous amount of money for her.

Henry was looking over his shoulder, scowling, as he stared at Zach.

"Eleven," Henry called out.

"Twelve," Zach said, his voice remaining calm.

Unlike Henry who shouted, "Thirteen!" His features had started to turn purple.

"Twenty." Zach calmly jumped to the higher amount and Henry's eyes nearly bugged out.

Christy wasn't sure if she was going to be able to stand as weak as her knees were at that moment. This was crazy.

"Do I hear twenty-one?" The moment the auctioneer looked at Henry seemed to draw out forever.

Henry folded his arms across his chest and scowled. "Let him have her. I'm done."

"Twenty going once, twice—sold to Mr. Zach Nikas."

Christy remained on the stage, stunned.

"You may join the winner now, Ms. Clarkson." The MC said and the escort took her arm again and directed her to the stairs leading from the stage and saw Zach waiting for her, that sexy smile on his face.

Her escort walked with her down the steps then turned her over to Zach.

"Are you crazy?" She spoke in a hushed tone. "Spending that much money on me?"

"Would you rather go with the gas bag?" Zach sounded amused as he took her arm.

"No." She looked into his dark eyes. "I just can't believe you spent that kind of money."

"You're worth every cent, Christy." His look was intense, hungry, and she felt heat throughout her. "Besides, the money goes to charity."

"How are you a bidder?" she asked. "You don't have a white boutonniere."

Zach shrugged. "It must have fallen off."

He rested his hand at the small of her back and guided her toward the ballroom doors.

She looked up at him. "Where are we going? There's still dessert and the dance. Drawings will be afterward if you want to win the car they're raffling off for the charity."

"I'd rather go someplace private." He moved his hand over the base of her spine, sending shivers through her. "I'd really like to spend some time with you and not have to share you with anyone."

That sounded good to her, being alone with Zach.

"Okay," she said. "I'm all for that."

When they reached the lobby, they stopped at the bell desk. She gave him her coat check receipt and he turned it and his own over to the bellboy. While the bellboy was retrieving the items, Zach gave his ticket to the valet to bring around his car.

The clerk returned with a man's coat along with her own as well as her purse. Zach tipped the bellboy then helped her into her coat before putting on his own.

He guided her out into the crisp D.C. night and she stuck her hands in her pockets to keep them warm.

"Is this yours?" she asked as a gorgeous silver Jaguar drove up to the curb. The valet stepped out and gave a slight bow to Zach.

"Do you think I borrowed it for the night?" Zach asked in a teasing voice.

The valet went to the passenger side and held the door open for Christy. Zach helped her into the low-slung car and the valet shut the door behind her.

After he tipped the valet, Zach climbed into the Jag.

It was then that the enormity of it all hit her. Zach had just bid on her and won. Earlier in the evening she had spilled out how much she wanted to be the woman in the pictures Zach had. What did she get herself into?

She swallowed. "Where are we going?"

"I thought we'd cap off the evening with a drink." He pulled the car away from the curb. "Have you been to Milonas before?"

"I run a successful business." She shook her head. "But not successful enough to even be able to afford to step over the threshold of that nightclub."

"Milonas it is." He glanced at her. "I think you'll enjoy it."

She nodded. "I have no doubt that I will."

As he drove she studied his profile, the way light and shadows played on his features as they drove through the city. He had long fingers and he wore a heavy gold ring on his right hand. She was very happy to see no ring on his left.

The leather of her seat was buttery soft beneath her palm as she looked at the sleek interior of the Jag. The perfection of his suit, the amount he had bid at the auction, the beautiful car, and the fact they were going to an exclusive nightclub that only the elite could afford, told her that he had done very well for himself since they were last together, eight years ago.

As she looked at him, it was hard not to think of the times they had made love. He was always so strong and controlling and rough when they did. She had loved it. She hadn't known about his kinky side for a while but later, some time after she broke up with him, she realized that questions he had asked her had been designed to test the waters. It wasn't until she found the pictures and learned what he liked that she ran.

She tried really hard not to dwell on those days, but it was hard not to imagine him naked. He'd had an amazing body then…to look at him it had to be even more incredible now.

"When we dated, you were studying business." She tilted her head to the side. "What did you end up going into?"

He glanced at her before returning his gaze to the road. "The restaurant business."

"Why am I not surprised?" She smiled at memories that came back to her of going to his home where his mother served up plate after plate of Greek food. "You always did like to eat." She looked him over. "Although you couldn't begin to tell by looking at you."

The corner of his mouth quirked. "Seems to me that you enjoyed my mother's cooking."

"Loved it." She smiled. "How are your parents?"

"Mitera," he said using the Greek name for mother, "as always thinks I'm too thin and not old enough to be on my own."

Christy laughed. "And what are you now, thirty-three?"

"Thirty-six." He shook his head. "She has never stopped being overprotective."

"That's right, you're five years older than me," Christy said. "What about your father?"

"Patri won't retire," Zach said. "He's still chief editor at their hometown paper." He glanced at her. "How is your grandmother?"

"She's a hundred and one now." Christy smiled. "Nothing can stop her."

The distance between the hotel and Milonas wasn't far, and within ten minutes Zach was pulling the car up in front of the nightclub. Immediately a valet opened Christy's door and helped her step out of the car. She held her dress and her coat down with one hand as she stood. The black coat was the length of her dress, and her dress was so short she was concerned about flashing her black panties at anyone who might be standing nearby.

"Mr. Nikas." The valet stood at attention, showing extreme respect to Zach as he walked around the car and handed the valet his keys. "Is there anything else I can do for you tonight?"

"This will be fine." Zach slipped a tip into the young man's hand.

"Thank you, Mr. Nikas." The valet jogged around the car and climbed in.

Zach placed his palm at the base of Christy's spine and even through the coat she shivered at the contact. The moment they entered the club, the hostess approached them and showed pleasure at seeing Zach and was polite to Christy. The blonde hostess helped them out of their coats and took them before she escorted them to a corner table with a view of the harbor.

The interior of the nightclub was elegant and rich in design and furnishings. Crystal lights winked from the ceiling at different levels, looking like stars across a black velvet sky. The lighting was low, the atmosphere romantic.

When Zach had pushed in her chair he took his own seat and settled back in it, watching Christy. She felt warm beneath his gaze and tried not to show how much he unsettled her... And how much he turned her on.

She wanted him to kiss her like he used to. Taste him and drink in his masculine scent.

He was even sexier than she remembered. She wanted to slide her hands over his chest, shoulders, and biceps like she used to and feel his hard muscles as they flexed beneath her palms. His short black hair needed to be mussed and she knew just how she would like to do it.

She would massage his back the way he liked, and rake her nails down his spine. He had taught her many things that he loved, with the exception of what had come between them. But he had pleasured her more than any man had since.

No one could ever measure up to Zach Nikas.

A server showed up at the table, knocking Christy out of her fantasies. The elegant woman had skin as fine as brown silk and eyes almost as dark as Zach's. She had a lovely smile as she looked at Zach.

"What may I get for you, Mr. Nikas?"

"We'll have a bottle of the Hirsch Vineyards Chardonnay," Zach said.

The server nodded and smiled again. "Right away, Mr. Nikas."

"Thank you, Brandi," he said and then she gave a little bow and left.

Zach turned his attention fully to Christy. His gaze locked with hers. "I've thought about you a lot over the years." He said it like he meant every word of it.

"Well, I told you already, I've thought a lot about you, too." Christy smiled. "It's hard to believe it's been eight years."

"So tell me, Christy." He leaned back. "What did you learn from your research?"

"I learned that it isn't so freaky, just kinky." She thought back to what she liked about the things she'd seen and read. "Losing control is appealing. Not to just anyone. To someone who is like you are, Zach. Strong, outgoing, accomplished, passionate about what you do and like."

He studied her as if examining every word she said and filing it away.

"Do you do it much?" She squirmed a little in her seat as she asked the question. She wasn't sure she wanted to know the answer.

"I have played with a lot of women," he said. "It's a part of the date for me, if I feel a connection with the person. It doesn't happen with everyone."

"Mr. Playboy, eh? Do you think you'll ever settle down?" she asked.

"I have no problem settling down." His eyes met hers and they were full of meaning. "When I find the right woman, I will."

She bit the inside of her lip before she spoke. "When I saw what you had— gags, blindfolds, cuffs, and so many other things…I didn't know what to think. And then the pictures of the bound women…and some of the equipment you used…"

"I've added a lot of play toys since then," he said. "It might frighten you off again… But it is a passion for me."

She swallowed. "Control is a passion for you, too, isn't it," she stated.

"Yes it is, Christy." He gaze was dark, intense. "Control my way."

"I am not into the master slave thing though," she said.

"Don't worry about that. It is not my thing either."

"I think I can handle whatever you've got." What was she saying?

His lips twitched as if he was holding back a smile.

At that moment, the server brought over the bottle of wine, showed it to Zach and poured just enough for him to taste. When he accepted it, the waitress poured them each a glass and left the bottle.

"To the auction." Zach said with his sexy smile as they toasted.

From the first sip of the wine, Christy knew it was an expensive one. It was an amazing wine with an incredible flavor.

"When I saw that you were being auctioned tonight, I had to come."

Christy's eyes widened. "You knew?"

"I had every intention of winning you tonight." Zach raised his glass to his lips. "That Henry Hawthorne never stood a chance."

Chapter 4

Christy's lips parted and she stared at him with complete and total surprise. "You planned this whole night?"

"Right down to having you sitting here with me and having a drink." He swirled the wine in his glass, holding her gaze with his own. "When I opened the program to your picture…let's just say that I had to see you. I had to have you."

She bit the inside of her lip before she spoke. "You always did like to control the outcome of everything that came your way."

"And I still do." He took a drink of his wine before setting down his wine glass. "Does that bother you?"

"Strangely, no." Christy studied him, remembering what it had been like when they had dated. "With you…I liked how you always took charge. I always felt safe and secure, and loved by you."

"Yes, I loved you." His expression grew serious and her stomach pitched as he echoed her statement in the past tense. "You tore my heart apart when you left."

"It was hard for me, too." She started to reach for her hair, automatically wanting to twirl it around her finger, but put her hand back in her lap.

"You still do that." He reached across the table and grasped a lock of her hair and let it slide through his fingers. "It's still spiraled from you doing that earlier tonight."

"You watched me?" she asked.

The corner of his mouth quirked. "From the moment you walked in with the blonde and the redhead. I couldn't take my eyes off of you."

"Is there anything else I should know?" she shook her head. "I don't suppose you watched me shower, too."

"As a matter of fact I did." He gave a sexy grin.

She pretended to act indignant, but she knew he could tell she hadn't seriously considered him actually doing just that.

"Mr. Nikas, is there anything else I can get for you?" the server asked as she stopped at their table.

"That will be all for tonight, Brandi."

She gave him a brilliant smile, bowed, and left.

"You must come here a lot." Christy followed Brandi with her gaze. "Everyone here seems to know you."

"They'd better know me." Zach gave an amused smile. "I own the place."

As many times as she had been surprised tonight, she may as well have left her mouth hanging open. "You own Milonas?"

He gave a slight nod. "And Passero's, downtown."

"I love Passero's. It's a great restaurant." Christy leaned back in her chair. "When you said you were in the restaurant business, I had no idea."

"Unless you would like some dessert or more wine," he said, "why don't we go to my place for a nightcap?"

Thoughts of being alone with Zach, totally and completely alone, sent tingles down her spine.

"I'd like that." She set her wine glass on the table and her fingers ached as she uncurled them. She hadn't realized she'd been holding it as tightly as she was.

"Good," he said. "We have a little catching up to do."

His home was so close to his nightclub that they could have walked. He lived in a house in a nearby exclusive community, which meant he was doing quite well. The fact that he owned Milonas and Passero's made that perfectly clear.

It would have made her uncomfortable if it weren't for the fact that it was Zach, someone she had known well and had loved.

He took her coat when they entered his home and closed the door behind them. He set the coat aside then took off his own, as well as his suit jacket.

Low lighting greeted them and she took in his home as they passed through the spacious foyer. To her left a staircase swept up to the second floor and just past that was a formal dining room. To her right was a formal sitting room.

They walked through an archway and into a large common room. It was casual and relaxed looking, with overstuffed leather furniture and a built-in entertainment unit with a huge flat-screen TV. This room was more like the Zach she knew.

Through a doorway on the right she could see the sleek lines of a modern kitchen. A hallway led away from the common room, probably to guest rooms or a home office.

He laid the coats and jacket over the back of the chair as if impatient to rid himself of them, and then he brought her into his arms.

The move surprised her, yet at the same time it didn't. She had wanted him to kiss her all night. The way he'd looked at her at the nightclub, she had the impression he'd been thinking the same thing.

Being in his arms was better than she remembered and when he brought his mouth to hers, his kiss was more amazing than the countless kisses she had imagined.

His kiss was searching, as if he was remembering her taste and the feel of their mouths together. She felt like she'd been transported back to the time when everything between them was amazing and fresh and new.

As he drew away, he cupped her face in his hands and studied her. Her lips were moist from his kisses and she almost begged him to kiss her again.

He slowly rubbed his thumb over her cheek. "It almost doesn't seem real having you here with me."

"It feels like a dream." She put her palms on his chest, feeling his heat through his shirt as she moved her palms up to his shoulders. "I've imagined this, imagined being with you again."

He continued caressing her cheek with his thumb as his dark eyes looked into hers. "I can't remember a time when I didn't think about you when I was with another woman."

She looked at him with surprise. "Do you mean that?"

"There have been a lot of women in my life, Christy." He brought his face closer to hers. "None of them were you."

The thrills that went through her belly caused a spiral straight to that place between her thighs. Even after all of these years, she knew him well enough that she didn't have to question what he just said. Zach Nikas didn't say anything he didn't mean.

"I guess we aren't waiting for the weekend at the resort," she said softly.

"This will make that weekend all the more exciting." He grasped her hair in his hand and pulled her hair back, causing her to gasp. "Are you sure you want to be here with me tonight, Christy? Last chance."

"I want to stay." She winced at the harshness of how hard he had pulled her hair. Yet at the same time it had a good sting to it.

And the mastery in the movement… He was already taking control of her and it turned her on so that her skin felt on fire.

He brought her to him for a hard kiss, nothing like the gentle reunion of moments before. This was harsh, forceful. He pinched her nipples hard through her dress and bit her lower lip, causing tears to sting her eyes.

She loved it.

The kiss was wild, hungry. He reached behind her and drew down the zipper of her dress. It fell in a silken caress down her body and around her feet, leaving her in her black bra and matching panties along with thigh-high silk stockings and her high heels.

He grabbed her by her ass and brought their bodies flush together. His cock was hard against her belly and knowing that he was as turned on as she was, sent an ache between her thighs. She held onto his biceps, digging her fingers in as if to hold on for safety from a coming storm. He moved his hand to the clasp of her bra and unfastened it.

Heat warmed her as he stepped away and took her bra with him and then he tossed it on the couch. He cupped her breasts and she sucked in her breath as he pinched her nipples again, harder this time, and she bit her lower lip to hold back a cry.

"Take off your heels." He stepped back and crossed his arms over his chest. "Now, Christy."

He looked serious and she knew she had better do what he told her to. She hurried to remove her heels. When she straightened, he said, "Take off your panties." She slipped them off and stepped out of them, leaving her in only stockings. "Now your stockings. Hand them to me."

A heady thrill caused her to shiver as he watched her with his dark eyes. They told her nothing, but the intensity of his expression made her obey.

Focusing on Zach, she slowly pushed down one stocking in a sensual movement. She could tell her teasing was working as his jaw tightened and his eyes seem to grow darker than they already were. She eased it over her foot then handed the stocking to him.

"Faster this time." His words came out dangerously low and she felt the urge to obey.

She hurried to take off the other stocking and gave it to him. He took her by her upper arms and turned her so that she was facing away from him, then pulled her wrists behind her back. She felt the silk of her stockings as he wrapped one around each of her wrists and tied it securely.

"Last chance." He rested his hands on her shoulders and moved his mouth to her ear. "Unless you've changed your mind, from this point on, you're mine."

Her heart beat a little faster. "Yes."

"Tell me you're mine." He brought her up close, her back up against his chest, and he pulled back her head again by her hair. "I want to hear it."

"I'm yours." Something like electricity sizzled through her as she spoke. He had her head pulled back so far that she could see his eyes as he looked down at her. He suddenly looked dark and dangerous.

"Yes," he said in a way that made her shiver. "You are mine."

Chapter 5

Zach smoothed her hair away from her face so that it hung down her back. He caressed her cheek with the other stocking, and as she felt its softness she parted her lips. He slid the stocking between her lips as he wrapped it around her head, gagging her, catching her by surprise.

He grasped her shoulders, turned her around, and looked down at her as he lightly caressed her shoulders and upper arms. "You are so beautiful, Christy."

With the stocking gagging her, she couldn't make a coherent response. She just looked at him, feelings of excitement, curiosity, and a little apprehension, swirling through her all at once.

He kissed the corner of her mouth and then moved his face so that his nose was buried in her hair. "And you smell wonderful, just like I remember."

His hands felt warm as he slid them from her shoulders downward, skimming the sides of her bare breasts with his fingertips, trailing them down to her waist and sliding his palms to her hips. The eroticism of the moment increased the ache between her thighs as he slowly moved them up again.

He raised his head and cupped one of her cheeks with his hand. "Now that you're mine again, I have so much in store for you."

She felt vulnerable, naked while he was clothed, her wrists bound behind her back and unable to say anything.

"Stay right there." He went to his coat and she watched as he took the belt from it and came toward her. What was he going to do with that?

He stepped behind her and the next thing she knew he was wrapping the cloth belt around her head, covering her eyes and taking away her sight. He tied it behind her head.

"I'm going to teach you a safe sound," he said. "You do know what 'safe words' are if you have been reading up on bondage, am I right?"

She nodded.

"Considering you can't speak, you will need a sound." He rubbed her neck as he spoke. "Listen to me."

He made an odd, very distinctive muffled sound, as if he was gagged, too. "You try it now," he said.

She made the same type of noise, changing the pitch of the sound like he had.

"Good girl." He took her by her arm. His voice was low, sexy as he spoke. "We're going upstairs."

It was unnerving walking without being able to see and unable to catch herself if she fell. She had to put her complete trust in Zach. And she did trust him. She knew he would never hurt her or let anything happen to her. Still, no matter that she trusted him, she felt timid as she walked forward, as if she might run into something.

The air felt cool on her body as they walked and her nipples were hard and tight. They stepped from the soft carpet onto the smooth and cool tile that she was certain was the foyer they had been in earlier. He guided her forward then stopped them.

"We're at the stairs." He put his arm around her waist. "Take a step up now."

As she stepped up she felt like she would fall endlessly down, as if there was no floor below them and no stairs in front of them.

Her foot stepped solidly on the stairs and then she tested her weight on it.

"Bring your other foot." He held onto her as she obeyed. "Now let's move a little faster.

She didn't know if she could move any faster, but he guided her up the stairs, almost forcing her to take each step.

"One more step," he said as he brought her to a halt.

She raised her foot and then stepped onto the floor. She couldn't help letting out a sigh of relief. A muffled sigh, considering she was gagged.

Zach guided her down a hallway and she heard the sound of a door opening and then her shoulder brushed what she assumed was a doorframe as they went forward.

He positioned her by her shoulders and then kissed her on the corner of her mouth. He moved behind her. "Naughty girl, your bindings are loose. I'll have to take care of that."

She tested the stocking and felt that it was indeed coming loose. A hard slap on her ass caused her to jump and give a muffled cry.

"No more of that," he said in a firm tone. "Now stand here."

The space he had just stood in felt empty when he walked away. Without her sight, her hearing seemed to be more sensitive. She heard the rustle of clothing, something that sounded like someone digging for something, and then the sound of metal clinking and something jingling.

She felt his presence before he spoke. "How are you doing, Christy honey?" Since she couldn't talk she nodded. "Good." He pressed his body close to hers and a thrill went through her as she realized he had stripped out of his clothing and she felt his naked skin against hers. "Do you like feeling helpless?" he said. "Do you like giving up control to me?"

She nodded again. She loved submitting to him, turning her personal power over to him.

He ran his hands down one leg as she sensed him crouching in front of her. She felt something soft yet hard that jingled as he secured it. Some kind of ankle cuff. He cuffed her other ankle and then stood, trailing his hands up her body as he did. He moved behind her and surprised her when he untied her hands.

"Considering you tried to get out, we need to handle you a little more stringently." He took one of her wrists and cuffed it with what felt like the same type of cuff that he had put on her ankles. She heard more jingling as he fastened them. He came around in front of her and clipped them together so that she couldn't pull them apart.

"Let's add a little something for punishment." He pinched one of her nipples and she made a sound of surprise.

Then something clamped on her nipple. If felt about the same as him pinching her. It wasn't unpleasant.

"That's not too bad, now is it?" he asked. She shook her head. "Let's tighten it so that you can really feel it."

She cried out behind her gag and tears wet her eyes from the pain. She squirmed and fought him as he pinched her other nipple, not wanting the clamp tighter. But he was stronger and faster and she cried out again.

He put his arm around her shoulders and leaned in close. "You said this is what you wanted. Do you still want this, Christy?"

A thousand times she had fantasized about this. She just had never felt anything like this before.

Even as tears wet the blindfold she nodded. She did want it.

"Good girl." He stroked her hair. "I knew you could handle a couple of little clamps."

She wondered what big clamps felt like then decided at that moment she didn't want to know.

Yet as she started to get used to the pain, it eased into a sense of pleasure.

"I love how helpless you look." He moved close and he put his hands on her waist and pressed his body to hers and she whimpered as his chest brushed the nipple clamps. He slid his palms on her ass and squeezed.

"I like control, Christy." His voice was low, firm. "I like to tell you what to wear, what to do. I please you by taking care of you and you please me by focusing on me." He nuzzled her ear. "Do you understand?"

She paused, then nodded. To give up that kind of control… She had always been a strong woman. She was successful, owned a thriving business…but she was willing to give up control in other parts of her life. In some way it sounded thrilling, exciting to have someone care for her like that.

He put his hands on her shoulders and lightly pushed. "I want you on your knees."

Her legs were shaky as she obeyed, but he kept his hands on her shoulders making sure she didn't fall.

"Now on your back," he said.

She paused but he guided her down onto the floor, holding her so that she didn't fall. "Bend your knees," he said when she was lying on her back.

He moved one of her legs so that her heel was touching her ass. Then he brought her wrist down to her ankle and clipped them together. He did the same with her other wrist and ankle, and he spread her thighs wide.

She had never felt more vulnerable or more turned on as she was at that moment as she waited for whatever he might do next. The women she's seen in pictures had been tied up elaborately with chains and equipment, and toys had been used on them.

What was Zach going to do now?

He moved so that he was over her, his knees between her thighs and his arms braced to either side of her head. He lowered himself and kissed her again. "I want you to try to get out again. And I want you to try hard."

She struggled, trying to slide her hands out of the cuffs at the same time she attempted to pull her wrists cuffs from where they were connected to her ankle cuffs. She couldn't budge anything yet she felt herself growing more excited with every struggle she made.

"Helpless, aren't you? The futile struggle." He moved so that their bodies touched but he still held his full weight off of her. "That's my girl."

His cock rubbed her folds as he moved against her. Heat suffused her body and she imagined how good it would feel to have him inside of her again. They'd had an amazing sex life before but she had never been as hot as she was right now.

"Do you want this?" He asked as he moved his cock to the entrance to her core and slightly pushed in.

Yes, she cried out in her mind but all she could do was nod. Please.

Totally at his mercy, she was spread out for him, unable to move, to see, to speak. Her senses seemed magnified, her skin more sensitive. Every touch made her feel more alive than she could ever remember feeling before.

She squirmed beneath him, begging the only way she could for him to take her.

He pushed a little farther in and her eyes grew damp behind her blindfold because she wanted him so badly.

He thrust hard, slamming himself inside of her. She cried out behind her gag at the sudden fullness.

She loved the feel of him driving in and out of her while she was at his mercy. Her orgasm was close, her body ready and waiting for her to tumble over the edge.

Sensations grew almost brutally strong inside of her, running toward her with the power of a freight train.

She came so hard she would have come up off of the floor if she wasn't in the position she was in. Her climax was so intense that it caused her core to spasm around his cock. Her entire body reacting to the orgasm, pulsing with it.

Zach moved in and of her then gave a low groan and she felt his cock throb inside of her. He pumped his hips a few more times and then he shuddered against her.

He reached behind her head and untied the stocking and pulled off her blindfold. She blinked up at him and he smiled. "Did you enjoy it?"

She gave him a teasing look. "Is that all you've got?"

Chapter 6

The day after Christy had stayed with Zach, she felt alive, yet on edge. She pushed her hair back from her face as she looked out the storefront window to the empty street. "Baubles and Beads" had been painted on the front window, the letters forming an arc. She looked at her watch. Early evening, almost time to close, and he was going to pick her up.

It was Saturday and he had wanted her to stay with him for the day, but she had a business to run. Her store manager was on a family trip, and the store wasn't going to open itself or make sales on its own. Not to mention a new employee needed to be trained.

A flutter went through her body at the thought of seeing Zach. She practically bounced on her toes, the excitement of seeing him again making her feel like she'd felt when they'd first met. He had been walking across the street to go to a Starbucks with one of his friends when he looked at her and their gazes met and held. Without taking his eyes from hers, he told his friend he would catch up with him later. And then he walked over to her.

That simple. One look and the next thing she knew they were dating. But she was young and inexperienced. When she saw the photos they scared her.

And when she confronted him he'd been honest and told her that's what he liked to do with women, what he wanted to do someday with her. He said he cared about her so much that he didn't want to frighten her away. He could tell by her answers to his questions that he needed to take it slow. Finding the pictures had not been in the plan.

It was enough to scare her into running.

But not anymore.

Her thoughts went back to last night and the things Zach had said. How he would tell her how to do her makeup and what to wear.

She looked in one of the store mirrors and straightened her crimson blouse and matching cashmere cardigan over her black slacks that he had dressed her in that morning when he took her by her house before work. Her long hair fell around her shoulders. Her brown eyes always looked bigger when she used makeup and she had to admit the colors he had chosen looked great on her. Shades of gold and bronze that she hadn't tried before, but were on her palette.

Her business and her independence were important to her. But maybe that was why she liked Zach being in control of her. She was so used to running her business and being the one in charge and making tough decisions, that it was exciting to have someone make all the decisions for her. Zach said he would take care of her. He loved control, but he was not selfish. Because he cared for her so much, something about that caused her to want someone she could trust, someone strong, someone like Zach.

She closed her eyes for a moment. Was she rushing into something that she would regret later? She had told herself she wasn't going to jump into another relationship after what Ted had done to her.

This isn't Ted. This is Zach.

Yes, this was exactly where she wanted to be.

It had been a busy day and seemed to drag on forever, and she spent most of her time dusting the knickknacks that crowded the store. She sold things she loved, like statues of mythical creatures, pewter figurines of warlocks, fairies, elves, and dragons, crystal balls, along with incense burners and every scent of incense that she could find. She had a huge assortment of beads for customers to make their own jewelry along with lots of other baubles.

As she dusted all she could think about was Zach. She was so anxious to see him again. This time they would have dinner at his home and then what else would he show her, do with her, to her. She could never have rushed into things so quickly with anyone else. Being together with Zach was amazing. She didn't think she could get enough of him.

At a quarter after five she walked out of the shop and her belly flip-flopped when she saw him parked in front of the store. He leaned up against his Jaguar, his hands braced to either side of him on the car.

Delicious. He looked so sexy in a dark suit that fit his tall form well. A smile touched his lips. His black hair wasn't as smoothly combed back as it had been last night. Now it was a bit mussed from the breeze and she could see it was a little longer than she had thought.

She turned away from Zach long enough to lock the heavy front door of her shop then walked up to him feeling like no time at all had passed since they had first met. "Hi."

"You look beautiful." His smile was sexy and slightly naughty as he looked at her. "I've been thinking about you all day."

"Funny, but I've been thinking about you, too." She reached him and he took her by her shoulders and kissed her. "Mmmmm…" She gave a happy sigh. "And that's what I've been waiting for all day."

He enveloped her in a snug embrace and he kissed the top of her head. "I have lots more planned for you than just a kiss."

"Good." She brushed his lips with hers. "You were holding back last night. I want to experience what you really like. I want to be like you picture me, in the same look and position that excites you the most."

His eyes were dark, his expression intense. "Be careful what you ask for, honey."

Her expression was serious as she said, "I'm ready. I want to experience what you love."

After he helped her into the car he went to the driver's side and climbed in then headed for his home. Like his nightclub, her shop wasn't far from his home and it took only moments to get there.

His home was amazing and she got a better look at it this time because she didn't end up with her clothes off almost as soon as she walked in. That was perfectly fine with her, but it was nice to see the place where he spent his days and nights when he wasn't working.

Or playing with other women.

She frowned at the thought. But something about those images aroused her also.

"What's wrong?" He paused just before they reached the kitchen.

"Nothing." She shook her head.

"Something is bothering you," he said. "I can tell you're not telling me the truth."

She looked away for a moment before turning her gaze back to his. "I was just thinking that you've played with a lot of women."

"That's true." He studied her, "And you've had sex with other men."

"Yes…" She bit the inside of her lip before she continued. "Is what you said to me last night something you tell other women? Do you tell other women that they are yours?"

"Only you, Christy. There is no one else that I am involved with right now." He took her into his arms and she caught his masculine scent and felt the heat of his body. "I don't tell them a lot of things that I told you."

She looked up at him. "Like what?"

"That I want to care for them in every way." He placed a kiss on top of her head. "I don't feel that way about other women. Okay?"

She nodded. "Okay."

He smiled, took her by the hand, and led her to the kitchen. She caught the smells of freshly baked bread, roasted vegetables, and other delicious smells.

"I ordered in from my restaurant. They don't deliver, but it is one of the bennies of owning the place." He opened up aluminum containers with fish and vegetables, and a bag with a baguette inside. "Your favorite. Swordfish."

"You have a good memory." She breathed in the smells. "Yum."

"I remember a lot of things." He said and his words held meaning to them.

They set the table with a place setting at the head and one to the right of it. Then they brought in the containers with their dinner.

"I'm glad it wasn't too much for you last night," he said as he arranged the containers on the table.

"Are you kidding?" She smiled at him as she set a bottle of white wine, along with two wine glasses, on the table. "It was amazing."

"I had plans to take it really slow with you," he said. "But it didn't quite work out that way."

She put her hand on his arm. "Don't hold back and do what excites you. I would love that."

With one hand, he reached for her face and pushed strands of her hair behind her ear. "I don't want things to move too fast for you and frighten you away."

"I've researched so much, watched movies, looked at pictures on this for the last eleven years," she said. "I have pictured myself doing so many things but I have never found the right person I could actually experience them with. Last night was just amazing. You won't frighten me away. I trust you. So please, I want you to do what excites you. I want to see that excitement in your eyes when you have me where you want me."

His dark eyes seemed to grow more intense. "You'd better be careful of what you ask for."

She gave him a teasing look. "So, Master Zach, are you afraid of me?"

Zach put his head back, looked up at the ceiling, and laughed. When he looked back at her, he said, "You're pushing me, are you? It actually excites me to hear you talk like this. You have just changed my plan for the evening."

She smiled but before she could sit, he said, "I want you to take off your cardigan and blouse."

She paused, her hand on the dining room chair. "You want me to eat in my bra?"

"No." He gave a dangerously sexy smile. "I want you to take off your bra, too." Shivers ran through her whole body at the thought. When she hesitated, he said, "Now, Christy."

He watched as she slipped off her cardigan and draped it over the back of a chair. The hungry look in his eyes told her that he was enjoying seeing her remove her clothing.

She met his gaze as she unbuttoned her blouse and put it aside with the cardigan. She reached behind her and unfastened her lacy bra and laid it on top of the blouse. Heat burned through her as she stood before him.

"Take off your slacks," he said. She took one look at his hard expression and hurried to slip out of her slacks, leaving her in panties, stockings, and heels.

When she put her hand on the back of her chair, he shook his head. "Not yet."

He had something in his hand. When he opened it on his palm was a pair of dangly things made of tiny silver bells that looked like earrings but with loops on one end.

"These are nipple nooses." He held one up. "You're going to wear them tonight."

She held her hands to her breasts. "My nipples are still sore."

"Christy," he said in a warning tone. "Come here."

She went to him and sucked in her breath while he pinched one nipple then slid one of the nooses over it. "That wasn't so bad," she said and then he tightened the noose so that she caught her breath. *That will teach me to say something like that out loud.*

The nipple ached now, but then it became a more pleasant ache than the nipple clamps had caused. He put the other noose on her opposite nipple and she winced when he tightened it.

"Let's have a seat." He pulled back her chair and then she sat, the little bells ringing as she moved. He took his own seat and looked at her with fire in his eyes. "Eat."

It felt naughty and unbelievably erotic to be sitting at the table and eating dinner without anything on but her panties and stockings and black high heel shoes while he remained in his suit. He didn't even take off his jacket, which seemed to separate them even more. He was the Dom. She was the sub, and she had to be kept in her place.

He raised his wine glass then rubbed it over each of her nipples, the cold making them feel even tighter.

When they were finished with dinner they cleared the table and the bells on her nipples jangled as she moved.

After everything was put away, he took her by the hand. They walked through his house and stopped at a door. "Are you sure you want more?"

She nodded. "Whatever you can give me."

"All right." He looked serious as he spoke. "Just remember that you asked for it."

She expected something fascinating to be on the other side of the door when he opened it, but it was just an office with a desk and walls lined with books on polished oak shelves.

"What are we going to do in here?" She looked up at him. "Play boss and secretary?"

He grinned and led her to the wall behind the desk. "Maybe another time."

Still holding her hand, he reached for a lion figure, moved it a little bit aside, then reached in and pushed something.

The wall started to move.

"No way." She looked at him in disbelief. "Like in a book or movie." She brought her gaze back to the moving wall. "How cool is this?"

"Very cool," he said and she smiled.

They stepped onto a landing and a flight of stairs led below. The staircase was beautifully done, polished oak and it stopped at another landing and then a door was at the opposite end. As they started to walk down, the wall closed behind them with a hard thump and locking sound. The bells on her nipples jangled in the quiet as they went.

When they reached the bottom, she looked up at him.

He studied her as if gauging how she was feeling at the moment. "Are you ready?"

"Yes." She nodded. "For everything you can give me."

He paused and gave her one more look before he opened the door.

Chapter 7

Christy's eyes widened as she took in the room and her heart started beating faster. Zach coaxed her forward, into the room, and her heels clicked on a polished wood floor and the bells jingled on her nipples.

Her skin prickled as she looked at things she had seen only on websites and pictures. She was nothing less than stunned. There was so much here. She wouldn't have known what most—if any—of it was when she and Zach were first together, but her research made much of it familiar. The more she had read about it, the more she wanted to experience it and now here she was and it was all Zach's.

Throughout her research, she had never seen anything so high quality and beautiful. It was all almost too much to absorb. He took her by the hand and began to give her a tour of his dungeon. Anticipation caused her heart to beat a little harder as she thought of what he might do to her with each of the items.

They went from one thing to another, him wanting to give her a taste of the devices. He treated his toys like a car collector treated his prized vintage car and he told her what he liked about each. She saw the locks, the keys, the extension of his control.

Every word expressed his desire for control and she wanted him to use them on her. To feel his toys, to be his toy.

Two walls were mirrors. Bondage furniture such as a spanking bench, crafted in burgundy leather and dark wood, was arranged throughout. A St. Andrew's cross was on one end and an iron cage on the other side.

"These are a couple of my favorites", he said point to the two chairs full of straps. One chair had a V-opening on one seat while the other chair had a dildo and a smaller plug that she assumed was an attached ass plug. "I can have you on here and watch you from five feet away and my toys will make you feel like I am inside you."

What he said was so erotic that she felt an ache between her thighs. She could picture herself right there with Zach watching, making her feel like it was him instead of the dildo.

Over near the corner were stocks with openings for the head and wrists, and it had rings at the base, which would secure the ankles. A saddle was on a machine and the saddle had a dildo and butt plug on it.

Christy pointed to the saddle. "You like the insertables don't you."

He met and held her gaze. "Just as important, I think, is that you will."

The thought that aroused her was that these were Zach's toys. He had accumulated them because he liked them. They gave him pleasure.

"Something that's good to understand," he said, "is that when I use these on you, it's not that they are simply restraints and control. They are extensions of me. When the restraints are holding your wrists and ankles, it is me holding them. A blindfold over you eyes, it is me covering them. A plug in your ass, it is me in there. I like it when you feel me all over. My control."

Zach's words caused a tingling in her belly. They would be more than just objects to play with, they were him exercising more of his control.

A bed was on the far side with a metal headboard with numerous rings on it. It also had a frame that was high over the bed. Chains hung from the overhead frame.

She was almost dizzy looking at what he had as she continued to stare at everything around her.

He explained so many of the devices and why he had them. It made her hot inside to hear him talk about them. He stopped and showed her some of his toys hanging on the wall—some things she recognized from what she had studied, some she did not. Floggers and whips that looked to be made of fine leather were among the items.

The way he described even the more unusual items excited her, like the shining silver stainless steel ass hooks. The half-inch stainless steel was in the shape of a fishhook but had a two inch rounded ball end that went inside the ass. On the opposite end was an eyelet that could be secured to something. He said it was much more ominous looking that it felt inside.

Below the items on the wall was a series of drawers and she could only imagine what was in them.

He opened a large drawer. "These are violet wands, and this is a tens unit. They channel electricity through your body in very erotic ways when used properly. The intensity can be controlled."

She had read about these devices. She pictured him using a violet wand on her. He might touch her nipples with it or any number of other places on her body. The thought excited her.

Another drawer held everything from feathers to clothespins to candles. Another held clamps, locks, and straps.

It was nearly overwhelming, how much he had.

"I had no idea of your collection of toys." She smiled. "I love all of this."

He smoothed her hair away from her face. "A toy is just a toy, but it is different when it is used on someone I care about."

The way he said it made her entire body tingle.

She spotted a camera with a big lens. It looked like a professional camera. She pointed to it. "Why is that in here?"

"I want to take pictures of you while we play," he said. "Just for us to look at. Is that okay?"

The thought of Zach photographing her while he bound and gagged her sent a shiver through her. It would add to the eroticism of the night.

She smiled. "All right."

He returned her smile then continued taking her on the tour.

She pointed to a doorway. "Where does that go to?"

"I have a private shower and bath in there," he said. "There's also a hot tub if you feel like going in it after we play."

"You have a desk in here," she said as she looked on the far side of the St. Andrew's cross. She hadn't noticed it earlier. The dark wood of the desk and the leather chair blended so well with all of the dungeon equipment. In front of the desk were two smaller leather chairs. It was like that corner of the room was meant to be unobtrusive.

"We can always play boss and secretary," he said in a teasing tone.

"Maybe we will," she said. "And that is one huge TV," she added as she spotted one near the desk, behind the cross. There were a couple of plain chairs nearby. "What do you use that for?"

"I'll show you, one of these days," he said.

On the left side of the room, thick black ropes connected through a series of pulleys hung from beams in the exposed wood ceiling. "There's something that I like about seeing you hanging there, helpless and swinging like a toy."

She could picture herself, swinging there for Zach's pleasure, and the thought sent a thrill through her.

A silver-linked chain attached to a hook above them hung near the set of stocks. Burgundy mats were scattered around the room.

When he finished with the tour, she was speechless. It was all so amazing, and so overwhelming.

He brought her into his arms and kissed her. It was a sweet and sensual kiss that set her on fire and she wanted more and more.

As he kissed her, his fingertips skimmed her back, causing her to shiver. He moved his hands up and down her sides and pressed her body close to his.

His kiss intensified. A hard, demanding, powerful kiss that showed her that he was already in control.

"Come on, Christy." He stepped back and gestured for her to walk to the wall of devices. She paused and looked up at him and he frowned. "Do as I tell you to. In here you obey me. There are consequences if you don't do as you're told. Do you understand?" She nodded but he shook his head. "I want to hear it."

"Yes." She cleared her throat. "I understand."

He took her by her arm and led her to the wall. "I don't think you do, but we'll deal with that later."

Her heart hammered and her mouth grew dry. What was she getting herself into? But this was Zach. She could trust him and she was excited to play with him. Still, it didn't mean she wasn't a little nervous of what would happen in this room.

"Take off your panties," he said and she obeyed and stepped out of them. Her whole body burned from the way he was looking at her now that she was just in her stockings and high heels.

He kissed her as hard as he was pinching her nipples, a deep, passionate kiss. "You look so good." He moved away from her and went to his drawers of toys and drew out a large ring with straps on either side of it.

"A ring gag." He raised it as he returned to her. "Open up."

She opened wide and the smooth but hard plastic ring clinked against her teeth as he inserted it and forced her mouth open wider so that the ring stood up behind her teeth and made it so that her jaws almost ached from how wide she had to keep her mouth.

He buckled the back of the strap and stood in front of her, holding her shoulders and looking into her eyes.

"Let's see your tongue," he said.

She stuck her tongue out through the ring in her mouth and he grabbed it between his lips and sucked.

"I love how you taste," he said. "Let's hear you tell me how it feels. Talk to me."

A few uuuhhuhhhh, mmphmmph, and other unintelligent sounds followed.

He smiled and sucked her tongue again to stop her. "That sounded so nice Christy. I love how you said that."

He directed her to walk to where the saddle was, next to one of the mirrored walls. "Take off your heels and climb on."

Nerves caused her stomach to flip-flop as she kicked off her heels. She put her foot in one of the stirrups and then he helped her to swing her other leg over. She imagined herself as back in the days of the Wild West where handcuffed prisoners were put on horses and taken to jail. She glanced at the cages and wondered if she'd be going to jail, too.

She stood in the stirrups, poised over the dildo and the butt plug built into the saddle, both of which had condoms that he had just put on them. Her breathing hitched as she watched while he took some gel and put it on the butt plug.

"That's just a small attachment, good for a beginner," he said. "Now ease on down."

She hesitated and he shook his head and frowned. She carefully moved down, letting the dildo slide into her pussy as he guided the plug into her ass.

The plug burned as it stretched her. "Relax," he said. "It will go a lot easier if you relax."

Relax?

She forced herself to breathe slower and let it slide into her slowly. It continued to burn for a few moments when it was completely in. But then it started to feel good. It was a full feeling that combined with the dildo had her feeling sensitized.

He went to the wall beside her and pressed a button.

The dildo and plug started to move.

She gasped and grabbed the pommel of the saddle and held on as the dildo and plug slowly moved in and out of her. She looked at the mirror and watched. The combination of seeing herself and feeling the plugs was amazing.

She closed her eyes, feeling the saddle dildo and the butt plug moving slowly in and out of her and there was nothing she could do to stop it.

At the same time she heard something like the sound of a camera taking pictures and she knew that's exactly what he must be doing.

The thought of him taking photographs of her like this made her feel even more excited.

"Can you feel me?" he asked.

She could only nod and moan a "yes".

She opened her eyes to see him sitting in a chair watching her, his camera now at his side. She loved his smile of excitement. She could see the bulge in his pants. The thought of how excited he was watching her made her wetter than she already was.

After about three minutes, Zach and the saddle started to fade as she fell into the feeling of the dildo and plug inside her. She was going to climax. She felt it coming closer and closer—

"Do not come." His firm tone startled her, pulling her concentration away from the plug and dildo.

But then her eyes started to cross and she started toward an orgasm again. The dildo and plug stopped.

"Remember our talk about consequences?" He held her gaze. "If you come without permission there will be repercussions. Do you understand?"

She bit her lower lip and nodded. "Yes." How could she not come? She was too aroused—it was impossible. She needed to focus on something that didn't excite her. She pictured Henry having her restrained. Him half naked, belly hanging out, smiling at her. Such a horrible thought caused the urge to subside.

"Let's get you down from there." He caught her by the waist and helped her so that she was standing in the stirrups, the plug and dildo no longer inside of her. Then he assisted her in getting off of the saddle and back onto the floor.

"That's my girl." He kissed her forehead and held her close for a moment, rubbing her back in slow circles, making her feel safe and secure. Her body throbbed from the experience on the saddle and it was like she could still feel the plug and dildo inside her. That was a whole different way to be saddle sore.

He nuzzled her hair. "Is my pretty little horsey rider okay?"

"Mmmuumph." She moaned through her gag.

"Did you enjoy my device?" he murmured in her ear. "Did you enjoy me inside you?"

"Mmmuumph." She moaned again as she nodded.

"I love hearing your sounds, Christy." He stroked her hair. "You did really well."

He bent over and licked her nipple while sliding his hand between her legs. He stroked her clit and again she wanted to come.

"Don't come, Christy." He stroked her clit harder. "Control yourself. You are excited aren't you?"

She nodded again. "Mmmuumph."

The fact was she was as excited as she had ever been. She loved it. She loved everything about Zach and the playroom. Not any playroom. His playroom.

He kissed her again then took her by her shoulders and turned her to face the stockades.

Her stomach dropped.

He gestured toward them. "Go stand by the stocks."

She looked at him then hurried to obey. The thought of being put in the intimidating device made her pulse jump with excitement and trepidation.

When she stood where he told her to, he had her bend at the waist. The nipple nooses dangled and the little bells jingled. He adjusted the stocks and raised the top part enough that she could put her head through as well as both wrists. Her belly twisted as he closed it so that she was locked in. There was no way to move.

"I love the helpless look of you bent over with your ass in the perfect position to take you just like this." He slowly stroked her ass cheek and she shivered from desire.

He trailed his fingers down the sides of her legs, teasing her, taunting her. Then he secured her ankles in the rings at the base, her legs parted. He could do anything with her in that position, including taking her from behind.

A highly desirous proposition.

He moved in front of her and crouched so that he could meet her gaze. "I love the helplessness in your eyes, but the sign of trust, too. Your trust in me excites me."

She loved that he liked how she looked and the way that he talked to her the whole time he had been securing her.

As she watched, he took off his suit jacket and laid it aside on one of the benches, then his dress shirt followed. He removed his shoes and socks next. She watched, hungry for him as he stripped off his slacks, leaving him in boxer briefs. There was something so hot about her being secured and played with by Zach while he was still in a suit and a tie, but it was time for those clothes to be gone.

Nice.

He had such a powerful body, his muscles sleek and solid. He walked into a closet and returned. He was wearing black leather pants now. They looked so good on his muscular body, his trim hips and his athletic thighs. His cock was a hard ridge behind the leather.

His expression was intense, almost fierce as he came toward her. When he reached her, he unlaced the leather tie on his pants and let his cock and balls out. The sight caused the ache between her thighs to increase. He moved his erection against the ring gag, through her parted lips.

"Suck my cock, Christy," he ordered.

She couldn't have done anything but obey as he slid his erection through the O-ring and into her mouth.

His cock was thick and long and she loved sucking it as he moved his hips against her face. She loved his scent, his taste. She wished she could touch him, but she could do nothing else. It felt so erotic being used for his pleasure.

"Good girl." He drew his cock out of her mouth then tucked himself back into his leather pants and tied it again.

With her being in the stocks, she couldn't see well but she was able to watch the lower part of him walk to his wall of devices.

He opened one of the drawers and brought out what looked like some kind of leather harness with big silver rings, then returned to her. He crouched down in front of her.

"Beautiful." He brushed her hair from her face and kissed the corner of her mouth.

He moved away and went behind her then started fastening leather straps around her waist and through her legs.

And then she realized what else he's been carrying—a butt plug. He pressed it against her anus and started to gently push. This plug felt bigger than the one on the saddle and she held her breath as he slowly pushed it in. She tried to relax but it was so hard. Again it burned and her eyes watered until it was fully inside her. He secured the straps and they held the plug in tight.

"Now," he said, "we will make this a little more snug."

She could see him in the mirror on the wall as he reached for the little rubber bulb pump hanging out the back of the plug. He squeezed it slowly three times. Each time she could feel the plug filling up in her ass.

She moaned through the gag.

"That should be enough." He patted her ass. "Can't get that out, can you? "

She wanted to say, "Are you kidding me? Get it out?"

He had her. Helpless, gagged, and plugged.

Yet at the same time it started to feel good. An extension of him as he had described it, as if it was him taking her in the ass.

He reached down and tightened the nipple nooses and she groaned from the increased pain. Then he bent to kiss her lips around the gag.

She watched as he moved back to the wall.

A flurry of excitement went through her at the thought that she was really doing this, really doing it with Zach. So far everything had been amazing.

He stopped to take a few pictures and it made her ache even more between her thighs. Something about it felt so naughty—she loved it.

After he set down the camera, he came toward her with a flogger.

Her anticipation turned to nervousness. Yes, she was really doing this and about to get flogged.

"I want to see you pink." When he reached her, he started caressing her body with the flogger's strips of soft leather. "Just for me."

Chapter 8

Christy shivered from the erotic sensation of Zach teasing her with the flogger, as she stood bent over and secured for him to do what he wanted to with her.

He went in front of her and crouched again so that she could see his face. "I told you there would be consequences for not obeying me immediately. Now you will be reminded so that you never do it again."

Zach started using the flogger on her in a way that told her he knew really well what he was doing. At first it didn't feel bad at all. But then after he concentrated on one area for a bit it started to burn and sting. A part of her thought how interesting that the pain turned into pleasure when he stopped flogging one part of her. But then he started it all over again on another part of her body and it stung and burned like crazy.

Tears wet her eyes from the harsh sting all over her backside, but she was also excited beyond what she had imagined.

"Good girl." When he was finished, he tossed aside the flogger running his hands over her body that felt hot everywhere a strap had touched. Then he slipped his fingers into her folds.

She caught her breath and squirmed against his hand, wanting him to continue. It felt so good. She was so sensitive, so close…

"That's enough." He moved his hand away and stopped touching her clit. "If you thought the flogger was bad, that's nothing compared to what I'll do if you come before I say you can."

A niggling of fear crept in, but she pushed it aside.

He took her out of the stocks. She felt relief that she was no longer stretched out and secured so tightly. He left the butt plug, the harness holding it in snugly. She could feel the continued pressure.

"How do you like it?" he asked after he removed the ring gag.

"I've never been so excited." She found it hard to explain how amazing it had been so far. "I love it. It's better than I ever imagined."

He kissed her long and slow and she sighed as he stepped back and walked to the drawers.

As she waited, he retrieved the same leather ankle and wrist cuffs that he had used on her last night, as well as a ball gag, and he returned. The rings on the cuffs jingled as he put them on her.

From inserting the new gag to putting on her cuffs, everything he did was sensual and slow, heightening her arousal that mixed with the small amount of fear she was experiencing.

Next he retrieved a thick leather collar with O-rings on it and secured that around her neck. She thought about all of the women she had seen and what had been done to them, and how much she had wanted to try those things. She was finally getting her wish. And she was getting it with Zach.

"How are you doing?" He moved in front of her and palmed her breasts, then pinched her nipples that still had the nipple nooses on them.

With the ball gag in, all she could do was wince and nod.

"On your knees on the mat." He guided her down, keeping her from falling as he did so. "Now lean forward so that you are on your shoulders, knees under you." He helped her so she would not fall forward. "Put your arms between your legs."

She wasn't sure what he meant but he helped her, having her lean forward so that she was on her haunches, her face to the mat, and her arms between her legs. He took off the lock that had held the two cuffs together, freeing her for a moment.

But then he said, "Put your arms through your legs and touch your ankles."
She had no idea what he meant.

He took one of her arms by her wrist and moved it down so that it was between her thighs. And then he forced her to move her arm down more, which caused her to have to lie on her shoulder. Then he locked her wrist to her ankle he did the same with her other wrist and ankle.

She was in the most vulnerable position she had ever been in her life. She couldn't move anything, her ass was up in the air, and her thighs spread wide.

"How are you feeling?" He stroked her shoulder. "Do you like being my toy to do whatever I want to?"

She nodded, her cheek rubbing against the mat, her hair over her face. It was all so bizarre yet it was amazing how it felt to be his toy.

He palmed her butt cheeks. "Look at this fine ass. I should take you just like this. Would you like that?"

Yes…she would love it.

She nodded and groaned. "Uhummph."

"You'll have to wait a little longer for that." He patted her ass. "But, I have something else in mind that you will love."

She couldn't see anything but she heard a buzzing sound and then something placed against her pussy. A vibrator. Not just any vibrator but the mother of all vibrators. One that was so amazing she was sure she was going to come almost at once.

"How is that?" He moved the vibrator over her clit. "Do you like that?"

She nodded. She loooved it. She could feel an orgasm charging forward, coming closer and closer—

"Don't come, Christy," he said. "Not until I give you permission."

Again? Is he crazy—?

The vibrator stopped. "Can't have you coming too soon."

No. Don't stop. She wanted to scream. That was the third time he had denied her an orgasm. All she could do was make sounds behind the gag that made no sense. Her body throbbed, her clit so sensitive that it seemed like the slightest touch would set it off. He continued to bring her close to orgasm and then stopping before starting again. Her groans of excitement told him when to back off.

After five minutes of the little orgasm denial game, he unlocked her wrists from her ankles and relief made her limp. Still she needed an orgasm so badly that her body felt like she might come undone.

She felt lightheaded as he helped her to her feet and directed her to the toy wall again. There he took off her wrist and ankle cuffs and replaced them with different kinds of cuffs that she had seen before but couldn't remember where. He also put a wide belt around her waist then added thigh cuffs. There were big O-rings on everything.

He went to another drawer and took out a hair tie then returned and jerked her head back as he gathered her hair in a tight ponytail.

When he finished, he grabbed her ponytail and pulled her head back as he kissed her at the corner of her mouth, and he pressed his rigid cock against her belly.

Then he led her over to the corner where the black ropes were hanging down from the pulleys. Now she remembered where she had seen the special cuffs. They were suspension cuffs.

He guided her toward the ropes that hung over a mat then paused to trail kisses along her jaw to her ear. He nipped her ear and her entire body felt like it was a mass of nerves, and every touch sent sensations straight between her thighs.

"Lie on your belly on the mat," he said as he drew away.

When she was lying facedown, he pulled her arms back and attached her wrist cuffs to her ankle cuffs in a hogtie. Then he started attaching ropes with heavy clips to the cuffs, including her thighs and her waist and he added a torso harness also.

What was he going to do now? Her heart beat faster. She loved the anticipation, the wondering. Trusting him.

"I love how you are handling everything." He caressed her shoulder and kissed the top of her head before getting up.

He went to the wall and pressed a button. She caught her breath as the pulleys raised her up, slowly, until she was about three feet from the floor. It was a wild feeling hanging from a beam in the exposed ceiling.

When she was suspended, he moved in front of her. "Do you like this?

She couldn't nod so she made an affirmative sound.

"Do you want more?" he asked.

Again she made a sound meaning yes!

He grabbed his camera and took multiple shots of her from all angles.

Again he set the camera aside and he untied the leather tie on his pants. He grabbed her by her ponytail, pulling her closer and undid the buckle on the ball gag and dropped it on the floor. He pressed his cock against her lips and she opened her mouth and he slid his cock in. He grasped her head and she bounced back and forth in the air as he moved her up and down his cock.

"Damn, but I love your mouth." He pulled out. "If I didn't have something better in mind I would come right now and you'd swallow every drop of my come. Wouldn't you," he stated.

Another affirmative sound as she sucked his cock. She would love to do that, love to do anything for him.

He moved away then came up from behind her, placed his hands on her ass, and pushed.

She gave a little cry of surprise and her head spun, and she felt almost dizzy. Yet free and exhilarating, too, and she wondered if that might be what it felt like to fly.

He pushed her back and forth like she was on a kids' swing, only in a much different position. In the mirrors she saw herself swinging and what she looked like with only her stockings on. Seeing herself like that made things even more erotic.

Another swing and then he caught her by her thighs from behind and held her still. He spread her thighs, grabbed her by her hips, and drove his cock inside her.

Her eyes felt like they were going to cross from the amazing feeling of him fucking her while she was suspended in midair. She moved back and forth in the air as he took her hard from behind, the sound of their bodies meeting a rhythmic slap.

She was so sensitized from all that he'd done to her and she could feel her orgasm bearing down on her like a landslide. It felt like every one of her senses was cut off except for feeling him pounding inside of her and the orgasm that was coming faster and faster toward her.

"Don't come, Christy." He continued to slam into her. "Remember, consequences."

By then she didn't care. She needed to come so badly and there was no way she could go back now. Her orgasm slammed into her. Her body jerked and her core contracted around his cock. She felt him throbbing inside of her even as everything pulsated within her.

She sagged, exhausted but happily sated, as he moved away and then he lowered her to the mat.

He released her from the hogtie and helped her to her feet, then brought her into his arms and kissed her forehead.

For a long moment he held her before drawing back and frowning at her. "I told you not to come."

"I couldn't help it." She gave him a pleading look.

He shook his head. "There is no excuse for not obeying."

"I'm sorry." She wasn't but it seemed like he was waiting for something.

"You're not sorry," he said, echoing her thoughts. "You will be."

He sounded so ominous that her stomach twisted.

He led her to the bed in one corner with the metal headboard with numerous rings on it. Chains hung from the overhead frame above it.

Whips and chains, oh my.

Her cuffs jangled as she walked and her nipple noose bells jingled. "Stand here." He took her by the shoulders and forced her to stay at the foot of the bed. He went back to the wall of toys and took some cloths out of a drawer and returned.

He picked up the ball gag that he'd dropped earlier and wiped it off with one of the cloths. "Open up." He pushed the ball into her mouth, forcing her jaws wide. Then she saw that the other was actually an eye patch blindfold. He put it on her, leaving her in the dark.

What did he have in mind now?

"On your back." He guided her to the bed. When she was lying on her back he fastened each one of her wrist cuffs to rings on the headboard.

Everything he did seemed more intense now that she couldn't see.

He attached clips and chains to her collar and secured them on either side of her so that she couldn't move her head.

Next, he raised one of her legs so that her ass was about six inches off of the bed and she heard the rattle of chain as he connected the ankle cuff to one of the chains dangling from the frame over the bed. He raised her other leg and did the same thing so that her lower back and ass were up off the bed. The butt plug was still in tight and it helped to keep her on edge.

It was an altogether unnerving experience as she heard him walk away, lying in the position she was in without being able to speak or see, her arms chained, too. He had said something about consequences. What would that include?

A snapping sound and an immediate sting made her cry out and tears flowed from her eyes. She heard another crack and felt another biting sting of a whip.

"This is what happens when you don't obey, Christy." He snapped the whip again and she cried out. "Do you understand now?" She nodded, frantic for him to stop.

He did stop and she heard the sound of the whip landing on the floor as he tossed it aside. "It hurt, didn't it," he stated.

She nodded, tears still wetting her eyes behind the blindfold.

His warm breath brushed her cheek as he came closer. He rubbed her ass with his palm as he kissed the corner of her mouth. "Is it starting to feel good?"

She thought about it for a moment. It actually was starting to feel good. The sting becoming a warm burn that faded into a sort of pleasure. She had read about that, just hadn't experienced it until now.

With the gag in she couldn't speak, so she nodded.

He moved away and then she felt him between her thighs. The soft glide of his hair as he lowered his face.

And then he licked her pussy. She would have come off the bed if she hadn't already been partly raised up from the bed.

He licked her folds and sucked her clit while moving two fingers in and out of her. In the dark behind her blindfold, with him going down on her while she was raised up, was an amazing experience.

"Don't come," he said when he stopped for a moment and she whimpered.

He rose up to stand between her thighs and he pressed her legs farther apart with his hips. She felt his cock pressing at the entrance to her core.

He reached for her breasts and pinched her nipples at the same time that he thrust deep inside her.

She gave a muffled cry and squirmed. The sensations were so intense, so exquisite that she felt like she was on another plane of existence.

"You're mine, Christy," he said as he continued pumping in and out of her. "You are mine."

She was his. He could do whatever he wanted with her and she would love every minute of it.

He fucked her harder and harder and she felt another orgasm on its way. She was so sensitive from everything he had done to her, and from the amazing orgasm she'd had when he took her from behind when she was suspended.

And his words—they added to the intensity of what she was experiencing. Zach telling her that she belonged to him.

Her orgasm sped closer and closer. She struggled to hold it back. She ground her teeth, fighting it, fighting it.

"Come, Christy," he said. "Come now."

She screamed. She'd never screamed before. This orgasm was too big, too powerful to hold anything back. Her body bucked and she twisted as he continued to pump in and out of her, drawing her orgasm out.

She heard Zach's shout as he came. Felt the throb of his cock inside her. Felt her pussy clench and unclench around him.

When she finally came down from her orgasm high he removed the gag from her mouth and his lips felt firm against hers as he kissed her. She felt him unclipping her legs and removing her ankle cuffs. Then he released her from the headboard. Her cuffs jangled as he tossed them onto the mat. Lastly he took off the blindfold.

She blinked as she looked up at him. He was looking at her so seriously, like he was concerned about what she would say.

"You still want to 'play' with me?" he asked in a low voice with that sexy smile on his face.

She looked at him and smiled. "I love, love, love this. What's next?"

Chapter 9

"When you come over, I want you to dress in the outfit I'm leaving on the bed for you." Zach's voice came over the line, low and sexy, sending a thrill through Christy's belly.

She squirmed in the chair in her boutique's office as she thought all they had done last night. Excitement blossomed inside her as she thought of having another incredible night. "I'll head to your place after my meetings."

"I'll be just a little late," he said. "You can use my key code at the front door." He gave her the numbers and she memorized them.

"All right." She smiled as she pictured him, tall and dark and hot. "Can't wait until tonight."

"Neither can I."

She pushed the "off" button and started humming and she walked from the back room to the front register of the boutique.

The day couldn't get much better than the way this one was going.

Christy wanted to bang her head against the steering wheel as she headed toward Zach's. She was ninety minutes early because one meeting ended before it started and the other canceled.

The meeting with her supplier, Henry Hawthorne, did not go well at all. He was snide, making remarks about selling herself to the highest bidder and going off to screw an old boyfriend.

Christy had told him where to shove his collector dolls, each and every one of them.

She sighed. Now she had to find a new doll supplier. She only sold the finest merchandise and Henry's had been from an exclusive designer. So not only did she need a new supplier, she would need someone who could supply her with something just as good if not better. It was going to kill her business for the shoppers who collected dolls from that particular doll manufacturer.

The ass.

She shook her head as if that would help her shake off the wrong turn her afternoon had taken. The appointment that canceled had been minor in comparison. It was probably better that they had. She wasn't in the mood for dealing with anyone right now.

Anyone but Zach.

The thought made her smile.

She had tried to reach him twice on his cell phone but no answer. He wouldn't mind if she dropped by an hour early, so she might as well get ready for him.

After she parked in his huge driveway, she went up to the front door and entered the key code. The lock clicked and she opened the door.

The house was warmer than the crisp afternoon and she took off her jacket and laid it over the back of a couch then walked to his bedroom.

On his bed was a beautiful black and bright blue accented corset with matching panties and silk stockings and a note with a other items—black shadow and slutty red lipstick, along with a few more things. The note was instructions on how he wanted her to wear the makeup. Next to all of that were the wrist and ankle cuffs they had used on her the last two times they had played, as well as the collar and a pair of extremely high heels.

She removed her clothing and the trials of the afternoon fell away as she slipped into the sexy clothing.

When she was dressed, she walked to a full-length mirror and studied her reflection. She smoothed her palm down the silky soft material, loving the way it felt against her skin. The corset pushed up her breasts and barely covered her nipples.

She put on the makeup, including the eyeliner and mascara that was with the black shadow, then put on the red lipstick.

Yes, she looked positively slutty.

She smiled at her reflection. She was already so hot for him that she could barely stand it and keep from touching herself. The cuffs and collar were all she had left to put on. They jangled as she buckled them, and then she put on the leather collar. She slipped the steep high heels.

Bring it on. She was ready.

A noise caused her to startle. Was that a woman's muffled cry?

There it was again.

She followed the direction she'd heard it coming from—Zach's office. When she entered the room she saw that his secret wall was open.

Another muffled cry.

Her heart pounded as she stood there. What was happening?

Could Zach be there with another woman?

She had to know. She slipped through the opening and started down the long staircase. The closer she got, the louder they became. Screams, cries, muffled sounds.

Her heart pounded hard and her skin grew hot. She moved in slow easy steps so that the jingling cuffs or the sound of her high heels wouldn't catch his attention. She had to see what he was doing before he knew she had been there.

She tried to keep her breathing even as she looked around the doorway.

A nearly naked, gagged woman was bent over a padded sawhorse, her legs spread, as a woman in a leather bustier paddled her. The woman over the sawhorse made a muffled cry behind her gag with every swat.

Her stomach clenched and she thought she was going to be sick.

He was cheating on her before they'd even really started.

Zach had his back to the door and he was holding his camera, taking pictures, just like he'd taken of her last night.

Christy didn't realize she'd made a sound until he turned to look at the doorway. She clapped her hand over her mouth, but it was too late.

She whirled to run up the stairs and almost fell in the heels. She kicked them off and started running up the stairs, trying not to slip in her stockings.

"Christy!" Zach called out from below as she reached the door into his office. "Let me explain."

Hell if she was going to listen to whatever lame excuse he might come up with.

The pounding of his shoes was loud behind her as she ran from his office to his bedroom. She needed to change and get out of here.

She slammed his bedroom door shut and was going to lock it, but she wasn't fast enough. He shoved the door open and she stumbled backward and tripped over her shoes and landed on her ass.

"Leave me alone." She almost shouted at him as he stood in the doorway. "Whatever stupid excuse you might have, I don't want to hear it. I've already caught one boyfriend screwing around on me, I don't need another."

"It's not that, Christy." He walked closer to her. "I—"

"Forget it." She scrambled to her feet and backed up to the bed. "Nothing you say will change things."

"I'm a photographer." He gave her a pleading look. "It's what I do."

"Sure you are." She grabbed her blouse and held it to her chest. "You told me you owned restaurants. Was that a lie, too?"

"I haven't told you a single lie." He reached her. "Listen to me."

"Forget it." She turned away.

He grabbed her by the shoulders. "Listen," he repeated.

"Screw yourself, Zach Nikas." She tried to get out of his grasp. "Or go screw your play toys who are in the basement waiting for you."

"Come down to the dungeon," He held her in a grip so tight she didn't think she could escape him and that thought made her angrier yet. "Let me show you what this is," he said. "I have things that can prove this is nothing."

To her surprise he released her arm and she almost fell.

She reached for her clothing but he grabbed them before she could. Furious, she snatched up her purse and said, "Fine. I'll leave like this."

He beat her to the door and wouldn't let her out. "If you won't do it my way on your own, I will make you."

She placed her palms on his chest and tried to push by him. "Get out of my way."

"Sorry, honey." He whirled her around and grabbed her wrists and pulled them behind her back. He had them clipped together before she could even catch her breath.

"What are you doing?" She struggled against his hold but he was too strong.

He pushed her onto the bed and she fell back onto her cuffed hands.

A tremor of fear went through her. He looked so intense and focused.

She scrambled backward on the bed. He took a clip out of his pocket, grabbed her by the ankle cuffs and dragged her back toward him.

"Let me go, Zach!" Even with her hands and ankles cuffed together, she struggled and fought him. He reached into a drawer and pulled out a ball gag. He has toys everywhere, she thought.

"No." She tried to get away but he pinned her down and forced the ball between her lips and into her mouth. He held her and secured the straps behind her head.

"If you're not going to listen to me, I doubt if you'll believe me if I do tell you." He brought her up to her feet. "So I'm going to show you."

She shook her head and tried to scream at him. He picked her up and threw her over his shoulder.

It knocked the air from her and she had to calm down to breathe. What was he going to do? Force her to watch him with another woman?

He carried her down the stairs, his shoes hitting each step hard.

The light brightened as he entered the dungeon. All she had to do now was make the women see that she was a prisoner. Unless they were into forced bondage…

The next thing she knew, Zach was taking her off of his shoulder then held her by the arm. He opened the top of a cage, picked her up and dropped her in. She landed on her back on one of the floor mats. She struggled and tried to cry out behind the gag.

It didn't matter, his strength was too much. He attached her wrist cuffs to a ring in the top of the cage so that she couldn't move them and couldn't take off the gag. Then he took the clip that was binding her ankle cuffs and attached it to the side of the cage so that she couldn't move her legs.

He kept his voice low, controlled. "That will keep you from thrashing around. Since you're ready to run anyway, I figure that as a last resort forcing you to watch can only help. It won't make it any worse. I hope you understand. I don't want to lose you because you don't understand."

She made muffled noises and he pinched her nipples, hard. Her eyes watered from the pain as he said, "Be quiet. Watch."

He slammed the door shut. Locking her in.

Chapter 10

He'd caged her. She couldn't believe he'd caged her.

Christy sat stunned for a moment as Zach walked away. Here she was, all dressed up for him, ready to play… now she felt different dressed like this and caged.

But far worse was that as far as she was concerned, this was cheating. He was playing with other women, and who knew what else.

When he moved out of the way, she saw him and the two women who were in the room.

He gave a nod in Christy's direction. "She's supposed to be here for the next shoot but wants to play a little since she's here early. It might add to the atmosphere for you ladies."

The blonde, slender, and almost naked sub was bound in ropes, her hands behind her back and a red ball gag in her mouth. From the look in her eyes, the sub seemed a little nervous at having Christy there while the Domme looked at Christy with amusement.

With long dark hair, the Domme was neither pretty nor unattractive, but somewhere in between. The woman was what some might call and Amazon in size—tall and big boned. The Domme wore a red and black corset with matching panties, and leather thigh-high boots. Her makeup was heavy, her lipstick a bright red much like the shade Zach had told Christy to wear.

The bastard. He probably had all of his play toys wear that color.

"Would you like me to take care of your slave?" the Domme asked Zach. "She looks like someone I would like to get my hands on."

"She'll be taken care of." Zach gestured toward the pulleys and chains. "Go for it, Mistress Donna," he said to the tall Domme.

Christy wanted to scream and tell them that she didn't want to be here, that Zach had taken her against her will. But the fact that she was dressed as a sub and wearing cuffs it wouldn't be farfetched to think that she was just playacting. Besides, they wouldn't care anyway.

She was going to chop off Zach's balls when she finally got free. And then after some slow, painful torture, she'd kill him.

Mistress Donna cuffed the sub in suspension cuffs then raised her up, by her feet so that she was hanging upside down. She was high enough that her face was even with the Domme's. The sub's blonde hair hung straight down and blood rushed to her face.

Zach began taking pictures like a photographer would with a professional looking camera, from all angles and positions.

Mistress Donna took the sub's face in her hands and kissed her as the sub hung upside down. It was a long, slow, sensual kiss. "How are you doing, Vicky?" the Domme asked in a low voice.

Vicky nodded.

When Mistress Donna stepped back from the kiss, she raised her hands and played with Vicky's nipples. The sub closed her eyes and moaned, looking like she was enjoying the attention.

The Domme walked away and returned with something. She talked to her sub in a low voice that was almost soothing, but Christy couldn't hear what she was saying.

The whole time, Zach continued to take pictures from every angle.

Mistress Donna had a remote for the suspension gear and she lowered the sub.

The Domme nuzzled Vicky's breasts with her face then began licking her nipples, teasing them into hard, taut nubs.

Vicky moaned from behind her gag as Mistress Donna licked and sucked her nipples. Even as she hung in the air, the sub arched her back and squirmed from the erotic sensations.

When she drew away, Mistress Donna reached for Vicky's nipples, continuing to talk to her with everything she did. She pinched them then attached nipple clamps with ball weights on them. The sub cried out from behind her gag and squirmed in her bonds as the weights hung down, pulling her breasts.

Christy winced at the thought of weights like that on her own nipples.

"Be quiet or your punishment will be more severe." The Domme took one of the floggers off of the wall and started flogging Vicky with slow, sure strokes. "I don't like a bad girl. You know that don't you?" Mistress Donna had in intensity to her voice now.

Vicky nodded as she cried out behind her gag.

"You deserve to be punished, don't you?" the Domme asked.

Again Vicky nodded and made a muffled sound.

"Will you ever play with another Dom's sub again without permission?" Mistress Donna said in a harsher tone.

Vicky shook her head.

More muffled cries came from the sub as Mistress Donna spun her around while flogging her. Somehow the Domme managed to make the whole thing look sensual… And hot.

Mistress Donna used the remote to lower Vicky, using the controller to pull on the torso harness to turn her right side up and then set her on her feet.

It didn't take long for the Domme to remove most of the sub's cuffs and the body harness. When all but the wrist and ankle cuffs were off, she told Vicky to stay put as she went to the drawers and pulled out a small harness. She returned and put the harness over the sub's face and strapped it on.

Mistress Donna put the handle of the flogger on one of Vicky's shoulders and pressed down, indicating the sub was to get on her knees.

As Vicky knelt, Christy realized that she'd forgotten for a moment about being in a cage, gagged, against her will. Watching the Domme and the sub was incredibly erotic and Christy felt an ache between her thighs that surprised her.

Zach didn't look at her, his focus on the Domme and her sub as he photographed the pair. He still wore all of his clothing, jeans and a T-shirt and running shoes.

He never touched Mistress Donna or Vicky and didn't interrupt them as they played.

Was this for Christy's benefit? Was he keeping his distance from the women so that Christy would believe that all he did was take BDSM pictures?

"Lower yourself to the mat." Mistress Donna rubbed Vicky's shoulder, as if soothing her with her hand as she helped the sub down. With her wrists cuffed behind her back, she couldn't have done it by herself.

Mistress Donna seemed to be tough with the sub, yet at the same time Christy could tell that the Domme genuinely cared about her sub.

"Don't move." Mistress Donna gave the order to Vicky in a firm tone. The sub just lay on the mat with her ass in the air, her knees slightly parted, giving a clear view of her pussy.

Heat in her cheeks, Christy looked away from the sub. She'd never seen another woman like this before. Instead, she watched the Domme as she went to the drawers, pulled open a drawer, and took out a stainless steel ass hook. She paused to put a condom on the hook, grabbed a bottle of lube then went back to her sub.

Christy's nipples tightened as she watched the Domme lube the hook then put the round ball of the hook up to the rosette of Vicky's ass. The ball was at least an inch and a half in circumference and the rest of the hook probably half an inch round.

Mistress Donna worked it and the sub moaned as the ball went in, leaving the curved part of the hook with an eyelet in one end.

"On your belly." Mistress Donna helped Vicky all the way down. Then she clipped the wrists cuffs to ankle cuffs, hogtying the sub.

"How are you doing?" Mistress Donna asked her sub.

Vicky made a sound like a little moan that sounded like a moan of pleasure, not at all like she wasn't enjoying this whole thing.

"Good, because I love it. Love how you look." Mistress Donna took a short chain and clipped one end to the eyelet at the end of the ass hook. Then she pulled on an O-ring at the top of Vicky's head harness and pulled her head back at the same time she clipped the chain from the hook to the O-ring, forcing the sub to keep her head back while the ass hook pulled deeper into her ass.

The entire time this was happening, Christy almost wished she had her hands free so that she could make herself come. It was all so hot and turned her on so much that she didn't know if she would have been able to stop herself. It wasn't a girl-girl thing… It was the sensuality, what the Domme was doing to her sub, and how she cared for her sub.

When Mistress Donna was finished hogtying her sub, she left to go back to the drawers, and she pulled out one of the incredible vibrators that Zach had used on Christy. The Domme put a condom over the end, plugged it in then returned to Vicky. She put the vibrator slightly under the sub's pussy so that it was resting on the sub's clit.

Mistress Donna turned on the vibrator and Vicky cried out behind her gag and squirmed.

"You like that, don't you," the Domme stated.

Vicky made an affirmative sound.

Mistress Donna turned off the vibrator and the sub whimpered. "Do you want more?" The Domme asked.

The sub made another sound of need.

"Will you remember my rules this time?

Vicky whimpered and Christy took it as another yes.

Mistress Donna turned the vibrator back on and the sub moaned behind her gag.

Christy squirmed in the cage. The whole scene made her want to be in the sub's place but with Zach handling the vibrator.

She frowned. No, she didn't. Zach was holding her against her will and he actually played with other women. She was just another play toy to him.

Vicky cried out behind her gag, drawing back Christy's attention. She saw the sub's body shudder and the sounds she made behind her gag.

"That's a good girl." Mistress Donna turned off the vibrator and set it aside.

When Vicky was fully free, gag removed, and unplugged, Mistress Donna hugged her and held her for a moment.

"Did you have fun?" Mistress Donna asked.

Christy heard Vicky speak for the first time as she nodded and said, "When can we do it again?"

Chapter 11

While Mistress Donna and Vicky took showers in the private shower room just off the dungeon, Zach went to Christy and opened up the cage.

"I'm going to take the gag off," he said, "because I have to leave the dungeon for a few moments and I don't want a gag to be in anyone when I'm not here. I wouldn't leave you alone at all if I didn't think you would be safe with the ladies here." His dark eyes held hers "Promise you won't bite if I take out the ball gag?"

"Let. Me. Out. Of. Here." Christy said the moment he removed the gag. She glared at him. "I'll scream."

He sighed. "Go ahead. I'll be back before they get out of the showers and no one will hear you here anyway."

Christy's insides burned as he left and they kept burning as he returned.

The women came back fully clothed in normal, every-day clothing. Vicky's hair was damp and she wore no makeup, and the Mistress's makeup was more subdued than it had been when she and her sub had played.

Christy would have screamed and begged them for help if she thought it would do any good.

"Thank you, Zach." The Domme went up to him. "We appreciate you fitting us in."

"Yes, thank you," Vicky said.

"You're welcome." He smiled and gripped hands with each of them. "You know your way out, ladies?"

"I think we can manage," Donna said with a smile and she and Vicky left.

After he closed the door behind them, he turned to Christy. She glared at him and would have spit fire if she it was at all possible.

He crouched down beside the cage. He was so handsome, with his well-cut Grecian features, his black hair that she almost forgot how mad she was at him, and broke down right there.

"I can't believe you locked me up." She yanked against her ankle and wrist cuffs. "You'd better let me out of here, Zach Nikas, or you will regret it."

"Just hear me out." He pushed his hand through her hair in a frustrated motion. "Give me a chance to explain."

"I saw what you're doing." She clenched and unclenched her hands. "You're 'playing' with other women."

"You still don't understand." He sighed. "Christy, I don't want to lose you again. I need you to believe me in this."

"What's to believe?" she snapped.

"Photographing BDSM play was one of my businesses." He raised the professional camera that he had set beside him. "This one happens to tie in with my passion. You can see I was fully clothed. There was nothing sexual between the women and me."

"Is that why you took pictures of me and you when we played?" Heat made her body burn. "Because of your business? Because of your passion?"

He rubbed his temples with his thumb and forefinger. "No. That was just for us."

"Unlock my wrists and ankles." She pulled against them and tried for another tactic. "Please."

For a long moment he studied her, then slid his hand into his front pants pocket and drew out a key. He stood and reached in and unlocked the locks from the cage at her ankles and her wrists, but he didn't take off the cuffs and he kept her wrists secured behind her back.

He helped her to stand inside the cage, then picked her up and set her on the floor.

She wanted to kick him in the shins and run, but she supposed that might be a little childish of her. Instead she took a deep breath and raised her chin. "Take off these cuffs, Zach, now."

He shook his head. "Not just yet."

Pain welled up inside of her. "I was cheated on once, Zach. I'm not going through that ever again."

"I'm not cheating." His gaze hardened. He took her by her upper arm and practically dragged her toward the large TV screen that hung on one wall, near the desk and chair. He pushed her down in a chair in front of the screen.

"What are you doing?" She frowned when he wouldn't let her stand. Before she could try again he clipped her cuffs behind her to one of the chair's spindles.

"You're going to watch this." He went to the desk and returned with a remote control. "What you'll see is everything from the start of the session to the end."

Since she didn't have a choice she set her jaw and stared at the screen. When it started, on the screen Zach was sitting behind his desk and Mistress Donna and Vicky were seated in front of it. The two women had their clothes on, the same clothing they were wearing when they'd left.

He had one set of papers in front of Donna, and another in front of Vicky. The onscreen Zach said, "Everything we do here is recorded from the moment you enter this dungeon to when you leave. This is for legal purposes only. I do not use the video for any other purposes."

"Okay," the sub said, and the Domme added, "Of course."

"Just so we understand each other," he said as he pointed to lines on the pages for them to read, "This describes the scene and what will happen and you are consenting to what will happen. It also says I have the exclusive right to use all the images that are taken of you."

"Understood," the Domme said and the sub nodded in agreement.

"Vicky, are you at least nineteen?" he asked.

"Yes." She had a soft, pretty voice. "I'm twenty-three."

"Let me see your driver's licenses, please, both of you." He took one from the sub then ran it through a special scanner that she'd seen somewhere else. It was obviously to make sure the license was legit.

He went through several other conditions then had each of them sign two copies of the forms. He gave them each a copy and kept one for himself, which he filed in a drawer.

"You ladies get ready, and I will make sure I'm prepared," he said as he stood.

Christy frowned as she stared at the screen, watching everything that was happening. Was he telling the truth? Or did he not participate in this one later, for her benefit?

"This part gets a little boring, so I'll speed it up," Zach said to Christy and he raised the remote. He fast-forwarded until the Domme and sub came out of the shower room and then let Christy watch as the session began.

It wasn't long before the onscreen Zach looked toward the dungeon door, set down his camera and left. The door was not onscreen, the camera only showing at an angle from the desk to the play area.

A little bit later, she heard Zach's voice and him telling the Domme and the sub, "She's supposed to be here for the next shoot but wants to play a little since she's here early."

And then from that point on the scene was as Christy had watched it unfold. He fast-forwarded once it got into the part that Christy had already watched.

The whole thing was recorded through the moment the Domme and sub left the dungeon.

Christy sat still as she let everything settle in her mind. Zach came up behind her and unlocked her cuffs.

She stood and looked at him, her chin raised. "All right," she said. "How do I know this isn't just an example of you photographing and not playing as a part of business?"

"Would you like to see another?" He walked to the set of drawers beside the desk and rolled open a drawer. It was full of DVD jewel cases. "Pick any one you want."

She followed him and looked in the drawer. The cases were labeled, numbered, and organized by date. She picked up one at random and handed it to him. "This one."

He took it from her then loaded the DVD into the player. Again he pointed the remote at the TV and a similar scene unfolded with a male Dom and a female sub signing papers, and then changing into latex outfits and playing.

"Well?" Zach paused it and looked from the screen to Christy. "Do you see all of the lighting in the room? It's set up for this. From time to time I rent this dungeon out to others from the same club that participated in the auction, I am just very discreet about this due to my other businesses. I started doing this years ago. I separate my business from my personal time here."

Christy frowned. "Are you telling me that you don't have photos of women you have played with yourself as you did me?

"I told you," he said. "I have dated women and this is a part of it. I am monogamous in a relationship."

"Where are the other photographs, with those women?" she asked.

"I deleted the photos for both women when we broke up," he said. "They asked me to and I did it."

She gestured to her surroundings. "Then why this huge dungeon with showers and a desk and a TV?"

"I did it for myself," he said. "I can afford it and I always wanted a dungeon, and I appreciate quality. I used it for my business and my fun. But now it doesn't get used a lot because I hadn't found the right woman."

She raised an eyebrow. "You're telling me that you don't play just to play for fun?"

"No, I don't." He shook his head. "I need the emotions involved to play. I used to do casual play, but it was empty. You may find that hard to believe, but that's the truth."

Christy studied him, trying to sort through what he was telling her and what her feelings were about it all.

He pointed to his laptop. "You can go through anything and everything you want to on my computer and in my archives in every hard drive I own. You will see nothing personal in there for the past two years, since I broke up with my last girlfriend."

"Do you have a website where you post some or all of these photos?" she asked.

"It's a website I sold. I no longer have it but it does have my old work on it. I no longer contribute to it." He touched his laptop. "Would you like to see?"

She shook her head. "Maybe later."

"Did you take video of us?" she asked instead of responding to what he'd said.

"No." He shook his head. "I did record every session so that I have a record of everything that has happened in this room including consent. This is the kind of business where you need to cover your ass. I have the consent on video because I don't know the submissive she was working over."

"When did you start doing this?" she asked, still trying to absorb the whole thing.

"About five years ago." He gestured to the room around them. "That's why I have such a large, well-equipped dungeon."

"That makes sense." She pulled at lace on her corset. "How often do you do this?"

"Quite a while ago it was once a week." He leaned back so that his ass was resting on his desk, his arms folded across his well-muscled chest. "I paid the models and prepared and posted the video and photographs on the website. It just got to where it didn't feel right. I didn't like to be a part of the website business. It was an issue with the last relationship I had and I just sold the business and quit. Now, like I said, it is infrequent. Maybe three to five months apart at most for old friends only who ask me to do it for them."

A part of her felt better now that she understood. But a part of her wasn't sure she could accept that he did this with other people, even if he didn't participate.

"Here's my portfolio." He handed her a large black book that had been on the file cabinet. "Look it over."

She opened the big book on his desk and started flipping through the pages, one at a time. The photographs were amazing. So clear and beautiful. It wasn't some hackneyed job for cheap thrills.

These were works of art. Each photo capturing a vulnerable moment from a sub or an expression of power from a Domme or Dom. The photographs were snapshots into the soul of the person he was photographing.

"Why didn't you tell me about all of this to begin with?" she said as she went through the book.

"I didn't want to scare you," he said and she looked up at him. "Like what happened when you discovered those pictures before I had a chance to slowly introduce you to my way of playing." He shook his head. "You have a bad habit of jumping into things before I can share them with you. You asked me about the TV and the desk. I told you I would tell you later. I fully intended to do that."

With a sigh she finished looking through the book and closed it. "I think you should have told me from the beginning."

"You're right," he said. "All that can happen now is that you decide to trust me." He put his hands to either side of him on the desk as he spoke. "And that you believe me."

She met his gaze. "I believe you, Zach. I'm sorry that I didn't listen to you and give you a chance to explain." She gestured around the room. "At the same time, I'm not sure I can handle this. That you have people over and watch them play in this room and more than that, you did participate in casual play with women here for your pleasure."

"Why does that bother you?" he said as he studied her.

She looked at him. "You're kidding, right? You have to be able to understand that."

"I quit doing the business when my restaurant and nightclub took off," he said. "I sold the website and I'm out of that life."

She waved toward the door. "Then what was this Mistress Donna and sub Vicky?"

"I told you. Donna was an old friend who did a few shoots for me in the past. Now I just do it now and then for certain people." He gestured toward the drawer of DVDs. "If you look closely at the dates for the past four years, you'll see the difference in how many shoots I did before selling my site and how many in the two years after. I've done maybe eight shoots in the past two years."

"Even eight is too much." She walked up to him and said, "I just need to think this through."

Chapter 12

Depression was not something Christy was used to. She wasn't really depressed she knew, but she was down.

She missed Zach.

This was far worse than the heartbreak she had gone through with Ted. Next to this, her experience with him was nothing.

Even though her initial relationship was brief, her heart belonged to Zach and it always would.

There was plenty to do around the store, so she kept herself busy, waiting for closing time as she worked through her mind what she should do.

Three days had passed since the episode in the dungeon with Zach and his side business. Three days since she'd told him she needed time to think things over. He had called the past two days but she had told him she wasn't ready yet.

Was she ready today?

She paused to brush a bit of dust that had settled on one of the mirrors she had for sale in her shop. She moved her hand away and studied her reflection for a moment. She looked tired, sad.

"Suck it up, Christy," she said to her reflection as she smoothed her hair away from her face. "You need to figure this out and make a decision. The right decision, whatever the hell that is."

Could she handle strange people going to Zach's and him watching them play? How could he help but get excited when watching what she had witnessed for herself yesterday? She didn't want him to be excited by anyone but her.

Anyone.

Was it jealousy? Or was this a genuine concern? Should she be accepting of anything and everything he did? Or should she stand her ground because it was something that bothered her so much?

She pushed her hand through her hair, feeling frustrated and lonely, like there was an emptiness in her life that she needed to fill. She missed him more than she had the first time she left him. It was like they were two souls that belonged together and were finally joined again then ripped apart just as fast.

But this... Could she do it?

"Damn." She rubbed her temples. Why did he have to put her in this position?

Zach was who he was. Did she have the right to ask him to change?

Three days and she was nowhere near being able to figure herself out. Since it had taken this long, it was a good sign that she couldn't accept this other business he had established. With such an elaborate dungeon that included a private bath and shower room, and even had a desk in one corner, she should have guessed that something was different. But all that she'd been concerned with was him and how much she'd wanted him and wanted to do for him.

Enough. She needed to put up or shut up. She needed to make her decision and save them both some more agony.

She adjusted her flowing skirt and peasant blouse, tightened the scarf around her waist, and started to go to the back room when the bells jangled at the front door. A draft of fresh cool air from the windy day made its way into the store.

Even though she didn't feel like smiling for customers, she fixed one on her face anyway and walked toward the front of the store. She paused and came up short.

Zach.

He was locking the front door and his back was to her as he flipped the

OPEN sign to CLOSED.

She frowned. "What are you doing?"

When he faced her, she caught her breath. The wind had tousled his black hair and he combed it through with his fingers. He was so hard in all of the right places, and even his cream cable-knit sweater couldn't hide the broadness of his chest nor could his jeans hide the power in his thighs.

His dark eyes held determination in them as he advanced toward her and she had the urge to take a step back. But she held her ground and raised her chin.

"I'm not sure I'm ready to see you." Her voice sounded softer than she wanted it to.

"You might not be sure, but I am." He reached her, but didn't touch her. "I'm not going to lose you again. I told you that before and I meant it."

Without intending to, she did take a step back as he advanced. "Zach—"

"I'm not taking no for an answer," he said as he towered over her.

Heat welled up inside of her. She set her jaw. "You'll take whatever answer I give to you."

"It had better be the right answer." He caught her off guard by jerking her to him then cupping the back of her head and bringing his mouth hard down on hers.

For a moment she was stunned, but then she tried to fight him, force him away from her. What right did he—?

His kiss became more intense, more passionate.

And then she was possessed by the kiss. It whirled her away and she couldn't think past the way his lips moved over hers, the way he tasted, the way it felt being in his arms.

Before she knew it, she was kissing him with just as much passion as he was kissing her. She found herself wild for him, needing him, wanting him.

She felt a loosening around her waist and realized the scarf around her waist was falling. But then he pulled back from the kiss and the next thing she knew, he was wrapping the scarf through her parted lips and around her head, gagging her.

Her eyes widened and she struggled, but he was so powerful. He managed to pull her blouse over her head and then he trapped her wrists, using the blouse to secure them together. Then he jerked her bra below her breasts. He did it all so quickly that she didn't have time to think.

She fought him as he moved her backward until her back hit a wall. Something fell and crashed to the floor with the sound of glass shattering.

He picked her up by her ass and forced himself between her thighs as he lifted her legs and he pushed her skirt up around her waist. She struggled, furious with him, but she could do nothing with her arms pinned between her backside and the wall.

And then she realized she was turned on. She was totally and completely turned on by his masterfulness, how he was taking control, staking his claim. She loved it. Loved being his to do with what he wanted.

Zach lowered his head and caught one of her nipples with his mouth. He sucked hard enough to make her gasp, then moved to her other nipple.

He reached between them and she heard the sound of his jeans unzipping and then she felt his erection pressing against the center of her panties. He pulled her panties aside and then thrust into her so hard that her eyes widened and she cried out behind her gag. He kept his eyes on hers as he fucked her hard and fast.

Zach felt so good inside of her. She'd missed him. Missed feeling him like this. Being a part of him like this.

Everything wound inside of her to a tight knot of pleasure that began to expand outward from her center. With every stroke she found herself growing closer and closer and closer to a climax that could tear her to pieces.

"You're mine, Christy." He growled the words, his features dark and intense. "Do you understand? You belong to me."

The possessiveness in his tone, in all that he said, heightened her excitement, sending thrills throughout her body. Something about his dominance, the way he was taking her, made her oncoming climax rush closer and closer.

"Answer me." He pumped hard, her head bouncing against the wall with every thrust. "Do you understand?"

All she could do was nod. She was his. He owned her heart and soul, and now he owned her body, too.

"Don't ever forget it." He reached between them and pinched her clit.

She screamed behind her gag as she came hard. Her scream would have been loud enough to rattle the windows if she hadn't have been gagged.

Everything dissolved… All she could do was feel the power of what had taken her by storm, an amazing climax that went on and on. Her mind spun and her body felt washed with heat, her whole being tingling in a way it never had before.

Zach slammed into her once, twice, three times more before he let out a shout and she felt his cock throbbing inside of her. She watched his face as he climaxed, the passion in his expression and in his eyes causing her to catch her breath. She felt like she might never breathe again.

As he came he slowed his strokes, pumping a few more times before he stopped.

He rested his forehead against hers, his breathing even harder and harsher than her own. His forehead was damp with sweat and she could feel perspiration on her own skin. His chest rose and fell while she didn't feel like her breathing would ever return back to normal.

"Come back to me, Christy." His words came out like a man who was desperate for water and begging for just one drop. "Please come back."

She didn't answer even though she wanted to say, yes, yes, yes! There was still the issue that was holding back her ability to actually go back to him. How could she ask him to give up something that he had a passion for just because she couldn't accept it? It wasn't fair to either of them.

When they had both calmed so that their breathing wasn't so hard, he let her down on the floor and he arranged her skirt. He freed her hands and adjusted her bra before pulling her blouse back over her head then untied her scarf from around her head then tied it around her waist. He smoothed her hair and smiled at her.

She looked up at him. He was so dark, so handsome. He was intelligent and caring, sincere, decisive, had a great sense of humor, so much that she wanted in a man and more. She loved how possessive he could be of her, making her feel wanted, needed.

And kinky. She loved his kinky side.

"I wouldn't have taken you against your will," he said. "I would have freed you if you hadn't stopped struggling. You know that, don't you?"

"Of course." She rubbed her palms up and down his arms. "You might kidnap me, but you would never force yourself on me."

"Do you really consider that kidnapping?" he said with an amused expression. "I thought of it more as detaining."

The corner of her mouth quirked. "Holding me against my will qualifies."

He smiled. "But it was for a good reason."

"Okay, okay." She picked at a thread on his sweater as she stood close to him. "I guess there was no other way but to show me."

"So you'll come back to me?" He sounded so hopeful, almost like a little boy asking his mother for something special.

She sighed. "I just don't know if I can accept that you have people there, playing, while you take pictures of them. Record them even."

"I'm not taking a 'no.'" He set his jaw. "We belong together, Christy."

"What about how I feel?" She moved away from him then turned and faced him. "This bothers me, Zach. I'm sorry, but it does."

Whatever he might be feeling was difficult to read as he said, "What you are saying is that it's my photography or you."

She winced. "It sounds awful when you put it like that."

He brought her to him in a rough movement that caught her off guard, and he gripped her upper arms. "I choose you, Christy."

"Do you really?" she asked, her eyes wide as she stared at him. "You would do that for me?"

It was like his heart was in his expression as he said, "I would do anything for you. You need to understand that."

She wrapped her arms around his neck and pressed herself close to him. "I don't want to take something away from you that you love, just because it's difficult for me to handle. That's why I've struggled so hard over this. It's not fair of me to ask that of you."

"I will do it for you." He drew back and met her gaze. "And I won't regret it, ever. You are what is important to me."

She looked up at him. "Are you sure?"

He smiled. "I wouldn't have it any other way."

Chapter 13

One year. I can't believe it's been a whole year.

Christy smiled to herself as she waved to the last customer of the afternoon. Today was one year to the day that she and Zach were reunited at the auction.

He was an amazing man and everything was just as exciting with him as it was the first day they met. She had moved in with him within a month of the time they got back together. He did everything for her like he had said he wanted to and she loved to do what he loved. He did things in a way that caused her to want to do things for him.

His focus on her needs, his attentiveness was incredible. He would bring home dinner, do things for her.

He respected her decisions, her opinions. He was interested in her business and proud of her for all she had accomplished. He was an incredible businessman and found new and better ways to promote her business and grow it. He had a way of thinking about things that she found amazing. At the same time, she had made observations about his business that he had taken seriously. It wasn't a one-way street with him. He simply took care of her.

Zach's strength became something she relied on and looked to. He was tough when they played and he pushed her, he was controlling in her life, but it was in such a loving control that he had that it made submitting to him, pleasing him, something she wanted to do. It was so perfect.

As far as she was concerned, she was sold.

She locked up the front door and went to the back of the store and into her office to check her email before leaving. He liked her full attention when they were together so she took care of business during business hours, and he did the same.

Her skirt slid up her thighs as she scooted into her chair. Today he had picked out the chocolate brown A-line skirt that settled mid-thigh and a cream-colored silk blouse with a matching cashmere sweater.

When she opened up her email she smiled when she saw one from Zach.

There's something special waiting for you on the bed. I want you to dress in it and wait for me… There's not much of it, but you will like it. Be in the dungeon with a blindfold on at 7:00 sharp. Sit on the red bondage chair. I will join you at 7:01.

She shivered with excitement. Whenever she received emails from him, telling her what he wanted her to do, she couldn't wait to get home and see what he had in store for her. What would he have on the bed for her to dress in? What did he have planned?

Zach had been right. There wasn't much too the outfit, but she liked it.

Christy picked up the bra and panties made of chain mail and leather or at least that's what it looked like it was made of.

After she took off her heels, she scooted out of her work clothes before slipping on the outfit. It had chain mail circling her breasts, a patch of leather on the crotch, and was trimmed in leather. When she looked in the mirror she had to admit she looked pretty darn sexy in it.

She glanced at the clock. Three minutes to seven. That gave her barely enough time to hurry to the dungeon and be ready for Zach just like he'd wanted. She practically bolted down the stairs, her bare feet pattering on the stairs as she ran.

When she reached the dungeon she went straight for the drawer of blindfolds before going to the red chair and sitting, then put the blindfold on.

With the blindfold on her sense of hearing was so attuned that she heard the faint sound of a footstep as he entered the dungeon. She shivered with excitement.

She heard the door open.

"Beautiful," he murmured and she felt his presence a moment before he caressed her face with the back of his hand. "I want you on your hands and knees and I want you to crawl toward my voice."

"Okay." Her heart beat a little faster as she eased off of the chair and onto her knees. It was so dark behind the blindfold and she could not see anything at all to peek at to help her make her way. Her nipples felt achingly hard against the cool metal of her chain mail garments.

"Over here." His voice came from her left and she started in that direction.

She moved her hips slowly and sensually as she went, drawing out both of their anticipation. She wanted him to want her so badly that he wouldn't be able to keep his hands off her.

"Come on, Christy." He sounded closer now. "You're almost here." She crawled a little farther before he said, "Stop right there."

Still on her hands and knees, she waited until he said, "Stand, but leave your blindfold on."

She stood, wondering what he had in mind for them.

"Take your blindfold off."

She reached up and untied the blindfold before letting it fall away. He wasn't standing before her.

He was on one knee in front of her.

Her first reaction was wondering what he was doing on his knee, below her.

Then she saw the small black velvet jeweler's box in his hand.

He smiled as he opened it.

She clapped her hands over her mouth, unable to believe what she was seeing. A diamond solitaire ring was nestled in the black velvet.

"Christy, I love you more than I could ever express," he said. "Will you marry me?"

Tears stung the backs of her eyes. "Yes," she said. "Yes, yes, yes!"

He stood and took her trembling hand and slipped the ring onto her ring finger. She flung her arms around his neck and tears escaped and ran down face she hugged him.

When he drew back, he smiled and brushed tears from her cheeks with his fingers.

She shook her head in amazement. "I can't believe you got down on your knees for me."

He gave a soft laugh. "I hope you enjoyed it because that's the first and last time you'll ever see me on my knees."

He kissed her. A long, slow, amazing kiss.

"I love you, Zach," she said as they parted from the kiss.

With a smile he said, "I can't tell you enough how much I love you."

"So why don't you try?" she grinned and he kissed her again.

"I would love to. Why don't you come over to my little chair here."

"Yes sir. Anything you wish"

Bought

Chapter 1

She'd never been up for sale before.

Imagine, the possibilities.

The pre-auction wine tasting mixer was in full swing. Roni McAllister tossed her long red hair over her shoulder and smiled as she made her way around the room. She intended to scout out the place and pick and choose which men she wanted to bid on her—men with triangle pins, preferably. She touched her own pin, an ornate circle and rubbed it for good luck.

She intended to get very lucky tonight.

The pins were for members of the Kink Club to recognize one another. A triangle meant a Dominant man or woman who would be a bidder, while a circle indicated a submissive who would be put up for sale. KC had infiltrated the elite charity auction thanks to one of the members on the Uptown Charity's board.

An overture of excitement carried on the busy hum of conversation, and a shiver went through her. She smoothed her palm over her abdomen, the satiny feel of her black dress a caress against her skin. She had designed the dress herself, an exclusive.

She glanced to her right and saw that one of her best friends, Christy, had been cornered by a hairy Pillsbury doughboy who was wearing a triangle pin. To Roni's surprise, Christy had shored up her courage and had put on her circle pin. Roni was just about to head over there to rescue her friend when a g-o-r-g-e-o-u-s man interrupted the doughboy. The way Christy looked at the new man, with pleasure in her eyes, let Roni know that there was something between the two, more than just a natural attraction. Gorgeous looked like he could more than handle doughboy.

Satisfied that Christy would be okay, Roni passed by Leslie, her other best friend, who had accosted the Navy SEAL she'd been after. *"Come with me. Come with me into my lair..."* Roni imagined Leslie saying. Unlike Roni and Christy, Leslie wore a triangle pin and was a bidder.

Roni looked away from Leslie and finished making her sweep, identifying no less than four good prospects. Now she would give each of them a chance to talk with her and she would interview them in her own way, determined that someone who excited her would bid on her.

Number One was a nice looking guy with a triangle pin and a Dom's confident demeanor. He had short dark hair and warm brown eyes.

The man had just turned away from talking with another woman with a circle pin when Roni held out her hand and introduced herself. "I'm Roni."

"Drake Pierson." He gripped her hand and smiled. He had a good smile, one you could trust. "Are you enjoying yourself tonight?"

"Most definitely." Roni smiled as he released her hand. "It's a beautiful night, an exciting event, great people. What's not to enjoy?"

He laughed. "I like your attitude."

"And for you?" she asked. "Meet any interesting people?"

"I've met you." He winked. "I think I'm done for the night and ready to bid."

"Oh, so you're a flatterer." Roni gave him an impish grin. "One of those."

"I like to consider myself honest." He raised his glass of wine and took a sip before he asked, "How long have you been with KC?"

She paused, surprised that he had brought the Kink Club up so quickly. "Not long," she said.

"How did you get involved?" he asked.

She shrugged off the unease she felt as he asked the questions. He was just curious. Wanted to know enough about her to bid on her. "A guy I dated was in KC."

Drake looked interested. "Did you play much?"

"Not really," she said. She and the former congressman she had dated had played a few times but he wasn't the right guy for her. She didn't always feel… safe with him. She wanted to play and know that she was safe. A little fear was always fun, but not the kind where one was afraid the guy was going to go out for lunch while leaving her in a vulnerable or even a dangerous position.

He nodded. "What do you like and don't like?"

Roni was beginning to feel like she was at a job interview. "Listen, it's fun talking with you but I feel like it's rushing things a bit, getting so personal."

"I'm sorry." He looked a little sheepish. "I find you exceptionally interesting."

"I'm flattered." She gave him a smile. "I suppose we should do that mingling thing."

He returned her smile. "I hope to meet up with you again."

"Perhaps we will," she said before she turned away and went in search of Number Two hot prospect.

Drake might have been at the top of her list if he hadn't rushed right into talk about play. A little too anxious as far as she was concerned.

Now for Number Two.

She went up to the blond, blue-eyed man, who wore casual sexy like a second skin. "I'm Roni," she said and she held out her hand.

He took it. "Craig Hendrix." He gave a lazy smile that would make a woman's toes curl, including hers. "What's the circle pin for?" he asked as he released her hand. "I've been seeing circles and triangles all night."

She'd been so blinded by his smile and good looks that she hadn't noticed he was missing a triangle pin.

"We've all been to various events throughout the year," she said as she gave the canned answer that they were to give any vanilla—someone not into kink— who asked. "The pins were for special donations made to various charities."

He gave a nod. "I see."

Craig was easily one of the hottest looking men she'd met tonight, but he wasn't a triangle and she was all about exploring the world of kink some more. For a brief moment she wondered if she might be able to convert him into a kinkster, but the chances of finding a man who met her needs in that area, among the vanilla crowd, were remote.

And there was something about Craig…something she wasn't sure about. She had good instincts and she intended to listen to them—even if they did seem a little off the wall at times. Her instincts told her that for whatever reason she should move on.

"I'd better get to mingling." For the second time Roni used the "mingling thing" as an excuse to move on. "It was good to meet you, Craig."

He gave a brief nod. "Likewise."

As she turned away from him she had the strangest feeling that she'd just pissed him off. Maybe she had cut any conversation with him short, but she didn't like to waste precious mingling time when she was trying to meet a few more triangles.

After she moved on she went to her next prospects. Number Three had great potential, Number Four not so much. This time she had made sure to check each man's lapel for a triangle pin.

She was searching the crowd for someone else to check out at the same time she was walking when she ran into a solid wall of man. She stumbled back and the man caught her by her shoulders. At five-eight most guys weren't that much taller than her, but this time she found herself looking up. Way up. The guy had to be at least six-four.

He had harshly cut features and an intense expression, hard, unyielding. His eyes were crystalline blue and so cool that she imagined herself shivering and goose bumps swept over her arms. He was sexy in a dark, mysterious kind of way—*really* mysterious.

Yes, she had just run into Mr. Tall Dark and Scary.

Well, scary if it had been anyone but her. It would take a lot to scare Roni McAllister.

She gave him a brilliant smile as he released her shoulders and she held out her hand. "I'm Roni."

A pleasant feeling traveled though her arm as he took her hand. His grip was firm, a man of confidence. "John Taylor." His voice was so deep and powerful that it made the most delicious flutters in her belly.

She glanced at his lapel. No triangle. Too bad, she would have loved to have this guy tie her up. She'd teach him how to smile.

"I'm not so sure you look like you want to be here," Roni said.

John raised an eyebrow. "Do you always say what's on your mind?"

She cocked her head as she considered his question. "Yes, as a matter of fact, I'd have to say that I do."

Was that the faintest quirk at the corner of his mouth? Had he almost smiled? Ooh, she loved a challenge and this guy would be a good one. He was intriguing and he had sex appeal.

"How did you end up here?" she asked.

He shrugged. "You could say that I was roped into it."

"You're kinda cute." Roni gave an impish grin. "You just need to lighten up."

He looked like he had no idea what to do with her.

That was okay. She could teach him.

A male's voice came over the sound system. "Ladies and gentlemen, please join us in the ballroom," he said. "The auction is about to start. Bachelors and bachelorettes, please meet behind the stage. Everyone else find a seat and we'll get started."

"Gotta go." Roni held out her hand again and he took it. She loved the tingles that traveled between them when they touched. "See you later."

He let her hand go. "You just might."

A pleasant thrill stirred in her belly. Just maybe she *would* be seeing him again.

She hurried backstage where everyone was getting ready. She didn't even have a chance to check in with Christy because her friend was nowhere to be seen and Roni was to be the second person auctioned off for the night. She saw Leslie in the audience, waiting to bid on the SEAL she was determined to get.

Excitement made Roni almost bounce on her toes as she waited for her turn. Thank goodness she didn't have to wait for too long. Patience wasn't one of her greatest attributes, and she had a lot of attributes.

She had never had a model's body and never would. She had a full and luscious figure and as far as she was concerned, if you've got it, flaunt it. Many men loved her curves—unless they had a thing for Twiggy-esque women. In that case, she wasn't missing anything.

"Roni McAllister!"

She walked from out behind the curtain and waved as she greeted the audience with a smile. The applause was generous and she felt her heart rate increase.

This is it.

"This Irish beauty is a fashion designer from Baltimore," the MC said as he gestured for her to show herself off. "Isn't she gorgeous?"

More applause as Roni walked across the stage like a fashion model would before returning to her spot.

"If you're lucky tonight, you will be spending a weekend for two at Half Moon Bay with Roni," the MC said. "Let's start the bidding out at one thousand."

At the same time, no less than four men indicated they wanted to bid on her. The lights weren't too bright and she was able to see the men as they bid. A couple of the men wore triangles, the other two did not. She spotted John sitting three rows back and found herself a little disappointed that he wasn't bidding.

However, Craig, the vanilla guy was bidding, despite the fact that she had come close to blowing him off. What would it be like to be owned by him for a weekend? Hopefully more interesting than their conversation had been.

The bidding reached twelve thousand and there was a pause before someone in the back said "Thirteen."

She knew that voice. It was John's.

A thrill went through her. Mr. Tall Dark and Scary had actually bid on her.

The next thing she knew, the auctioneer pounded his gavel and said, "Sold. To Mr. John Taylor."

Another shiver of excitement made her almost jittery as she was escorted from the stage and down the stairs to where John waited for her.

"Hi, cutie." She grinned at his perplexed expression when she called him cutie. He really didn't know what to do with her. *All the more fun for Roni.*

"Planning on staying for the after auction dessert party and dance?" she asked even though he didn't look like a dessert guy much less a dancing guy. With his dark presence she was surprised he was even here.

"I didn't get a chance to eat dinner before I came." He moved his gaze around the room. There was something deliberate and calculating in the way he looked at everything. "I think I'll get something in the lounge."

"Mind if I tag along?" She smiled as he looked back to her. She had planned on staying to chat with her friends afterward, but something about John made her want to spend some time with him. "It will give us a chance to get to know each other before our weekend away."

"I hope you like bar food," he said. "What I want is a good burger, fries, and a beer."

Now that seemed to suit him better than a suit and tie and an exclusive charity auction no matter how good he looked in a suit. It wasn't that he didn't look like he should be there, it was more that he looked like he'd be happier in some place casual like a bar, knocking back a bottle of beer instead of sipping from glasses of wine.

"Sounds good to me." She fell into step beside John as he started toward the doors leading from the ballroom and out to the lounge. "I'm ready."

Chapter 2

Before joining John in the lounge, Roni excused herself to go to the ladies room. When she came back out of the restroom, she nearly ran into Drake, the Dom she'd spoken with first out of all of her prospects.

He smiled when he saw her and came to a stop. "I apologize for getting too personal with you earlier," he said.

Something about him and his sincerity sent a pleasant warmth through Roni. "That's all right. I guess we can be a little enthusiastic about what we love."

"I find you very interesting," he said. "I wasn't able to bid high enough but I'd like the chance to get to know you better."

Yes, he had been way too forward when they'd first met. But, should she give him another chance? He was good-looking and sexy. He had just touched too soon on a subject they both enjoyed. He had an allure about him that drew her in.

"Sure." Before she could change her mind she opened up her purse that she had picked up at the coat check after the auction. She found a grocery receipt and scribbled her name and phone number on the back of it. "That's my mobile number." She handed him the paper. "You can call me pretty much anytime."

"Great, Roni." His grin seemed to light a spark in his eyes as he slipped the receipt into the inside pocket of his suit jacket. "I'll call you."

"All right." She gestured toward lounge. "Meeting my buyer for a drink now. I'd better go."

"That's something else I wanted to mention. I've heard about that guy." Drake looked troubled. "You need to be careful."

"What do you mean?" She frowned.

"Just watch out for him." He stared in the direction she had gestured to. "I'm worried about you."

"I'll be fine." She put her hand on his arm. "Don't be concerned about me."

"Can't help it." He shook his head as she moved her hand away. "Just be careful, okay?"

"Sure." She didn't know what he was talking about, but she'd get her own read on John. "I'll talk with you when you call tomorrow."

Drake nodded. "Have a good night."

I intend to.

She parted ways with him and headed to the hotel's bar. John was in a lounge chair in one corner. He might be a man of few words, but he was what some might call broodingly handsome. Dark and dangerous looking, his jaw set, he looked like a caged tiger ready to tear into its handler.

Drake's words came back to her—when he'd told her that she needed to be careful around John.

Roni mentally shook her head. He might look almost fierce right now while doing something as simple as reading a menu, but she didn't feel like she had to worry about him harming her. Although she did wonder what it was that Drake had heard about him.

She watched John as she walked in his direction. He'd taken off his suit jacket and had laid it over one of the two other chairs at the table, rolled up his shirtsleeves, and took off his tie. The shirt was white against his tanned skin and it pulled tight over his powerful shoulders. She could tell that beneath the material that he was cut, every muscle well defined.

Damn, he's hot.

"Hi," she said when she reached the table.

He gestured toward the chair without the suit jacket. "Have a seat."

What would she have to do to get a smile out of the man?

Goal number one.

Roni slipped in and sat across from him. She picked up the menu on the table in front of her.

"I'm a little hungry." She leaned back in her chair. "Just an appetizer would be good."

The server appeared and asked for their drink order. To no surprise, John ordered a pint of Guinness along with a double cheeseburger with fries. Roni went for the sweet potato fries and a rum and Coke.

The server left and Roni crossed her legs at her knees. "How did you get involved with Uptown Charity?"

John shrugged one shoulder. "A friend told me about it."

She watched him as she asked her next question. "Why this one, a battered woman's shelter charity?"

He focused on her as he responded. "My mom took my brother and me to the shelter with her when I was nine. I owe them my mom's life."

"Oh." Roni felt a little taken aback. "I'm sorry if that was too personal to ask."

He shook his head. "No problem."

"I'm glad it doesn't bother you to talk about it." She had the feeling that wasn't something he shared with everyone. "Why did you buy me?" She tilted her head, genuinely curious.

He leaned back in his seat, folded his arms, and studied her. "I don't know."

Roni almost laughed. He really didn't know what to do with her.

"I'll tell you why." She gave him a teasing grin. "Some part of you likes that I'm outgoing and can talk enough for the both of us."

"You've got the talking enough for the both of us part down," he said and she knew he was teasing her. She swore she saw a muscle twitch in his jaw as if he might smile.

She did laugh this time. "Don't worry. I promise not to drive you too crazy." *Maybe.*

The server arrived with their drinks. When he left, Roni sipped her rum and Coke while John took a drink of his beer.

"What do you do for a living?" she asked when she set her glass down.

He lowered his beer mug and the glass made a *thunk* as it hit the wood. "Security."

"Securities or security?" She was sure she knew what he'd meant, but she liked pushing him.

"I make sure people and things stay safe," he said, then he turned the tables on her. "You're a fashion designer," he stated.

She was going to ask him how he knew when she realized the auctioneer had announced it to the whole room. "I work for an upscale clothing manufacturer."

"How long have you been doing that?" He looked interested in hearing about her career.

Maybe the beer was loosening him up, now that he was asking questions. She had the feeling that he had a knack for asking people the right questions to find out what he needed to know.

She scrunched up her nose as she thought about what he'd asked. "I graduated from a fashion college in New York City nine years ago and was hired right away by a Manhattan manufacturer. I worked there for three years then moved to Baltimore and have worked here for the past six years."

Their food arrived, cutting off their conversation. John's huge double cheeseburger and fries were laid out in front of him and the basket of sweet potato fries was set close to Roni.

When they were alone again, she picked up a sweet potato fry. "Do you just have the one brother?"

"Yes." He took a huge bite of his burger. When she waited for him to elaborate, he paused in between bites. "He lives in Baltimore."

Roni couldn't help smiling around him. He had a tough exterior but she could see that below it was something soft, something she wanted to get to know better.

"I have a huge Irish family in South Boston." She shifted in her seat. "My father's a cop and my mother is a stay at home mom. I have three brothers and two sisters and a boatload of cousins."

She shook her head and smiled. "We all grew up trying to talk over each other. My parents didn't raise shy, reticent kids."

When Roni had said "cop" she thought she saw a flicker of something in John's expression but he continued eating.

They spent another hour with Roni drilling him with questions about his past and present and John turning things around on her so that she was answering his questions instead.

He polished off his burger and wiped his mouth with a napkin. "What made you decide to put yourself up on the auction block?"

"To help the charity," she said. If he wore a triangle pin she would have told him more.

He took a drink of his beer then studied her like he knew she wasn't giving him the complete truth. "Tell me about the circle and triangle pins," he asked as if she had just said her thought out loud.

She started to give the same answer that she'd given the vanilla guy back at the wine tasting. She changed her mind. "I have a feeling you'd see straight through me if I told you anything but the truth."

He continued to study her, waiting. Again she had the impression that he was good at this. Waiting for her to say something and letting her spill it all out.

"Everyone wearing a circle or a triangle belongs to an exclusive club, the Kink Club, or KC as we like to call it." She watched him for a reaction but his facial muscles didn't even twitch. "A triangle means the person is a Dominant while the circle indicates a submissive." She had the weirdest feeling that he already knew all of what she'd just told him.

His gaze moved to her pin and returned to her. "You like tie-up games."

"Are you good with rope?" She couldn't have stopped herself if she'd wanted to as she teased him.

She could swear the corner of his mouth quirked when she said the words. *Ha.* She'd get him to smile yet.

He gripped the handle of his beer mug. "As a matter of fact I am."

"Then we have something in common." She grinned. "You like to play with rope and I like to be tied up."

She picked up a fry and pointed it at him. "You more than know your way around a couple of ropes, don't you," she stated. "I have a feeling you know exactly what the kink club is and you were testing me."

He tossed his napkin onto his empty plate. "We'll keep it to the fact that we both like rope."

She ate her last sweet potato fry. "Okay. For now."

"You're wearing a circle, but I'm not sure you're much of a submissive," he said, bringing the conversation back to circles and triangles.

She shrugged and wiped her fingers on a napkin. "Just because I'm outgoing and like to have fun doesn't mean I won't submit to the right man."

He looked over the rim of his beer mug. "What's your idea of the right man?"

With her eyes locked with his, she said, "The right man for me is someone confident, in charge, intelligent, and successful."

She couldn't tell what he was thinking as he looked at her. "Successful as in money?" he asked.

"No." She shook her head. "Success means someone who is successful at what he does. That can be pretty much anything. Someone who takes pride in what he does and works to be the best that he can at it. Money has little to do with it as far as I'm concerned. I don't care about that. I care about being with a man who has goals, whatever those goals might be, and he strives to reach them.

"Take my family," she continued. "My mom worked hard to raise six children and I believe she was good at what she did. She was and is successful. My father is a cop and he is good at what he does. He's successful. My brothers are all military and they work their asses off to be good at what they do. And you know what? That's success.

"One of my sisters is a school teacher and the other is studying to be one." Roni went on, passionate about how she felt. "And you know schoolteachers don't get paid nearly enough. But if they're good teachers, strive to be good at what they do and send children out into the world prepared to face what comes next, that's success."

After a pause, John said, "People usually equate money with success."

Roni pushed her hair over her shoulder. "That's pretty shallow thinking."

He gave a slow nod. "You're right."

"I know I'm right." She smiled. "And there's even success in BDSM. A successful Dom is one who is passionate about play and is careful and safe. And no matter how tough, the Dom really cares about the welfare and wellbeing of his sub."

John pulled out his wallet and put cash with the bill on the table. "How are you getting home?"

"I'm planning on catching a cab," she said as she started to get up from her chair.

He frowned. "There's a serial killer out there and you shouldn't go anywhere without friends."

A slow chill rolled down her spine. "I heard about that on the news."

"Come on." He got to his feet and grabbed his suit jacket and tie. "I'll give you a ride."

Chapter 3

Roni watched patterns of porch lights that winked through the trees as John guided his truck down the street to her home. She had already given him her address and house number.

He pulled his truck into her driveway and put it into park and she said, "It's still early, so come on in. I have beer in the fridge."

She was afraid he would say no but he gave a nod. "All right."

A spark of excitement went through her. The fact that he'd said yes felt like a small victory. She opened the door to his truck and was trying to decide the best way to get down without tripping over her heels when John appeared and helped her out.

When she was solidly on her feet she looked up at him. "Thank you." On impulse she reached up and lightly kissed his cheek. His light evening stubble was rough against her lips.

She didn't give him time to react. She hooked her arm through his and walked with him along the path to her front porch and up the stairs that squeaked with every step. By the time they reached the door she had her key in hand. He took the key from her before she had the opportunity to use it and he opened the bolt lock and the door lock.

As he held the door open for her, she noticed that he casually looked up and down the street and wondered why. It was like he was surveying his surroundings, making sure everything was clear. The entire way home he had continued to check his mirrors as if watching to make sure they weren't being followed.

You're being silly, she told herself.

"Take off your jacket and make yourself comfortable," she said as she gestured toward the couch and chairs in her living room. "I'll get the beer."

She passed the grandfather clock and entered the kitchen through the pair of swinging doors. A six-pack of Heineken was in the fridge and she grabbed two bottles before returning to the living room where John was relaxing on the couch. He'd taken off his jacket and tie and had laid them on a chair near the front door. She smiled and handed him a bottle of beer and set her own bottle on the coffee table.

"I have to get this dress off and get into something else." She headed toward her bedroom and looked back at him. He had an eyebrow raised. "Don't worry," she said. "I don't plan on putting anything racy on to seduce you."

"Too bad," he murmured and she grinned and disappeared into her bedroom.

She was tempted, really tempted, to go out in her corset and panties, just to get his reaction, but decided not to and went for a long button-up silk shirt in emerald green that she used for a nightshirt, and she rolled up the sleeves.

When she returned to the living room, John had the TV on and was watching highlights of the day's games on ESPN.

"Color me not surprised." Roni laughed as she approached the couch. He looked at her and something flared in his eyes, something like lust. Maybe the shirt was sexier than she had intended.

"I'll take your empty." She leaned down to pick up his bottle from the coffee table and as she did she looked at him to see that he was staring at her breasts. She glanced down and felt a rush of heat to her cheeks when she saw that her top button was undone and there was a clear view of her cleavage. She rushed to grab the bottle and almost tripped over his feet when she stepped away from the coffee table.

"Oops." She held her free hand to the top of her blouse. "I'm forward, I know, but that was not intentional."

He gave her a dark look that she couldn't read. "I enjoyed the view."

She wasn't used to feeling embarrassed, but then she'd never flashed a man in quite the same way before. "Take mine and I'll be right back." She gestured toward the Heineken she'd put on the coffee table for herself.

He leaned forward and took it and she thought she saw amusement on his features. As she walked to the kitchen she couldn't help a grin to herself. Amusement was a step closer to a smile.

After she snagged herself another beer, she walked from the tile that was cool beneath her bare feet to the soft carpet in the living room. He still had the sports news on but turned it off when she reached him.

He looked so hot and sexy as he studied her, dark sensuality in his eyes. She sat on the couch, next to him, and put her feet up on the coffee table. She twisted the cap on her beer and tossed the cap onto an end table before she took a long drink. She'd always enjoyed the flavor of beer over wine or anything sweet.

John took a drink then lowered his bottle. "How long have you been with the Kink Club?"

"Close to five months." Roni tilted her head. "I dated a congressman who introduced me to the club. He was fine at the beginning and I got my first taste of submission and I know I like it."

"Things didn't work out, I take it," he said as she took a long drink of beer.

She lowered her bottle. "Nope. Cheating bastard."

John raised his beer and she watched as his throat worked while he swallowed. She had not submitted to someone like him. He was a man's man. Thoughts of him and being tied up by him made her skin hot and caused an ache between her thighs.

"What about you?" She sloshed beer around in her almost empty bottle. She was starting to feel pretty mellow. "I think you know exactly what KC is."

He drained his bottle then set his empty on the coffee table. "Yeah, I know what the Kink Club is."

When he didn't elaborate, she said, "So are you? Into kink?"

"I like it hard and rough." The way he said it made wild tingles shoot throughout her. "And I like rope and cuffs. I like control. Is that kinky enough for you?"

"We have a lot in common." A shiver went through her. She raised her bottle to cover her sudden nervousness, only to find it was empty. "I'll grab another couple of beers."

Hard and rough. Butterflies went crazy in her belly as she walked to the kitchen. She could easily picture getting naked with John and submitting to him. She wasn't one to rush into things, but the way he talked and looked right now, she wanted to be his tonight.

When she returned, she gave him his beer then opened her own and sat facing him with one leg tucked under her. His gaze dropped to her breasts again as she took another drink, but she pretended not to notice.

She was a little tipsy, the butterflies she'd been feeling now bouncing around like drunken moths in her belly.

People at the auction had to know John or he wouldn't have been able to be there. Her friend had said all the bidders were known well by someone on the auction board. He had to be safe.

"When I was dating whatshisname," she said. "I discovered something about myself."

"What's that?" John asked.

"I get excited when I experience fear." As she said the words, his expression didn't change but she felt a subtle shift in something in the air. "Not crazy stuff... But fear. Including being out of control to someone."

"I didn't know the congressman well when we first played," she continued. "I got the taste of being out of control to someone that I barely knew."

"Is it something you think of often?" he asked.

"I do." She nodded. "When it's someone I don't know well, it is a different type of excitement that is amazing. As you get to know someone in the right relationship, the submission gets better, but that certain excitement and fear from the early times can't be recreated the same way. That might sound crazy, and some would say it is dangerous." She raised her hands. "There you have it. True confessions."

Yes, she was drawn to it. She wanted the feeling that she thought about alone in her bed. She wanted to experience that excitement now and she wanted it from John.

"Stay here." She set her bottle on an end table as an idea—a rather naughty idea—came to her, and she stood again. "I'll be right back."

She hurried to her garage where she found packages of new rope and then went back inside and handed the packages to John. He took them with a wary look in his eyes.

"I want you to show me how well you know how to use rope." She stood and held out her wrists. "Come on. Put your money where your mouth is."

He stood and suddenly he seemed so tall and almost intimidating. Giving this man, a virtual stranger, some rope and letting him tie her up... She might as well be offering herself up as a sacrifice to the gods.

It was crazy what she was doing but she trusted her instincts. They had always served her well in the past. Okay, there was the congressman, Mr. Cheating Dickhead, but he had introduced her to KC so that had worked out just fine. She had only gone to a couple of the club's events with him, but they had been exciting and fun.

She kept her arms outstretched, her wrists in front of her as he took a rope out of one of the packages. He clasped her wrists in his hand and jerked her close to him, so close that she could feel his body heat, smell his masculine scent and her heart started pounding in a rapid beat.

"Are you sure you want to do this?" His heated expression was doing dangerous things to her body. "Once I start, I don't stop."

She loved the way he said it, the power in his voice, and the meaning in his words. Yes, she wanted this.

She shivered with excitement, she said, "I know I do."

Instead of tying her wrists in front of her, he turned her around and took both of them behind her.

She bit her lower lip as she felt him making secure cuffs out of the rope, wrapping it around each wrist so that the cuffs were about two inches wide. He pulled at her hands, testing the rope and she felt how snug and secure they were tied.

Fear mixed with excitement as he began tying her arms at the elbows behind her so tightly that they were almost touching. Her arms started aching but she didn't complain—she loved how he was taking control.

When he finished he gripped her shoulders. "So you like fear do you?" He gave a low laugh close to her ear that sent chills through her. "Well, you're getting what you asked for."

She swallowed as more chills rolled through her.

"I can show you fear." He slid his hands around her throat and lightly squeezed. "I could do anything to you right now. Isn't that right?"

She swallowed, her breathing quickening as he increased pressure. "Yes." She had to gasp the word.

He kept his hold on her neck and lowered his head and kissed her. It was a hard kiss, fierce and primal. It made her head feel like it was spinning.

When he broke the kiss he met her gaze, fire in his eyes "You tend to talk too much." He kept the pressure even as she nodded. "I'm going to fix that."

He picked up the additional rope then hooked his arm around her neck and drew her backward toward her room. When he reached her room, he kept his arm around her neck as he set the rope on top of her dresser then searched her upper drawer. He pulled something out and caressed it along her cheek to her mouth. She felt the silky softness of one of her panties as he moved it over her lips. He forced the panties into her mouth and secured them with more rope.

She looked up at him as he turned her around to face him. An almost exhilarating sense of fear shot through her when she saw the look in his eyes.

He brought his palms to her breasts and her eyes widened at the dark sensuality in his expression. The heat of his hands traveled through the satiny material and her nipples tightened.

"I think this is why you flashed your breasts at me." He began massaging them as his gaze held hers. "I think you had every intention of seducing me." He grabbed her long hair and her scalp stung as he jerked her head back. "Isn't that true?"

Her head was back so far and so tightly that she couldn't nod or shake her head. With her arms pulled back like they were it caused her chest to thrust out.

He lowered his head and cupped her breast with his free hand as he brought his mouth to her nipple.

She gasped behind the gag. It felt so wonderful with his hot mouth sucking her nipple and wetting the fabric. He moved his hand to her other breasts and sucked that nipple, too.

When he raised his head, he jerked her hard against him and she felt his rigid erection against her belly. "I want to fuck you, and there isn't anything you can do about it if you wanted to." He lowered is mouth to her ear. "But we both know that's exactly what you want."

He kept her head pulled back and nuzzled her neck as he started to unbutton her nightshirt. With every one that came undone, her blood rushed in her ears. When the shirt was completely unbuttoned, he let it fall open and expose her breasts and her silky black panties.

"You look so beautiful, so helpless." He caressed her curves then raised his hand and let her hair slide through his fingers. "I love the color of your hair."

One erotic thrill after another went through her as he fondled her nipples then moved his hand down her belly and slid it into her panties. Her eyes widened and her breath caught as he slipped his fingers into her folds.

"Wet." He rubbed her clit and her eyes nearly crossed from the pleasure he was giving her. He moved his hand out of her panties and she almost whimpered, wanting him to touch her again.

"I'm not finished with you." He grabbed the rope he had left on her dresser and released her enough to begin binding each of her breasts. He looped the rope around the back of her neck, then, around her upper chest and each shoulder so that her shoulders were pulled back. He then began to wrap the rope around each breast before finally tying it off.

The rope was snug so that her breasts were firmed up, her nipples hard and prominent. He tied the rope so that her upper body was in a body harness like she had seen in pictures. She had never felt such a restrictive tie.

"You're gorgeous." He surveyed his handiwork as he caressed her. "I love your body. I want to fuck you until your eyes cross and the only thing you see is me as I take you."

Her heart couldn't seem to slow down. She felt a little frightened, but mostly so turned on that she wanted him to take her. Now.

"You like fear?" his voice was almost menacing as he caught her face in his palms. "You'd better be afraid. You have no idea what you've gotten yourself into."

Roni's heart beat so hard it almost seemed to hurt her chest. He was right. She didn't know what she'd gotten herself into. This might not be harmless fun like she had thought from the beginning. She was reckless and she really should know better.

For all she knew he could be the serial killer.

Now that's just stupid, Roni.

Still her breathing was so fast she thought she might hyperventilate.

He moved his hands to her shoulders. "Tell me you want it. Tell me you want my cock inside of you."

Despite her fear and the wildness of her thoughts, she wanted him so badly she could taste it. She nodded.

"That's what I thought." Again he hooked his arm around her neck and pulled her into the living room.

Her thoughts were wild, crazy. What was he going to do with her?

He reached the couch and pushed her down so that she was hanging over the back of the couch, her cheek against the soft leather. Her arms were still tied behind her and her shirt opened all the way so that her bare breasts pressed against the couch cushions. The gag was so tight that she felt the rope rubbing the sides of her face.

It wasn't hard to imagine that she was taken captive by a man who was going to take her whether she wanted him to or not.

The brush of his slacks and his erection against her backside sent a thrill through her core. A zipper hissed and then the rustle of fabric and he was pressing his cock against her panties. It felt long and thick and hard and she ached between her thighs, wanting him to take her now. He shoved her shirt up and over her hips then her pushed her panties down. He knelt and took them from around her ankles and did something with them before he rose back up again.

He bent over her and his breath was warm on her neck. "You'll notice that with your elbows secured, your shoulder tied back, and your wrists secured to the harness, you have no leverage. Go ahead. Try and get away. Fight me. And I want to hear you, too."

He was right. With her arms back and her elbows tied she had no leverage, but she kicked back with her heels and hit him in the shin and he cursed. She made muffled sounds as she tried to get out of his grasp.

As she struggled, she heard the sound of a package and knew he was putting on a condom. Her excitement grew and she fought him even harder.

He put his knee between her thighs and forced her legs so that they were wide apart. She bucked against him.

"That's not good enough." His breathing sounded tight as he pinched her nipple. "Fight me."

The more she fought, the harder he became against her backside.

And then he thrust his cock into her core and she cried out behind her gag. It felt so incredible having him inside her. He was so big and the more she struggled the more excited she became, the more erotic it felt.

He pumped his hips against her and she felt his slacks against her naked ass. With each movement she made it seemed to magnify every sensation that she felt. He slipped his hands between the couch and her skin and grabbed her breasts. She cried out behind her gag as he pinched her nipples.

She could feel an orgasm rising up in her, heading out of nowhere.

"I know you want to come." The man knew far too much about how she was feeling. "But you're going to wait until I tell you that you can because I'm not through fucking you."

She groaned and tried not to think of how deep he was burying himself inside of her, how hard he was taking her.

It was impossible. She felt it coming at her, faster and faster.

Then he stopped and spanked her hard. She shrieked from surprise and pain, the gag muffling her cry. He spanked her again and again and she felt his hard thickness inside of her and the contrast of pleasure and pain made her whole body quiver. Tears leaked from her eyes from the combination of so many incredible sensations.

Her orgasm came closer and closer even though she fought it down. He started fucking her again.

He leaned over her back. "You can come now."

A muffled cry escaped her as she climaxed hard and long. It seemed like the vibrations would cause her to become undone.

He made a hoarse sound as her body trembled from her orgasm and she felt him throb inside of her.

"Damn," he said as she started to come back to herself. He braced his hands on the couch to either side of her. "Best investment I ever made."

Chapter 4

It was the best night of sleep she'd gotten. Ever.

Roni rolled onto her back and stared up at the ceiling and smiled. John Taylor was so much more than she had imagined. She looked at the pillow next to her. Too bad he wouldn't stay the night but that was understandable. He'd said he had to go to work in the morning.

Hell, they'd barely met.

And they were getting together again tonight. She had invited him for dinner and he had accepted. With sex like that she'd be inviting him to dinner every night.

She stretched, a long luxurious stretch. What a fantastic way to wake up on a Sunday morning. It had been a while since she'd had sex and last night had been *great* sex. She was nicely sore in all the right places. Nothing like being bought and used for his pleasure.

After making a pot of coffee and pouring herself a cup, she curled up in her robe on the sofa—the same sofa she'd had wild sex on last night—and powered on her iPad. It was her favorite place to read the latest happenings, and she pulled up the local news site.

She frowned when she saw the headlines. The serial killer had struck again last night, sometime after John had left her house. She thought about his warning and was glad he had brought her home rather than her catching a cab and coming alone.

A slow chill rolled over her as she read. Last night's victim was the fifth in the past two months. What was even more disturbing was the victim profile just released by the FBI.

All the women had long red hair, were between five-six and five-nine in height, mid thirties, single, business professionals, and lived within a tri-state area that included Maryland, Delaware, and Virginia.

Goose bumps broke out on her forearms and she shivered.

Determined to avoid getting caught up in thinking about the uncanny similarities of the victims to herself, she perused the rest of the news. Despite her efforts, her mind kept going back to the serial killer, along with tempting thoughts of dying her hair blonde.

Frustrated with herself, she turned off the tablet and set it aside. She had never been one to get caught up in the news. But man, this was weird.

She grabbed her cup of coffee from off of the end table and was headed into the kitchen when her phone rang. She scooped it up off of the kitchen table and read the caller identification screen.

LIZZY.

Or Elizabeth as her older sister preferred to be called. She hated the nickname her brothers and sisters had given her as they were growing up.

"Hi, Lizzy." Roni grinned to herself as she answered.

"Bite your tongue, little sister." Lizzy's response didn't have the kind of enthusiasm that it normally did. "I saw the news about the serial killer in your area."

"Yeah. That." Roni poured her now cool coffee into the sink. "Find a man who has a thing for redheads and what does he do? Dices them up."

"I'm worried about you." Lizzy blew out her breath. "Living alone, fitting a profile like that... Talk about a miniscule portion of the population and the guy is whacking them off? I don't like it."

"Not so crazy about it myself." Roni poured herself another cup of coffee as she held the phone between her ear and her shoulder. "But there's no sense in worrying about it. Besides, it's like looking for a needle in a haystack, trying to find women to fit his profile."

"But he's finding them."

Roni dumped cream and sugar in her coffee. "I'm fine and I promise to be careful. Just don't tell Mom and Dad. Both of them will worry too much."

"I won't," Lizzy said. "But then I won't have to because Dad reads the papers."

Roni groaned. "Downplay it, okay?"

"You be careful."

"All right, Ms. McAllister." Roni said her sister's name in a singsong voice, like one of her students might. "And I'll bring an apple to school Monday morning."

"Very funny."

"Thanks for calling." Roni took a sip of her rapidly cooling coffee. "Give everyone hugs and kisses."

"I will."

After they hung up the phone, Roni took a long drink of her coffee then set it aside. The morning had started out so awesome. She had to get her mind onto the more important things.

Like tonight when she and John got together again.

Roni selected a head of lettuce and set it in her basket as she picked up a few things from the produce section at her neighborhood grocery store for her dinner with John. After choosing some tomatoes, garlic, and onions, she moved on to grab some lasagna noodles then ricotta and mozzarella cheeses along with other ingredients to make lasagna. She chose a nice merlot from the selection in one corner of the store.

She'd spent the day catching up on things she hadn't been able to take care of during the week while she was at work. E-mail, bills, laundry, yadda yadda yadda. She couldn't wait to see John later that evening. He'd said that he would be at work until late that afternoon and would call her when he got off. She wondered what security company he worked for.

After her last load of laundry was in the dryer, she had headed to the grocery store. She enjoyed grocery shopping. It was kind of relaxing, taking her time as she made her way around the grocery store. Especially when it was for something special like tonight.

After she picked up a pint of sorbet from the freezers she went to the dairy case. She was taking a half-gallon of milk off of the shelf when someone bumped into her. The carton slipped from her fingers and slammed onto the floor, a flood of milk rushing from it.

"What—" She turned to see who had just hit her from behind.

It was Drake Pierson from the auction last night.

"Roni?" He sounded surprised to see her, then said, "I am so sorry. Not exactly the way I envisioned us meeting again."

"Never dreamed I'd be ankle-deep in milk." She shook her head. "But you know what they say about not crying over it."

A store employee said, "You can leave it, ma'am. I'll take care of the mess," as Roni started to pick up the now empty carton.

Drake's brown eyes were warm as he smiled at her. "I am glad to see you, though."

"Nice to see you, too." Roni returned his smile. Drake had the good looks of a male model—not to mention the body—but a down to earth presence.

She pushed her basket out of the employee's way so that the milk could be cleaned up. She cocked her head to the side. "What are you doing here?"

He raised a loaf of Italian bread that she hadn't noticed he was carrying. "It would go great with that pasta and sauce ingredients you have there," he said with a nod to her basket.

She nodded. "It would indeed."

"How about inviting me over and we can spend a little time getting to know each other," he said with a hopeful look.

"Tonight's not good." She would be *really* busy with John. At least that was the plan.

He sighed and with mock sadness shook his head. "My hopes dashed."

With a laugh, she said, "You still have my number?"

He reached into his back pocket and pulled out his wallet. "Safely in here."

"You can call me later this week, if you'd like," she said. Who knew if things weren't going to go well with John? She hoped they went great, but it never hurt to have backup. And as hot as he was, Drake would make excellent backup.

"I will do that." He returned his wallet to his back pocket.

"I'd better get home before my sorbet melts." She took another half-gallon of milk out of the dairy case and put it into her basket.

"Did you walk or drive?" He fell into step beside her as she went to the closest checkout lane.

"Walked." She parked the cart and started putting items onto the conveyor belt, and they moved toward the cashier.

"I'll walk you home."

She glanced at him and the hopeful look on his face. What would it hurt?

Well, for one it would encourage him. For two he might ask to come in and she would be getting things ready for dinner for John.

"I'm fine," she said. "But thanks."

He handed her the Italian bread. "You should take this."

"Thank you." She had completely forgotten about getting some bread herself.

After she paid for the groceries, she turned to say goodbye to Drake. "It was nice seeing you," she said. "Next time without the milk."

He laughed. "Yes, agreed."

She picked up her bags and headed out the door. She looked over her shoulder as she walked out but he was gone.

Chapter 5

The doorbell rang and Roni looked into the peephole, saw John, and she smiled. She opened the door and she caught her breath. He looked so sexy in a blue shirt with Levis and a pair of running shoes. His short sleeves drew attention to the power in his arms and the fabric fit his muscular chest just right. She liked the way his short hair curled a little above his ears and the piercing intensity of his blue eyes.

"Hello, beautiful." He leaned down and kissed her as she held the door open. It was a kiss filled with a day of pent-up passion that they both obviously felt.

The kiss rocketed her blood pressure. Who cared about dinner when she had one hell of a man on her doorstep?

"Hi," she said when he drew away. She wasn't sure she was going to be able to breathe for a while.

"Smells great." He sniffed the air as she let him in and she thought she heard his stomach rumble. "It's been a long day and I haven't eaten much."

So much for pre-dinner diversions.

He swung a duffel bag off his shoulder and put it on the floor by the couch. "Mind if I leave this here?"

"Sure." She smiled and headed toward the kitchen. As he followed her, she looked over her shoulder. "How was work?"

"Not real great." He shook his head. "Got called out of bed almost as soon as I got home."

"Wow, you've been up awhile." She paused and faced him. "What happened?"

He shrugged. "Security issues." It was clear that was about all she was going to get out of him about work.

"You must be exhausted," she said.

Another growl of his stomach. "Right now I'm more hungry than anything."

She gestured to the kitchen table that was already set for two including wine glasses, the bottle of wine, and a slender taper candle. "Have a seat. Dinner is ready."

"I'll help you get everything to the table," he said.

He carried out the pan of lasagna while she took the bowl of salad and the basket of garlic bread—which she had thanks to Drake.

As she lit the candle, she could tell it wasn't easy for the hungry man at her table to hold himself back while waiting for her to join him.

He insisted on helping her sit, took his own chair, and then he served up lasagna on both of their plates while she took care of the salad.

John wasn't real chatty to begin with and he was even less so when he was as hungry as he appeared to be as he ate. There was nothing like having a man who appreciated a good home cooked meal.

"This is great," he said after a few large bites. "I think it's probably the best lasagna I've had."

"Thank you." She smiled and dug into her own dinner.

When he stopped to take a drink of merlot, he said, "How was your day?"

"Not too eventful." She thought about her day and running into Drake. She certainly wasn't going to mention him. "Took care of some odds and ends that I needed to catch up with and went to the grocery store and made dinner. That was the extent of today's excitement."

"I could use a day like that." John wiped his mouth with his napkin. "Doesn't seem to be in the cards. If one particularly big problem was solved it would make my life a whole lot easier."

He paused as he seemed to be working something over in his mind. "Did you walk to the store?"

"Yes." She set her fork down. "I always do. Why?"

With a grim look he rested his forearms on the table. "It's too dangerous to be walking anywhere on your own. That means *anywhere*."

She frowned. "It was only to the store and it was broad daylight."

He shook his head. "Doesn't matter. If someone is looking for a person with your description, he's going to spot you day or night. All he needs is to figure out where you live."

Chills rolled up and down her arms. "You're talking about the serial killer and the fact that I fit the profile for his victims."

He continued to study her. "That's exactly what I'm talking about."

"I can't just live in fear all of the time." She clenched the stem of her wine glass. "I can't hide away waiting for something to happen."

"If it will keep you alive, then you should do exactly that." His tone was firm, decisive. "Stay in hiding until the bastard is caught."

"Who knows how long that will be?" she said. "How long would you expect me to be in hiding?"

"As long as it takes," he said.

Like hell, she thought. She wasn't about to spend her days shaking in a corner.

Instead of voicing that aloud, she changed the subject and gave him a seductive look. "Last night you said something about cuffs."

His gaze turned dark, filled with all of the danger, fear, excitement, and the unknown she could ever want. Yes, something about him scared her on some level. She wasn't sure what, just that there was an air of danger around him.

"I'll help you clean up the dishes," he said in a low tone. "And then I'll show you exactly what I've got."

While they finished putting away leftovers and washing dishes, the excitement within her grew. Every time their hands touched or his body brushed hers, new thrills tingled throughout her.

After she dried her hands on a towel, she turned from the stove to find

John inches away. He took her by the shoulders, drew her close, and kissed her.

She sighed, feeling something intangible deep inside of her. The man knew how to tie up a woman but her woman's intuition told her there was more to the man than what he appeared to be at face value.

He tasted so good, a masculine taste with a hint of the merlot they'd had with dinner. He moved so that her back was up to the countertop and he pressed his erection against her belly.

"Do you know what I'm going to do with you?" he murmured in her ear.

"Tie me up?" she said hopefully.

He gave a soft laugh. "If it were only that easy for you."

Intrigued, she looked up at him to see a smoldering look on his features. A look so hot and sexy that it made her knees weak.

A shiver raced across her skin. "What do you want me to do?"

He held her by her shoulders and then stepped back. "Take off your clothes."

"In here?" She looked around the kitchen and back at him.

"Don't make me wait." There was a warning edge to his tone that caused the butterflies in her belly to return. Still a small niggling of fear from doing something as daring as letting a virtual stranger tie her up. Again.

His expression was dark as he watched her take her clothes off. She removed her blouse and then her bra and something flashed in his eyes when her breasts were bared. He flexed his hands and looked like he wanted to touch her but he didn't move.

She smiled inwardly and kept her gaze focused on him as she pushed down her skirt and let it drop to the floor, leaving her only in panties. She hooked her thumbs in the waistband then wiggled out of them and pushed them aside with her foot when she dropped them to the floor.

When she was naked, she straightened and let her breasts jut out. She had a full figure, including large breasts, and men loved them. She had no problem using them to her advantage. His throat worked as he swallowed, but that was the only sign that he was affected. It was good enough for her.

"Come here." The words came out with such power that she felt the urge to hurry. She forced herself to walk slowly to him to make him wait just a little longer.

He reached into his back pocket and pulled out a pair of what looked like real police-issue handcuffs. Her eyes widened and he took her by one wrist and turned her around so that both wrists were behind her back. They made a metallic sound, almost like a zipper, as they were closed to fit her wrists. The metal was cool against her skin.

His warm breath tickled her nape as he pushed her long hair over her shoulders and kissed the back of her neck. "You're beautiful, Roni. I love your body, love what it does to me to see you naked for me, and you not knowing what I'm going to do to you next."

She enjoyed the erotic feel of his jeans against her bare ass as he pressed himself against her. He moved so that he was standing in front of her again.

The next thing he pulled out of his back pocket looked like two huge zip-ties connected together. He bent on one knee and put one ankle through one loop and her other ankle through the opposite loop so that her ankles were cuffed together.

He rose up and grasped her by one arm and escorted her into the living room, like a police officer taking a suspect away from a crime. She couldn't take very big steps with her ankles tied so she shuffled her way there. He brought her up short in front of the bag he had brought with him.

"Stand right there." His voice was deep and filled with something almost menacing that made a queer sensation slide through her belly and she shivered. He hadn't hurt her last night and he could have. So what reason did she have to be afraid?

He opened the bag and she saw exactly what she should be afraid of.

Chapter 6

Battery cables.

With big clamps on the ends.

"What are you planning on doing with those?" Her voice shook a little.

"They make great nipple clamps." He said it casually. "I like to use things you can find around the house.

"Uh-Uh." She cleared her throat. "I draw the line at battery cables."

He grabbed a handful of her hair and jerked her head back. "There's not a whole hell of a lot that you can do about it, is there," he stated.

"Please don't." Genuine fear raced through her as he reached into the bag.

Relief made her knees weak when he brought out a ball gag instead of the cables. But then she realized she wasn't going to be able to say anything at all if she didn't want him to do something.

He put the ball to her lips but she kept them shut. He cupped the back of her head and forced the ball gag into her mouth. She gave a muffled sound and tried to shake her head but he made her be still as he fastened he gag so that it was secured firmly.

She couldn't stop looking at the battery cables with the big copper clamps. He wouldn't… Would he?

Again he reached into the bag. This time he pulled out a roll of duct tape and he tore a small piece off and put it over one of her eyes. She shook her head, not wanting him to take her sight, but he forced her to be still and put tape over the other eye.

She was naked, couldn't walk or use her arms, and she was in the dark. She couldn't talk, couldn't see. At least she could hear. The ticking of the grandfather clock was almost welcome.

Her heart raced as he rustled around in his bag then returned to her. A pause and then he was pressing something into one of her ears. An earplug. He filled her ear with another one and the ticking of the clock was silenced.

She tried to slow her breathing and prayed that John wasn't sadistic enough to put those battery cable clamps on her nipples. What did she really know about him?

She felt him press his body against hers and realized he was naked now. He grasped her hips and rubbed his cock on her belly, mimicking what she wanted him to do—minus battery clamps.

Fear of the pain she would feel made her tremble. She liked playing a lot and she didn't mind a little pain. Key word: *little.*

What was he doing? How far would he take this?

He nuzzled her neck and she thought she heard him murmuring words but she couldn't hear. He ran his hands along her body, stroking her, making her want him despite her fear.

When he stepped away she nearly cowered from the thought of what he might do to her. Then she felt his erection brush her belly at the same time he pinched one of her nipples. She held her breath and then something clamped down on her nipple.

She screamed behind her gag, her eyes watering beneath the pieces of duct tape on her eyes. The pain was intense enough to make her shake. And then he grasped her other nipple and then another clamp was put on it.

Pain radiated through her breasts and to her body. A part of her had thought the pain would be worse, that the teeth of the clamps would dig into her tender breasts. This hurt like hell but it wasn't what she had expected.

She felt his body heat and he pulled one of the plugs out of her ears. "I love how you look. Love how much trust you put in me no matter how misguided that trust might be. Because you really don't know, do you, Roni?" She shook her head and he gave a soft laugh. "You should be afraid."

He put the ear plug back in and she wondered how she had gotten herself into this. It all started with an auction, something totally innocent and fun. Well, she had expected kink to be involved but she just hadn't thought it through well at all.

She stood in front of the couch as she waited for what he was going to do next. Her jaws hurt from the ball gag and her eyelids felt sticky from the duct tape. The pain of the clamps had receded a bit, but not enough to make her feel comfortable.

Where did he go? She'd been standing there for a few minutes without him touching her. He was making her wait. Making her wonder what he was going to do next. He'd been away from her for a while. What was he doing? She couldn't see or hear him to know if he was even there. Had he left her?

Something hard slapped her ass and she cried behind her gag. The pain made her eyes water even more than they already had. He was paddling her with something hard. It felt like he was taking a two-by-four against her ass.

She whimpered, knowing it wasn't going to do any good but hoping that he would show her some mercy.

Then she realized that she wasn't feeling as much pain anymore on her nipples and the swats weren't a lot more than spankings from a paddle. She still cried out with each one but they had become more whimpers than anything else.

When he stopped swatting her, he took her face in his hands and kissed the corner of her mouth by her gag. He removed the earplugs. "That wasn't so bad, now was it?"

She paused or a moment, thinking about it. Her fear had been the most intense part of the whole thing. Wondering what he was going to do next, keeping her constantly on edge.

"I want you on your knees." He held her by her upper arms, helping her since she couldn't do it by herself with the ankle cuffs on and making sure she didn't fall.

He unfastened the ball gag and pulled it out of her mouth. She was about to give a sigh of relief when he replaced the gag with his cock.

She made a cry of surprise that was muffled by his erection. He cupped the back of her head with his hand and forced her to go up and down his cock. She started to suck, loving the feel of him, the taste of him, knowing that she could drive him crazy with her tongue, lips, and mouth.

The metal cuffs on her wrists were starting to chafe as she bobbed her head up and down and she felt as if they were being rubbed raw.

He clenched his hand in her hair. "I'm going to come in your mouth. And you're going to love it." He tightened his grip in hair, pulling it on her scalp. "Isn't that right?"

Another muffled sound came from her. Yes she would love to do whatever he wanted of her.

Somewhere her fear had left and she felt only excitement. Or that her fear had led to this magnitude of excitement. She found herself wanting more of whatever he could give her.

Minus the battery clamps.

He fucked her mouth a few more times and then came with a rumbling groan. His come spurted into her mouth and she swallowed it while she continued to suck.

When he stopped her, he pulled his cock out of her mouth. She licked her lips and wondered what he was going to do next.

After he did something with her ankle cuffs and removed them, he helped her to her feet. She started to say something but he shoved the ball back into her mouth and secured it. She still couldn't see and she couldn't talk, and she had no idea what he was going to do to her next.

He guided her so that she was sitting on the couch, her cuffed hands between her back and the cushions. He shifted and then he pressed her knees apart with his palms. She waited, wondering what he had in mind, when she felt his head between her thighs and he licked her pussy.

Surprise and pleasure combined as he flicked his tongue over her clit. She squirmed beneath his mouth, loving the feeling of being locked away while he went down on her.

She felt her climax coming on, racing toward her, a feeling so amazing that she didn't know if she would be able to handle the exquisite ride.

Her orgasm ripped through her and she moaned and whimpered behind her gag. He kept licking and sucking her until her body stopped bucking and she pressed her legs together around his head, telling him that she couldn't take anymore.

When he raised his head she sagged against the couch. He pulled the tape from her eyes. She thought that the duct tape would stick to her lashes or hurt her skin, but it didn't at all. She looked up at him with exhaustion. She hadn't seen him naked before and his body was even more amazing when he was in the flesh. He grasped her nipple and she looked down to see that he had put clothespins on her nipples.

"You're a tease," she said as he removed the other clothespin. "You had me believing you were really going to put those battery cable clamps on my breasts."

The corner of his mouth quirked. "Who says I won't? There's always the next time."

"You're assuming there is a next time." It was her turn to tease as he adjusted how she was sitting on the couch and he removed her wrist cuffs with a key.

He brought her wrists in front of her and massaged them then raised her hands and kissed the backs of them. "How about you agree or I put these cuffs back on you and we can start all over again?"

She laughed. "Okay, okay you win. There will be a next time. Just no clamps, okay?"

He gave her a devious look. "We'll see."

Chapter 7

"KC is sponsoring a party at Sir Thomas's dungeon tonight," John told Roni over the phone as soon as she said "hello". It was two weeks to the day that they had met. He added, "I'd like you to go with me."

Disappointment rolled through her. "I've got a cold." It actually came out as, "I'b got a code." She dabbed at her nose with a tissue. "Stayed home from work."

"That's too bad, honey," he said. She was amazed he had understood her congested mumblings. "Need some chicken soup?"

Despite the ache in her head and her stuffed-up sinuses she smiled. "Would love some."

"I'll be over this afternoon," he said before he disconnected the call.

It had been a great couple of weeks. They had spent time together or had met up with each other every day since he had bought her at the auction. She had never expected to find a man who turned her on like he did, or got to her in the same way he had.

They were supposed to be on their weekend to Half Moon Bay, but John had some issues to deal with at work that he couldn't get away from and they had rescheduled for another month from now. It worked out fine since she had ended up with a cold.

She shifted her position on the couch and snuggled into her thick terry robe and her favorite quilt that her mother had made. She grabbed another tissue before reading the news on her iPad. She wanted to ignore the stories written up about the serial killer, but it seemed to be staring her in the face every time she went to the news.

New information had been leaked to the press. The victims had all been tied up with intricate rope bondage skills. For some reason that made her think of John tying her up and it caused a strange shiver to travel down her spine.

Enough. She set the tablet aside and snuggled under her blanket to wait out the cold.

The doorbell jerked Roni awake from dreams of having all of her hair chopped off and stuffed into a bag. She had been running from someone holding the bag of hair in one hand and rope in another.

She shrugged out of her blanket, thinking it would be nice if John had a key, but it was far to soon in their relationship. It had the feel, though, of having been together for months rather than weeks.

When she peeked out the peephole, she saw that it was John and she opened the door. He walked in and enveloped her on a one-armed hug and kissed her on the forehead.

"I'm sick." She playfully pushed him away. "I don't want you to catch it."

"I don't get sick." He raised one of his hands and she saw that he was holding a paper bag.

"If I could smell anything I'd bet that was chicken soup." She closed the door behind him and followed him into the kitchen.

"Then you'd bet right." He set the bag on one of the counters and pulled out a large thermos.

"Don't tell me that's homemade." She came up beside him. "Or is it?"

"An old family recipe." He reached into a cabinet, grabbed a bowl, then proceeded to fill the bowl with soup.

"Mmmmm." She hadn't felt like eating all day but the soup looked delicious. "Homemade noodles?"

"Egg noodles." He pulled a soup spoon out of the cutlery drawer. "My grandmother and then my mom made them when I was growing up. Really simple."

He carried the bowl to the kitchen table and helped her sit before he took a seat across from her.

"Why aren't you eating?" She blew on a spoonful of soup with noodles and pieces of chicken.

"Made myself a chicken sandwich." He motioned to her spoon. "I know you like to talk but try eating."

She couldn't help a smile at the way he liked to tease her. She ate a spoonful then said, "This is amazing. I swear I'm feeling better already."

"Just eat."

After a few bites she asked, "Are you going to that dungeon thing tonight?"

"My plan was to go with you." He shook his head. "It's always fun to go and see a few people I know and watch a little. But since you aren't going I should get things done."

Maybe she shouldn't have, but she felt pleased that he wasn't planning on going without her. She still felt stuffy but she really did feel better after polishing off the bowl of soup.

When she was done he asked her if she wanted more then took her bowl to the sink when she declined and said she would save it for later.

"Are you staying?" she asked. "You're already germ infested now."

"I really do have some things that I need to take care of," he said. "But I'll call you later."

She followed him to the front door. "Okay."

He kissed the top of her head again then let himself out of the house and closed the door behind him.

She returned to the couch with her box of tissue and snuggled into her quilt to read while she waited out her cold.

"Yes, the man who bought you at the auction is here and he's with another woman." Leslie spoke over the music in the background. "I thought you were seeing each other."

"I thought so, too." Roni gritted her teeth. John had given her every impression that he wasn't seeing another woman. "I think I'll drop by and see for myself."

"Sure you want to do that?" Leslie said.

"You bet I do." Roni pressed the OFF button and found herself shaking. She didn't think her shaking had anything at all to do with her cold.

As a matter of fact right now the fire in her veins had replaced the achy feeling with energy. She'd have to get angry more often whenever she came down sick.

She pulled her hair back with a clip, put on a little lipstick and mascara so that she didn't scare anyone with her pale complexion, and pulled on a nice skirt and blouse. She might be headed off to murder someone, but she wanted to do it in style.

Her Prius had more get up and go than most would expect, but it didn't seem fast enough at all as she raced to Sir Thomas's Dungeon. She intended to catch him at it before he left.

She almost marched right past without paying but she caught herself and stopped long enough to fork over the money to get in. Twenty was a cheap price to pay to rip off someone's head.

What she didn't expect was how bad it hurt to see him talking with another woman. She was a redhead, about Roni's age but slender. She wore a collar and John was holding the leash.

The pain in her heart was like something hot and hard was lodged there. She had known him for a short time, but it had been long enough that she had fallen for him. *Yeah, stupid me*, she thought. *Stupid me.*

She couldn't take it anymore. She turned away and found Drake standing behind her.

"What's wrong?" He looked at her with concern. She shook her head but he looked past her. "That's the guy who bought you at the auction."

Pain stabbed behind her eyes but the last thing she was going to do was cry. "Yep. That's him."

"Did you two have something going on?" He studied her intently. "Is that why you didn't return my call last week?"

"I'm sorry." She dug in her purse for a tissue, afraid her nose was going to start running. "I just didn't want to lead you on when John and I seemed to have something going on."

Drake looked grim. "You deserve better than that."

She nodded. "Yeah. I do."

He gave a nod in the direction of the entrance. "Why don't we go somewhere a little quieter?"

"Okay." She glanced at John one more time and saw his surprised expression when their gazes met and it caused something to twist in her belly. She turned away. "Let's go," she said to Drake.

Just as they reached the entrance she heard John calling out her name. "Roni," he said. *"Roni."*

She ignored him but he reached her, caught her by her shoulder, and turned her to face him.

"What are you doing?" She shrugged off his hold. "Why don't you go back to your little playmate?"

"Let me explain." He kept his grip on her arm. "I couldn't focus on work and I needed to get away so I came here and met up with a friend who has a new sub." He raised the leash as he indicated the woman behind him. "My friend was called back to his restaurant for a little emergency and asked if I would stay with her until he got back. Being alone makes her nervous so I am just watching her while he is gone. It is not a big deal."

Roni looked past his shoulder and saw that the slender redhead behind John.

The redhead raised her hand and wiggled her fingers. "Hi."

Confusion made Roni's stuffy head spin. "That's all this is? Why didn't she go with him?"

"Look at what she's wearing," John said. "He wasn't taking her to his restaurant dressed like this."

Roni looked over the collared submissive. She had a small leather bra on and also wore leather brief type shorts, stockings, and high heels. The thought of the sub walking into a nice restaurant dressed like she was, let alone even in a car driving, was amusing.

"I would have called you but I figured you were resting and I didn't want to disturb you." Still holding the leash, he put his free arm around Roni's shoulders, hugged her to him, and whispered. "Look at her. Do you think she's my type? Besides, as far as I'm concerned, you and I are exclusive."

She took a deep breath and smiled. "Me, too." She leaned into his shoulder. "I'm sorry. When Leslie called and said you were here with another woman, I sort of lost it."

"I would have lost it, too," he murmured as he leaned down and brushed his lips over hers. "Just trust me, okay? If anything happens, give me the benefit of the doubt."

She sighed. "Fair enough."

It occurred to her then that she had forgotten about Drake. She looked in his direction.

He was gone.

Chapter 8

"I bought this just for you." John held a leather hood in his hands. "You deserve one of your own. I picked out my favorite one."

"I've never worn a hood before." Roni swallowed as she looked from the object back to him. "But I've seen them in some movies that I've watched online and I've wondered about the experience." She felt like she was babbling as she spoke. "I read a discussion about them too that a lot of people who are claustrophobic can't handle them. I've never been claustrophobic, but... What if I can't breathe?"

"Relax." He picked up the leather hood from off of his bed. They were in his bedroom in his apartment. "Once you get used to it, you'll like it."

"I've seen them and I know people who love to play in them." She met his gaze and his intense blue eyes. "And I know it's about the look as well as about control. But I don't know if it's for me."

"Roni." He had a stern note to his voice. "You *will* wear it."

"Please—"

He quieted her by pulling the hood over her head. She gasped and felt a moment of panic as she was encased in the leather. She forced herself to breathe. *People use these in play all of the time. I'm not going to suffocate and*

John won't let anything happen to me. I'll be just fine.

There were openings for her eyes and mouth, and small round holes where the nose was, to breathe through. To look at the hood on the outside, it was actually rather cool looking, with the eyes and sensuous looking lips showing through.

She decided to focus on his naked body instead of the hood. He had one of the finest male bodies she'd ever seen. Every muscle was defined, from his sculpted biceps to his taut belly to his athletic thighs. Strength and power radiated from him. His skin was a few shades darker than hers, the hair on his arms golden against his tanned skin.

He pulled her hair through a hole in the top of the hood, leaving a long ponytail. Then he took time lacing the hood up in the back. She could hear the sounds of the lacing amplified as he slowly tightened it snug. He turned her around and adjusted the mouth and eyes then turned her again and tightened it a final time. She could feel the snugness of the leather as it encased her head. She found that she could breathe easier than she'd thought. She peered out through the eyeholes and it was a bit like looking in from another world.

"You're doing great." He caressed the hood. "I love how you look. I love how it isolates your beautiful eyes and your mouth." He put a collar around her neck and buckled it in the back so that it was snug and not too tight. "Some people do have trouble handling it well the first time wearing it. Others love it. You are handling it well."

She pulled against the rope binding her arms and wrists behind her back. "Who says I'm handling it well?"

He hooked his finger in an O-ring at the front of her collar and brought her close for a kiss. She sighed. It was weird kissing him through the hood but something about it was hot. "I love that you're doing this for me." He caressed her naked body from her breasts to her hips and back. "I love the way you look and knowing that it's you inside of there, just for me.

"I love doing it for you." Knowing how he felt about her being encased by the hood made it exciting. There was something about him restraining her and taking away her senses and controlling even her appearance, transforming her into an object for his pleasure…it actually excited her. She wanted to please him more than any man she had ever met.

"I have more in store for you. Lots more." He went to a duffel bag that he kept things in and brought back two nipple clamps with a chain connecting the two. Her eyes widened, but she remained still, waiting for him. When he attached the first one she cried out. He didn't give her any time to adjust to the first clamp before he put on the other one. It was just as painful and she couldn't hold back a groan.

He moved her in front of the mirror so that she could see herself as he caressed her breasts. She looked sexy and bizarre.

"I love how you look... Amazing." He tugged on the chain between the nipple clamps and she gasped.

From the top of the dresser he picked up a leather gag the pressed it into her mouth and she heard it snap into place. She pushed on it with her tongue. It was there until John wanted it out.

"Love it." He squeezed her breasts as they looked in the mirror.

There was something about the slow deliberate way that John went slowly taking away her senses. Transforming her into his own object for pleasure that excited her. She loved that he picked out this hood for her and he loved her inside of it. She loved pleasing him.

But then he raised a matching leather blindfold and she shook her head. He caught her to him and turned her around to buckle the matching blindfold on. Now it was dark, so dark that she felt locked away, a more intense feeling than when he had put patches of duct tape on her eyes.

Her heart beat faster as he took everything away from her again. Almost all of her senses.

"You're doing great." He hooked something to the O-ring on her collar and she realized it was a leash when he started leading her around.

It was so dark with the blindfold cutting off her eyesight and blocking out any light at all. Part of her was afraid she would run into something, but a greater part of her knew she could trust him to guide her safely along.

She felt a subtle shift of air against her bare skin and knew they had entered a larger room. The air felt cool but his body heat radiated off of him.

All along she had to force herself to not think in terms of suffocation but on the fact that she could breathe easily.

He tugged on the leash and she moved forward until he grasped her upper arm and said, "Stop." Then, "Take one more step."

She obeyed and when she took a step forward she felt something soft against her ankles and knees.

"Kneel." He guided her to the floor with his hand on her shoulder. She eased down, trying to maintain her balance with her hands tied behind her back. When she was on the floor, he slowly pushed her forward. "I want you lying over the ottoman."

So that's what she was in front of. She'd noticed it when she first walked into the room. It was large, about two feet by three feet in size and overstuffed so that it was well cushioned. She leaned over so that her face and upper chest were against the ottoman. He helped her move so that she pushed up and then she was lying over the piece of furniture with her ass in the air.

He secured a spreader bar between her ankles so that she couldn't move them. Then he unbound her wrists. Before she could feel any sense of relief, she heard the ominous sound of chains and then he took each wrist cuff and fastened them to something. She tried to pull her wrists away and heard the rattle of the chains and could not move her hands.

His hand was warm on her ass as he slid his palm down. She felt the press of something against her anus and she stiffened.

"Relax." He smoothed his hand. "You know it's so much easier when you do."

Yes, she did know. She let her whole body relax and felt the stretch and fullness of him gently pushing the butt plug into her. When it was in, she heard the sound of him pumping the plug up with air so that it expanded inside of her and she felt so full that it made her feel even more excited.

Then he pulled on the O-ring on top of the hood and she heard the sound of a chain rattling through it. He pulled her head back and secured the chain to her ankle cuffs so that her head was held up.

She could hear him in front of her.

"You can't move," he said. "You're all mine."

Yes, she was his. She loved being his.

"I adore how you look." He stroked her arm as he spoke. "So sexy. So hot. So helpless. You're amazing looking. I love putting you in another world, a world of isolation where all you think about is me and what I have in store for you. You will see that being isolated in there will heighten all of your senses. You will be more aware of touch and sounds.

"You are wondering what I will do next aren't you?" And then his voice deepened becoming almost harsh. "Aren't you?" He pulled on her head chain bringing her head back more.

She groaned. "Mmuuummmph."

"A little pleasure my little sub," he said. "Then I have a surprise for you."

She shuddered with excitement. What did that mean? What was next for her?

He caressed her from her naked ass to her thighs, his callused palm rough against her soft skin. He slid his hand down then slipped his fingers between her thighs and into her wet folds. He stroked her clit and she gasped behind the gag and then she moaned as he continued to rub it.

She fell into the sensations. Her hearing was muffled and she felt locked away. When he stopped she was disappointed, yet wondering what he had planned next.

He crouched close enough that she heard him speaking close to her ear. "I'm going to leave you for a while."

Her heart rate bounced. Alone? He was going to leave her alone? Fear of a different kind went through her. She didn't want to be left alone.

"You won't know where I am or how long I'm gone." He stroked her shoulder. "You won't know if I've come back or I'm still away. You'll lose all sense of time and place."

She had read about subs entering some kind of state where they lost track of time and lost sense of themselves. Sub-space? She had read about it, and she understood how that could happen and she wasn't sure she wanted to go through it herself.

"I'll see you later." He kissed her shoulder. She wanted to shake her head but she couldn't the way she was tied down.

She tried to calm herself. If she didn't she might hyperventilate and that wouldn't be good.

For a long time—at least she thought it was a long time—she lay over the ottoman. Thoughts of anything on the outside just seemed to vanish. It was like the hood blocked out the world and it was just her alone. Somehow that was peaceful and calming.

She came back to herself as she heard voices, more than one. Maybe even three.

The sounds made her heart start pounding. The voices sounded close but she couldn't make out what they were saying.

John wouldn't have brought anyone into the room with her lying naked and bound, would he?

No. No way.

But the voices seemed to get louder until it felt like they had to be in the same room as her. She heard male laughter.

Fear made her freeze up. What was happening? What was John doing?

Even though the voices sounded like they were close, she still couldn't understand what they were saying. They had to have been talking about the naked and bound woman in the middle of the room.

More laughter, and then she clearly heard John as he said, "Have at it, guys. Go ahead and have some fun."

Roni screamed behind her gag and fought against her bonds. They had to see that she was here unwillingly. Would they care?

She had always liked the fantasy of being used by more than one man. But it had been a fantasy. Now she couldn't do anything about it.

With everything she had, she struggled but couldn't move.

Her breathing came faster. She really was afraid she was going to hyperventilate.

Then she heard John's voice, close to her ear. "Keep trying to get out, Roni. I love watching the futile struggle. I will enjoy watching you with my friends."

She felt a hand stroking her thigh and skimming her folds and she stilled. One of the men was touching her.

Despite her fear and the fact that she didn't think she wanted to be fucked by more than one man, she grew wetter than she had been and felt an ache in her pussy. The thoughts of the men taking her and the reaction her body was having shocked her into breathing hard again.

Then someone worked at unfastening the blindfold. The light was bright at first but then she saw John with a smoldering look in his eyes.

"How do you feel now?" he asked. "Scared?"

She made a muffled sound. He had to see by her eyes that she was terrified.

He raised an iPod and showed it to her. She blinked and tried to make sense of why he was showing her an iPod. He pressed the on button and she heard the sound of muffled male voices coming from a stereo.

She sagged in relief. He had been screwing with her. She was going to punch him when she got free. One thing that she had to admit was that he got her good. It was probably the most scared she had ever been.

He adjusted the way that he was sitting and she saw that he had put a large mirror in front of her and she could see just how bizarre she looked.

"I'm not finished with you yet." He moved away and she didn't feel his presence anymore.

She waited in her confined world he had her secured in, so thankful that he had only been carrying out what she loved to feel… Fear. Maybe she'd had enough fear for a while.

A hard strike across her thighs nearly had her choking on her gag as she cried out. Again he did it and again. He swatted her with what felt like a riding crop, just enough for her eyes to water from the pain. The sensations, mixed with how she had been feeling moments ago left her feeling raw… And incredibly excited.

He stopped swatting her and moved behind her and between her thighs and she watched him in the mirror. He grabbed her by her ponytail and he pulled her head back. She felt the press of his cock against her and then he drove into her.

She watched in the mirror as he fucked her hard, slamming up against her, so hard that she felt as if the motions could break her bonds. He rode her, holding onto her ponytail.

Harder. Harder. Harder yet. It felt so good, so intense as he took her and being able to see herself like this added to it all. She felt the slide of him inside her, his thickness and his length and felt the butt plug filling her up. She felt all of him and she didn't want him to stop.

But her orgasm was coming. It charged toward her faster than she wanted. She tried to hold off but she couldn't.

She climaxed hard, her whole body vibrating beneath him. He kept on fucking her, causing her body to shudder with aftershocks.

His shout was muffled through her hood as he came. She felt him throb inside her, felt him pump in and out a few more times. Then he relaxed, bracing his arms so that he was over her, his cock still inside of her. She felt the sweat of his skin over her own hot flesh.

She sighed with exhaustion and relief and she watched him as he unfastened her wrist cuffs and removed the spreader bar from between her ankles, and removed the plug.

When she was free, he brought her into a sitting position on the ottoman and pulled off her hood.

She felt dazed for a moment as she returned to the present and the real world, and a sense of euphoria overcame her, unlike anything she had ever experienced before. She looked up at him and smiled.

He sat next to her, brought her into his arms, and held her.

Chapter 9

It wasn't possible to get tired of sex like this. How would it ever be possible to settle for plain old vanilla?

Roni smiled to herself as she rolled out of bed around ten. Before dawn John had received a call and he'd had to leave his apartment for some kind of emergency. She had lain around in bed for a while after waking up, enjoying the pleasant afterglow of great kinky sex before she had to decide how she was going to spend her Sunday.

Decisions, decisions.

She headed into his bathroom and took a shower, enjoying the feel of warm water pounding down on her skin. His shampoo and shower gel reminded her of him and she loved the scents.

When she climbed out of the shower she toweled herself off in one of his thick burgundy towels, then used his brush on her long wet hair. If she had known she was going to spend the night, she would have packed a little bag.

After she was dressed, she wandered from the bathroom and through his apartment. It was comfortable and homey, a feeling that wasn't always possible in an apartment, especially for a guy, from her experience. It had three bedrooms, one of which he used for an office and the other for an exercise room. That explained his ripped body.

She wandered to his exercise room and pictured him working out on the weight machines or jogging bare-chested on the treadmill. Very nice visuals accompanied those thoughts.

As she was passing by his office she noticed the door was open. It hadn't been yesterday. She wasn't planning on going into his office because she didn't want to invade his privacy. Even though the door was open she didn't intend to look, but something caught her eye. She pushed the door open and her heart started thundering.

There were pictures on a corkboard on one wall.

 Pictures of dead women. Women who looked like her.

She couldn't stop staring at the pictures even as her stomach churned. Almost in a trance, she walked closer and saw the sightless eyes, the naked bodies bound in white ropes.

Her whole body trembled as she held her hand to her stomach and started to back out of the room. Before she could get through the door, she noticed the large map with red dots on an adjacent wall. She paused and looked more closely. Dots punctuated the map in areas across three states. Her mind spun through it all as she mentally notated the cities where the red dots were. All cities where women with her description had been murdered.

Slowly her gaze moved to the desk. On it was John's iPad. Her hand shook as she reached for it. She wasn't sure why she had to look at it but something compelled her to pick it up. When she powered it on she saw what he had been looking at the last time he used it.

On it was a picture of her.

Chills rolled over her body and she held her hand to her chest. According to the date on the digital photograph, it was taken sometime before she had met him. The image was of her leaving the building of the manufacturer that she worked for.

Everything fell together.

John had known exactly who she was before he met her.

He had pictures of dead women who looked similar to her.

He had an aerial map showing the three states where the murders had been committed with red marks signifying the location of each killing.

She clasped her hand over her mouth, holding back a scream.

John was the serial killer.

Terror ripped through her and a crawling sensation went up her spine. She dropped the iPad on his desk and slowly turned around, praying that he wasn't behind her.

He wasn't. She bolted for his bedroom where she had left her purse. Her hands trembled as she tried to find her phone. When she finally located it, she was shaking so badly that she fumbled with the phone and dropped it on the floor and it bounced under the bed.

She looked to the doorway and then got down on her knees and reached for the phone. When she picked it up she saw that the screen had cracked from having hit the floor hard. Still on her knees, she punched in 9-1-1 and prayed that it would work.

A tiny measure of relief when through her as an operator answered and asked what the nature of her emergency was.

"I know who the serial killer is, the one killing women with red hair." She felt herself hyperventilating. "I'm in his apartment. I'm afraid he's going to come back soon."

"What is the address you're at?"

"I—I don't know." She looked around frantically, like it would suddenly appear. She couldn't think, couldn't remember what his address was even though she had driven to it multiple times since meeting John. Then it came to her. "I'm in an apartment at 555 Bal—"

The phone was suddenly ripped from her hands. She looked up to see John standing over her as he pressed the **OFF** button.

"Don't kill me." She scrambled away from him and her back hit a corner wall. "Please."

A concerned look overcame the grim expression that he'd just had. He crouched in front of her. "I'm not the serial killer, Roni."

She shook her head. "I saw all of the pictures and the map on your wall. Women who look like me." She pressed herself farther back into the corner. "And you have a picture of me. From before I even met you."

"I can explain all of that." He held his palms down, like telling her to calm down. "I'm FBI. It's my job to track down the killer. What you saw was my work."

"FBI?" She looked at him, her mind not able to process what he was saying. "You said you're in security."

"You could say I am." He moved a little closer and she tried to push herself back. He held his hands up to tell her he didn't have anything in them and that he wasn't going to hurt her. "I protect people and eliminate threats. Working in security is my cover."

She shook her head trying to shake her thoughts in line. "But you have a picture of me, taken before I even met you."

"I can explain that, too."

"Was I an assignment or something?" Things just weren't computing. "I didn't think someone in a law enforcement career could spend twelve grand in a charity auction."

"It depends," he said. "As for me, I had an inheritance about three months ago. It's more than I can ever do anything with, so I like to spend it on charitable causes."

"Why would you be working then?" She was still having a hard time processing.

"Because I like my work." He sighed. "Come out from there and trust me, Roni. If I was going to hurt you I would have by now, don't you think?"

Her fear was starting to lessen. It was true—if he was the killer she'd probably be dead right now and be a picture on his wall.

She flinched as he reached into his back pocket and pulled something out.

"Shhh." He drew out a wallet. "I'm just going to show you my credentials."

She watched as he opened the wallet and she saw a badge and his picture along with his name.

"Come on, honey." He stood, pocketed his wallet and held out his hand. "Let me explain everything. We'll sit down and I'll get you a drink and we'll talk."

Her legs trembled as she stood, using the wall for support as she rose. When she was standing she still didn't want to go forward and didn't want to take his hand.

"Come on, honey." He extended it further. "It's okay."

Her pulse was slowing and reason was starting to come back to her. She trusted John. She knew in her heart that he would never hurt her. Just seeing those pictures and that map had shocked her. It never occurred to her that he could be in law enforcement and be working on the case.

She took a deep breath and reached for his hand. When his hand grasped hers he drew her to him and enveloped her in his embrace. At first she stiffened but then she relaxed and pressed her face against his shirt and breathed in his comforting scent.

"I don't blame you." He rocked her a little as he held her. "Those pictures are shocking and not just anyone would have them on his wall."

"I guess you're not just anyone." Her words were muffled against his shirt.

He drew back and her gaze met his. "No, I'm not."

With his arm around her shoulders, he escorted her to the door of his office. "Stand here. I don't want you to have to see the pictures again but I want to show you a couple of things."

She remained in place, a part of her still wondering if she should run. Her heart was still pounding but the adrenaline rush that had powered her fear was starting to subside.

He returned and he showed her an FBI award certificate and a plaque, both with his name on them. "These are just a couple of things. If you want more, I can show you more."

"That's fine." She took a deep breath. "I think I'm okay now."

"Good." He put his arm around her shoulders again and guided her to the kitchen and then to the table where he helped her sit down. "First things first," he said as he drew his phone out of his pocket and then he punched in a number.

"This is Special Agent John Taylor," he said to whoever was on the other end of the line. "I need someone to contact Baltimore police and let them know that a call that came from my home address to 911 and it has been taken care of."

He listened to whoever was on the other end of the line then proceeded to give more detailed information. When he was finished, turned off his phone and pocketed it again. His gaze met Roni's. "How about that drink now?"

She gave a deep, shuddering sigh. "I don't care how early it is, that's exactly what I want."

"It's almost noon." He took a bottle of vodka out of the pantry, along with a few other things, and tomato juice out of the fridge. "Good enough time as any."

He made her a tall bloody Mary and handed it to her then fixed one for himself.

The glass was cold in her fingers, condensation already forming on its surface. "Can you start from the beginning?" she said after she took a long drink and felt the burn of alcohol as it made its way down her throat.

"The beginning?" He leaned back in his chair and pushed his hand through his hair. "I was called in after the third murder was committed. It became an FBI matter once the killings extended to three states.

"I specialize in serial killers," he went on. "I have a pretty good record, but this one has been a bitch." He shook his head. "Not that they aren't all bad."

She swallowed more of her bloody Mary before she asked, "How did you end up with a picture of me?"

"You were in the auction pre-program as being one of the women and men who were to be auctioned off." He gripped his drink. "Two of the women murdered were in KC, the only connection we've been able to find so far. If the other three were involved in any way, we haven't been able to determine the links. You did match the profile of the woman he likes. Red head. Mid-thirties. Curvy. The only things that are a constant are what you've read in the paper."

"So you followed me?" She gripped her glass with both hands. "Or had me followed?"

"Yes." He gave a slow nod. "I followed you."

"So what was this?" She held her hands out. "You bought me to protect me? And had sex with me to keep track of me? That doesn't even make sense."

"No, that wouldn't make sense." He looked at her with the same kind of expression he'd had when she'd met him, when he'd looked like he'd gotten over his head. "Something about you made me want you and I didn't want any other man to get his hands on you."

"And then you didn't know what to do with me." She couldn't help a little smile. "But then I showed you."

"Yes, you did." He shook his head. "This—you, me—went places it never should have gone."

"How do you feel about that?" Her voice softened. "Do you think it was a mistake?"

"No." There was a fierceness to his tone. "Nothing about you is a mistake, Roni."

The way he looked at her made her heart beat faster. "I'm glad," she said. "I wouldn't want you to have any regrets."

"I don't have a single one." He reached out and laid his hand over hers. "Well, maybe one."

She raised an eyebrow. "And what's that."

His voice was low as he said, "That I didn't meet you sooner."

With a smile she said, "Me, too." She thought for a moment and said, "How do you just happen to be into kink?"

"It was one of the reasons that I wanted to be on this case," he said. "I knew about KC and I like a little kink. I could be more active in the group and observe things and talk to people inside without raising suspicions."

After a moment she changed the subject back to something she needed to know. "What about the killer? Do you think he's a member of KC? Was he at the auction?"

"One of our leads is a member of the KC but his alibis have appeared solid." John frowned and shook his head. "Something about the guy just isn't right. We don't have the manpower to keep an eye on him and the other more suspect individuals in the case."

"Who is it?" she asked then realized it was a question that wouldn't get her anywhere.

"I can't discuss that type of information." He pushed his hand through his hair again. "I wish I could." He leaned close to her. "Let's just say I'd like you to steer clear of Drake Pierson. If you see him around at all, you get somewhere safe and call the police and me."

A slow chill rolled through her. "I bumped into him at the grocery store the morning after the auction."

The line of John's mouth grew tight. "He approached you? What happened?"

"I was getting a carton of milk and he was right there when I turned around and I dropped the milk. He—he had a loaf of bread and wanted to invite himself over." She rubbed her arms, trying to chase away the chill. "He offered to walk me home but I said no."

John's expression grew darker. "Has he made any other contact?"

"I saw him at that dungeon party." Her cheeks warmed. "Where I thought you were with another woman." John gave a nod for her to continue. "He wanted to go someplace but then you talked to me and he disappeared."

"Does he know where you live?" John grasped her upper arm, surprising her.

"I don't think so." Confusion clouded her brain. "Oh." Her eyes widened. "He has my phone number."

"Damn." John cursed something worse under his breath, too. "You need to stay here. With me."

She started to protest that she'd be okay at home, but she saw the wisdom in what he was saying. "Okay. I just need to get a few things."

He gave a nod. "I'll go with you."

Chapter 10

Another week went by and then another. The killer hadn't struck again and she hadn't run into Drake Pierson. She started to feel more relaxed. John had said Drake's alibi had panned out, and he was currently out of state on vacation, staying with a relative in Boston.

John was still concerned about Drake, though. He'd said something about the guy just didn't sit right with him.

It was after work on a Friday. It had been a long and trying day, but like always when she came home to John's house, she was able to leave her problems on the doorstep. She sat down in his recliner with her iPad, wishing that he were home. She would be happy to make his day far more enjoyable.

An email popped into her inbox and she looked to see that she had a message from him. "Speak of the devil," she murmured. She loved getting messages from him. Sometimes he emailed her or sent her text messages just to tell her that he was thinking about her. Other times it was to give her instructions on something he'd like her to do that would liven up their evening.

She opened up the email and read it.

I left a package for you in the closet, on the shelf above my suits. I want you to put on the handcuffs, hood, and blindfold, plus something else I've left you.

When you're ready, lie on the bed with your wrists cuffed together. Leave the ball gag on the bed.

I'll be home at 7:00. Be ready by 6:30. I like the thought of you waiting there, secured and blindfolded, waiting for me and thinking about me.

She smiled and replied to his message:

I'll be waiting.

She glanced at the time on her tablet to see that it was around five-thirty. She set the tablet aside, went to the bedroom and into the closet, and reached up on her tiptoes to grasp the box he'd left and took it down. It wasn't too heavy and she carried it to the bed and opened it.

Inside was a wide collar with an O-ring in the front and D-rings on each side. She had seen these used before. It was a posture collar that restricted head movement. Also in the box were sets of ankle and wrist cuffs, a small lock, and a red hood that had an O-ring on top of it. She set those aside and saw that John had picked out some very sexy lingerie for her. A red and black corset, with matching panties and stockings.

He had wanted her to be ready early and she intended to make her man happy.

Her man. She liked that. Liked it a lot. She hoped that he thought of her as his woman.

She stripped out of her clothing and slipped into the lingerie that he had left her. It was silky and erotic against her skin. She felt sexy and wanton and so hot for him she could hardly stand it. She loved the fact that he had bought it for her and he had picked out just this for her to wear. There was something hot about a man buying a corset, panties and stocking for her.

She still had plenty of time so she sat down to read a little more and kept an eye on the clock. She wanted to be ready when he'd told her to. For all she knew he was going to come home early and check to see if she had obeyed him.

After she climbed onto his king-sized bed and pulled on the hood and blindfold. She had gotten so used to the hoods he had that she actually enjoyed being inside them and had started to look forward to wearing them. It was hard to explain to anyone who hadn't experienced wearing a hood. It made her feel like she belonged to him somehow. She was his property.

When the hood and the blindfold were on, the ball gag on the bed beside her, she locked her wrist cuffs together with the small lock that he had left. She settled back on the pillows and closed her eyes as she waited.

Only a few minutes seemed to have passed by when the bed dipped and she heard the muffled sound of the bedsprings squeaking. He had come early like she'd thought he might.

She started to tell him hello, but he pushed the ball gag into her mouth. He did it so hard that it mashed her lips against her teeth and she tasted a bit of blood.

He pressed a cloth to the nose holes in the mask and she tasted and smelled something odd. A mere fraction of a moment passed and then she slipped away.

"Wake up, princess."

Roni felt groggy and out of it as she heard him speak. Everything was dark.

Something felt strange and odd, almost like she was floating yet bound, and she tried to think through the fuzziness in her mind. Then she realized she was hanging, her body somehow suspended. She could feel rope against her bare skin she felt a kind of rope body harness.

She was wearing a blindfold now and not the hood, and the ball gag was in her mouth. She tried shifting her head and neck, but the posture collar kept her head from moving and the D-rings had been secured to either side of her neck.

John had drugged her and suspended her. Apparently he was taking their play to a whole new level. Was this yet another way to cause her to experience fear? It had been a couple of weeks since the last time he had scared her. She could still remember how freaked out she'd been when she thought he had brought other men into the room.

"Are you awake now?" His voice was still low, hard to hear, as if he was talking from a distance. With her head and neck secured she couldn't nod, so she made a sound behind her gag to answer his question.

"Good." He unfastened the gag and she licked her lips as he moved his hands to her blindfold and removed it. She blinked and her eyes unfocused and the focused.

It wasn't John looking at her.

It was Drake.

Raw terror ripped through her and she instinctively pulled against her bonds. "No." She tried to control her breathing as she stared at him. "Please, no."

"That's a big yes, honey." He reached out and pushed her and she swung back and forth and she felt like she might fall even though she could tell she was secured to well. "Isn't this perfect? I like redheads and you like fear. Before I kill you I'm going to give you a lot to be afraid of."

She stared at him, her heart beating so hard it was going to come out of her chest. Drake. The killer was Drake and he had her. He really had her.

Her voice shook and she almost couldn't speak because she was having a hard time catching her breath. "Did you hurt John?"

Drake brushed the question away with a wave of his hand. "I've got a better way to deal with that dick. I ditched a few things in his apartment that will be considered evidence that he's the real killer." He gave a smile that was in no way handsome. "When I'm finished with you I'll drop you in the dumpster. His fingerprints are going to be all over your collar and cuffs. He might be facing the death penalty for what he's going to be accused of doing to you and the other poor girls."

Adrenaline pumped through her body and she trembled from it. She could see just enough to tell that she was in some kind of basement and a door was just at the top of a rickety looking staircase.

Could John possibly find her here? Where was here?

She struggled to find something to hold him off. "How did you know I was at John's apartment?"

"I've been intercepting your email for some time which is how I found out about your taste for fear." Drake smiled. "It wasn't hard to figure out where you lived. Broke into your house a couple of times while you were at work."

He reached for her and squeezed her shoulder. "I like computers. It was not too hard to set up to tap into your router and follow your emails. I've been monitoring it, waiting for the perfect time. The plan the dick laid out today was too perfect."

She bit the inside of her cheek hard as she tried to figure a way out of this. "Please don't do this. I'll let you do what you want but don't do this."

"What would be the fun in that? I like fucking with my women. Figuratively and literally. So I will fuck with you for a while."

Cold fear made her start to tremble. "Please let me go, Drake."

"I don't like hoods too much so I took yours off." He tugged at strands of her hair. "I don't like how it covers up your pretty hair and the fear on your face." He picked something up and then she saw that he had a butcher knife with a gleaming edge. "I'm going to cut some of your pretty hair for a souvenir to go along with the rest of my collection. While I'm at it, I might just carve your face a bit. You are so beautiful and I will love seeing my mark, on you."

He moved closer and held up the knife and repeated, "So beautiful."

Roni screamed as loud as she could, putting everything into it that she had.

Drake slapped her, cutting off her scream, the power in his swing so hard that she felt dizzy.

"Shut up, bitch." He shoved the ball gag back into her mouth, mashing her lips against her teeth and she tasted blood again, only this time more.

He picked something up and raised it so that she could see. It looked like a policeman's baton. "I can snap every bone in your body with this. Do something as stupid as that again and I start with the bones in your face first.

"But right now I want to play." He set the baton down then raised the knife and put it to her cheek—

The door at the top of the stairs exploded inward.

John stood at the top of the stairs with a gun aimed at Drake. "FBI. Don't move."

Roni's heart leapt.

Drake looked shocked but the knife was already at Roni's face. He shifted fast enough that he had it pressed against her throat, hard enough that it bit into her skin and she trembled as she felt a droplet of blood roll down her throat.

"Put the weapon down." The expression on John's face was murderous. "Move away from her, Pierson."

"You are going to let me out of here or she's dead." Drake spoke with a calm, even tone, as if he was talking about getting himself a cup of coffee. "And she's coming with me."

He pressed the knife tighter against her throat and she felt more blood trickle down. "Throw your weapon over here. Slowly. Then I want you to come down here."

John kept his eyes on Drake as he tossed his gun. Drake caught it and then pointed it at John.

Roni's terror rose. She looked from John to Drake and saw death in Drake's eyes. He wasn't planning on letting either of them out of here alive.

"Hands up." Drake waved the gun at John. "And take it real easy walking down those steps. Wouldn't want you to have an accident."

The stairs creaked with every step that John took until he was at the bottom. He stood there with his hands still raised.

"I'd love to hear how you found the basement door." Drake said. "It's well hidden."

"Not hidden well enough," John said in a growl.

"You heard the bitch scream didn't you." Drake's jaw tightened.

John said nothing, just stared at Drake.

"Take her down." Drake stepped aside, gun still on John. "Don't move too fast."

John met Roni's gaze. Without words he seemed to be trying to tell her that everything was going to be all right and that they would get out of here some how, some way.

He moved to her and started by crouching and untying the rope from the cuffs on her ankles. When they were free he moved up to her knees and to the rope cuffs on her thighs. If it wasn't for the rope body harness she would have been feeling more pressure on her elbows and wrists.

When he reached her arms he murmured, "I'm going to get you out of this."

Drake chuckled from behind John. "Go ahead and delude yourself and her, Special Agent Taylor. It's going to be hard getting her out of anything when you're dead."

Roni swallowed down her fear. They would get out of this before Drake had the chance to kill either of them. She had to believe that.

John untied the ropes that had been secured to the posture collar then took the collar off and let it drop to the floor. She felt a moment of relief to be able to move her head and neck again. It was only a flash of relief. It was hard to feel anything but fear in their current situation.

He turned to Drake when she was hanging from only the body harness. "I need to cut her down so I can catch her."

"You'll just have to let her fall then." Drake shook his head. "You're not getting the knife if that's what you're angling for."

"I'll be fine." Roni said. "Just get me down from here."

With a grim expression, John moved directly in front of her. "Hook your legs around my hips."

Drake looked on with what seemed like interest. "Go on," he said.

Just feeling John so close was in some way comforting. He worked on the rope tying her body harness and then she fell backward.

He caught her in one arm right before her head could hit the floor. He brought her back up and set her on her feet. She was unsteady at first after having been hanging. Circulation slowly returned to her limbs.

Drake barely gave her a chance to recover before he pointed the gun at John. "Push her over here."

John met Roni's gaze. "It's going to be okay."

He released her and she refused to budge. Instead she got in front of him. "I'm not letting him kill you, John," she said as she stared at Drake.

Drake gritted his teeth. "You're both going to die anyway, princess. So it ends now for both of you or I get the opportunity to play with you a bit."

"Go." John gently pushed Roni. "I'll be fine."

No way was she going to let Drake murder John. She moved toward Drake, not knowing what she was going to do, just knowing that she was going to do *something* to help both her and John.

When she got close enough to Drake, he grabbed her arm and jerked her to him. She was off balance and almost fell but he kept her on her feet. As he jerked her to him, she spotted the policeman's baton that he'd threatened her with earlier, sitting on a small table beside them.

"This is it, Special Agent Taylor." Drake cocked the gun as he pointed it at John. "Say goodbye."

Roni grabbed the baton and with a two-handed grip she swung up as hard as she could beneath his wrist.

The baton hit him dead-on. A shot rang out as bone snapped. He screamed and dropped the gun.

John lunged for Drake, but Drake grabbed her by the throat and jerked her to him with his good arm.

"I'm going to break her neck," he shouted.

She clenched her fist and brought it down on his wrist.

Drake screamed in pain again and Roni jerked herself away from him. She landed on the floor, near the gun.

She scrambled for the gun as Drake grabbed the butcher knife from where it had fallen on the floor and raised it up as John was coming down on him.

She wrapped her fingers around the gun's grip, pointed it at Drake, and pulled the trigger.

Drake went still.

A hole was in his forehead, a single drop of blood rolling down his skin.

Chapter 11

Roni reeled her line back in as John was casting his as they sat on the mid-sized boat they had rented for the day. They were alone out on the water where John had driven the boat. Their weekend at Half Moon Bay was almost over and she hated to see it end.

It was two months after the ordeal with the serial killer and it seemed like life was back to normal.

John brought his line in again and then took both of their poles and set them aside. He brought her into his lap and hugged her close to him.

"You know I love you, don't you?" he said once again with a smile.

"And you know I love you." She smiled and kissed his cheek that was rough with stubble. "Now that we have reestablished that fact, why don't you show me what you have below deck?"

"My pleasure." He rose up with her still in her arms and she laughed and held onto him.

He carried her down the stairs and she felt the gentle rocking of the boat when they were below, he carried her to the bed and set her on it. "Take off your clothes."

She was delighted to. She pulled her shirt over her head and tossed it aside then wiggled out of her shorts, leaving her in her leopard print bra and matching panties. Then she unfastened her bra and pushed down her panties and stepped out of them.

After what she went through, being restrained by a sick murderer, John had been concerned that playing bondage games would bother her. She had explained to him that this was different and she didn't have any of the feelings she had experienced during the ordeal.

She knew that with John she was safe and bondage was something that they both enjoyed. She wasn't going to let a lunatic ruin that for either her or John. She wouldn't let him put a dark mark on their lives.

Over the weeks she had worked hard to occupy her mind with other things if they strayed toward things she didn't want to dwell on. When they played, it was easy to forget everything but what mattered—each other.

"What did you bring?" she asked as he dug in the duffel bag he had taken on board with them.

John pulled rope out of the duffel bag as well as cuffs and a short spreader bar. His muscles flexed as he moved and she enjoyed the view. He took a pair of what looked like fishing weights out and set everything down then put the cuffs on her.

"Come here." He gestured for her to come to him and then he picked up the fishing weights. She saw that they were connected to nipple clamps.

"Ow," she said as she looked at them. She could already imagine what they felt like.

He shook his head. "No complaints."

She bit her lower lip and stood in front of him. He leaned over and sucked one of her nipples before putting on the clamp. She cried out at the feel of the thing as it squeezed her nipple and the weights intensifying the feeling. He sucked the other nipple then put the clamp on and she cried out again.

His scent of sunshine and the ocean enveloped her as he kissed her, a sweet, sensual kiss.

He took her by the hand. "Let's go." In his other hand he held the spreader bar and something else that she couldn't see.

She reached out and took his hand and he led her back up the stairs and into the cool California sunshine. The wind caressed her naked body, her nipples already hard and aching.

The metal rings on the cuffs jingled as she walked. When they reached the railing at the bow, he used rope to secure her cuffs to the railing and then put the spreader bar between her ankles and attached it with clips to the cuffs.

He positioned her so that she was bent over the railing with her legs spread, the weights hanging from her nipples. The breeze was cool as it brushed her folds. He moved behind her and pressed something hard against her anus. She held her breath as he slowly pushed a butt plug inside of her.

The plug started vibrating. She caught her breath as he pressed himself to her and his cock was hard as he rubbed it against her folds.

She thought she heard the sound of a boat in the distance and her heart started pounding a little. What if they were caught? The danger of it added to her excitement.

He caressed her body from her breasts down to her ass and back. "I love your body." He tugged on the weights and her eyes watered. "You are so beautiful and you're mine."

"Yes." She pressed back against him. "I'm all yours."

She heard the rustle of his zipper then felt his hard cock against her core. He thrust inside of her and she moaned from the exquisite pleasure. The erotic feel of him taking her while she was naked and out on the water, with the sun kissing their bodies, and the breeze caressing their skin, and the boat rocking on the calm ocean.

He took her at a slow, easy pace and her climax started to build inside her. Everything grew even more intense and she fell into the incredible sensations.

In and out, harder and harder.

She felt her orgasm starting to crescendo, closer, closer—

Brilliant light flooded her mind as she climaxed and cried out. He pulled on the weights on her nipples as she came and the pain somehow added to her orgasm. Her body jerked and her core spasmed around his cock.

He shouted as he came and he gripped her hips tight in his big hands.

Her limbs felt weak and she needed his strength to hold her up. He undid her bonds, took out the plug and removed the clips and set them aside on the deck. Then he took her to one of the deck chairs and cuddled with her in his lap.

She laid her head on his chest and he kissed the top of her head.

"The best investment I've ever made," he said.

Imagine the possibilities, went through her mind as she remember her thoughts the night she met John.

"Yes." She smiled and looked at him. "It certainly was."

Claimed

Chapter 1

Leslie Adams smiled as she slipped through the crowd of people mingling before the exclusive charity auction in Washington, D.C. The air smelled of elegant perfumes and diamond jewelry glittered in the room's low lighting. An undercurrent of energy seemed to run just below the surface of the night's event.

But what she was focused on was a man across the room.

"SEAL is on the menu tonight," she murmured to herself as she watched him. "That Navy man is *mine*."

He was even sexier in the flesh than he'd been in his photograph. His features were well cut and his skin tanned, showing he was outdoors quite a bit of the time. She could almost feel how soft his short dark hair would be as it sifted through her fingers. His muscular body would feel smooth and hard against her palms. His suit fit him well and he wore it with ease, as comfortable in it as he no doubt was in a wetsuit.

Thoughts of how he would look with his suit off had her running her tongue along her lower lip and caused a tingling between her thighs. His body would be buff and perfect beneath his clothing and she would be happy to lick his naked body all over. She wondered how he had been roped into allowing himself to be auctioned off for charity.

She couldn't believe her fortune. She loved her men tough, strong, and sexy, and from what she'd read, Rick Pierce appeared to be all of that and more. After studying the auction program and reading through the information about him, she all but had him tied up with a nice red bow as a present to herself.

Tying him up was the plan.

She needed to talk with him, but if he was only half of what was described in the program, she wasn't about to let anyone outbid her tonight. No one.

Her silver dress felt slinky and sexy against her skin and with her white-blonde hair up, the air in the room was cool at her nape. She reached up and ran her finger along the edges of the decorative triangle pin on her left shoulder. It signified she liked to top submissives from KC, the Kink Club. The tougher they were, the more desire she had to control them. She'd never come across a man since Michael who'd had the power to make her submit to him.

That will be the day.

Thoughts of Michael always made her stomach pitch and she stuffed thoughts of him back into the box she always kept them in.

She was several feet from Rick when a man stepped in front of her and blocked her path. She had been so focused on the SEAL that it took her a moment to register that the man in front of her was one of the most sought after male models in the industry. He was with a competitor's agency. At one time she would have given her firstborn—if she had one—to have Armand Moreau with her own agency.

"Leslie, dear." He took her hand and brought it to his lips. "What a pleasure."

He had been in the auction program as one of those individuals being auctioned off, but she'd had no intention of purchasing him for a weekend alone so hadn't given him a lot of thought.

"Armand." She smiled despite the fact that she wanted him to be gone so that she could continue on to her prey. "It's good to see you. Now if you please excu—"

"I see that you are a bidder." He indicated the white corsage on her shoulder, near her triangle pin. "How wonderful. No doubt you saw that I have given myself up for auction to benefit this event." His French accent was heavy, his rather large ego intact.

For a moment she thought about what it would be like to tie him up and have him at her mercy. She doubted if he could take what she would have in store for him if she purchased him during the auction. It might actually be quite interesting to find out.

But she wasn't into more than one man at a time, and right now her goal was a certain SEAL named Rick and this man was in her way.

"You are bidding on me, no?" He said the words as if it was a foregone conclusion.

"I am certain the ladies will be fighting over you tonight," she said.

"Yes." His look was what she might define as smug. "But I would only be happy to have you in my arms this weekend."

She raised an eyebrow. "Then it will be a lonely weekend for you."

He frowned. "Are you not bidding?"

"I am." She gave him a tight smile. "But I'm going to leave you for the ladies who would give you the appreciation you so richly deserve."

And she would bid on someone with considerably more intelligence, not to mention a physical prowess Armand would never have in the same way Rick appeared to. Besides, she didn't "do" male models anymore, she reminded herself. To a one, none of them had been able to handle her.

"I am disappointed." He took her hand and kissed the back of it again. "If you change your mind…"

"Enjoy the auction, Armand." She extracted her hand from his. "I look forward to seeing you another time."

"As do I." He glanced over her shoulder. "There is Dahlia. I must say hello." He took Leslie by her shoulders and kissed each cheek before moving away from her. "Dahlia, darling," she heard him say and she shook her head in amusement.

"Hi, Leslie," Kelley Bachman said from behind her.

Leslie turned and smiled at her good friend. "You made it."

"I was a little worried I wasn't going to be able to." Kelley pushed her golden blonde hair away from her face. "You know how Dr. Brown likes to keep me late whenever possible."

Leslie put her hand on her friend's arm. "Maybe it's time to transfer into another area of the hospital."

Kelley smiled. "You're right. It's just been so hectic lately. Work just never lets up."

"The nerve of people getting sick." Leslie laughed. "I don't know how you handle being a nurse. It takes someone pretty special to have that as a career."

"I love my job." Kelley raised her glass of wine. "If it wasn't for Dr. Jeffrey Brown being after me all of the time, I'd be perfectly satisfied right where I am."

Leslie touched her hair to make sure it was still smooth. "Have you thought of filing a sexual harassment suit?"

Kelley shook her head. "It hasn't gotten to that point. He's done nothing that would qualify as harassment. He just does everything he can to keep me close. It's in his eyes though, but you can't file a claim based on the way someone looks at you covertly."

"Anyway," Kelley went on as she brought her fingers to the circle pin she wore, signifying she was a submissive in KC. "We're here for fun and I intend to enjoy myself and hope that the right guy bids on me." She looked at Leslie's triangle pin. "Have anyone in mind that you're looking to bid on?"

"A Navy SEAL." Leslie gave Kelley a naughty grin. "Just think of the fun I'll have."

"Nice." Kelley laughed. "You always did like the best of the best."

Leslie gave her a quick hug. "Good to see you, honey."

Kelley hugged her back. "Go get him."

When Kelley moved away, Leslie looked to where the SEAL had been standing, but he was no longer there. Disappointment eased through her but she slowly pivoted to see if he was nearby but she didn't see him anywhere.

"Excuse me." A deep voice from behind her had her turning to face whoever had spoken.

It was the SEAL.

The moment that his tawny eyes met hers almost took her breath away. Her heart started to pound and her blood warmed as his gaze swept over her from head to toe.

His presence was almost magnetic, as if she could move closer to him and her body would fuse with his.

Tingles ran up and down her spine. She'd never had this kind of reaction to any man. Ever.

Must have been too much wine.

She put on a sensual smile, doing her best to make sure her reaction didn't show on her features. She was good at that, putting on one face for the world while on the inside she was feeling entirely different.

His lips curved into a smile so sexy it made her shiver inside.

"Rick Pierce." When he clasped her hand, a flood of heat rushed through her. His hand was much larger than hers and his grip had a natural power to it. In his eyes was a confidence that for a moment made her wonder if he was a man who could control her and that she would actually permit to control her.

Of course not. No man would.

"Leslie," she said as she looked up at the tall man as he released her hand. "Leslie Adams."

He wasn't wearing a circle pin, which would ID him as a submissive from KC, but she could teach him the ropes. Literally. She had a thing for luring in men who had never experienced BDSM. As for this SEAL, she'd heard Navy men knew how to tie all kinds of knots but that didn't mean he could get out of hers. She planned to see.

"I saw you in the auction program." She cocked her head. "How did a Navy boy like you end up being auctioned off for charity?"

"My sister is on the committee." He had an almost boyish expression, as if a little embarrassed to be up for bid. "She asked me to help out and I've never been able to refuse my little sister."

A server stopped with a tray of glasses filled with bubbly. "Would you like a glass of wine?" he asked.

"Yes." She accepted a glass from him that he picked up from the tray. "Thank you."

He touched his own glass to hers. "To new friends."

She took a sip then lowered her glass and smiled. "I know many of those on the board," she said. "Which one is your sister?"

He lowered his glass. "Jessica Pierce."

"Ah." Leslie nodded. "With the dark hair and tawny-gold eyes, I should have guessed."

"That would be us." Rick shook his head. "Jess and I take after our father. My brother, Mark, is blond-haired and blue-eyed like our mother."

"How many siblings do you have?" Leslie asked.

"Just the two," he said. "Little sister, big brother."

"Hard to imagine you having a 'big' brother." She let her gaze drift over his easily six-four frame.

"Mark and I are the same height and build, but he'll always be my big brother." He raised his glass in a gesture that meant it was time for her to answer some questions. "What about you? Any brothers or sisters?"

She took a sip of wine before answering his question. "I'm an only child."

"You were lonely growing up." He stated the words in a way that made her feel like he'd just seen straight through to her soul, as impossible as that was.

It was as if he had seen the layers of loneliness, hurt, and pain that had accompanied her childhood. It was good she didn't have any brothers and sisters to go through what she had. At least the cold indifference of her parents hadn't gone any farther than her.

She shrugged off his statement. "You don't miss what you have never had. Besides, who needs siblings when you have a bevy of nannies at hand?"

He looked at her for a long moment. "I apologize for bringing up something that bothers you."

She took another sip of wine "It doesn't."

He continued to study her. It wasn't unnerving, it was almost comfortable being under his scrutiny.

"Are you currently on shore leave or whatever they call it?" she asked.

"I'm an instructor in the physical education department now," he said, "at the Naval Academy."

"Ah." Leslie nodded. "In Annapolis."

"That's the place." He set his wine glass on a tray on a stand beside the table of cheeses and fruits for the wine tasting. "You know what I do for a living," he said. "Tell me about your choice in careers."

She laughed. "I sort of fell into it but it has become a passion. I own a modeling agency with my partner, Raul."

"Now that's an interesting career," he said.

"Sure, if you don't mind putting up with egos and demanding and emotionally charged young men and women," she said.

He nodded. "Tell me, Leslie, what are you looking for tonight?"

She didn't miss a beat. "A strong man."

The corner of his mouth quirked into a smile. "Is that your criteria?"

It was her turn to study him. "I love strong men who challenge me. Most men can't handle me."

He looked at her with some amusement on his features. "Apparently you just haven't found the right man."

"I don't think that's possible." Leslie gave a soft laugh. "But perhaps I can find one who is fun to play with for now."

"Play with?" He laughed. "That's an interesting approach. So why don't you think it's possible?" he asked.

"I like to control situations and most men have trouble keeping my interest," she said. "I imagine you have had a lot of relationships."

"I like to have fun but I'm not really into relationships right now." He shrugged. "And you are looking for a playmate as you say. Might be perfect."

"So you're a love 'em and leave 'em kind of guy." She toyed with her wine glass as she flirted with him. He was like her.

"I wouldn't say that." He held her gaze. "Maybe I just haven't found the right woman. Not to mention, my choice in career has made it tough."

As she looked at him, she wondered if perhaps he could be someone she could settle down with. She mentally shook her head. Not likely. After a while, relationships bored her.

"Ladies and gentlemen, please join us in the ballroom," came a man's voice over the sound system, interrupting her train of thought. "The auction is about to start. Bachelors and bachelorettes, please meet behind the stage. Everyone else find a seat and we'll get started."

"My cue," he said.

"I will see you afterward." She put on her most sensual smile. "Plan on it."

As Rick left her, she made her way into the ballroom and found a seat in front of the stage. She settled back in her chair as she waited for him to be announced. She casually glanced around her to see what other women were in the crowd who would be interested in bidding on him. Several women would be bidding on the few men in the auction, so there would be competition. But of course she would win. She was determined to.

Her gaze met Daniela Danesworth's and her hackles rose and her neck prickled with heat. Daniela owned the modeling agency that Armand worked for, and she found pleasure in competing against Leslie whenever possible. Daniela knew that Leslie didn't give up easily. If Daniela was going for the Navy SEAL tonight, it was going to cost Leslie a small bundle to win.

But that didn't matter. Leslie faced the front again and settled into her chair. Rick was worth every penny. Besides, the money went to a good cause, a shelter for battered women and their children.

About halfway through the auction, the auctioneer said, "Ladies, we have a special treat for you. Captain Richard Pierce of the US Navy."

Rick walked out from behind the curtain and gave a casual wave as the crown applauded. He looked comfortable and confident. He didn't carry himself with an arrogance about him like she had expected from one of the Navy's elite. She had always heard that SEALs were confident to the point of arrogance because they had to be to do their job. They were the best of the best and sent into the worst situations a war had to offer. Their arrogance was well earned.

"Captain Pierce is a Navy SEAL and has graciously taken on a new challenge." The auctioneer smiled. "One of you ladies is his next assignment as he joins you in Cabo San Lucas, Mexico for a weekend for two."

Leslie's heart beat just a little faster as adrenaline kicked in. Bidding brought with it a thrill, an excitement, that she didn't feel with anything else. It was a challenge, something she could conquer.

Bidding started low enough that multiple women bid on Rick. As the dollar amount increased, eventually only Leslie and Daniela remained.

"Fourteen thousand dollars." The auctioneer took Daniela's bid. "Do I hear fifteen?"

Leslie indicated that she had raised the bid.

She glanced at Daniela whose mouth was tighter than normal. She wanted the SEAL and she was clearly frustrated that Leslie continued to bid against her.

The bidding reached seventeen thousand. Leslie bid eighteen. This time when the auctioneer looked at Daniela, the woman gave a shake of her head.

Leslie smiled to herself. The SEAL was hers.

The auctioneer instructed Rick to meet Leslie at the bottom of the stairs leading down from the stage. He reached the bottom stair as she came up to him. He held out his arm and she took it.

"You are persistent." He smiled down at her. "I knew from the moment that bidding started that the other woman wouldn't be able to beat you. You like to win, don't you," he stated.

"Absolutely." She returned his smile. "Do you plan on staying for the after auction dessert party and dance?"

They came to a stop at the ballroom doors as he shook his head. "I can't. I leave for the airport. I have a redeye to California."

She schooled her features to avoid showing disappointment. "Then I shall see you when we leave for Cabo."

"I'll meet you there," he said. "Until then I'll be in California visiting my parents."

She held out her hand. "I will see you then."

He smiled. "I'm looking forward to it, Leslie."

Just his smile and the way he said her name made her stomach twist in the strangest way and she felt a little unnerved, off-kilter, in a way that she never had before. There was something about the toughness of the man that combined with a certain depth of person she rather liked. He just might be perfect for her.

She straightened her shoulders and returned his smile. "I'm looking forward to it, too."

He gripped her hand before leaning down and brushing his lips over her cheek. He smelled good, a natural scent that was all man. Sexy and sinful all at the same time. Her cheek tingled where he kissed as he drew away and she resisted touching her fingers to her face.

"Goodbye, Rick," she said as he took a step back.

He gave a brief nod before he turned and walked away.

Chapter 2

"I love the flowers." Leslie smiled as she looked at Rick's image on her laptop at her kitchen table. Over the past two weeks since the auction, their Skype conversations had become an almost daily occurrence. She drew a yellow rose out of the bouquet of assorted yellow, white, and orange flowers. She brought the bloom to her nose and breathed in the wonderful scent. "Yellow is my favorite color."

He smiled in return. "I had a feeling you would like them. Yellow suits you."

She twirled the rose as she looked at his handsome face. "Thank you."

When they talked, she was always struck by how good-looking he was but even more appealing was that he had a great personality that made him easy to talk to about her day, her friends, her business, her co-workers, and even the models she worked with.

The one thing she wouldn't talk about was her family. What she had to say about any of them wasn't worth sharing. Why ruin a perfectly good conversation?

And of course Michael. She never talked about the bastard.

When she asked him, he shared a little of what it was like serving as a Navy

SEAL and as an instructor at the academy. There wasn't a whole lot he could tell her because the things he had done were highly classified.

In his voice she could always hear the respect, admiration, and appreciation he had for his fellow SEALs when he spoke about some of the guys he had worked with past and present.

He told her more about his parents, brother, and sister, and it was obvious he cared for them and loved them. He'd had the kind of upbringing that she always wished she had. Being born with a silver spoon in her mouth had not been a pleasant upbringing. Not when that spoon was shoved down her throat all of the time.

Over the years, both she and Rick had traveled around the world. Her modeling business took her places and she could afford to vacation in exotic locations. He had traveled because of his career. They compared notes on places that he was allowed to talk about and she told him stories about some locations that she'd been to. Both enjoyed their travels to most destinations, although she didn't really know what he thought about some of his more secret missions.

After all the time they had spent talking, she felt like she knew him.

And she knew that she wanted him.

Even though most of their communication had been over Skype and phone, there was a definite chemistry between them.

She smiled at his image on her laptop screen. "I've never asked you what made you decide to join the military."

He leaned forward, closer to his webcam. "When I was going to college I saw a feature on a soldier. I listened to what that guy said about his sense of duty. He ended up losing a leg and didn't regret it. He said he wanted to make a difference and serving his country was doing just that." Rick leaned back again. "It struck a cord in me. I was set on a business career and it hit me that I wanted to do the same thing as that man. Make a difference."

"How did you choose the Navy and to train to become a SEAL?" she asked.

"I studied every branch of the military." He looked dead serious as he spoke. "The place I believed I needed to be was where I could do the most good. To get there, I knew I had to become a SEAL.

"After I graduated from college," he continued, "I enlisted and went through extensive training. When I finished training I was deployed to places I can't speak of to serve my country. I would do it all over again in a heartbeat."

The man was unbelievable. "That's pretty amazing."

"It's not any more important than our boys who are on the front line," he said.

Modesty was something she found endearing about Rick. He never took credit for things he'd done. Teamwork was important to him.

When she asked him to tell her more, he gave her a good idea of what he had been through to make it as a SEAL. It was almost too much to take in. It wasn't just combat training but so much more. She loved that he was so tough. A man's man.

He changed the subject and asked her about her day. She told him some of the things she dealt with daily. Considering what he'd gone through they seemed like petty little things in comparison. But he made her feel like what she did was important and it mattered in its own way.

After awhile, she said, "Are you ready for me in Cabo, Rick?"

"You have big plans for us don't you," he said in a teasing voice.

"Well, we've Skyped enough that I feel like I know you…" She pricked her finger on a thorn on the rose and set it down. "We can skip all of the awkward getting to know each other."

"So," he said, "just a hello at the airport when you pick me up and then I jump you when we get to the hotel… Is that your plan?"

"No." she shook her head. "I thought you understood me better. You pick me up and I jump you at the hotel."

He flashed his adorable grin. "You are an aggressive one, aren't you."

His smile made her feel almost like a schoolgirl with a crush. "Only when I sense a connection."

He rubbed the stubble on his chin. "Is this a 'come into my parlor said the spider to the fly' situation?"

"I'm shocked." She pretended to be offended. "What type of person do you think I am?" Then she gave him what she knew was sensual smile. "To answer your question, yes, the spider and fly story does fit. Frightened yet, Mr. Tough Guy?"

He laughed. "Should I call you black widow?"

She had to admit that he had that right. She'd been a black widow to many. Love them and leave them as she moved on to her next. Although she hadn't really killed anyone. Yet.

A part of her wondered if this one would be different. Maybe she wouldn't dump Rick when she was through with him. She knew deep down that she could not keep running from relationships because of one major hurt. But something about leaving them wanting and moving onto the next was fun. And safe on her emotions.

Maybe if someone stood up to her... But that would set her up for hurt. She'd been hurt enough after what Michael had done to her.

"A black widow..." She tilted her head to the side. "Yes, that's me. You didn't answer my question. Frightened yet?"

"Frightened of you?" He raised a brow. "Naw. You actually sound fun."

"We have talked on Skype and at the auction about what I'm looking for." She might as well spell it out. "I want a man to be a man. I don't like wimps, but I like to control things."

Rick leaned back in his chair, giving her a clearer view of the upper half of his body. "You have used the word 'control' a lot. Do you mean just in bed?"

"In a lot of things," she said. "On top in bed, yes, but also in business and in relationships."

She wasn't sure if he was amused or just curious when he asked, "So it is obvious from what you have said that you like kink. So how much kink?"

She nodded. "You're pretty good at guessing games aren't you? Do you know what power exchange is?"

Rick cocked his head. "I think I can put two and two together, but why don't you tell me since you are in charge here."

"We both know you are stronger than I, but you relinquish control because you want it and you trust me."

He did look amused now. "In other words, when a man lets you tie him up."

She gave him a sensual smile. "I love to restrain a strong man, but that is only a part of it. It's an amazing high."

"I just like to have fun." He grinned. "It's been a long while but a girlfriend and I played tie-up."

Leslie raised an eyebrow. That was unexpected. "Who did the tying up?"

"I did." He shrugged. "It was only one time. She was adventurous enough to try but it didn't do anything for her."

"What about you?" Leslie asked. "Did it do anything for you?"

"I thought it was hot," he said. "But she didn't get into it so that was that."

Leslie picked up her rose again. "And since then?"

"I guess I just haven't found the right partner." Before she had a chance to respond, he asked, "What else can you tell me that I might find surprising?"

She looped a strand of hair around her finger. "I love fetish wear."

He was obviously intrigued by his expression. "What kinds of fetish wear?"

"Cat suits, leather, latex." She pushed the strand of hair over her shoulder and held the rose between the fingers of both hands. "And I adore lingerie. I have tons of it. I could open up a store with all of the panties, corsets, garter belts, and countless other things in my collection."

"You're kind of like a fantasy, aren't you?" He grinned.

She smiled. "Be careful what kind of fantasy you want."

"You're working hard to frighten me off." He smiled and shook his head. "There are layers and layers to you, Leslie," he said. "I have a feeling that I've only scratched the surface."

She sniffed the rose's perfume again then looked at him over the rose. "You have no idea."

Chapter 3

Leslie felt the change in the air the moment she stepped off the plane and onto the ramp in the Los Cabos International Airport. She had checked her bag, and two plane changes later she hoped it was still with her. She carried a large tote with an extra change of clothing and a few personal items just in case.

She made her way toward baggage claim and held her purse close to her body on one side and gripped her tote on her other. She had picked out a pair of white capris to wear with navy blue slip-on shoes as well as a navy blue boat-necked shirt with gold anchors embroidered on the sleeves.

Just as she reached baggage claim a tall form caught her attention as Rick strode toward her.

No man could possibly ever look as good as him. He wore a black polo shirt, snug Levis, and athletic shoes. His skin was tanned, the muscles in his arms well defined, and the power in his presence was undeniable.

She couldn't help a smile as he hugged her and gave her a kiss on the cheek. "Did you check-in anything?" he asked.

"Two bags." She glanced toward the carousel. "There they are. The hot pink ones with the *Diva* luggage tags."

He raised an eyebrow. "Diva?"

She shrugged. "It was unique and matched the suitcase. Besides," she said. "I work with a bunch of divas and I know them well."

"Two bags for a weekend?" he asked with clear amusement.

"A long weekend," she said with a quick grin.

"Damn, what do you have in here?" He raised one of the two heavy bags he easily pulled off the conveyer belt.

"That is a surprise." She had plenty of surprises in store for him.

After he grabbed her bags, he walked with her outside. The balmy air brushed over her and a light film of perspiration coated her skin from the warmth of the late afternoon sunshine. She pulled a pair of big sunglasses out and pushed them onto her nose then dug a floppy hat out of her tote and adjusted it on her head. No sense in burning her fair skin.

They headed to where he had parked his rental car, a red Mustang. "Perfect," she said as he loaded her suitcase into the back of the car. "A hot man and a red Mustang. Can't beat that combination."

Rick gave her a quick grin. "Don't forget a beautiful woman."

She smiled back at him. "I'm ready for a mojito. How about you?"

"You're on."

The trip to the Pacifica Resort in Cabo took about fifty minutes. The desert scenery on the single-laned highway was completely different from what she was used to in Baltimore, but she loved it. A paved high coastal drive, that was beautifully landscaped, took them straight to the resort.

The resort itself was gorgeous and appealing, the perfect getaway for their extended weekend trip. The glittering crystal blue sea was visible through magnificent floor to ceiling glass windows.

"I have been so ready for this weekend." She looked up at Rick from under the brim of her floppy hat. "As you know from our conversations, it's been a trying couple of weeks at the agency."

"While I've been basking in the sun at my mom and dad's in San Diego," he said as they walked to the registration desk.

"Talk about an extended vacation." She laughed. "Every time you told me about the weather in California, I went through a fit of jealousy."

They came to a stop at the desk. "You don't strike me as the jealous type."

"When it comes to men and most things, I'm not. I don't have time or reason to be." She looked out the windows at the gorgeous views. "But this…" She raised her arms to encompass the view. "Who wouldn't be envious?"

The woman behind the registration desk asked their names in heavily accented English. Rick responded in fluent Spanish, the words rolling off of his tongue as if he was born to the language. Leslie knew the language marginally well, but in no way did she speak it as well as he did. She enjoyed listening to him. He had a beyond sexy voice that she could listen to for hours—and had during their phone and Skype conversations.

When he finished talking with the woman, she gave him two key cards and instructed them on where there rooms were located.

"They gave us a connecting suite," he said as he easily carried his and her luggage to their rooms.

"I understand Spanish, but do not speak it very well," Leslie said. "How did you become so fluent?"

He shrugged. "I grew up in San Diego which isn't far from the Mexican border and I took classes in high school. Most I learned in the service, though."

The charity provided separate rooms for the winners in the various resorts that were included with each auction. Leslie planned on only one room getting any use on their stay. His. Or hers. Whichever came first.

The suite was gorgeous, the sitting room also having floor to ceiling windows. "It's magnificent," she said as she moved to stand beside the window after dropping her purse, tote, and hat onto the couch.

She heard the thump of the suitcases as he set them on the floor and then felt his presence as he moved up behind her. He put his hands on her shoulders and started massaging them as they looked out the window at the sparkling sea.

"Geez, what do you have in those suit cases?" He laughed. "You wearing a suit of iron on the trip?"

"No, but you might be," she said.

She leaned back against him, feeling as if they had done this a thousand times. "It's simply amazing." Even though she had been around the world, she always felt some kind of awe when in the presence of some of nature's wonders.

She turned just enough to look up at him. "What's first?"

"So you aren't throwing me into bed right away?" he asked.

"There is plenty of time for that." She laughed.

"Let's head out for dinner then." He smiled down at her. "I'm starving."

The walk down the beach to Restaurant Row on the marina was fun and they found a restaurant with a thriving atmosphere. An energy spread through the city signifying it was Friday night and time to seriously party.

It was early enough in the evening that they didn't have to wait to be seated. Apparently all meals were cooked tableside in the restaurant. It was an amazing thing to watch and the food tasted fantastic.

She and Rick never seemed to run out of things to talk about which she found invigorating. He was someone who could keep up with her intellectually.

How would he match up with her sexually? That was something she intended to find out and soon. She liked that he was adventurous and open to some fun games, but for her it was more than a game. She simply loved control. Whether he could or wanted to handle her would soon be found out.

All in good time…

Partying on the marina was really getting into gear by the time she drained her second mojito. They left the restaurant then stopped at a nightclub and listened to the live band. She learned that Rick was a great dancer the moment he escorted her out on the floor.

The night was still young when she took his hand and led him outside. "Let's go for a walk." She slipped off her shoes and carried them as they headed toward the water. Moonlight glittered on the sea, the silvery moon seeming close enough to touch.

The air smelled fresh and clean and cooled her skin. She had read that the temperatures in the desert dropped at night and she found herself rubbing her arms with her hands to chase away the chill.

He draped his arm around her shoulders and pressed her close to his big body and his heat warmed her. She rested her head on his shoulder as they walked along the beach, the wet sand cool beneath her feet.

"I'm having an incredible time already." She gave a happy sigh. "And the trip has only just begun."

"It's a lot of fun to be here with you, Leslie." He squeezed her to him. "Considering you own me for the weekend, what do you have in store?"

She raised her head and looked up at him and gave him a teasing look. "You have no idea, sailor. But you are all mine to do with as I choose."

He held his free hand to his chest. "Be gentle with me." She saw him wink in the moonlight and it made her smile.

"You may have gone through hell with your SEAL training," she said. "But you've never dealt with the likes of me."

"You keep talking like that and I might have to hire a bodyguard." He stopped and brought her into his arms and stroked her cheek with the back of his hand.

"Now you're not afraid of little ole me are you, Rick?"

"Let's just say I am looking forward to you proving it," he said.

Chapter 4

Leslie felt a thrill low in her belly as Rick took her hand and they walked back to the resort. Her nipples tightened beneath her blouse and she bit the inside of her cheek. She'd never had such an immediate reaction like this, before she'd even started to play with a man. At least not for as long as she could remember.

Sexual tension hummed between them all the way back to their suite. When the door to the suite closed, Rick brought her into his arms and pressed her up tight against him. He brushed his lips across hers before settling in for an amazing kiss. A passionate, earth shattering, primal kiss that rocked her to her toes.

She loved his taste and his scent that filled her until she was almost intoxicated with it. His body felt warm and hard against hers.

He drew away and his gaze held hers. "You might have paid for me," he murmured, "But I claim you, Leslie."

Excitement tingled beneath her skin as he moved his palms over her body.

She smiled and took his hands in hers, drawing him in the direction of her bedroom, on one side of the suite. He smiled back at her, a look so sexy that she couldn't help herself from stopping and kissing him again before continuing on into the bedroom.

When they reached the bed she lightly pushed him so that he sat on the edge of the mattress. She kicked off her sandals and climbed onto his lap, and her skirt hiked up to her hips as she straddled him.

He cupped the back of her head and kissed her again, a kiss of passion and intensity. He moved his hands down to her ass and rubbed it through her panties, and she found herself whimpering from the need to have him. And then he slowly moved so that he was on his back and she was on top of him. Then he rolled, causing her to gasp in surprise and she found herself beneath him.

"I think I'm dizzy now." She laughed and tried to tickle him into letting her back on top.

"Not ticklish." He grinned down at her and then he laughed when she tried pinching him. His body was so muscular, so hard, that she had a hard time finding a good spot. "I bet you're ticklish." He captured both of her wrists in one of his hands and pinned them above her head. He held her down with his body weight and she couldn't move. She tried to wiggle out of his hold and then he started tickling her with his free hand.

"Nooooo." She giggled and squirmed to get away from his fingers that were finding all of her most sensitive spots. She couldn't stop laughing even as she begged him to stop. "Please let me go. I promise I won't try pinching you again."

He lowered his head and kissed her. She sighed from the sheer pleasure he was giving her. She went from giggling to moaning, wanting him, needing him.

When he raised his head, he smiled down at her. "What's this tying up that gets you so excited?"

She had a hard time catching her breath enough to talk. "I love it," she said when her breathing returned to normal. "I told you how it excites me to have someone big and strong let me take control."

He looked both intrigued and amused. "So you would like to tie me up."

"I would love it." She felt a twinge of excitement in her belly. "I didn't expect it this soon. I didn't want to be too pushy or controlling." She grinned. "The first twelve hours anyway."

He rolled over so that she was on top of him again and she sat so that she had her knees to either side of his hips and his cock was pressing against her center. She loved that he was already so turned on.

She moved her hands over his muscular chest. The power she felt beneath his skin was such an incredible turn on that she found herself biting her lower lip. He had strength enough to crush her, but that strength would be hers to play with as he turned over control.

"Let's take off your socks and shoes." She slipped off the mattress and stepped back as he sat up and kicked off his shoes. She moved closer and peeled off his socks before taking his hand and pulling to get him to stand.

When he was up, she pushed his T-shirt over his head then skimmed her palms over his bare skin. "Can't wait to see what else you have under these clothes."

She smiled to herself when he audibly sucked in his breath as she scratched her fingers over his jeans along the length of his cock. It felt hard and thick and she was ready to let it come out to play. She unfastened the top button then drew the zipper down. His breathing came a little more rapid and she swore she could hear his heart pounding.

He may be a tough Navy SEAL, but ultimately he was just a man when it came to the right woman.

His Levis dropped to the floor and then she pushed down his boxer briefs to uncover his cock. "Damn," she murmured as she wrapped her fingers around it. "Nice."

Now that he was fully naked, she stepped back for a moment to admire him. He didn't look so amused. Now his eyes burned with passion and she knew he wanted to step forward and take control of her. He did a remarkable job of holding himself back.

She guided him toward the left side of the king-sized bed, near the headboard, and pushed him down. The bed rocked beneath his weight as he dropped onto the mattress.

"Let me see you now." His voice was almost hoarse with desire.

"In good time." She went to one of her bags and rummaged in it before pulling out two pairs of leather handcuffs and long white rope and metal clips.

He raised an eyebrow as she carried them to him. "Come on, big boy. Let me see your left wrist."

"I can't believe you brought that." He laughed.

"Oh, this and more," she said. "I could tell in our Skype time that you were up for adventure, so I figured what the heck."

He shook his head and grinned. "I wonder if they checked your bags."

"Sure they did." She shrugged. "I don't care though. One of the ladies checking actually looked rather excited."

He held out his wrist and she buckled on a cuff. He was being a good sport, at least so far, and it was a high knowing that he was doing this just for her.

Of course he had no idea what she had planned for him.

She'd secured rubber-coated black chain around the legs of the bed before they'd left for dinner—she'd told him she was going to her room to freshen up. All she had to do was snap a clip to the chain and a ring on his cuff on each side of the bed and he would be ready for her.

He watched as she knelt and brought the chain up to his wrist and secured it.

"You brought *chain*?" he said with humor in his voice. "To *Mexico*?"

"You'd be surprised what I have in those bright pink bags. I told you this stuff and more." She grinned. "Move into the middle of the bed."

He obeyed and she went around to the other side, buckled a cuff to his right wrist and stretched his arm out so that his arms were secured to either side.

She watched him for signs of unease that he was turning over control to a woman but he remained at ease, with the exception of his cock that was still standing at attention. She returned to her bag and pulled out a pair of leather ankle cuffs. He raised his head enough to watch her as she put the ankle cuffs on him then used clips to attach them to chains at the foot of the bed.

She loved how the big, strong, confident man had turned control over to her without a complaint, without worrying that she would hurt him.

When she had him spread-eagled on the bed, cuffed, in all his naked glory, she found her own heart pounding faster. He was so sexy with his dark hair and tawny eyes as he watched her with hunger in his gaze.

"I'll be right back." She gave him a seductive smile before grabbing up one of her bags and taking it with her into the bathroom.

It didn't take her long to get ready for him. As she came out, he gave a low whistle when he saw her in her leather corset and panties.

"Damn, that's hot." He seemed mesmerized by her breasts that were pushed up high, and didn't seem to notice the riding crop in her hands until she was standing over him. "Be kind to me, Mistress," he said in a teasing tone.

She brought the crop down lightly on one of his thighs then used it a little harder and a little harder yet. She loved that he didn't make a sound. No matter how hard she used the crop, he just watched her without flinching.

"My, my you're tough." She climbed up onto the bed and knelt with her hands to either side of his head. Again he seemed transfixed on her breasts that were nearly spilling out of the corset. She reached down and grabbed his balls and squeezed. Hard.

His gaze moved from her breasts to her face, the only indication that he felt something. She held onto his balls and smiled. "I want your complete attention, do you understand that?"

"Sure." His expression still showed no sign that she might have been causing him any pain. She squeezed harder. No change in the way that he was looking at her. Not a twitch of a muscle or a vein bulging on his forehead. Nothing. "I'm all yours." Even his voice was clear with no hint of pain.

This might call for more drastic measures.

She eased off of the bed and returned to her bag of tricks. She pulled out some of her favorite instruments of torture. Clothespins tied to twine.

"I love these." She returned to him and drew the clothespins out. They were on rough twine and she watched him as she slowly started applying the clothespin zipper, one clothespin at a time, around his balls and even around his cock. She made it last, putting each one on slowly, making the whole thing an erotic torture.

Except that it didn't seem like torture to him. He didn't even wince. Most guys were whining and sniveling by now, but Rick was taking everything she dished out.

She loved it.

Wimps and men with baggage were such a turn-off. She'd dumped men for begging and whimpering.

"How do you like this, big man?" She kept hold of the end of the twine as she moved up enough that she could brush her lips over his. Then she raised her head, gave a devious smile, and pulled on the string, ripping away the clothespins like a zipper.

As she watched his face she thought she saw a tic in his jaw, but she wasn't sure. She kissed him again then went back to her bag.

Next she chose silver clover nipple clamps. She climbed onto the bed and moved up and knelt between his thighs. "These might pinch a little." She clasped one on each of his flat nipples. "They might not hurt so much at first, but—" She tugged on the chain connecting the clamps and they automatically tightened when they are pulled. Still no obvious reaction. "Every time this is pulled, the tighter the clamps will get."

"Got it," he said and winked, and she shook her head.

When she went back to her bag, she bypassed the ball gag and took out a pair of red panties and a nylon stocking. Yelling didn't seem to be something she had to worry about other guests in the resort hearing as she played with Rick, but she liked the idea of using her panties as a gag. The man was a definite challenge.

She stuffed her panties into his mouth and wrapped the stocking around his head four times through his mouth and tightened it keeping the panties in place. She looked down at him and smiled. His eyes were heavy lidded and she knew he was turned on without him saying a word. Then she picked out a length of thin rope and went back to the bed and moved between his thighs again.

"This won't hurt, much." She started tying up his balls with the rope, winding it around his ball sac. Round and round she wound it between his cock and his balls, separating and stretching his balls down and further from his body. They hardened like limes.

His erection remained hard as she played with him. "You love all of this, don't you," she stated.

As he silently watched her, she lowered her head and licked the head of his cock. This time he twitched and she smiled. She knew how to get to him.

She gripped his cock in one hand and squeezed his tied-up balls at the same time she started going down on him. Her eyes locked with his. His jaw tightened and a sheen of perspiration soon coated his body as she sucked and licked his cock.

There was always a way to get through a man's defenses.

But she didn't think *she* could take much more. It was the first time she had ever wanted a man so badly she was almost shaking with it. She moved off of the bed and slipped out of her leather panties then pulled out the condom she had slipped into her corset earlier, in her cleavage. She got back on the bed and knelt beside him as she opened the package and tossed it aside. Her hands trembled as she rolled the condom onto his cock.

She eased up his body and straddled him, settling with her knees to either side of his chest. She never expected to move this fast, but the Skype sessions had excited her and she wanted him. She knew he wanted her, too. As much as she wanted to ride him, she restrained herself and moved her lips to his ear.

"I'm going to fuck you." She nipped at his earlobe and stroked his cock at the same time. "There isn't a thing you can do about it. But I know you want me, so that isn't a problem, now is it?"

He moved his head from side to side. Definitely not a problem. She rose up and looked down at his tawny gold eyes. *Lion's eyes,* she thought. They were dark with hunger and she knew he was dying to be inside of her.

She shifted so that her pussy was over his cock and rubbed herself on him. He was hard against her folds and she felt herself grow wetter. She reached down and placed the head of his cock against her core.

Even as she ached to have him, she took her time, drawing it out for the both of them.

Her hips rose and then she slammed herself onto him. His eyes nearly crossed as she moved up and down his cock and she had a hard time hanging on and not climaxing. She didn't want to come yet. She wanted to enjoy the sensation of him filling her up, of his cock thrusting in and out of her core, his big muscled body moving beneath her. She grasped the chain to the clover clamps on his nipples then pulled.

He shouted behind his gag and she didn't know if it was because his nipples hurt or he was close to coming.

Everything rose and rose inside of her. Colors seemed to intertwine in her mind and her body trembled from the power of her orgasm rising inside of her. She cried out as she climaxed, forgetting for a moment that she could be heard by neighboring resort guests.

Her whole body seemed to clench and unclench as her orgasm carried on. For a moment she lost sense of herself as her entire body throbbed.

The next thing she knew, she was beneath Rick. She gasped in surprise. How had he managed to free his wrists and ankles?

He had to have figured out how to undo one of the clips. She should have used locks. Once he had one hand free, it would have been easy to get the rest of the cuffs off while she had been lost in orgasm La-La Land.

She struggled and tried to get free but he had her pinned down tight with his body and one hand securing her wrists again. With his free hand he unwrapped the stocking from around his head and pulled the panties out of his mouth and tossed it all aside.

His gaze was burning hot when her eyes met his and a drop of sweat rolled down the side of his face.

He drove his cock into her core and she cried out with surprise at the intensity of his movement. He fucked her hard and fast, and she felt him deep inside of her.

Another orgasm came charging toward her as he drove in and out. She cried out even louder this time and she heard his own shout as he climaxed along with her.

Everything pulsed within her and her whole body seemed to spasm with her orgasm. It throbbed and throbbed and she didn't think she'd ever come down from the incredible high. She didn't want to come down.

He wrapped her in his arms and rolled her onto her side and looked into her eyes. "Honey," he said. "You can try to tie me up anytime."

She smiled feeling satisfied and amazed at how wonderful she felt. "I plan to," she said as her whole body relaxed and she felt more sated than she had ever felt in her life. She snuggled up against him and slipped into a deep sleep, dreaming of whips and chains and this time she wasn't the one in control.

Chapter 5

The sun was barely coming up as Leslie slipped her feet off the mattress and onto the floor. She'd teach Rick for escaping and taking control of her like he had.

When she was out of bed she glanced at him. He had one arm across his eyes and the other stretched out beside him. His bare chest rose and fell with deep, even breaths and she was certain he was still asleep. A sheet was tangled around him and it barely covered his early morning erection and her mouth watered as she thought about a great way to wake him up.

But she had other plans.

She knelt beside the bed and found one of the leather handcuffs on the floor. It was still attached to the chain and she wondered at how well he had managed to get away. She'd always heard that SEALs were the best of the best.

Of course that didn't mean she couldn't do her best to take back control.

It was amazing how he had gotten out last night. Thoughts of that moment sent a thrill through her belly. It had been incredible when he suddenly had her in his control.

He had taken everything she had dished out without one word of complaint, without one whimper. He had let her restrain him and play with him. He hadn't had to give up control at all. He could so easily crush her with his superior strength. But he was a man of confidence, a man willing to give up control and not feel threatened by her.

This time she would use locks, once she had him secured. She picked up the cuff that was attached to the chain then checked to make sure he still looked asleep. She slowly moved the cuff toward the arm he had sprawled out beside him. She reached for his wrist—

He snatched her arm so fast and sudden that she cried out in surprise. Her head spun as he grabbed her and flipped her onto her back. Suddenly she was looking up at him and he had a look of satisfaction on his face.

She tugged on her arm and she felt the metal cuff biting into her wrist. Somehow he had cuffed her in the same motion that he put her onto her back.

Before she even realized what was happening, he was cuffing her other wrist on the other side of the bed.

Her eyes widened. Rick had chained her to the bed. *He* was the one who was supposed to be chained.

This had gone wrong in a hurry.

The bed dipped and Rick sat on the mattress beside her.

"Good morning." He smiled and she saw a mischievous spark in his eyes. *Uh-oh.*

"I figure that I owe you." He traced a path from her throat to her cleavage that was still covered by the corset.

That didn't last long. As soon as his hand reached the corset, he pulled it down, releasing her breasts. She caught her breath as cool air tightened her nipples and they immediately ached for his touch. As if reading her mind, he lowered his head and sucked one of her nipples. She moaned as the exquisite sensations flowed throughout her. She loved her nipples being sucked and licked. Her next favorite thing to a man going down on her. He moved his mouth to her other nipple and gently bit it, causing her to gasp. He placed his hand on her flat belly as he teased the taut nub with his tongue and teeth.

He raised his head and looked down at her and the corner of his mouth curved into a smile. "You're one beautiful woman, Leslie." He pinched her nipple, causing her to gasp. "And you sure know how to show a guy a good time."

She would have smiled if her eyes weren't watering and her nipple didn't hurt so much. She obviously didn't have the same kind of stamina when it came to pain as he did.

He moved his mouth to hers and softly kissed her. "Don't you love paybacks?"

She groaned. "I told you I like to be in control."

"Too bad." He trailed his lips along her jaw and then down the curve of her neck to the hollow of her throat. "I always win, hon. Don't forget that."

"Oh yeah?" she said.

"Uh-huh." His mouth was occupied with her nipple again, causing her to arch her back from the pleasure. He bit down hard enough to make her eyes fly open and caused her to cry out in surprise.

A tough Navy SEAL she was not.

"Rick." She moaned as he licked her other nipple. "I don't like to be out of control."

"Get used to it when you're with me." He looked down at her again. "Even when you think you're in control, I really am."

"That's not true." She squirmed beneath his mouth and hands, loving the feel of it but fighting the want and need rising up inside of her. *She* was supposed to be on top. That's how it was for her. After Michael—

No, she wasn't going to think about him. Especially not now.

"Tell me, Leslie," Rick said as he nuzzled the curve of her neck. "What makes you so determined to be in control with men?"

It was as if he had read her mind. She had tried to figure herself out for a long time. She believed that it had to be Michael. She always liked control, but not in a relationship. Once he had been her Dominant partner and she'd been his submissive. It had been the only time she had let a man be in control and it had been amazing in the initial stages. But after their relationship ended, she swore she would always be in control from that point on.

"I belong on top." She tried to get out of his grip.

"I am going to enjoy this." He moved his mouth close to her ear. "And so are you."

"Ha." She kicked at him but he grabbed both of her legs. She couldn't begin to get out of his grip the way he had her. He easily picked up the leather cuff that was still attached to the chain at the foot of the bed and cuffed one ankle with it even as she fought to get her legs away. When that one was done he had an easy time of cuffing her other ankle.

He tightened all of the restraints so that she couldn't even wiggle. Her heart beat faster and she bit the inside of her cheek. How was she supposed to get out of this? She wasn't Houdini like this man seemed to be.

When she was secured, he moved up and braced his hands to either side of her chest and looked down at her. "How does it feel, Leslie?"

"I don't like it." A bald-faced lie. She was so turned on that she wanted to squirm from need.

He gave a soft laugh. "We'll see." He brushed his lips over hers and she couldn't help a sigh of pleasure. Then he eased off the bed and she turned her head enough to see that he was going through her bag of tricks.

She swallowed as he pulled out a red ball gag and a black blindfold and carried them back to her.

"Ohhh. Look at this. Never used one of these. Can't have you making too much noise so let's try it out." He put the ball gag to her lips. She refused to open her mouth. He pinched her nipple and she gasped in surprise and he pushed the ball into her mouth. He raised her head enough that he could buckle the back of the gag. The corner of his lips turned up into a smile. "That will keep you from complaining about not being on top."

She made a sound of argument as he put the blindfold over her eyes, a sound that he ignored. When the blindfold was on, he kissed the corner of her mouth. "There. That's better."

Her thoughts spun. What was he going to do now that he had her down tight?

He moved his mouth to her ear again. "You'll see," as if he knew what she was thinking. He inhaled deeply then ran his lips along her jaw then nuzzled the curve of her neck.

Shivers ran along her spine as he kissed a trail down to the valley between her breasts. Something about not being able to see enhanced sensations because all she could do was feel his every touch. She thought about this strong man having her helpless. The thought sent ripples of excitement through her whole body.

She gasped behind her gag when he sucked each of her nipples again, before moving his palm over the corset on down to her belly. His hand felt warm against her skin and she wanted him to move it lower and lower. He eased down her body and pressed his lips to her bellybutton, his hand on her thigh. She bit down on her gag and squirmed as he dipped his tongue into her bellybutton. It felt like there was a straight line between there and that place between her thighs that was dying for him to touch.

He moved on and she thought she was going to go crazy as he nuzzled her mound and she heard his audible inhalation. He blew on her curls and she held her breath as she waited for him to go down on her. She wanted his mouth and tongue on her so badly she could barely stand waiting.

Instead, he kissed her inner thigh and began moving his lips along the inside of her leg to the back of her knee. She groaned, loving the exquisite sensations. He continued on, over her calf to the inside of her ankle then the instep of her foot.

Perspiration broke out on her forehead and her breathing came more rapidly. He was going to kill her.

He slipped her big toe into his mouth and he sucked. She gasped behind her gag, unable to believe how incredible it felt with him sucking her toes, each and every one of them. He moved his mouth to her other foot and started the torturous experience all over again. He sucked one toe at a time then kissed her instep before trailing a path of kisses up the inside of her leg to her thigh.

Her heart beat faster and her mouth was dry. He pressed his lips to the soft skin between her folds and her inner thigh.

Please, she begged in her mind, feeling almost delirious with it. *Please.*

He ran his tongue over the soft curls covering the lips of her folds, then slipped his tongue into the wetness.

She cried out from behind her gag and she nearly came at once. She managed to hold back her orgasm, but she knew she wasn't going to last much longer. Her entire body was like one giant nerve.

He licked and sucked and slipped his fingers into her core. She wished she wasn't blindfolded so that she could look down and see his head between her thighs. She felt the softness of his hair and the abrasiveness of his stubble as he went on licking her while pounding his fingers in and out of her pussy.

She couldn't hold on any longer. She didn't want to hold on. If she hadn't already been blindfolded, her vision would have gone dark as her orgasm exploded through her. She screamed as she came, her voice muffled but her cry going on and on. Her whole body jerked and shook with her climax like it was never going to end.

In the back of her mind she realized he wasn't going down on her any longer and she was able to catch her breath again. A moment's reprieve and then he straddled her shoulders, removed the gag, and pressed his cock to her lips, then pushed it into her mouth.

She caught her breath in surprise as he started pumping his hips and forced her to give him a blowjob while she was tied up. It made her feel even more excited and her belly tingled all the way down to her clit.

Before he could climax he moved away, off of the bed, and she heard the sound of a package being opened. He was putting on a condom and the thought that he would be inside of her again sent more thrills through her belly.

The bed dipped from his weight. He settled himself between her thighs then drove his cock inside of her.

Another cry rose up in her as he fucked her, thrusting in and out so hard that the headboard banged against the wall. Her body was so sensitized that she came almost at once, and she didn't think she could take much more as the second orgasm took hold of her.

She wished she wasn't blindfolded and could see his face. She wanted to see his expression when he came.

A few more strokes and she heard his groan and felt the throb of his cock inside of her. In and out a few more times and then he pressed his body to hers. She felt the sweat of his skin as it mingled with hers and thought she heard their hearts pounding as one.

Chapter 6

The shower felt delicious. If only Rick was in it with her—that would make it exceptional.

She hummed to herself as warm water rained down on her and she washed her hair with rosemary mint-scented shampoo and scrubbed her body with soap of the same scent. When she finished she grabbed a towel, dried off, and stepped onto the thick rug outside the shower door. The bathroom was filled with steam and the mirrors fogged.

The sound of a voice coming from outside the bathroom caught her attention. Was Rick back from his jog already? It didn't seem like that much time had passed. Had she lost track of time? That or the sound had been her imagination.

She picked up her brush and ran it through her wet hair. She paused when she heard a hard thump, as if something had been thrown across the room.

What in the world?

With her wet hair lying about her shoulders, she wrapped a thick towel around her body and opened the door from the bathroom into the bedroom. She heard another noise, this one coming from the suite's sitting room that connected hers and Rick's rooms. She frowned and walked through the door leading out of the bedroom to the sitting room.

Three men were in the sitting room.

Leslie started to scream but a man with a short scraggly beard and small dark eyes pointed his gun at her. "Shut up and come here." His English was coarse and thickly accented.

Adrenaline ran through her veins and her heart pounded in her throat as her whole body started to shake. She clenched the towel around herself and took a step back instead.

He gave a low growl. "Come here, bitch."

Her body continued to shake as she stepped toward him.

Scraggly-beard laughed and said in Spanish to the other two men, "A bonus, my friends. A beautiful woman." He used his gun to wave Leslie closer to him. "Comprende Española?" he said to her.

She shook her head. Even though she was terrified, a part of her realized that if they thought she didn't understand Spanish maybe she would learn something from them when they talked to each other that would help her.

"Is anyone else here?" the man asked her.

She shook her head again. "No," she said while she prayed that Rick would come back soon.

The man grabbed her by the wrist and jerked her to him. He ripped her towel away, leaving her naked and it felt like he had stolen away her last defense. She folded her arms across her breasts and shivered as she stood in front of him.

To her right a man was going through her bag of toys that he had obviously taken out of the bedroom. He laughed and pulled out Leslie's metal handcuffs along with her leather restraints. "We can use these on the señorita if she doesn't do as she's told," the man said in Spanish as he tossed the metal ones to scraggly-beard.

"Convenient," scraggly-beard said. "Now where are your jewels and your money?" he asked in a harsh tone as he swung the cuffs back and forth.

"In the hotel safe in the bedroom closet." She swallowed. "I'll give you the combination. Then please let me go."

He laughed and shoved her so that she stumbled. The back of her legs hit the couch and she fell onto the edge of it. "Maybe we will let you go after we enjoy your body first." He shrugged. "Or maybe we don't let you go. There is a market for beautiful American women."

Cold washed through her at the reality that these men could rape her like he'd just threatened, and they could also sell her. She'd heard about women being abducted and sold, and turned into sex slaves. The thought made her want to vomit. She glanced at the other two men who looked at her with raw lust in their eyes.

Come back, Rick, she prayed silently. *Please come back.*

The man with the gun spoke to one of the other two men. "Check the closet." Scraggly-beard turned back to Leslie. "The combination."

She paused for a moment, her mind suddenly blank.

"*The combination,*" he shouted.

It came to her and she rushed to get the numbers out. "Five-five-zero-one."

The man with the gun nodded to one of the other men, a thin man wearing a dirty white wife-beater T-shirt. The man went to the bedroom, shoved the door open, and disappeared. She heard the distinctive hard click of the lock and door opening.

The man shouted in Spanish from the bedroom, "Much money and jewelry."

"Excellent." The man with the gun approached Leslie and her heart pounded impossibly faster. "Now we have fun."

She felt exposed, vulnerable, and helpless. Three men with at least one gun against her, a naked woman. They were going to rape her. She could see it in their eyes. She'd never been so scared in all her life.

Scraggly-beard set the gun on an end table and started to unzip his jeans

Terror ripped through Leslie, giving her strength. She shot her foot out and rammed her heel into his groin as hard as she could.

He screamed and dropped to his knees. The other men grabbed her and she screamed. One of them slapped her so hard that her mind spun. She tasted blood in her mouth and realized her nose was bleeding. The other man grabbed her around the neck from behind and pulled her up against him.

"*You,* I will kill," scraggly-beard said in English.

At first, Leslie thought the man was talking to her.

Then Rick spoke in a deadly quiet voice. "I am only going to tell you once. Let her go."

She looked up to see him standing in the doorway to the suite. Fear for him rose up inside of her. What if they shot him?

The man she'd kneed in the balls had already retrieved his gun from the end table and had it pointed at Rick. The arm around her throat tightened.

"You are not telling me anything," the gunman said to Rick. "Close the door. Then on your knees, hands behind your head." The man walked toward Rick, keeping his gun steady. "Or she dies."

Rick looked calm as he got to his knees. He showed no fear, no doubt. As if he was just biding his time.

The man with the gun pressed it against Rick's forehead. "Get the handcuffs we found," the scraggly-beard said to the thin man without taking his eyes or gun off of Rick. "Use those to cuff the gringo."

The third man kept his arm around her neck while the thin one went to her bag and retrieved her police-issue cuffs. The man with the cuffs walked behind Rick and knelt down to cuff his wrists.

What happened next was a blur. Rick snapped his arm up and grabbed the barrel of the gun, pushing it away from his face and ripping it out of scraggly-beard's hand. The gun went off and a lamp exploded as a bullet hit it. The man lost his hold on the gun and it dropped on the floor beside them.

With his opposite arm, Rick flipped the thin man over his shoulder, wrapped his arm around the man's neck, and twisted. Leslie heard the sickening pop of bone as Rick snapped the man's neck then released him.

In virtually the same motion, he brought straggly-beard down, slamming the man's head against the floor. The man scrambled for the gun that was now beside him and grabbed it. Rick wrenched it from his hand. He put a bullet through the man's skull.

He surged to his feet, gun still in hand, and started toward Leslie and the third man. He came to an abrupt stop.

"I'll kill her!" The third man sounded shrill as he tightened his arm around her neck, choking her. Then her blood chilled as she felt the cold metal of a gun barrel pressed against her temple. That was why Rick had gone still. "Put down the gun."

"Don't listen to him. He won't kill me." Leslie clawed at his arm around her throat as she could barely talk. "He knows you'll kill him if he does."

Rick looked at the man as if calculating his next move. His face was impassive, no expression that she could decipher. "Let her go," Rick said. "And I'll let you live."

"I do not believe you." The man behind her trembled against her back. He tightened his arm around her throat some more and she clawed harder at his arm. "I saw what you did to my brother and my friend."

"I will let you live," Rick repeated as he took a step forward. "Put the gun down."

"Don't move!" The man swung his gun around and pointed it at Rick who was now only about three feet away.

Leslie kicked the man hard in the shin with her heel. It was enough to distract him and he took his eyes off of Rick who took two long steps toward them. Rick easily kicked the gun out of the man's hand who then lost his grip on Leslie. Rick drove him to the floor and gripped him by his throat before slamming his fist into the man's face. He screamed.

Rick raised his fist again but went still as voice shouted, "Police!" accompanied by the sound of guns being cocked. Leslie and Rick snapped their attention toward the doorway.

"Put your hands behind your head," a man in a uniform shouted in English. "And get to your feet. Slowly."

Four men stood just inside the doorway, all in Mexican police uniforms, all with guns trained on Rick.

He did as he was told and slowly rose. An officer tossed the towel that had dropped on the floor to Leslie and she wrapped it around herself with shaking hands.

One of the officers jerked Rick's hands behind his back and cuffed him. Another officer cuffed the man on the floor and dragged him to his feet.

"Wait." Leslie looked at the officer that looked like he was in charge and she gestured toward Rick. "He saved my life. These other men were robbing me and were going to rape me. They also threatened to kill us both."

"We will determine if your statement is true or not." The man in charge gave a nod toward her closet. "Put on some clothes. We are taking you to the police station."

Leslie did as she was told, hoping they weren't stepping farther into a nightmare.

"I already told you everything." Leslie felt exhausted as she spoke to the police officer. What had started out as a wonderful morning had turned so very wrong. "We're tourists. Those men broke into our suite. You know the rest."

She had wondered at how fast the police had reached the hotel and their room. One of the officers explained that one of the housekeepers had recognized the men and saw them break into Leslie and Rick's room. The men had not seen the housekeeper and she was able to notify the hotel manager who contacted the police.

Leslie looked in the direction they had taken Rick when they'd been escorted to the station. "Where is Rick?" She hadn't seen him since they had arrived and her stomach churned at the thought of what could be happening to him.

The officer frowned and opened his mouth to speak when another officer caught his attention and spoke in rapid Spanish.

"We spoke with our contact in the United States." He lowered his voice and continued in Spanish, but Leslie could hear and understand the man. "This Rick Pierce is a Navy SEAL and an American hero. If we cannot prove that he did wrong, we must release him."

The officer who had been grilling her stood, suddenly looking nervous. "I believe the woman is telling the truth. Release Señor Pierce."

Leslie slumped with relief. With all of the horror stories she'd heard about people getting caught up with the Mexican authorities she'd been so afraid that this was going to end up even worse than it already was.

The officer had called Rick an American hero. Was that what they considered SEALs to be? It certainly was to her. Or could it be something more?

Whatever was said on the phone call certainly worked. The attitudes of the Mexican police changed. She was told that Rick's paperwork was being processed and he would be released shortly. Her passport was returned to her as she waited for him.

It seemed to take forever, but finally Rick came into the room she was in. She practically ran to him and threw herself into his arms. "I don't think I've ever been happier to see anyone in my life," she said and brushed away a tear that rolled down her cheek.

"Are you okay?" He gripped her by the shoulders and studied her. "They wouldn't tell me what they had done with you."

"All they did was interrogate me." *Over and over again.* "I'm fine."

"It's a damned good thing." He kissed her hard.

"Thank God you're all right." She put her head against his chest. "I was so worried about you."

"Nothing to worry about." He kissed her again. "Let's go."

She nodded and he looped his arm around her shoulders.

"They said they found out that you're an American hero." She looked up at him as they walked. "They released you in a hurry after that."

Rick shrugged. "I guess being a SEAL carries some weight in some places and with some governments."

"They said specifically 'American hero,'" she said.

"Whatever it takes to get me out." He pushed open the door, leading them into the sunshine. "They just wanted to get me free."

"Well, you're a hero to me." She rested her head against his chest. "Thank you for saving me from God knows what."

"I'm just grateful you're okay, honey." He kissed the top of her head. "It scared the hell out of me to see those men with you."

"I don't think I've ever seen someone look as calm as you did," she said.

"I never had a doubt I'd get to you before they could hurt either of us," he said. "But seeing you like that—I never want to see that again."

She sighed. "That makes two of us."

When they reached the hotel, they went to the front desk. All of their bags had been moved to a new suite after the investigation and clean up.

It was already evening. The ordeal had taken the greater part of the day.

After Rick unlocked the door, she tossed her purse onto the couch.

"I need a bath." She was still trembling as she turned to Rick. "A nice, long hot bath."

He brushed his lips over hers and it helped to calm her. "Mind if I join you?"

She managed a smile. "Your tub or mine?"

With a gentle smile he said, "Which would you prefer?"

Without hesitating she said, "Yours is just fine. I'm still shaking."

He wrapped his arms around her and hugged her close. "I'm here, and while I'm here, I won't let anything happen to you. Do you understand?"

She loved the strength of his hug and the safe feeling it gave her. She had never met anyone like Rick.

He kissed her then took her hand and led her in the direction of his room. "I'm ready for that bath."

The rectangular jetted tub was huge and had backrests on both side of it. She ran the water until it was almost hot, stripped out of her clothing, and eased into the tub. She sighed as her body sank into the warm water and closed her eyes.

The water sloshed and she looked up to see that Rick had ditched his clothing, too, and was climbing into the tub. He sat across from her and looked as pleased to be in the hot water as she was.

"Furry little seals love water, don't they?" she said with a slight smile.

"As do big SEALs." He gave a groan that told her he was very happy to be in the tub with her.

"Mind if we stay in tonight?" She played footsies with him in the water and he grabbed one of her feet. "I think after today I would like to just relax."

"Agreed." He started rubbing her foot. "We can order room service."

She sighed with pleasure as he massaged her foot. The gentle massage helped to relax her. Between that and the warm water, she wasn't trembling as much.

"Oh, that feels so good," she said. "Please don't stop."

He smiled and after a moment picked up her other foot and started massaging it. She closed her eyes and reveled in the feeling of his touch.

The water had cooled by the time they decided to get out. He grabbed one of the thick, fluffy towels and dried her off. She was happy to stand in front of him and let him towel dry her. He made short work of drying himself and then tossed the towel aside and led her into his bedroom.

She looked at the bed. "I think I could happily pass out right now."

"Lie down." He gently pressed her toward the bed. "On your stomach."

She climbed onto the bed and obeyed him. He straddled her and started massaging her neck and back.

"That feels sooooo good." Her muscles started to relax and she felt as if she could melt right into the mattress. "You are an amazing multi-talented man. Did anyone ever tell you that?"

He leaned over and kissed the back of her neck. "You are so beautiful, Leslie." She turned over as he moved off of her. He sat beside her and stroked her cheek. "I've never met anyone like you."

She caught his hand in hers and held it to her cheek. "You're unlike anyone I've ever known, too."

He eased down so that they were lying side-by-side and he leaned close and kissed her. With a soft moan she kissed him back, loving his taste, loving the feel of his body close to hers. His naked body was warm and hard beneath her touch as she moved her palm down his chest to his abs and then up to his shoulder again.

His hands were callused and rough as he stroked her softer skin. His touch was amazing, making her body feel alive again. He gently palmed her breasts, and she sighed as he rubbed his thumb over first one nipple and then the other.

"Make love to me." She moved her mouth to his and kissed him. "Make love to me."

He shifted his body and then his body was in between her thighs. She gasped at the feel of him inside of her.

She wrapped her legs around his hips, drawing him closer. His movements were slow and easy as he began taking her. She moaned with pleasure as he eased in and out of her.

She arched her hips, encouraging him to increase the tempo. He started moving at a faster pace as he looked down at her and their gazes locked.

The moment stretched on as he pumped in and out of her. She gasped and cried out to him. "Faster, Rick. Please, faster."

He started moving at a faster rate and she felt an orgasm starting to rise within her. It came closer and closer, filled with the promise of something extraordinary.

Perspiration broke out on her skin and her breathing increased. His body felt heated against hers and she felt his sweat mingling with hers.

He never took his eyes from hers and when she felt like she couldn't hold on any longer he kissed her hard.

Her orgasm rocketed through her and she cried out against his mouth. Her body shook and trembled as fireworks exploded in her mind. She had never known what that meant or what it was like until this very moment.

His strokes became stronger, harder, as her body vibrated with her climax. Just when she thought it was over, another one took hold of her and she cried out again.

With a groan his body shuddered against hers. She felt his cock throb inside of her, drawing out her second orgasm.

When he came to a stop, he pressed his hips tight against hers and held it for a long moment. And then he rolled them both onto their sides facing one another.

"You know how to relax a girl don't you, Rick Pierce. Thank you." She smiled and caressed his cheek. "That was beautiful."

He took her hand in his and kissed her knuckles then drew her into his embrace.

Chapter 7

Leslie adjusted her black latex corset as she looked into the mirror of her bedroom in her home in Maryland. She had promised Rick that she would dress up in some of her favorite fetish wear just for him.

She turned and looked over her shoulder in the mirror and checked the smooth lines of the tight black latex pants that went with the corset. Latex molded her ass just right. After fixing her hair, she pulled on a pair of four-inch heels.

After their ordeal, they had still enjoyed the last of their weekend in Cabo. The beach, sun, drinks, and good food, helped take her mind off of what had happened.

Dinner had arrived fifteen minutes ago. She wasn't crazy about cooking but she had nimble fingers for dialing the phone and a pile of menus from places that delivered. Tonight they were having Thai.

The doorbell rang. Her heels clicked on the hardwood floor as she headed along the hallway, down the sweeping staircase, and to the front door. It was the first time he had been to her home since they had known each other. Before she answered, she looked through the peephole to see that it was definitely Rick. He was so hot looking that her mouth watered. He was holding a bouquet of flowers and a bottle of wine.

When she opened the door, she wanted to just stand and take him in. He wore a dark blue shirt that was snug on his muscled body along with Levis. His short, dark hair looked so hot on him and his tawny eyes were warm and inviting.

She crooked her finger, telling him to come toward her. "Come in, said the spider to the fly," she said in her most sultry voice.

"Damn." Rick shut the door behind him and she saw the appreciation in his eyes. "You look unbelievable. Turn around. Let me look at the back of you."

Leslie took a few steps, turned, and pivoted around on her heels as if modeling on a runway. Then, with her hand on her hip, she stood and looked at him with her most sultry look.

"Now, turn around again and stop," he said. When she showed him the back she heard him whistle. "That is as hot an ass ever poured into pants like that. I love the shiny tight latex and how if forms to your perfect ass. Just amazing"

She faced him then walked toward him. "Let me take those before you drop them." She almost grinned at the distracted look on his expression. From the sound of it, he definitely loved the way she looked.

"Oh." He looked at her again and handed her the colorful bouquet that he was holding. "I don't think I'm going to be able to keep my mind on anything but you." He shook his head. "Not that I've been able to stop thinking about you at all."

Something in the way he said the words made her feel almost shy. "I want to put these in water." She turned away from him and headed for the kitchen and felt the burn of his gaze on her backside.

When they reached the kitchen she set the bouquet on the counter and heard the thump of the bottle of the wine as he set it down. She turned to look at him and he brought her into his arms and kissed her.

She gave a soft moan from the exquisiteness of his kiss and the way it made her feel deep inside. The way he kissed nearly curled her toes. He moved his palms up and down the smooth latex covering her body and his hands seemed to burn through the latex to her skin.

He drew his head back and smiled down at her. "No matter what you're in, you look amazing." He stepped back enough to take a look at her up and down. "How hard is this to get out of?"

She laughed. "If you're worried about access, don't. Special zippers and Velcro are in strategic places."

With a grin he kissed her again. "I've always been good at special missions."

While she put the flowers in water, he uncorked the bottle of chardonnay and poured a glass for each of them.

"That will go perfectly with dinner." She opened one of the paper bags filled with Thai food.

"Smells terrific." He peeked into the second bag then moved his gaze over her, taking her in from her head to her polished toenails. "My stomach is growling, but I still think I'll have a hard time doing anything but look at you."

The table was set for two and all they had to do was carry out the food containers and sit down and eat.

While they enjoyed their dinner, she teased him by leaning down to tug on one of her high heels, moving so that he got a good view of her cleavage. While they ate she did her best to find ways to taunt him sexually, wanting to make him as hot as she was. She touched his hands whenever possible and brushed her knees against his.

In turn he ran his fingers along her arm and placed his hand on her thigh, close to her mound.

He cleared his throat. "So what kind of mission am I going on tonight?"

"A top secret mission." She whispered the words as if someone might hear.

His expression heated her through. "My favorite," he said.

"It involves going into dangerous places." She gave him her most serious look. "Places you might not make it out of."

He smiled. "I'm up to the challenge."

She leaned back in her chair. "I'll bet you are."

After they cleaned up and she tossed empty food containers, Rick left the room. She put the vase with the bouquet of flowers on the table then left the kitchen for the living room.

Just as she walked through the door from the kitchen he grabbed her, startling her into crying out. She was standing one moment and the next she was on her back with him on top of her, straddling her, her arms pinned over her head.

He started tickling her and she broke out into giggles as she tried to get away from his hands. She laughed so hard that she could barely catch her breath when he finally stopped.

"So much for my dominance over you," she said between breaths.

He kissed her and she sighed into his mouth. The man was the most amazing kisser. When he raised his head he smiled as he looked down at her. "What's our mission tonight?"

"If you'll let me up," she said, "we'll deploy."

"I'm well trained and ready for anything." He gave her a quick grin and helped her to her feet. She took his hand and led him up the staircase.

"You have an incredible home." He looked around him with interest. "This place must have been here since colonial times."

"It has." She nodded. "My family tree is deep in New England and has roots as far back as the Mayflower."

"It's impressive." He looked down at her shoes. "How do you manage these stairs with those heels?"

"Practice," she said.

He made a sound of approval "They're so damned hot on you."

They reached the second floor and she tugged his hand. "This way."

She led him down a hallway, past her suite of rooms, to a locked room at the end of the hallway. She let go of his hand and reached into her cleavage that was held up with the latex corset, and pulled out a large brass key.

"I think you'll enjoy this," she said as she looked over her shoulder.

He raised an eyebrow, definitely intrigued.

When she let the door swing open, she followed his gaze around the room while he took in her various toys and unusual bondage furniture.

"Wow. Nice surprise." He looked at her. "You're really into it. Where did you get all of this?"

"I wouldn't have invested in all of this. I have it because a good friend gave some pieces to me." She gestured to one side of the room. "That cage, the St.

Andrews cross, the bondage chair, and the stocks next to it. He bought them and did a room up to surprise his wife for her birthday. The day before the occasion, she told him she was leaving him for another man. He just couldn't stand seeing it so he gave it to me. I know the cage might seem a little too far, but if nothing else it adds to the ambience. Actually, the sight of a naked man tethered in a cage would be nice foreplay to me."

"It all looks brand new." He looked away from the toys to her. "Have you use most of it?"

She shook her head. "Haven't found the right sub."

"Or man to use it on you." He walked over to a sex swing and pushed it. As it swung back and forth he looked over his shoulder. "We are definitely using this."

With a laugh she stepped into his arms. "Oh, yeah?"

"Yeah." He lowered his head and kissed her.

The feelings that rolled through her shocked her. This guy was changing the way she felt about bondage and domination. He was transforming her. He made her feel safe, secure, maybe even loved.

She no longer wanted to control him… She wanted him to control her.

The feelings she had were all so different. She was a dominant woman and she just didn't turn over control, total control, to any man. But she didn't feel dominant around Rick. Not at all. All the equipment in the room was for her to use on a man she would discard when he couldn't handle her or wanted to get closer emotionally. Now she wanted it used on her. Used on her by Rick.

The experience in Mexico had changed her, too. She had never felt so protected as she did with Rick.

A part of her thought about telling him but she knew it was too soon to start talking about things like that. She wasn't even sure why she felt this way, much less what to do about it.

"What do you have planned for me?" He rubbed his hands up and down her upper arms.

She bit her lower lip before she spoke. "Something changed and it doesn't feel right to top you."

"Good." He cupped her face in his hands. "Because it feels right for me to take control of you. I love it. And I know that you do, too."

She nodded, feeling strangely exhilarated as she looked up at him.

"I have a lot of goodies here, and then some." She gestured at the short but wide cabinet where she kept a lot of her toys. She had some things on the surface and others in the drawers and toys hanging from the insides of the open doors.

"Perfect." He took her by the arm. "Come on."

She followed him to the cabinet, excitement stirring in her belly like a hundred butterflies. He rummaged in the drawers and pulled out the red ball gag then pushed it into her mouth and buckled it behind her head.

The way he was taking control made the butterflies in her belly go crazy.

Next he pulled out a fur-lined pair of leather cuffs, and a metal clip. He moved behind her and brought her wrists back and secured the cuffs then clipped them together.

He ran his palms up and down her latex-covered body as he came around to face her. "Now to search for those strategically placed zippers and Velcro." He palmed her breasts and found the latex cups that were attached with Velcro. He tore them off and tossed them aside, leaving cutouts around her breasts.

"Love it." He lowered his head and sucked one of her nipples. She squirmed, wanting to touch him. And most of all wanting to feel him inside of her.

She wondered what was next when he went back to her cabinet. He took a large jeweler's box off of the surface of the cabinet where she kept some of her nipple clamps. "What do we have here?"

A groan slipped out of her mouth from behind her gag. She'd never had the clamps used on her. She loved to use them on men but her own nipples were so sensitive that she winced at just the thought of them on her.

Her eyes widened as he brought a pair of silver clamps with red tassels hanging from them. *Not those*, she thought to herself, then remembered she had used clover clamps on him and was grateful he wasn't doing the same to her. Still…

When he reached her she tried to swallow but couldn't with the ball gag in her mouth. "Beautiful nipples." He played with one while he leaned close and kissed the corner of her mouth. He slowly closed a clamp around her nipple.

She couldn't hold back a muffled cry as he did it and then whimpered again when he put the other clamp on.

After he put the clamps on, he gestured toward a kneeling bench. "I want to see you on that."

She walked to the bench, steady on her heels from years of practice. She moved onto the padded kneeling surface and he helped her lean forward so that her top half was on the bench, her ass in the air, her hands cuffed behind her back. She winced from the pressure of the clamps on her nipples against the padded bench.

He rubbed her ass with both palms and they felt warm through her latex pants. Then he pressed her thighs apart with his hands and she felt tingles of desire where he touched her.

"Mission accomplished." He located the zipper and she caught her breath as he unzipped the latex pants at the crotch. Cool air brushed her exposed folds and she moaned as he slid two fingers inside of her. "Mmmmm. I love this outfit."

At that moment she *really* loved it, too. She got lost in the sensations as he reached up and slipped his hands beneath one of her breasts with his other hand.

"Yeah. Nice." After a few moments of erotically teasing her, he moved away.

She almost whimpered, already missing his touch. She heard him rummaging in the cabinet drawers, but didn't know what he was getting because her back was to him.

A hard swat to her ass with a paddle and she yelped in surprise. Another swat had her eyes watering her. He had taken everything she had dished out to him and she felt like she had to try her best to hold back any cries no matter how muffled they woul dbe.

In between swats he rubbed her ass, rubbing in the burn. Her eyes were damp when he finally stopped and leaned over so that he could whisper in her ear. "That's for teasing me while we ate dinner."

Paybacks were, indeed, a bitch.

But she found she loved it. Every bit of it.

He moved his hips between her legs and she felt his erection through his jeans and her latex pants. He slowly pumped his hips and she moaned again from need.

"I want to try out that swing now." He helped her up so that she could stand and he took her by her elbow and led her to the swing.

Excitement swirled through her as he unclipped her cuffs and had her lie on her belly on the swing, her ass in the air. He went around to her front side and clipped her cuffs together again. He returned to stand behind her and she heard the sound of a zipper before he pushed his hips between her thighs.

Tingles prickled her skin as he rubbed his cock against her bared folds. "Beautiful," he murmured. "Can't wait to be inside you again."

She couldn't wait, either.

It felt so exciting to be at his mercy. Gagged, clamped, in a sex swing. She felt like she was floating and ached between her thighs as she waited for what she prayed would come soon.

"I'm going to fuck you hard." The way he said the word made her pussy ache even more.

He drove inside her in a fast, powerful thrust. Her eyes widened and she gave a muffled cry. As he pounded in and out of her she bounced in the air and was lost. Lost in the feel of him taking her. Lost in the buoyant feeling of swinging in the air and being brought back up against him again.

Her orgasm came flying toward her, too fast to control. She couldn't hold back. As it rocketed through her she screamed behind her gag. Rick continued to slam into her hard and fast.

She came a second time and a third and he was still driving in and out of her. And then he shouted as he climaxed.

His cock pulsed inside of her and he came to a stop. He pressed himself tight against her and held her by her hips. She hung from the swing feeling limp and exhausted, and completely sated.

He helped her to her feet and took off the wrist cuffs. She held his arms to keep from slumping into a pile of sweet satisfaction. He tossed the wrist restraints aside then removed the nipple clamps and the ball gag.

"Wow." She smiled up at him. "That was amazing"

"You are amazing." He cupped her face with his hands and brought his mouth to hers for a sweet, sweet kiss.

She rested her head against his chest as he held her and she squeezed her eyes shut. After Michael she had sworn off relationships that were anything more than playing around.

And now what was she doing?

She was falling for Rick. And she was falling hard.

Chapter 8

"Are you sure about this?" Rick studied Leslie as they stood inside the foyer of her home. "I've never been to something like what you're telling me this is. Some kind of wild BDSM party."

"Where's your sense of adventure?" She grinned. "I thought all of you Navy SEALs were up for anything."

"My sense of adventure has some limits when it comes to civilian to life." He shook his head. "I don't think there's a thing we've gone through that will have prepared me for a big wild bondage orgy."

She put her hands on her hips. "It is *not* an orgy. Just because people are into BDSM doesn't mean they like group sex."

He gave her a pointed look. "But some do."

"Yeah, well." She smiled and tugged on his arm as she encouraged him to go out the front door. "I'm not into that kind of thing. So come on and you'll get to meet some of my friends."

He looked her over, admiring the black leather miniskirt she wore, as well as the corset she had on beneath a short leather jacket. "I don't want to let you out of my sight looking like that, so I guess I'm in."

"Good." She locked the door behind them and they headed toward his black SUV that was parked by the curb. It had been several weeks since Cabo and they had been seeing each other as often as they were able.

"Tell me about this place," Rick said as he drove them toward a rural part of Maryland, their headlights the only light around.

"It's simply called 'the farm.'" She looked out into the darkness as they continued beyond the city limits. "KC, I mean the Kink Club, holds an annual party at the farm. It's a lot of fun."

Rick grunted.

"A guy named Garth owns it." She looked from the window to Rick. "He was on the auction board. He organized KC's private involvement."

"So he probably knows my sister." Rick didn't sound like he approved.

Leslie laughed. "There's no doubt since they both work on the board."

Even though Rick seemed a little unsure of all of this, he was still fun to talk to and he loosened up as they drove to the farm.

The place was lit up like a Christmas festival as they reached the road leading up to the two-story farmhouse and drove toward it. From a distance the lighting looked like a hundred fireflies dancing about.

The truck bounced in ruts along the road then Rick found a place to park that was a good distance away because there were so many vehicles parked outside the main gates.

It was cool outside and she was thankful for her jacket, although her bare legs beneath her leather mini skirt were chilled. He held her hand as they walked toward the buildings, his grip helping to steady her on the uneven surface in her four-inch heels. She wanted to poke him in the side for his lack of enthusiasm. It wasn't dampening hers, and she knew he hadn't intended it to. He just wasn't crazy about the idea of being here.

"Leslie." Garth stepped out of the darkness and she jumped in surprise at his sudden appearance.

She laughed. "You nearly gave me a heart attack coming out of nowhere like that."

"Sorry." He kissed her cheek before straightening.

He turned his gaze on Rick. "And this is the Navy SEAL you were so hot for at the auction."

She looked at Rick and grinned. "Yes, all of my friends knew that I intended to win you."

He looked amused and extended his hand to Garth. "I'm Rick."

"Garth." They seemed to be sizing each other up as Garth shook Rick's hand.

Dressed all in leather, Garth was a tall Dom and a lot of people found him almost intimidating. He happened to be a very sexy bald man with a goatee. He was big and extremely muscular. She and Garth often traded innuendos and she teased him about letting her be his Domme and he would shake his head and tell her that he'd like to see her on her knees as his sub. It was all in good fun.

But tonight she didn't want the banter in front of Rick.

"Have you seen Christy or Roni tonight?" she asked Garth before he could get anything else in. "Are they here?"

He gestured toward a group of tables on the south side of the house. "Saw them over there with their Doms."

Leslie raised an eyebrow. It had been a while since she'd had a chance to speak with either of them. She knew they were in committed relationships, but neither woman had referred to her man as a Dom. Curiouser and curiouser.

"Good to meet you," Garth said to Rick as he took a step back.

Rick gave a nod. "Likewise."

Leslie gave Garth a little wave then took Rick's hand and they walked toward tables with kerosene lanterns on them for light, each one turned low so that it was a more intimate atmosphere.

Laughter and voices came from outside and inside of the farmhouse. Rick might have lacked enthusiasm about coming, but she was sure that once he was here for a while that he would fall into the spirit of the event.

The farmyard was extensive with a huge barn that they could see outlined in the lighted yard as well as what looked like pens for animals and out buildings.

Leslie swept her gaze over the yard. There had to be close to a hundred partygoers participating in various activities outside and probably another fifty inside. She recognized a lot of the partyers. The same people tended to attend various events, some more than others.

People they passed were in various stages of dress and undress, but all of them with some form of clothing on, no matter how scant.

Women in latex cat suits; men in black leather; women with pasties on their nipples and tiny skirts; men with bare chests and leather straps across their bodies; corsets and bustiers; chain and leather outfits; fishnet and thigh-high boots; and any other possible form of what might be considered to be clothing.

There were pony girls pulling carts and puppy boys on all fours walking with their Doms holding their leashes. Some women were dressed like schoolgirls and others in French maid costumes. There were men dressed like women, same sex couples, as well as heterosexual and bisexual couples.

Leslie tugged on Rick's hand as they walked through the rows of tables. He looked around them and seemed to be analyzing everything as they went.

As they walked, female and male subs and Doms waved to Leslie or stopped them to say hello. Each time Leslie smiled and said it was great to see them and then she and Rick moved on. She did her best not to take the time to make introductions or they would be there all night.

"You sure know a lot of people here." Rick looked at her.

She shrugged. "There are a lot of good people here, but when I think about it, my reasons for coming were pretty shallow." She moved her gaze over the activities and felt a little like an outsider looking in for the first time ever. "I don't need to be here for the same reasons."

"What's that?" Rick said.

"My friends and I would go trolling for guys, trying to make the right connections." She spotted a couple of her former subs and the males waved at her. She gave them a little wave back. "They never measured up to what I really wanted in a man. I wanted a male I could control. Thing was if the male wanted his life directed, I would lose respect for him and it was over."

"What were you looking for in a man?" Rick asked.

She looked up at him. "I guess in many ways I didn't know. I just knew when it wasn't right and I would move on."

Then she heard a familiar voice. "Les." Roni called out "Over here."

Leslie smiled and squeezed Rick's hand as they walked toward Roni and the dark, mysterious man who had won her at the auction. Beside her sat Christy and the very hot man who had bid on her. After the auction, Leslie had learned from Roni that Christy and the man had shared a past together.

The men stood and shook Rick's hand as Leslie hugged Christy and Roni.

"So good to see you." Leslie smiled at her friends then shook the hands of their men as introductions were made. Roni's guy was John while Christy was with Zach.

"Wow." Leslie sat on a bench seat at the table across from her friends. "That auction turned out to be amazing for all of us."

Roni smiled at John. "Most definitely."

Christy nodded and put her head on Zach's shoulder. "Couldn't have happened any better."

Roni gestured toward Kelley Bachman, whom they were all friends with. She was with a group of people who were watching a pony girl race in front of the barn. "Kelley was bid on by a really hot guy, too, but he's been out of town since the auction. If she's as lucky as we were… Well, we'll just have to find out."

They laughed and talked for a while. John was an FBI agent and Zach owned a couple of exclusive restaurants. Roni was a fashion designer and Christy owned a popular downtown boutique.

Rick was a little quiet but friendly and sociable. Leslie had never been around him with other people, so she hadn't known what to expect. Some people were more talkative one-on-one than they were in a crowd.

They had been laughing and talking a while when John looked at Rick and said, "I thought you looked familiar and now I know why."

Leslie glanced at Rick and he seemed to be bracing for something.

"You're the Navy SEAL who was decorated with the Navy Cross a few months ago." John smiled. "It's great to meet a true American hero."

Leslie's eyes widened. "You didn't tell me that."

"That's amazing," Christy said.

Zach nodded. "It's an honor."

"Wow." Roni smiled. "I've never met a real hero before."

Even in the dim light of the kerosene lantern, Leslie thought Rick was blushing. He raised his hands like he was pushing away the compliments. "I'm no hero," he said. "I was just doing my job."

"You went far above and beyond, my friend," John said then looked at Leslie. "Don't let him fool you. He may be humble but he is a hero."

Rick looked distinctly uncomfortable. "There are many men and women in the service who are true heroes."

"Shhh." Roni put her finger to her lips. "At these things no one uses last names or says anything about knowing the person outside of the event."

"Sorry about that," John said.

Rick shook his head. "No problem."

John looked at Leslie. "This one's a keeper."

Chapter 9

"Why don't we check out what's going on inside?" Zach said, saving both Leslie and Rick from further embarrassment by John's comment.

Roni stood. "Let's go." She had dark red hair and a full figure and looked great all in leather. John seemed to agree as he stood behind her and palmed her ass, causing her to jump and laugh. Roni was exuberant and fun but she loved to submit to the right men. Looked like John might be that guy. Leslie had heard a story that he had saved Roni's life, a story she wanted to hear more about.

"It'll be fun looking at everything." Christy stood, too, and grasped Zach's hand as he got to his feet. Christy wore tight leather pants and a leather bustier. Zach settled his hand at her waist and drew her close to him. Christy had been new to KC but she seemed to have taken to the lifestyle really well. Leslie could tell by the way Christy was with Zach that he was her Dom and was protective of her.

Rick got up with Leslie and she took his hand again. He seemed even quieter, probably due to his discomfort with the praise lavished over him just moments before. But he squeezed her hand and she gave him a smile as he looked down at her.

"You're beautiful," he said.

"You're pretty hot yourself." She let go of his hand and gripped one of his tight ass cheeks. "Yes, you're definitely all that and more."

They paused for a moment to watch the pony girls trotting in an arena. Leslie didn't see Kelley. She'd hoped to say hi to her friend.

"What do you think?" she asked Rick as he observed the action that was taking place in the arena.

"Explain to me why those women are acting like horses," Rick said.

"They're called pony girls," she said. "It's all about control and bizarre looks."

"Control and bizarre looks?" His gaze followed one of the pony girls who pranced nearby. A pony boy was also in the ring. "I thought I'd seen everything."

"Pony girls often wear modified horse tack like bridles with bits, harnesses, and are usually outfitted with special hooves," Leslie said. "They usually have a butt plug inserted that has a horsetail coming out of it."

Rick looked like he might be intrigued by the whole thing.

"They might have manes and elaborate headdresses." Leslie gestured toward a woman who was exceptionally outfitted. "Sometimes they wear horse masks or horse hoods."

"Most of them are standing up," Rick said. "Only a couple are on all fours."

"Yes." Leslie nodded. "Pony girls usually walk upright and are often used to pull carts that carry their Doms." She looked at Rick. "They're normally well trained. During their training sessions, they're taught how to act like ponies—whinnying, high stepping, and prancing are just a few things that they learn."

"Let's go inside." Leslie tugged on Rick's hand, pulling his attention away from a harnessed pony girl with pasties on her nipples. She didn't think it was the girl, so much as it was the fascination he had watching what she was doing.

Before Leslie and Rick went into the house with their friends, he paused to watch a woman in a schoolgirl outfit on the grass who was on her knees and in stocks. A Dom erotically flogged her bare ass and he was leaving red marks on her ass and thighs. She was crying out with every stroke.

Someone said, "Put a gag on her and that'll shut her up." Those standing around laughed.

By her expression, it was obvious that the woman loved the attention.

Rick shook his head, looking amused. "Yep," he said. "This definitely wasn't in the training manual."

"You must have lived a sheltered life," she said in a teasing voice.

He smiled. "If you call never having had any experience around BDSM as being sheltered, I guess so."

Leslie laughed. The last thing in the world a SEAL could be was sheltered, but she liked introducing him to something he wasn't very familiar with.

They walked into the house that looked pretty normal, save for the unusual way that a lot of people were dressed. The lights were low, people clustered in groups, talking and enjoying the evening.

Leslie, her friends, and the men they were with all looked vanilla in comparison to almost everyone else in the spacious front room.

The Kink Club paid for the catering and women and men wearing skimpy leather outfits carried serving trays and moved throughout the room with hors d'oeuvres. There was a bar in a corner of the room where wine, beer, and well drinks were provided.

Rick raised an eyebrow as he got a good look at some of the furniture. "There's a woman who's a lamp."

"And those men are serving as a coffee table." She pointed toward two tightly bound men, each on all fours, with a table on their backs. She gestured toward someone in a stuffed armchair with his feet up. "And there's a human ottoman."

She could tell that Rick was holding back his amusement when he saw a couple of nearly naked human end tables, too.

"Let's go upstairs." Roni raised her voice and pointed to the ceiling. "The real fun stuff is up there."

Rick looked hesitant but Leslie gripped his hand tighter and drew him along with her and they headed up the stairs.

The farmhouse was a big place and upstairs there were six bedrooms. Each had been transformed into a different theme.

The first room had a St. Andrew's cross and a man was strapped to it while a female Domme used a whip on him, drawing out every strike of the thin leather. Red welts patterned his torso and legs. The man cried out with each lash.

When it came to players at the club, they had to adhere to the guidelines of safe, sane, and consensual BDSM. If they didn't they were out. There were dungeon masters and mistress in each venue. Wearing black armbands, their job was to make certain everything was safe.

A woman was bent over a spanking bench, being paddled by another Domme. A chain dangled from the ceiling that a third person hung from while being flogged by a male Dom.

In the far corner was a set of stocks with a sub being struck with a riding crop by a Dom.

Male and female Doms and their subs were waiting for their turns.

"Ah, here's the debauchery." Rick looked down at Leslie. "You do know that if one of us was to get flogged in here, it wouldn't be me."

She hooked her arm in his and smiled. "No worries. I've never gotten into public spanking."

"That's probably because you always liked to do the spanking," he said. "In the past."

"Yes." She rested her head on his shoulder. "In the past."

They went to the next room where a male and a female were using rope bondage and giving a demonstration on good techniques. The hogtied female did not look like she was going anywhere soon.

"Interesting." Rick observed the intricate rope bondage being used on several subs.

"Take notes," Leslie said with a smile.

He glanced down at her. "Believe me, I am."

After watching some of the rope bondage for a while, they moved on to the third room. In it subs were suspended and played with by their Doms and Dommes. A couple of Doms were teaching how to suspend safely.

"Suspension can be dangerous if not done right," Leslie said to Rick.

"Have you ever been suspended?" he asked. "Other than the sex swing you have."

Thoughts of Michael came to her but this time she didn't feel the pain and anger that normally went along with memories of him. Maybe she was over what he'd done and able to move on.

"Yes, I've been suspended," she said. "But it was a very long time ago."

"You have something to tell me, don't you," he stated. "Something you need to get off your chest."

She was quiet for a moment then she nodded. "Yes. I will tell you sometime when we're alone."

"Good." He squeezed her hand. "I'm here for you."

She smiled. "Thank you."

A fourth room had subs who had been put into various devices, like stocks and cages.

Rick looked over five cages, side-by-side and there was a man or woman in each cage. He glanced at Leslie. "I think I'd like to put you in yours. In private."

Pleasant heat swept over her at the thought of Rick caging her.

He gave a devious grin before turning his attention back to what was going on in the room.

A Domme had her sub in a set of stocks and was using a cupping set on the female's breasts.

Rick looked puzzled. "What is that Domme doing?"

"There are Asian techniques where cupping is used to treat illness, sore muscles, injuries, and other things. There are different ways of doing it." Leslie nodded toward the Domme. "She's using suction cups with a gun that takes out all of the air in the cup and sort of sucks a little of the skin and flesh in that spot into the cup. In BDSM play it's another method of controlling a person's pain and pleasure.

"She's doing it on that woman's breasts." Rick looked at Leslie. "That's gotta hurt."

Leslie nodded. "Believe me, it does."

"I thought you didn't let anyone do anything to control you," Rick said.

She shrugged. "I'll tell you about it sometime."

The fifth room had Doms using things like violet wands, clothespins, and other interesting items and techniques while topping their subs.

Room number six was wax play. Massage tables were lined up and on them were women with naked breasts and men with bare chests. Doms and Dommes were dripping different colors of candlewax onto the subs' bodies, some in intricate patterns.

"I love wax play." Leslie looked up at Rick. "There's something so sensual about creating a masterpiece on a sub's body."

"Doesn't it burn?" he asked. "Wax can get hot."

"Certain types of waxes can be used that don't burn the skin," she said. "Baby oil is normally rubbed on each person's body to make the wax easier to remove."

After touring the upstairs events, Christy and Zach decided to enjoy the spanking room while Roni wanted to experience wax play with John.

"How about practicing using some rope bondage on me?" Leslie said to Rick. "Breast-binding is fun and any number of other things."

"I'm hungry," he said. "How about we go for some of that barbeque that I'm smelling right now."

"Barbeque sounds good." Leslie tried not to feel disappointed that Rick wasn't into doing any of the upstairs activities. Maybe later they would. Come to think of it, she was pretty hungry, too.

As they walked outside, Rick said, "All of the toys are fun and I enjoy exciting you by what you love."

"Wow. You get into this more than I thought," she said.

"I told you that I liked it," he said. "I never found anyone who wanted to play so I never pursued it." He looked down at her surprised expression. "Hey, I'm a male. What male doesn't look at the Internet? I always enjoyed the bondage sites, so I'm not a complete newbie to it."

"I didn't realize you had a real interest in it," she said. "I thought it was more curiosity."

"I don't find that the public thing is something I would probably do unless you were turned on by it," he said, "it seems to lose some of its intimacy with everyone around, but the thought of doing it all with you excites me. Watching all of this is actually a kind of foreplay. There are things here I find hot and would love to try with you."

"Like what?" she asked.

"Never thought I would like the collar and the leash, but that is a hot look," he said. "It is a bit of a contrast for you. In control, independent, but I would love to pull you around at the end of a leash."

Leslie smiled. "I can't believe I am actually saying this, but being at the end of a leash with you would excite me. Just about all of this excites me, but it takes it to another level when it is with someone you are connected with."

"So, it takes it to another level for you with me, huh?" he said.

She hooked her arm through his. "Let's just say you are in the exciting phase for me."

"Oh, the phase right before being discarded on the heap of males you have gotten rid of."

"I should never have told you about that." She laughed. "I will admit that you would be the hottest looking male in that pile."

"Thanks for that image." He shook his head but had an amused expression. "Good to know what phase I am and that I will eventually be in the discard heap."

How different you are Rick Pierce, she thought. In some strange way, she could not tell him how she felt though. It was as if there was an element of control deep in her that wanted him to wonder… If he even did. Another part of her wanted to think that there was nothing to this. It was all about guarding her feelings.

After she and Rick found paper plates and filled them with barbeque ribs, bread rolls, potato salad, deviled eggs, and roasted veggies, and each grabbed a can of soda, they found an empty table in a far corner of the farmyard. She scooted onto the bench across from Rick and they dug in.

"So good." She sighed as she pushed her nearly empty plate aside.

He had gone back for seconds and had just polished off the rest of his dinner. "Excellent." He set his plate and plastic fork aside like she had, then folded his arms on the table and leaned forward. "Why don't you tell me now about whatever it is in your past that bothers you so much?"

Taken by surprise, her lips parted but nothing came out.

"You can do it, honey." His tone, the way he looked at her, somehow gave her courage she hadn't had for a long time.

"I was a sub once." She studied Rick's features but there was no change in the way he was looking at her.

"Go on," he said.

"His name was Michael." She looked up at the millions of stars in the sky that were so clear out here in the country. She turned her gaze back to Rick. "I loved him. At least I thought I did."

"What happened?"

She glanced down at her hands, so small after having stared up at the heavens. When she looked at Rick again, she said, "He was having affairs with other women." She shoved her hair behind her ears. "It hurt so much that I swore I would never let myself care again."

"That's when you started topping." Rick didn't look judgmental, just concerned.

She nodded. "Bondage, domination… It's a part of me that I couldn't push away into some corner. I've found domination to be almost healing."

"Almost," Rick said.

With a nod she said, "Almost."

Talking about Michael made her feel like a weight had been lifted from her chest and she actually felt like smiling for the first time when she thought about him. He wasn't worth her anger and she should have realized that a long time ago. It was time for her to move on.

They were quiet for a moment and she looked into his gaze, wanting to tell him how she felt now but the words wouldn't come.

"Why don't you ever talk about your family?" he asked.

She frowned. "Because there isn't anything positive to talk about."

He didn't look like he was going to let her put him off. "Maybe that's something you need to get off of your chest, too."

"I suppose." She sighed. "I grew up with very wealthy and very absent parents. I was raised with a host of nannies and tutors then sent off to boarding school as soon as I was old enough. My father was a mean bastard and my mother was a social snob." Leslie pushed her hair out of her face. "Getting pregnant with me was the last thing on earth she wanted. She had surgeries to get her body back in shape but it was never quite the way she wanted it to be."

Everything rolled out of her so fast she hadn't been able to stop herself. She clenched her fist on the tabletop. "I wasn't wanted and it wasn't the best upbringing any child could have."

He reached across the table and squeezed her hand. His touch was almost healing. It was like he took the bad feelings, the bad memories and drew them into himself then disposed of them. It was the oddest, yet wonderful, feeling.

"I didn't realize how much I needed to get that out." She took a deep breath. "I don't talk to anyone about my parents or Michael."

"I'm here for you whenever you need me, Leslie," he said again. "You got that?"

"Yes." She nodded and gave him a smile. "Thank you."

"Come on." He stood and went around to her side of the table and helped her out of her seat. "Let's head on home."

Rick walked with her as they went back to the farmhouse to dispose of the used plates and flatware. Then he put his arm around her shoulders and they walked out to the parking area, ready to head home.

It felt good to be with him. So good that a flash of a future for them came to her. She could picture the two of them sharing a life together.

He was turning her world upside down and she couldn't be happier.

Chapter 10

They arrived at Rick's house shortly before midnight. Leslie was so turned on by all of the things they had seen at the party that she could barely keep her hands off of him. Hell, she could hardly keep her hands off of him, period.

The moment they got through the door, Rick slammed it shut behind them and wrapped his arms tight around her. He brought his mouth to hers and claimed her with a hard passionate kiss as he squeezed her ass and ground his erection into her belly.

Her breathing came faster as she kissed him back and she clenched his shirt where it was tucked into his jeans and she tried to pull it out. She had to get his clothes off.

"Hold on, honey." He caught her hands in his. "I have plans for you."

The way he said it made her heart pound faster and caused thrills to zip from her belly to that place between her thighs.

He gripped her ass and lifted her and she hooked her thighs on his hips and wrapped her arms around his neck and held on.

Excitement made her squirm in his arms as he carried her down the hall to his bedroom. The moment they reached his bed she kissed him hard and they fell onto the mattress, still kissing.

It was obvious he was controlling himself as he drew back and got to his feet. His tawny eyes were dark with passion.

She sat up on the bed and braced her hands on the mattress to either side of her as she watched him, her heart thumping.

He grasped one of her legs and sensuously moved his hands down her calf and braced her foot on his thigh. He unbuckled the four-inch heel and it thumped on the carpet when he tossed it aside. He removed her other shoe, too and ditched it, as well.

"Lie back." He gently pushed her down so that her knees were at the edge of the mattress and her calves were dangling over the edge. He bent over and reached for the button on her leather skirt and unfastened it, then drew the zipper down. He tugged off the skirt, leaving her in her leather corset and black panties.

She watched him, feeling hungrier for him than she ever had.

He slowly caressed her, bringing his palms down her belly to her panties then grasped the hem and eased them down over her hips and thighs then over her calves and feet. He dropped the panties near her skirt then he pressed her thighs wide apart with his hands. She was bare for him from her waist down and the way he looked at her made her feel beautiful.

The heat of his expression burned through her as he leaned over her again. This time he tugged her corset down below her breasts. He put his knee between her thighs, resting it on the mattress, then leaned forward and caught one of her nipples in his mouth.

She grasped his head in her hands as she arched her back, wanting more of the incredible sensations. She slipped into the moment as he licked and sucked her nipples, she clenched her fingers in his hair.

When he pulled back she let her hands slide away from his hair, feeling bereft of his touch as he moved away. She needed his touch so much she could hardly stand it.

"Wait right there." He pushed back from the bed and went to his walk-in closet.

She didn't move. She wasn't planning on going anywhere but where he was tonight.

He returned, carrying a duffel bag. Butterflies bounced around in her belly at the thought of what might be in that bag. He dropped it and it made a loud thump on the floor. Then he grasped her hand and pulled her to her feet.

Her mind spun with excitement as he kissed her. He caressed her arms from her shoulders to her hands and back and a loving way that made her feel special. She felt a little off kilter, her knees weak from the amazing kiss.

He steadied her then picked up the bag, set it on the bed, and reached inside of it. He pulled out a new pair of red leather cuffs and a red leather collar with O-rings around it.

"You've been shopping," she said with a smile.

"I have a few things in my bags of tricks." He buckled the collar on her neck first "You can't be the only one with toys."

"Where did you get everything?" she asked as he secured one of the cuffs to her wrist.

"I have my methods." He finished putting on the other wrist cuff before clipping the cuffs together. "You, however, are talking far more than you should be." He leaned down and dug in the bag and brought out a red leather gag with a rubber insert, and matching red leather blindfold. He took her by her shoulders and turned her around before buckling the gag behind her head, the insert in her mouth, keeping her mostly silent.

While she still had her back to him, he leaned over and picked up the blindfold, putting it on and securing it tightly so that her world was dark and she couldn't see anything. She loved the way it felt, in the darkness with him in control.

"Can you see any light?" he asked and she shook her head. "Try to talk," he told her.

She attempted to make some kind of intelligible sound but all she could do was make muffled noises.

"Turn around and brace your hands on the bed." He guided her down so that she could obey him. More rummaging sounds and then he was pressing something against her anus. She automatically stiffened and grunted into her gag. Only one person had used butt plugs on her, Michael, and it had been a very long time ago.

"Relax." He caressed her ass with his palm and she took a deep breath. She felt the cool lube on the end of the plug before he started inserting it. "Just relax," he repeated.

She imagined how good it was going to feel and then he was pushing the plug up and into her. At first it ached as it stretched her. He moved slowly until she was used to it and then pushed it in farther.

Then the plug was in. "Mmmmmm." She made the sound, loving the feel of the plug.

"Not done yet," he said.

She heard the sound of a hand air pump and then felt the plug started inflating with it, filling her up and her eyes widened. When it was inflated, she felt herself grow wetter, the feeling turning her on and making her more excited and she made another sound of pleasure.

He helped her to straighten then took her by her shoulders and started turning her around and around until she became disoriented and had no idea what direction she was facing any longer. There was a tug on her neck and then the sound of a metallic click and she realized he had put a leash on her and tugged. She loved that she was doing what he liked. Being at the end of his leash was so exciting, so hot.

With another firm tug on the leash he led her somewhere in the room then took her by her waist and pushed her up against a door.

What door, she wasn't sure. She heard him adjusting something at the top of the door and then she had to stand on her tiptoes as he stretched her arms high over her head and attached her wrist cuffs onto some kind of door hook.

As she stood there, he kissed her around her gag while he played with her nipples. She felt discomfort from her position, but incredibly aroused at the same time.

It was so hot to be totally controlled by this man, so exciting.

He moved away but now she couldn't see what he was doing. Her senses were heightened because she couldn't see, she could only listen.

It was quiet for a moment and then he moved close enough that she could feel his body heat close to hers.

"You have the prettiest nipples," he murmured before he slipped nipple nooses on her. He tightened one and she gasped at the pinching pain. At least they weren't clamps. She shifted on her toes and she winced as he put the other one on and tightened it, too.

He moved his callused hands over her body, caressing her all the way to her hips and back to her breasts.

Her arms ached as he made her stand on her tiptoes. But then he unhooked her wrists and relief rushed through her arms and legs when she was back on the floor again.

He reached down and inflated the butt plug a little more and she gasped at the stretching sensation. When she felt that it was as big as she could handle, he stopped and moved his lips to her ear. "How does that feel? Does it feel good to have something so big and hard in your ass?"

She nodded and made a sound of pleasure, telling him that she loved it.

He moved in front of her and unclipped her wrists then pulled them back behind her and clipped them again. After she was secured, he tugged on the leash forcing her to walk forward. She knew that he would not let her run into anything, but still, being unable to see made her hesitant.

"Come on." His tone was masterful and it sent thrills through her. She loved him taking control. Loved it.

She hesitated again as he pulled the leash but he tugged harder and she gave in to trusting him. She felt a shift in the air and realized they had passed from one room into another. The floor was carpeted, soft beneath her feet and then she felt cool tile and she realized he was leading her into the kitchen.

He guided her forward then stopped her and played with her nipples. "Kneel," he said and helped her so that she wouldn't fall. "I should put you on all fours and make you lap water from a bowl. Then you would be my little puppy girl."

Being his puppy girl sounded exciting, sending pleasant thrills throughout her.

"Stay," he said.

She didn't know where he thought she might go with her hands bound behind her back and a blindfold on, while sitting on her knees. The butt plug made her feel even hotter.

He opened the refrigerator and she listened to the rummaging sounds, wondering what he was doing. A dish clattered on the table when he returned along with what sounded like silverware. What had he brought back?

Something smelled like chocolate. He removed her gag and then took a chair close enough to her that his knee brushed her breast.

"Open your mouth." He pressed something cool against her lips and when she obeyed he slipped a spoon into her mouth.

Whipped cream. Smooth, creamy, delicious.

He pulled back on the spoon and kissed her, his tongue slipping into her mouth as he tasted the whipped cream.

He leaned back and said, "Again," and she opened her mouth and he slid the spoon inside.

Chocolate cake. The most incredible, moist chocolate cake she could ever remember tasting. "Mmmmm." It was nearly orgasmic. Again he kissed her and tasted her.

Then he pressed a maraschino cherry to her lips and she let it slide in. It tasted sweet and delicious and he kissed her again.

"I have another treat for you." He tugged on her leash and moved her so that she felt his knees on either side of her. He had her between his thighs and he was lowering her head. She opened her mouth, knowing what kind of treat she was going to get.

He pushed his thick cock into her mouth and she made a sound of pleasure. She loved doing this for him. It made her feel both powerful and feminine at the same time. She hummed as she licked and sucked him and he clenched his hands in her hair and moved her up and down his length.

When he pulled her head back and his cock slipped from her mouth, he put another bite of chocolate cake in her mouth before having her go down on him again.

It was an intoxicating blend of eroticism as he fed her cake while blindfolded and then had her suck his cock in between bites. He was so thick, so hard.

And then he swept her up into his arms and carried her in what she guessed was the direction of his bedroom. Her heart began to pound faster and faster and liquid heat filled her veins.

He laid her on the bed, pressing the butt plug in tighter. She heard rummaging and then a low hum. He moved between her thighs and then placed something against her clit at the same time he thrust his cock inside of her.

She almost came up off the bed. She'd never felt anything like it. He had put some kind of super vibrator against her clit and was pressing it tight against her with his body as he fucked her.

It was one of the most amazing things she'd ever felt. There was no holding back her orgasm, even if she had tried. The combinations of him taking her with the butt plug inside her ass, while the vibrator stimulated her pussy, made her come so hard and fast she didn't even expect it. Her cries were loud as her body bucked and jerked beneath him.

He pounded in and out of her and then gave a sound like a low growl as he came. He moved in and out then pushed aside the vibrator and it fell to the floor as he pressed his groin tight to hers.

Her body was still pulsating as he rolled over and brought her into his arms and kissed her. She gave a happy sigh and snuggled into his arms and let herself slip away into a deep and wonderful sleep.

Chapter 11

Leslie covered a yawn as she walked through the house toward Rick's kitchen. She could smell the coffee he'd made a mile away. She was dressed in what she'd worn last night. She would have loved to roll around in bed all day but she had to get home and take care of a few things.

She smiled as she thought of last night. She had almost told him how she felt but she didn't know how to say it. She'd never told a man that she was in love with him except Michael.

Because she had never been in love before except for him.

In lust, yes. Infatuated, yes. But real love, never.

Even if she felt comfortable, how was the best way to tell Rick? Did she just blurt it out over coffee? Did she wait until a romantic evening out? Or did she tell him in bed when it was just the two of them snuggling together? It was probably best not to say anything. Why did she have to be like this?

She mentally shook her head. "I won't think about it for now."

When she reached the kitchen she saw a clean mug sitting by the coffeepot like he'd told her there would be, and next to that was a jar with sugar and a small carton of half-and-half. She put liberal amounts of both into the coffee that she poured and then walked out of the kitchen, looking for Rick.

She thought she heard his voice and her heels sank into the carpet as she walked to the opposite side of the house where he had shown her his office. She reached the office door. Rick was on his cell and was listening to someone on the other end of the line.

She started to knock softly on the doorframe to let him know she was there, but then she stopped.

Rick pushed his hand through his hair as he spoke into the phone. "I thought I had more time to wrap things up in Annapolis."

Leslie tilted her head, wondering what he meant.

Rick paused to listen. "Yes, sir." He frowned. "I'll get out there immediately."

Another pause. "Thank you, sir," Rick said after a moment then ended the call.

He looked up and saw that Leslie was in the room. "Hi, honey."

"You're going on a trip?" she asked.

"Not exactly." He sighed.

A slow chill began to creep up her spine. Something was wrong.

He dragged his hand down his face. "Orders came through yesterday. I'm being transferred to San Diego."

She felt like all of the color had drained out of her. Rick was leaving and he hadn't said a single word to her. He had just let her fall in love with him like she meant nothing to him. Nothing at all.

Her hand shook and a little coffee sloshed onto her wrist. "When were you going to tell me that you're leaving?"

"Tonight," he said. "I just got my orders a few days ago and that's where I'm headed. It was supposed to be another position at Annapolis and not San Diego. It was also going to be a month, but now it is immediate. The guy I'm replacing just went into the hospital. They want me there as soon as possible."

She found her whole body was shaking with anger and pain. She stepped forward and smacked her coffee cup on his desktop before she could drop it and coffee splattered onto some of his papers. "How can you act like it's nothing?" She clenched her fists at her sides. "So you screw around with me and then you just leave without giving a damn about how I feel?"

"Like I said, I just found out," he said. "I've been trying to figure out this whole thing."

She took another step back then straightened her spine. "Goodbye, Rick. Have a nice life."

"Wait." He went after her and caught her by her shoulder. "We need to talk."

She swung around and jerked away from him. "I don't want to hear it. Not a word."

He followed her as she went to the front door and picked up her purse from where she'd left it. "Don't go," he said. "We'll work this out."

She grabbed the doorknob and gave him one last look. "I need time alone. Don't call me. Don't stop by my house."

"Let me give you a ride home." Concern was clear in his voice.

"I don't need a ride." She stuck her hand in her bag and jerked out her cell phone. "I'll get a cab."

"Don't leave like this, Leslie." He followed her down the steps. A part of her realized he was in his boxers and T-shirt. "Please don't leave like this."

She turned her back on him and pulled up the phone number to call a taxi, pressed send, and held the phone up to her ear. She gave the address of a store down the street to the dispatcher and she started walking.

Rick called after her one last time and she could feel his gaze on her.

She never looked back.

Leslie climbed up the stairs to her home. It had been an exhausting day at work with spoiled models and one emergency after another. A broken nail, a five-pound weight gain, a missing collection, an injured runway model with a limp, and preparation for tomorrow afternoon for a big show in New York City, made for one hell of a day. She'd have to fly from Baltimore into JFK tomorrow and she wasn't really in the mood for a fashion show.

For the past two weeks Rick had called, left voice mails, sent emails, and sent her text messages. At first she listened to his voice mails and read the messages, but then she couldn't take it any longer. Her heart hurt far too much to open it up to any more pain. Look where it had gotten her.

He hadn't taken the hint. He wouldn't give up.

She rubbed her temples as she entered her home and let the door slam shut with a hard thump behind her. She dropped her purse beside the door and faced her living room, and came to a complete halt.

A vase was on her coffee table and it was filled with a huge bouquet of colorful flowers.

A vase that hadn't been there before.

Someone had been in her house.

She took a step back. Her spine prickled. Someone was behind her. She started to scream when a hand clamped over her mouth and a strong arm pinned her up against a hard body.

Terror ripped through her.

"It's me, Leslie." Rick's voice made her sag in relief. At the same time she wanted to kill him for scaring her. "I'm not taking my hand off of your mouth unless you agree to shut up and listen. Nod if you understand."

She was tempted to bite his finger but she nodded.

He moved his hand away and took her by the shoulders and turned her around. He looked so good she wanted him to hold her close. She wanted him to kiss her. But she couldn't let herself allow that.

"I want to shake some sense into you." He gripped her shoulders tighter. "But let's start with dinner before the manhandling begins."

A feeling of excitement rose up inside of her. Rick was here. *Here.* She would have smiled if her heart wasn't aching in her chest. She tamped down her excitement. "It's been a long day. I'm sorry but I really am not in the mood for dinner out."

"Then we'll order in." He pulled his cell phone out of the holster on his belt. "Why don't you get out of your work clothes and get into something more comfortable."

"And a quick, hot shower." She rolled her shoulder as she spoke. It didn't look like he was going to leave and she needed to clear her head before they talked.

Thirty minutes later, she caught the rich smells of Italian food when she walked out of her bedroom and down the staircase. Pasta with red sauce and warm garlic bread.

Her entire body hummed with awareness of him as they put the rigatoni, bread, and salad on the table, along with a bottle of merlot. She was hungry but didn't feel a lot like eating. For a little while it was quiet between them as she made herself eat. The wine went down easier than the food and the warmth of it as it passed through her helped bolster her resolve and her courage.

When they started talking, it was about anything but the two of them. He asked about her friends whom he had met, how things were going at work, what had she been doing. He answered her when she asked him how he liked his new position and what it entailed.

After they finished eating, he brought the conversation back to the two of them. "Did you listen to or read my messages?"

She sighed and set her fork on her plate and met his gaze. "At first. But it just got to be too painful."

"I didn't know if you did so I came back to talk to you," he said. "You will listen to me, Leslie. I'm not going to throw away what we have."

"Had," she said.

"No." His jaw grew tight. "It's still there and you know it."

"I can't open myself anymore to this kind of pain." She shook her head. "I should never have let myself fall for you. What I went through with Michael—I didn't want to ever experience that again."

He frowned. "I'm not Michael."

"No," she said. "You're not. This is a hundred times harder than it ever was when I broke up with him. Can't you see that I just can't take this anymore?"

"It's not like that with us." He clenched his fist on the tabletop. "You have someone right now who loves you and wants to make it work."

"How can it work?" She shook her head. "You're in San Diego now and I'm here."

His expression was intense, almost fierce. "People work out long distance relationships all of the time."

"Not me." She shook her head. "I don't do long distance."

"What are you going to do?" he said. "Go through the rest of your life being afraid of being hurt?"

She swallowed and didn't say anything.

Rick put his hand over hers. "I need you."

There was pain in his voice and his words sent a strange feeling through her. She hadn't seen it from his side at all. She had only been feeling her own pain.

He stood and clasped their hands together and pulled her to her feet. He put his forehead to hers and they stood there for a long moment.

"I love you, Leslie." He raised his head and her lips parted as she tried to absorb his words. "I love you."

"I love you, too, Rick." The words came easier than she had thought they would. "But the distance…"

"Come with me." He cupped one side of her face and brushed her hair behind her ear with his other hand. "I would stay here if I could."

She closed her eyes for a moment before opening them again. "I have my business."

"Can you telecommute?" he asked.

"If it was that simple I would consider it." She reached up her hand and put it over his as he caressed her face. "But with this business I have to be right here. I can't do this from thousands of miles away."

He studied her, his tawny eyes searching hers. "Let's give the long distance thing a try for now until we can figure something out."

"Figure what out?" She never cried but she heard tears on the edge of her words. "It won't work. That's that."

Rick let his hands slide away from her and he stepped back. "Think about it. Please."

She looked down and then back at him. "I've been going over everything in my mind for the past two weeks. I just don't see it."

"If you're not going to listen voluntarily, I'm going to make you listen." He grabbed her around the waist and she made a sound of surprise as he threw her over his shoulder.

"What are you doing?" She tried to push herself up a little but he kept her down as he headed up the stairs.

When they reached the top he went straight for her toy room. He was so strong that he was able to hold her and grab something that she couldn't see since she was behind him. Then he swung around and carried her back through the door and to her bedroom.

"I am not letting you go." He set her on the bed and she bounced a little on the mattress, and she saw that what he had grabbed was a bunch of rope.

"Oh, no you don't." She attempted to scoot off of the bed but he caught her by her wrist and efficiently bound her wrist to one of her bedposts. *"Rick. Don't."* She tried to get up but he grabbed her other wrist and tied it to the opposite bedpost. She struggled to kick him but had her spread-eagle, her ankles secured to the bedposts at the foot of the bed.

He straddled her. "When I claim something," he said as he braced his hands to either side of her head, "it is mine."

She bit her lower lip. No, she couldn't allow herself to feel anything more for him. Much less let him claim her.

"I won't let you go, Leslie." He lowered his face so that it was closer to hers. "You are mine."

He kissed her hard and moved his free hand up to her breast then back down to her thigh and he grasped the hem of her skirt and pulled it up to her waist. "I need to be inside of you again. I need to make love to you."

"I need you, too." She pressed herself up against the hard ridge of his erection. "Now."

He reached down between them and unzipped his jeans. She squirmed, wanting to help. He wasn't moving fast enough for her but he had her wrists bound.

When he had his cock out she felt it press against the center of her panties. He pushed them aside and thrust inside of her.

Her eyes widened and she gasped at the sudden feel of him. He ground his hips hard against hers and she moved in rhythm with him.

He took her harder and faster. Everything wound up inside her belly and she felt her oncoming orgasm as he thrust in and out of her. She held back, not wanting to come too soon.

"Come with me, honey," he said.

She cried out with the power of her orgasm, his words all she needed to set herself free.

He untied her and brought her into his arms like he intended to never let her go.

Chapter 12

Leslie settled herself into her window seat on the airline set to take off for JFK from Baltimore. She had to get to New York City and prepare for the afternoon's fashion show then return to Baltimore in the evening.

She had left a note on her pillow for Rick to read in the morning that she had to leave town. In her note she told him to give her time and space to figure it all out.

Thank you for an amazing night, she had written in the note. *But don't pressure me. Give me time.*

She looked out the small window to the tarmac below, as the plane started moving down the runway. It gained speed and then the powerful bird was in the air.

You're so messed up, Leslie Adams, she told herself.

What was she going to do? Keep running? Go through life scared because of one jerk?

Was she going to keep going through one guy after another, trying to fill that empty void inside of her?

Such a shallow, unfulfilling life she had in front of her.

Unless she went with her heart.

Unless she went to Rick.

It took her two more days to work everything out in her mind.

Another two weeks to get things in motion.

Leslie sat at her desk in her modeling agency as she stared at the papers in her hand. She looked up at her partner, Raul.

"Are you sure this is what you want?" Raul said as he leaned back in his chair, studying her. "You've worked hard to help build this place to what it is today."

"Yes." She took a deep breath raised the pen. "It's absolutely what I want."

With a flourish she signed her name on the line, signifying the end of her career in the modeling business.

She hadn't expected to feel the power of relief that flooded over her. She hadn't expected the smile that came to her with the sweep of the pen.

"Yes," she said again. She stood and pushed the papers over to Raul. "It's exactly what I want."

He got to his feet as she did and she gave him a quick hug. "I'll stop by when I'm in town," she said. "You haven't seen the last of me."

"I will miss you." He kissed her on each cheek then stepped back.

Feeling happier than she'd ever felt in her life, she walked out the door of her office. She waved goodbye to people she had worked with for years but didn't stop to talk with anyone. It was time to track down a certain Navy SEAL.

She had never loved anyone like she loved Rick, and he had made it clear that he loved her. She had been stubborn, unwilling to give up what was ultimately a shallow life.

With Rick she could have something richer. A life with someone who loved her.

San Diego sunshine warmed her bare arms and legs as she stood with her suitcases at the front door of Rick's apartment. The taxi sped away behind her and a breeze ruffled her skirt.

A twinge of nervousness made her belly ache.

Maybe she should have called and told him she had changed her mind. That she had sold her interest in her business and was coming out to be with him.

Maybe this was a bad idea, showing up on his doorstep without making sure he still wanted her.

The feelings of doubt came out of nowhere and she set her suitcases down. This was stupid.

She raised her hand to knock on the door.

It opened before she ever had the chance to knock.

Rick stood in the doorway, looking amazing. Her heart felt full at the sight of him and she smiled, wanting him to sweep her into his arms, yet wondering how he was going to react.

"It's about time you got here." He picked up her suitcases. "You're almost late for dinner."

She blinked as he swept up the two large suitcases she had brought with her and followed him inside the apartment. She closed the door and he dropped her suitcases with two large thumps.

He grabbed her to him and took her down to the floor.

Her lips parted in surprise as she found herself pinned beneath him, his hips between her thighs, her arms stretched over her head, her wrists clasped in one of his hands.

He brought his mouth to hers and kissed her so hard her head was spinning. He groaned and kissed her like he'd never get enough. She didn't think she could get enough of him. Ever.

"You do realize," he said when he raised his head. "That if you're just here for a visit, I'm not letting you go back. Even if I have to hold you captive, you're not getting away from me again."

She smiled. "I'm here to stay, Rick."

"It's a good thing." His smile filled her with something warm and good. "What about your business?"

"I sold my interest to my partner." She couldn't stop smiling. "I'm a free woman."

"You're not free," he said. "You're mine. I claimed you, remember?"

He kissed her hard, his breathing harsh like her own. "I love you, honey," he said.

"I love you Rick." She knew she could never say it enough.

He grinned and rolled onto his back with her on top of him. He wrapped her in his arms and she knew she was right where she needed to be.

Taken

Chapter 1

It was like the lottery in a way. Either she would win or she wouldn't, depending on who bought her at the auction tonight. Whatever happened, her fate for one weekend was in someone else's hands.

Tonight was for fun. Fun she needed in the biggest way. Her gaze moved around the room of people at the wine and cheese mixer and she smiled. No matter what happened, she would enjoy herself.

Kelley Bachman slipped into the elite crowd. The whole room sparkled like one big diamond and she felt almost blinded by the glitter and dazzle of the wealth in the room.

She moved away from her friend Leslie, whom she had just been talking with, wishing she had Leslie's cool confidence and the easy way she seemed to manage her life.

Is anything ever easy? Kelley mentally shook her head. Not for her.

She was everyone else's pillar of strength. From raising her brothers and sisters, to working off her ex-husband's debts, to being head nurse at a large hospital, she was always in charge.

She took a deep breath and shook off the tension that always seemed to be with her as she repeated to herself, *Tonight is for fun.*

Yes. It was all about her secret fantasy… A dominant male bidding on and winning her at the auction. A Dom who really liked to take control so that she wouldn't have to do anything but please him. That was exactly what she wanted. One weekend of letting someone else make all of the choices in her life would be heaven. And one weekend pleasing someone else however he wanted her to would be amazing.

There were probably better ways to go about finding a male dominant who would fulfill her fantasy, but when she heard about the auction and the inclusion of a group that she'd belonged to a short time—a group that practiced BDSM— something stirred deep inside her that she hadn't felt before. Something almost primal. A need she had to be taken, to belong to someone.

Hopefully the right man would get her. There was an element of danger that excited her. Giving up control to someone she didn't know well was a hot thought. She had to have a connection, though. If that wasn't there, it might be a long weekend. Worst case, she had her own room on the weekend of the trip and there was always the headache excuse.

A cool breeze in the room brushed against her bare back and she shivered. Her sparkly red dress scooped all the way down her back to the base of her spine. It was sexy, glamorous, and far more daring than anything she'd ever worn before. She glanced at her left shoulder to make sure her ornate gold circle pin was still there and she saw it glinting in the low lighting.

The circle would tell any dominants at the auction that she was a submissive. The Kink Club, KC, had multiple members who were discretely participating in the exclusive charity auction. Doms wore triangle pins and tonight there were several men and women with triangles in attendance.

And some of the men were *really* hot.

Unfortunately, she had arrived late, thanks to the doctor who had kept her overtime at work. She hoped she'd have time to meet a couple of interesting dominant males before the auction itself started, but she wasn't sure there was enough time left.

She wandered through the crowd, trying to avoid catching the attention of anyone who did not have a triangle pin. She ducked past a man who didn't have one and caught sight of someone just a few feet from her who took her breath away.

Nate Davis. Her heart beat a little faster. She hadn't seen him since the night of the party at his home two years ago.

He looked better than ever.

Not only that, to her pleasure she saw that he was wearing a triangle pin—he was with KC.

About five-eleven, well over her five-four inch height, he had dark blond hair and sage green eyes. He was talking with a woman, an obvious submissive, with a circle pin, and he had the sexiest expression when he smiled at whatever the woman was saying. She remembered him telling her he was into mixed martial arts and it was clear in his bearing and build.

There was a sense of power about him, and that power had always attracted her and tonight it drew her in, making it almost impossible to do anything but get closer to him. Hopefully the woman would move on so that she would have a chance to talk to him. She had always felt some kind of soul-deep attraction to him, one she didn't fully understand but tonight she intended to investigate it.

She moved a little closer then held herself back as she watched him listen to the woman who was talking animatedly and without pause. Kelley couldn't hear them, but by the woman's expression she was more than attracted to him. Kelley wasn't sure about him, though. Was he just flirting back or did he have a strong, genuine interest in her?

Nate raised his gaze and met Kelley's. He winked.

Warmth heated her cheeks and she bit the inside of her lip. It was almost as if he was telling her something, telegraphing to her that he was amused by the woman he was talking with and that he wanted Kelley to wait for him.

That or he was amused with her.

Her face grew hotter and she debated on whether to move away or stand her ground and take the chance that he could be interested in her again. The man made the choice for her by excusing himself from his conversation and moving toward Kelley. In the background she saw the disappointed woman staring at her with an expression that bordered on anger.

"You weren't planning on leaving without saying hello, were you, Kelley?" The man's smile was even sexier up close and personal as she gave her full attention to him. "After all, you never said goodbye."

Another warm flush went through her. She returned his smile as her cheeks cooled. "I wasn't going anywhere."

"What happened the last time?" He didn't act upset, just curious. "After our lunch together and after the night of the party, I thought that you were interested. But you never returned my calls."

Lunch had been fun and so had the party. He owned a medical supply company and had thrown the party for his clients. That night they had talked and talked and talked.

She'd had an incredible time with him but she thought she owed it to Ray to give their relationship another try.

She looked down for a moment then met his gaze. "You caught me on the rebound. My then boyfriend wanted to get back together right after we went out. At the time I thought I loved him. I just didn't know how to tell you. I didn't handle it well with you. I am sorry."

"I saw you in the auction program." He referred to the booklet that had been put together with pictures and bios of all the men and women who were being auctioned off tonight for charity. "I take it you're single now."

"Yes." The attraction Kelley had felt when she first knew him seemed to double as he spoke. She had been totally smitten with him. If it hadn't been for Ray... Things could have been different.

She had always loved Nate's voice and she imagined what it would be like to have that voice commanding her, telling her what to do. It was a pleasant fantasy that she allowed herself to indulge in.

"Do you still work at the hospital?" he asked.

"Yes," she said. "I haven't seen you stop by there."

"My company lost the contract with the hospital," he said. "When the big staff change happened, someone brought in a medical supply company they had already been working with."

"I thought about you a lot." She wasn't sure if she should say it, but she let it out anyway. "When I broke up with my ex-boyfriend, I thought about calling you."

"Why didn't you?" He looked genuinely curious as well as interested.

"I wasn't even sure you'd want to talk to me since I never returned your calls," she said.

"I would have welcomed your call. It was a long time before I could get you out of my mind." The look in his eyes told her that he meant what he said.

"And look at you now." He looked her over from head to toe in a way that made her feel attractive. "It's great that you're here. And you are with KC. I am surprised, but I love that you are."

"You being with the club surprised me, too," she said. "I'm really glad you're a part of it."

He still looked amazed. "How long have you been with KC?"

She tilted her head to the side as she thought about it. "A few months. There's something about it that concerns me about being seen in public. I'm not very open about my personal interests."

"I understand and can relate to that." He glanced around the room. "Everyone here who's involved with KC is to be discreet."

Kelley gave a nod. "That's what I was told."

"It's been a while since I've been active," he said. "What made you decide to get involved in the auction?"

"I needed something fun. Exciting." She pushed a wave of blonde hair over her shoulder. "Something different. And not only is there the potential for fun, it's all for a good cause with the charity."

His lips curved into the sexy smile she'd seen him wear before. Only this time there seemed to be something added to it, something even hotter. "What kind of exciting?"

With a laugh she said, "I'll tell you because I'm sure you'll get it, considering that you're involved to some extent in the BDSM community. As crazy as my life has been, anything that gives me pure release, an escape from being in charge of everything, will be heaven. Someone I can trust…someone to whom I can turn everything over to."

"You want a man to be in charge of you?" He lowered his voice and it had a sexy timber to it. "Someone to make all the decisions in your life."

That hadn't been exactly what she'd said, but it was what she wanted, and this man had seen right through to her deepest desires.

"What about you?" she said.

"I don't want a man making my decisions for me," he teased her and she smiled. "What I am looking for is a woman who wants to be cared for." He seemed to grow a little more serious. "I appreciate you being so open and direct. Usually it takes a while to learn that someone has those kinds of interests. Personally, I need someone who needs what I can give her in every aspect of her life."

Little tingles ran up and down her spine. "Then we make a good match." She hurried to add, "For one weekend, anyway."

"One weekend," he said in agreement although something told her that he was looking for more than that.

Seeing him again, and finding out that they had more in common than she'd thought, excited her in a way that she hadn't expected.

"Ladies and gentlemen." A man's voice said, over a sound system. "Please join us in the ballroom. The auction is about to start. Bachelors and bachelorettes, please meet behind the stage. Everyone else find a seat and we'll get started."

"It's been fun talking with you." She smiled. "I hope to see you later."

He took her hand and squeezed it. "You can count on it."

The way he said the words sent a thrill through her belly.

His words repeated in her mind. *"You can count on it."*

In her crazy life she didn't count on anything that she didn't have some form of control over. But something told her that if she could count on anyone, it would be Nate Davis.

Chapter 2

Kelley waited behind a curtain for her name to be called and then she would walk onstage. She rubbed her arms with her hands, feeling a sudden chill that caused goose bumps to rise on her skin.

Now was the time to wish for a little luck and a man named Nate Davis.

"Kelley Bachman!" came the booming voice of the MC.

She pushed her hair over her shoulder, took a deep breath, and walked onstage. As she stood by the auctioneer she tried to peer into the crowd but at first the lights were too bright for her to get a really good look. She thought she saw Nate but wasn't sure.

What a great Dom he could turn out to be. Something about him made her excited. Made her believe that relationships could be real and honest.

It's silly to get your hopes up, Kelley. She mentally shook her head. "Kelley is a nurse at a local hospital," the auctioneer was saying. "One of you lucky gentlemen will get to take the lovely nurse to San Francisco for a getaway weekend."

The bidding started out at a fairly high number. She had heard the unbelievable amounts that were paid for earlier bachelors and bachelorettes, and had been curious how much she would go for.

As the bidding went on, Kelley tried not to squint to get a better look at who was bidding on her. Instead she just smiled and waited until the auctioneer hit the gavel and said, "Sold, to Mr. Nate Davis."

Butterflies looped around in Kelley's belly as she was escorted to the steps leading from the stage. At the bottom of the stairs, Nate waited and he was smiling. She smiled in return as she met his gaze.

He glanced at his watch. "It's early. Would you like to head out for a drive around the city?"

She nodded. "I'm in no rush to get home."

Downstairs, she waited for him in the lobby while he went to get their coats and her purse.

"Hey there, hot mama." A man spoke from behind her.

She ignored him and hoped that Nate would hurry.

Two men came around to face her, crowding her personal space, and she took a step back.

"Wanna have fun some tonight?" The taller of the two men said. He had dark hair and a goatee. He was the one who had spoken from behind her. He pointed to his crotch. "Come and get some of this, baby."

Heat burned her cheeks. She tried to turn away but the shorter man stepped in front of her.

"What do you have under that dress?" The shorter man leered. "Come on, show us."

She glanced around her in the huge, almost empty lobby, looking for help. She would scream if they came a step closer.

She heard Nate's deep voice. "Someone needs to teach you boys some manners." He stepped in front of her and got within two feet of the men. "I think that might just be me."

Nate's presence was powerful and intimidating. He made her think about a tiger ready to slam into the men and tear out their throats. It was easy to see his mixed martial arts training in the way that he held himself, the controlled tension in his bearing.

Both of the men backed up. "We were just having some fun," the taller one said.

Nate took another step toward them. "You come near her again and I will take you apart."

The shorter man shoved the other guy. "Let's get out of here."

They both took off. The taller guy looked over his shoulder, as if making sure they weren't being followed.

When they were out of sight, Kelley took a deep breath and turned to Nate. "Thank you."

He took her by her shoulders. "Are you all right?"

"They didn't hurt me." She was surprised to find she was a little unsteady on her feet.

"You're shaking." He rubbed her upper arms. "It's the adrenaline kicking in. If I could have taken those two out, I would have."

"I know." She straightened and managed a smile. He'd been her protector, had chased off the two men from what could have been a really bad situation.

He picked up their coats and her purse from where he had laid them on a nearby couch and after he helped her put her coat on, they headed out the front doors. He'd already had the valet bring his car around. He assisted her in getting into his gorgeous silver Mercedes and pulled away from the curb and headed away from the hotel. The car was so smooth riding that it felt like they were gliding along the road. She didn't know a lot about cars but it beat her Toyota by a long shot, and she loved her Prius.

Thrills of excitement went through her belly while they talked as they drove around the Tyson's Corner area just outside of D.C. She loved the time they spent together in the car and found herself more than looking forward to the weekend in San Francisco that went along with the auction. If she read it right, he seemed just as attracted to her as she was to him, as if their relationship had continued instead of ending two years ago.

After they had driven around for at least an hour, Nate said, "I've moved since you were last at my home for the party. Would you like to stop at my new house for a tour, and maybe a drink?"

Anticipation hummed in her veins. She had thought about asking him into her home when they returned but had wondered if it would be too forward and too much too soon. He'd just taken care of it for her.

She smiled. "Yes."

It wasn't long until he turned onto a road with huge homes set back aways with long drives. She could barely see the lights in the homes because there were so many trees.

He pulled into a driveway and directed his car toward an old colonial home. Before she could say anything, he said, "Welcome to my place." He was at her side of the car and opening the door before she could. He helped her out of the car.

She looked over the front with its big white columns and shuttered windows as they walked up the short flight of stairs to the front door. He unlocked the door and escorted her into his home. Once they were inside, he helped her slip out of her coat and he put it and his own in a coat closet near the front door.

"I love your home," she said.

He looked down at her. "I enjoy it."

The place was filled with colonial furnishing and décor and she admired everything she passed. When they entered a room toward the back of the house, she blinked, a little surprised. This room was warm and inviting, and altogether modern. As she took in her surroundings, he slipped off his suit jacket and laid it over the back of a couch.

"Would you like a drink?" he asked.

She shook her head. "I think I probably had enough wine at the party. I'll get sleepy if I have more."

"How about that tour?" He held out his hand

She took it and a shiver traveled through her at his touch. "I'm ready."

It was like going through a colonial museum. He showed her books and letters and items passed down through his family for generations as well as other things he had purchased as a collector. The furnishings were unique to the period as well as all of the fixtures.

At the end of the tour, he brought her down a well-lit hallway to a set of doors that opened into a sitting room.

"Welcome to my favorite space." He looked down at her as they stood in the doorway. "To the left, through there, is my bedroom. This is the sitting room, an old-fashioned term, I suppose for a private living room."

Kelley looked at her surroundings in the large. Rich furnishings filled the place, including a divan, a couch, and a couple of chairs, along with a large wardrobe cabinet.

She turned her gaze back to meet his and looked into his sage green eyes. His masterful presence stirred the primal desire in her that needed to be quenched. With his jacket off she had a better view of his physique and she wanted to touch the power she knew she'd find when he removed his shirt.

But then she didn't need him to take it off to feel power emanating from him. It surrounded her, stroked her, seduced her. Here was a man she knew could control her in every way she desired.

She wanted him to kiss her so badly she could taste it.

Instead, he gestured to the couch. "Have a seat."

Disappointed, but still hopeful, she sat, holding down her short dress so that it wouldn't climb up her thighs, and he sat next to her.

They talked for a while about how things were at the hospital and a bit about the accounts he was working with for his medical supply business.

Their conversation was easy and casual and she really enjoyed talking with him.

After a while, the conversation came back to KC and BDSM, a topic that she was more than pleased to explore.

"Do you play often?" she asked.

He trailed his fingers along her arm. "Only if I'm with the right person."

A little shiver ran through her at his touch. "What do you like in a woman?"

"I like obedience." He moved his fingers slowly up and down her arm. "So I don't need a cattle prod to force compliance."

Her eyes widened. "Do you have a cattle prod?" she asked, hoping he didn't.

"No," he said. "But I do have other items which produce the same effect."

She was almost afraid to ask but did anyway. "Like what?"

He studied her. "I will show you in time."

"Tell me what it is." She needed to know. "Please."

"Full of curiosity and interest, aren't you." He raised a brow. "All right. I'll get one of the things out for you that I use."

He walked around the couch, behind her, to the wardrobe. She found herself curious at exactly all he might have in the big cabinet. When he returned he was carrying what looked like a briefcase. He placed it on the coffee table before he sat next to her on the couch.

She glanced at him. "What's in that?"

He flipped open the two catches and opened the case. Inside was a violet wand along with several attachments.

"Have you ever had a violet wand used on you?" He took out the wand with its round glass globe attachment. He ran the smooth globe down her arm and she jumped, expecting a shock, but he hadn't turned it on.

"I've never seen one." She watched the globe, not able to take her gaze from it. "I read a story where one was used. That was pretty intense and exciting."

"You can decide for yourself just how intense and exciting it is." He moved the globe to just above her elbow and turned on the wand.

She jumped and reflex had her jerking her arm away from the globe. "Ow." It was like getting a good electrical shock from an exposed wire. "You didn't even touch me with it."

"The shock sensation is created when there's an arc between the body and the wand," he said. "If I actually touched you with the wand, you would feel more of a warm sensation than a shock."

"The warm sensation sounds better," she said.

"I think I'd have to tie you down to get the full benefit out of using this on you," he said in a teasing tone. He brought the wand to her knee and slowly rolled it up to her thigh and she felt a pleasant warm sensation.

The thought of him tying her down gave her all kinds of possibilities to fantasize about.

Not to mention he was *hot*. His eyes held intelligence that she found exceptionally attractive, even beyond the strong line of his jaw and his muscular build.

"I loved your directness at the auction tonight and telling me what you are looking for, Kelley," he said as he smoothed the wand up her arm, spreading the warm sensation. She watched the wand rather than looking at him. "Normally I wouldn't jump right into this," he said, "but you did, so I will." She looked at him and saw the sexy curve of his smile. "What do you love most when it comes to bondage and domination?"

She was caught a little off guard, but she shouldn't have been. "I love confinement."

He studied her with interest. "What kind of confinement? How extreme?"

"Any kind." She watched as he moved the wand so that he was rolling it down her calf then she returned her gaze to him. "I love the feeling of having my movements completely restricted."

"What have you had done to you before?" He looked more and more intrigued as she spoke.

"Mostly rope bondage along with a hood. Spandex, leather or maybe even latex." She felt herself growing excited just talking about it. "And one time I was in a sleeping bag and bound from the shoulders down and I was wearing a spandex hood and a blindfold. I like feeling as if I'm inside a cocoon. It's indescribable."

He set the violet wand on the coffee table. "What else do you like?"

It was amazing how open he made her feel. She felt a strong draw to him and a comfort level so great that she found it easy to tell him her darkest secrets. He didn't need the wand to draw the answers from her because she wanted to tell him. Besides, she knew he wanted to hear them. No doubt he imagined doing to her all of what they talked about.

She tilted her head to the side. "Everyone likes different levels of pain. I want my limits tested. There's something about being helpless, knowing someone has the power to do what he wants." She paused. "It would be really exciting to have new experiences and to be taken to the edge. There is something about the rush from the mix of fear and trust." She shook her head. "I really can't believe I am telling you all of this. I don't know what there is about you, but when you ask a question, I just want to tell you."

"I like that you are so open," he said. "Your interests match many of my own."

"It's fair to say that you are intoxicating," she said and he laughed. "What do you want?" she asked, turning the tables on him.

"A woman I can take care of." The way he looked at her as he spoke sent thrills through her. "Someone willing to take my direction and let me make the decisions. Someone who will trust me in whatever I say. But that kind of connection all takes time and trust."

She smiled. He was looking for what she was. She wanted a man who would take care of her and he wanted a woman to take care of.

He stood and held out his hand and she grasped it and let him pull her to her feet. When she was up, he didn't step back. He stayed close, within inches of her. Butterflies tumbled through her belly as she felt the warmth of his body heat and inhaled his masculine scent.

He moved his face close to hers and paused as if waiting for her to say no to a kiss. Instead, she reached up and brought her mouth to his. He gripped her upper arms and kissed her.

His lips were firm and he tasted of wine, and something about it sent her mind reeling. She wanted more than a sweet kiss and she wrapped her arms around his neck and pressed her body close to his. She shivered when she felt his erection and the knowledge that he was aroused caused an ache between her thighs.

Too soon he drew away. Her lips were moist and they tingled from his kiss.

She opened her eyes and looked into his. "That was amazing."

He smiled. "I thought so, too." His expression changed a little, like he was concerned. "I'm worried."

"About what?" She tilted her head to the side.

"If we stay in here much longer I won't be able to keep my hands off of you." He looked serious. "I want things to be right between us now that I know your secrets."

His words caused her to smile and made her more sure of him than ever. Maybe it was crazy, but she didn't care.

She touched her finger to his chin. "Don't be concerned, I'm not worried." She reached up and murmured in his ear, "Nothing is going to happen that I don't want to happen."

He shook his head. "Not tonight."

"Why not?" She looked at him with surprise.

He kissed her hard then pulled back and met her gaze. "I thought about playing, but you want it too badly."

She frowned. "Why is that a problem?"

"I control what we do or don't do, Kelley." He cupped the side of her face in his hand. "You need to understand that the only control you have is the word 'no' or your safe word if you don't want to do something. When it comes to anything else, I will decide what it is and what time is right.

"For now," he said, "let's get you home."

"You're taking me home?" She felt a little deflated. "Are you disappointed in me?"

"Not at all." He squeezed her hand and started leading her toward the doorway. "This might be the hardest thing I've ever had to do."

Chapter 3

"Come by my home tomorrow night at seven." The last words Nate had said to Kelley when he dropped her off at her door were clearly an order. "I have something in mind for you."

All day she felt excited and couldn't wait to see what he had planned. She should have had no problem getting to his home on time, after she had a chance to shower and change. Her shift at the hospital was supposed to end at five, but one of the doctors had insisted she assist him—even though he could have gotten any other nurse—and she arrived home forty-five minutes late.

Instead of being on time, she barely made it to Nate's house at seven-thirty after taking a rushed shower and dressing in a hurry. She had picked out a short black dress with sexy lingerie with the possibility of an exciting night ahead. She hoped he wasn't going to send her away again at the end of the evening, wanting and needing.

On the drive to his home, she thought about last night and how attracted she was to him. Somehow just being around him made her want to please him. There was something about him that called to her in a way she'd never felt before.

After parking in his huge driveway, she went up to the house and rang the doorbell.

When he opened the door, he brought her into the entryway then smiled and kissed her. She sighed into the kiss, enjoying the power and mastery of it.

"I'm glad you're here," he murmured as he drew back. "Have you eaten?"

She nodded. "I had something a little while ago."

"Would you like a drink?" he asked.

"Sure." She could use something to settle her nerves a bit.

After he put her coat into the closet, he escorted her to his modern family room. He went to a wet bar in one corner and she paused in the middle of the room. An enormous television screen took up one side of the room and the furnishings were cherry wood, the leather couches and chairs overstuffed.

"Have a seat." He bent down and she assumed he was looking in a small fridge. "What would you like to drink?"

She settled on the couch. "I'll go with white wine if you have it."

He picked out a chardonnay and poured them each a glass before he settled on the couch with her.

It wasn't long before she relaxed and found herself laughing and talking. It wasn't so much the wine as it was the company. She really enjoyed being around him.

"I promised you that I had a few ideas in store for you," he said after they had been talking for a while. "Are you ready to see?"

He escorted her upstairs to his sitting room and brought her around to face him. He brought her into his arms and kissed her. His kiss was fierce and hungry and almost scared her with its intensity.

When he drew away, he took her hand and led her to an antique table along one wall and her belly flip-flopped. He had laid out things along the table that made her wonder what he had in mind. There was a blindfold, a ball gag, a spandex hood, wrist and ankle cuffs, a collar, a paddle, a flogger, a butt plug, and some kind of harness.

He turned back to her and took her in his arms. "You know what I want to do to you, don't you?" he said in a low voice.

She nodded. "I think so."

As he held her tight, he kissed her again, a kiss that melted her to her toes.

He moved one of his hands down her back, along the zipper from her neck to the base of her spine and back again and her skin tingled wherever he touched her.

She found herself breathing harder and she felt a combination of excitement and fear. What was he going to do? Did he plan to use everything on the table on her?

He broke the kiss, raised his head, and looked into her eyes. "Tell me what you want."

"I want you to take control." The words just came out easily. "Total control. I want you to use me for your pleasure."

"I usually take it slow but I can't believe the energy you have," he said. "You're sure? Once I get started I'll push you to your very limits."

She took a deep breath and nodded. "Yes."

Nate gave her a sensual smile as he pulled down the zipper to her little black dress. Heat rose inside of her as he moved his hands over her ass and clenched the dress's hem. He drew the dress up over her hips then ran his hands over her silky panties.

"These feel so nice," he murmured as he massaged her ass through her panties. "I want to see them."

Her heart beat faster and she reached up to one shoulder of her dress and she started to slip her arm out of the sleeve. He helped her move the dress down over her black corset and slid it over body until it dropped to the floor and she stepped out of it. Now she wore only the corset, panties, thigh-high stockings, and her high heels.

"You are amazing." He brushed his hands over the tops of her breasts that were pushed together by the corset and that gave her remarkable cleavage. He moved his mouth to hers as he pressed his body against her.

As they kissed, his fingers found the corset's ties at the back and he loosened them. He raised his head and her heart thumped as he made the corset loose enough to pull over her head and set aside.

She almost couldn't believe that she was doing this so soon after seeing him again. One day and here she was, almost naked. There was something about him. She wanted him and didn't want to wait any longer. She had to have him take control.

"I love that you have them pierced." He looked at her nipple rings, his gaze even hotter now. He pinched her nipples then lowered his head and licked her nipple and the ring.

She rested her hands on his shoulders, tilted her head back, and reveled in the feeling of him licking and sucking her nipples. The rings made them even more sensitive and she grew wetter between her thighs.

He smoothed his hand down her belly to the ring at her belly button and he tugged on it. "Love it."

She gave a soft sound of pleasure. It felt like the ring was attached directly to her clit.

"Kick off your heels." He pinched her nipples and she hurried to obey and stepped out of her high heels, making her even shorter compared to his height.

"I'm going to leave these on." He moved his hand away from her belly ring and stroked her stockings at her thighs.

He looked at her, clearly waiting for permission. She swallowed then nodded and he smiled and slipped his fingers into the waistband of her panties and pushed them over her hips and down to the floor, too. He kissed her again as he tugged hard on her nipple rings.

Her eyes watered a little, but she loved the feel of him taking control.

He guided her to a couch and had her stand in front of it. The couch was a divan, with no back to it, only cushions on one end. "Stay right here," he commanded.

She watched as he went just steps away to the table with all of the items he had shown her.

When he returned he was carrying the leather wrist and ankle cuffs along with the collar and a couple of locks, and he set them on the couch beside her.

Nervousness swirled through her belly as well as a thrill that she was doing something so incredibly naughty and kinky with him already. It was like she couldn't stop herself. The excitement was intoxicating.

His fingertips brushed her skin as he moved her hair out of the way then fastened the collar around her neck. It was a wide collar with numerous rings on it. He lowered his head and moved his lips along her chin to her mouth and kissed her. He tasted so good, felt so good, and she loved his scent. Warm, masculine.

She wanted him to remove his clothing, but at the same time there was something erotic about being naked while her Dom was dressed. Still she hoped he would take off his clothes at some point. With his shirt on he was hot. She could only imagine what he would look like with nothing on.

He drew away and took one of her wrists in his hand, brought it to his mouth, and pressed his lips against her skin, causing her to shiver. He took a cuff and buckled it onto her wrist, making sure it was snug. There would be no slipping out of that cuff. He grasped her other hand and brushed his lips over her knuckles before fastening a cuff firmly around that wrist.

His gaze held hers as he rubbed her nipple between his thumb and forefinger, pressing against the ring. The sensation was exquisite. He brushed his lips over hers.

Gently he pushed down on her shoulders telling her he wanted her to sit on the couch. The cloth felt soft beneath her bare ass. He went down on one knee and took one of her feet and rested it on his thigh as he fastened a leather cuff around her ankle. The second cuff was secured next and then he lowered her foot to the floor and placed his palms on her thighs. His hands felt warm and were so close to the juncture of her thighs that she ached for his touch.

"Stand." He took one of her hands and brought her to her feet as he stood. "I want you to turn around and bend over, your palms on the couch, and your legs spread."

She obeyed him, feeling unbelievably hot as she braced her hands with her ass up, the air caressing her between her thighs.

He left and she heard the rustle of clothing, then felt his presence behind her when he returned. He grabbed her by her hips and caressed his cock against her ass. She let out a soft moan at the feel of his erection, already wanting him inside of her.

Something cool pressed against her anus and she realized what he was going to do—slide the butt plug into her ass. She tried to relax, knowing from what little experience she had that it would be easier if she did.

When the plug was fully in, she breathed a sigh of relief and also of pleasure as she felt the fullness. She wanted it. Had to have it. Like he was some kind of addiction she had and she needed to feed it.

"How does that feel?" He rubbed her butt cheeks as he spoke.

"Good." She let herself enjoy the sensation as he used the harness she'd seen to strap in the plug so that it would stay in.

He didn't tell her to get up so she remained bent over, waiting for his instructions. The plug started to vibrate and she cried out in surprise. When she had seen it on the table she'd had no idea it was a vibrating plug. He gave a soft laugh and rubbed her ass again. The vibrations stopped and she let out slow breath.

He helped her straighten then turn, and she got her first look at him naked. He nearly took her breath away.

"You're gorgeous," she said as she drank in his incredible physique, every muscle carved to perfection beneath smooth tanned skin. He wasn't body-builder muscular, but it was obvious he worked out and the fact that he was into mixed martial arts was easy to see.

And his cock… Big and thick enough to fill her completely.

"Lie on the couch." He eased her down so that she could sit on the couch then lie back and rest against the cushions. "Don't move."

The plug went even deeper from the pressure of lying on her backside and she enjoyed the feeling that it gave her as she waited.

He took three steps to the wardrobe. This time he brought back silver chain. She watched as he took lengths of chain and secured them around the wooden legs of the backless couch. Then he took the chains and clipped them to her cuffs so that her wrists and ankles were chained down. There was something intimidating about hearing the rattle of chain as he secured her.

Everything was in his hands now and she was at his mercy. She bit her lower lip at the thought that there was no getting out of the cuffs and chains. No escape.

"Let's pick out a safe word," he said. "I don't think you'll need it, but it's always best to have one."

She nodded. "How about something easy like 'medical'?"

"Medical it is."

When he had her chained to the couch, he stepped away again and went back to the wardrobe.

When he returned, he was carrying the violet wand. She wasn't sure if he was going to use the warm fuzzy feeling or give her a shock, so she found herself a little uneasy yet excited at the same time.

The globe flashed brilliant violet light and at the same time electricity shot through her arm. She jumped at the shock.

"I'll consider going easy on you." He moved the wand away. "Providing you can be quiet while I enjoy using this." He raised an eyebrow. "Think you can do that?"

"Yes." She nodded. "I can be quiet.."

He gave her a look that was sensual but dominant.

She nodded and bit the inside of her cheek. Was she going to regret telling him that she wanted her limits tested? Was he going to do just that with the violet wand?

He brought the wand near her fingertips and she tensed. Then he rolled the wand up her arm and the tension eased out of her. He moved the wand away, teasing her with it by letting her watch the globe without bringing it too close to her skin.

Even as she didn't want to be shocked, she loved that he was in control and doing what he wanted with her. That in itself was a complete turn on.

Still, she held her breath as he brought it down close enough to zap her toes but slowly and sensually slid the bulb along the soles of her feet..

"You're being a very good girl." He gave her a sensual smile. He brushed his lips over hers then moved his free hand to her mound. He slipped his fingers into her wet folds and she barely held back a moan. Then he moved his hand away from her clit and shocked her at the back of her knee.

She almost lost it that time and she bit the inside of her cheek. He'd caught her off guard and she'd had such a hard time keeping herself from screaming..

He touched her nipple with his fingertips, She jumped as if his hand was electric and he was about to give her a powerful shock.

To her relief he just pulled on her nipple ring and didn't shock her.

He smiled and lowered the wand toward her bellybutton and its ring. She tensed, her eyes wide. He held it high above her navel as he looked at her, but then she felt a measure of relief as he moved it away then caressed her belly with the globe, filling her body with warmth. Then he turned off the wand and set it aside.

"Good girl." He smiled and kissed her before meeting her gaze. "This time I was teasing. I wanted to show you that I can do whatever I want. You are powerless. There will come a time when I will really use it on you, but not now."

She watched as he rose and she took in how incredible he looked. His body would be firm and solid against hers, his hips fitting perfectly between her thighs. His cock would feel so good inside of her. Her nipples were hard and she ached between her thighs as she imagined him taking her.

"Are you ready for more?" he asked.

Being used for his pleasure heightened every sensation she'd been feeling. It might scare her at times, but she loved that he loved it.

"Yes," she said.

"Good answer."

He unchained her then had her turn and lie vertically on the backless couch so that she was hanging over it with her ass in the air again. He splayed her wide, reattaching her cuffs to the chains, only this time one wrist cuff was chained to the head of the couch while the other was secured to the bottom. He did the same with each ankle cuff.

When he finished, he showed her a ball gag. "I'm going to use this on you. Since you won't be able to say your safe word, you need a safe sound. Do this if you want me to stop."

He made a muffled but distinct sound. She copied it and he gave her a nod of approval. Then he took the ball gag and pushed it into her mouth, causing her jaws to stretch, and he buckled the strap behind her head. He slipped a blindfold around her head and everything went dark.

"Love how you look like this." He palmed her ass cheeks before slipping his fingers into her folds and stroking her clit. She gasped in surprise then gave a soft moan of pleasure. "You're so wet."

Not being able to see made her all the more aware of what he was doing and it enhanced what she was feeling.

He moved his fingers away and she waited to find out what he would do to her next, as she ached from need made even more powerful by his touch.

A hard swat to her ass had her crying out behind her ball gag. Another swat and another followed as he spanked her. She cried out with every slap of his hand against her soft flesh.

"Did you forget how to be quiet?" He spanked her again.

She shook her head.

"Prove it," he said.

Another hard swat and she fought to hold in the sounds as she bit down on the ball in her mouth.

Her eyes watered as her backside stung. He rubbed her ass cheeks, the sting turning into a warm burn.

She heard a low hum and then felt the most powerful vibration she had ever experienced against her pussy.

"This is a Hitachi." He moved the vibrator over her clit and down then up again. "I can make you come as many times as I want you to and there's nothing you can do."

She couldn't stop squirming as he held the Hitachi to her clit. With the plug in her ass and the vibrations on her clit, the sensations were incredible. An orgasm rushed toward her, so fast and sudden that there was no holding back. She cried out behind her gag as she came, her body jerking and heat flushing over her body.

He moved the incredo-vibrator away and she relaxed into her orgasm. But then her butt plug started vibrating and he pressed the Hitachi to her clit again.

She had never come so fast or hard with a second orgasm as she did right then. Her body hadn't even recovered from the first climax and she was screaming again.

Her body was so sensitized the sensations magnified, that she knew she couldn't handle anymore. When he drew the vibrator away and the butt plug stopped vibrating, her body sagged in relief.

He put the Hitachi against her clit again.

"Nooo." She tried to beg him to stop but it came out nothing more than a muffled moan.

She came within seconds. She trembled with the sensations that had her nearly weeping. It was almost too much to take.

The hum of the vibrator stopped but she still begged him in her mind not to do it again. She didn't know if she could survive another orgasm. The pleasure was too intense.

She heard another sound, this one like a package opening, and she wondered what he was going to do next.

His cock pressed against her backside and he grabbed her hips. Before she had a chance catch her breath, he slammed his cock inside her.

He fucked her hard, the feeling so good as he drove in and out. The ass plug and his cock made her feel beyond incredible.

At the same time she was so sensitive that every movement he made took her that much closer to pushing her over the edge again.

Then the butt plug started vibrating and she couldn't hold back any longer.

Her fourth orgasm took over her body. Behind her blindfold, light seemed to spark in the darkness. She felt almost semi-conscious from so many orgasms in such a short period of time. Her core contracted around his cock, every spasm sending shockwaves through her.

He kept driving in and out of her, taking her hard and fast. She continued to ride the wave of her last orgasm, afraid she was going to pass out from too much pleasure.

Then he shouted and he pumped in and out several more times as she felt his cock pulsating inside her. He groaned as he finally stopped and she gave a mental sigh and went completely limp with exhaustion.

He braced himself above her and she felt his cock still thick inside of her. She heard the sound of him breathing over her shoulder before he drew out of her and took off her blindfold.

The light seemed bright despite the room's fairly low lighting and she had to blink away the stars still sparking behind her eyes. She felt almost dizzy.

"That was beautiful," he said as he unbuckled the ball gag. "Seeing you come so many times was amazing."

She groaned. "I thought I'd die of too much pleasure."

He gave a soft laugh. "You think that was great. Just wait until you see what

I have in store for you next time."

The thought of a next time made her smile as he unchained her. When she was free of the chains, he helped her so that she was sitting on the couch and he sat facing her. She felt dizzy and her mind seemed to spin.

She leaned against him and rested her head against his chest as he wrapped his arm around her shoulder, holding her close. "That was incredible," she said.

He kissed the top of her head. "There's plenty more where that came from."

She managed a laugh. "I don't know if I can survive you."

"Believe me." He squeezed her tightly to him. "You can and you will."

"Yes, sir," She felt herself beginning to drift off, feeling so sated and exhausted. "Just give me a chance to recuperate."

He stood and brought her up with him, then scooped her up into his arms and started toward the doorway to his bedroom. His bed was large with a metal frame built around it as if the bed should have a canopy. He settled her on the mattress then moved around to the other side and slid onto the bed next to her.

He drew her into his arms and held her close and she sighed with pleasure. It felt so good to be in his arms. His fingertips were warm against her skin as he caressed her and his masculine scent swept over her. She loved it.

With a smile she snuggled into his embrace. He held her like he really cared about her and he kissed the top of her head and squeezed her tighter to him.

"Do you have to work at the hospital tomorrow?" he asked.

She shook her head and bumped his chin with the movement. "I have Sunday off."

"Good." He sounded genuinely pleased. "I think I can come up with something fun for us to do if you're game."

"I am very game." She gave sigh as she found herself slipping away, unable to stay awake much longer.

"Sleep well," he said as he stroked hair from her face.

"Mmmmm," was all she managed before she was off to dreamland.

Kelley woke up to a sensual kiss and Nate between her thighs. She felt his cock, hard against her folds.

When their gazes met, he took her wrists and pinned them over her head with one hand then positioned his cock at her core.

"I'm going to fuck you." His voice was low and deliberate. "I want to be inside of you."

She nodded. "Please."

He thrust inside of her and she gasped at the sudden fullness. He rocked between her thighs and she wrapped her legs around his waist and held him to her.

She loved how he was taking her. Just a good, hard fuck. No toys, only the two of them sharing this moment together.

A climax built inside of her and the harder he thrust the faster it charged toward her. When it exploded within her it was colors and light and something more than she had ever felt before.

He came just moments after she did and he let out a restrained growl as his cock throbbed inside of her. As she came down from her orgasm high he kissed her. A long, lingering kiss. Then he rolled onto his back with her snuggled against him, her head on his chest, and she drifted away.

Chapter 4

"I want to take care of you," was what Nate told her the following morning—which was how she found herself on a shopping spree that afternoon. A shopping spree that he had insisted on.

Kelley sat across from him on the outside terrace of a deli after they finished shopping for lingerie. "Can't wait to see you in that red and black corset and stockings," he said after taking a bite of his sandwich.

She pointed her soupspoon at him. "You just saw me in it."

"For about two minutes." He gave her a sexy smile. "I can't wait to see it on you again, this time just for me."

She smiled as she dipped her spoon into her vegetable soup. "I haven't had so much fun in ages."

It wasn't having a man buy her clothes and other things. It was because he was a man who wanted to take care of her. A man who made her feel special.

All the responsibilities she had in her life she was able to set aside to spend time with him. She would have to return to reality soon enough. For now she was thoroughly enjoying her time with him.

"I especially like the stockings with the line going up the back of the leg," he said. "Hot."

"You're such a man." She laughed. "I bet you're looking even more forward to seeing me *out* of it, too."

He grinned. "Are you ready to head on out?"

She raised an eyebrow. "In a hurry for something?"

"Who? Me?" He gave her an innocent look. "Of course not, but if you just happen to be done I say we head straight for my place and you climb right into that outfit."

"Hmmm." She pretended to think about it as she set her spoon in her empty bowl then gave him a quick grin. "You're on."

On the way back to his home in his car, they laughed and talked. It was easy being with him and sharing things about her life that she didn't share with anyone else.

"How is your mom?" he asked. That first night in the car she had told him that her mother was ill.

"I called her on my cell phone yesterday on my way to your house," she said. "She seems to be doing better."

"Good." He looked at her then moved his gaze back to the road. "I'm glad to hear that."

"You really care, don't you," she said.

He glanced back at her. "Just because I'm a Dom who likes BDSM doesn't make me heartless."

She smiled. "Heartless you are not."

He answered her questions, too, about how his life was growing up in the D.C. area, his family, and his career.

She liked that they didn't spend all of their time talking about BDSM play. Other than the two times she had shared her interests with him, and the first time they played, they hadn't talked about it.

When they arrived at his home, he carried in the bags of lingerie and some really cute dresses that he had insisted on buying for her. He had great taste and everything that he'd had her try on she'd loved.

They went upstairs to his bedroom and he set all of the packages along one wall and she laughed at how many bags there were. "This is ridiculous," she said as she looked from the bags to him. "I can't believe we did that much shopping."

"I can." He gave her a soft kiss. "I loved doing it with you."

She smiled. "Now to put on something sexy for you."

He moved behind her, brushed her hair aside, and kissed the back of her neck. "Wear the red and black."

"Okay." She shivered at the feel of his lips against her skin. "Just give me a moment."

"Meet me in my sitting room when you're ready." He left and closed the bedroom door behind him.

She went through the bags and pushed aside black, royal blue, fuchsia pink, and purple lingerie before locating the red and black. She also found the stockings with the line up the back.

The corset was pretty with red lace over red satin, and it was trimmed with black piping and black satin. It pushed her breasts together in a most enticing way that made her feel even more feminine and sexy. The matching red and black panties were smooth and silky feeling. One at a time she slid on the stockings, rolling them up to her thighs, careful to keep the seam straight.

When she was dressed, she pressed her hand to her belly to settle the butterflies, then opened the door and walked into the sitting room A thrill went through her as she saw him. He filled out a collared shirt and jeans so well.

"You are gorgeous." His eyes seemed to be a darker green as he took her in. "Come here." He motioned for her to go to him. When she reached him, he took her into his arms and kissed her.

She sighed into the kiss, loving the feel of his lips and tongue against hers and she loved his taste. She slid her arms around his neck as he kissed her and drank in his masculine scent. It drew her in like nothing else could.

He eased his hands up and down her sides, caressing the satin corset, then moved his palms down to her panties and cupped her ass. He pressed her hard against him and thrills went through her belly as she felt the hard ridge of his cock.

When he raised his head and broke the kiss, she tilted her head back to meet his gaze. She smiled as he stroked hair from her face. "Let me see all of you." He stepped back and turned her around. "Just beautiful."

He brought her around to face him and she smiled. "I love the lingerie.

Thank you."

"I have plans for you," he murmured and glanced beside them at the table that he had put items on yesterday.

A shiver went through her. Tonight, on it were several things that he had used on her, like the cuffs and collar, but there were a few other items. A roll of Saran wrap, nipple clamps, surgical scissors, and a different kind of butt plug than what he'd used yesterday. What would he use the plastic wrap for? If he used it.

"Seems a shame to undress you." He brushed her hair over her shoulders. "But I need to see all of you for what I'm going to do."

He moved his fingers to her waist and unzipped the side zipper then removed the corset and laid it on over a chair. Slowly he pushed down her panties and she stepped out of them. He reached for the collar then slid it around her neck and buckled it, then secured each leather cuff at her wrists before clipping the cuffs together.

When he was finished, he took her by her upper arm and moved her to stand by the backless couch. "Wait here."

She watched him as he stripped out of his clothing. He looked so hot as he straightened and she got a good look at his body again. There was much power and confidence in his bearing that turned her on as much as his muscular form did. And what a nice package he had.

After he finished undressing, he moved back to the table then returned, carrying the huge roll of Saran Wrap. "Are you familiar with using plastic wrap for mummification?"

"No." She shook her head starting to feel a little trepidation. "I've never been mummified.

"There are a lot of ways to mummify, and plastic wrap is one of the ways. It's a form of edge play." He touched the side of her leg. "Stand still, feet together, arms at your sides."

She did as he told her and he knelt and began wrapping the plastic around her ankles. Her heart thumped a little harder as he wound it around and around and around. He took his time, slowly wrapping her. By the time he reached her knees, there was no way she could move. He had her hold up her arms then wrapped the plastic over her hips and around her waist.

He stopped to play with the ring at her bellybutton, darting his tongue inside. It felt like her bellybutton was attached to the place between her thighs and it sent tingling sensations throughout her. Then he told her to put her arms at her sides and pinned them to her with the wrap.

The more snug the wrap became the more her heart pounded. She tried to move her legs and arms but she couldn't budge them. She couldn't even wiggle her fingers.

When he got to just below her breasts, warmth rolled over her as he lowered his head and kissed her while at the same time he played with her nipple rings with one hand. His kisses were delicious and made her feel somehow secure, and his touch caused her to squirm with need.

"Your skin is so soft." He ran his lips along her jaw, causing her to shiver with desire.

He drew back. "Take a deep breath and expand your chest. It will help you breathe easier when I'm done."

"Okay." She inhaled and waited while he continued with the wrap.

Keeping a slow pace, he continued wrapping the plastic around her, reaching her shoulders then moving on to her neck.

As he began wrapping her face, both fear and excitement rolled into one big ball in her belly. He made sure she could breathe, leaving all her mouth and her nose uncovered. The wrap felt strange around her head and she closed her eyes right before plastic covered them. When she opened them again it was distorted, like looking through shattered glass.

It was amazing how much she loved the confinement. It felt secure yet erotic, too, knowing that she was naked and he could see her through the wrap.

"I'm going to lay you down on the couch now," he said.

"Okay." She couldn't nod but she was glad she could talk

The next thing she knew, he had lowered her so that she was lying on her back on the couch, snug in her own world. She felt the smooth edge of the surgical scissors when he cut slits where her breasts were and the air cooled her nipples. Then something tugged on her nipple rings and pain shot through her causing her to give a little cry, mostly from surprise.

She enjoyed the cocoon-like feeling and imagined that she was a butterfly that would break free at any moment. She loved the helpless feeling it gave her.

A tug and then she felt the surgical scissors again, this time at her mound and a little below, exposing her there. He slipped his fingers into her folds and she gave a moan as he stroked her wetness.

He straddled her and moved up so that she could feel him right at her upper shoulders. Then he pushed his cock through the opening where her mouth was and she took him into her mouth. He slowly pumped his hips, moving his cock in and out of her mouth. She sucked him, loving the way he had taken control of her and now was using her for his pleasure.

She was a toy to him now. A plaything that he could use however he wanted to. She loved it.

He pulled his cock out of her mouth then moved down and brought his mouth to hers and kissed her as he played with her one of her breasts and the nipple ring on it.

"How are you doing?" he murmured when he drew away. "How do you like being my little prisoner?"

"I love it," she said and he kissed her again before moving down her body.

He reached her pussy and licked. She gasped and moaned as he licked and sucked her.

It felt so good, and somehow more intense with her locked away, unable to move anything but her mouth. The sensations caused her body to shake with need as her climax came closer and closer. It grew and grew and she knew she was close to losing it.

Her orgasm burst through her, sending a flush of heat throughout her body. Pleasure radiated from between her thighs to her belly and even through her mind, so much that she didn't think she'd ever come down from the high.

When she started to come down she felt him using the scissors to cut way the wrap from her lower half. When the wrap was off from the waist down, he pressed her legs apart and spread her thighs.

"I'm going to fuck you." He moved his cock to the entrance to her core. "I want you to experience my control over you."

She wiggled her lower half. "Yes, please."

He drove his cock inside of her. She cried out with pleasure at the feel of him moving in and out while she was still partially locked away in her cocoon. He fucked her slowly, easing in and out of her body, drawing out everything. Through the wrap she could only see the distorted image of him and she loved not being able to see him while he took her.

Another orgasm started to rise within her. Then out of nowhere it hit her and she came hard. It felt like she was flying as she cried out and she didn't know if she would come back down.

"That's it." His voice was rough as he continued pumping his hips against hers. "I love to hear you when you come."

He gave a low growl and then she felt the throb of his cock inside of her as he came. He pressed his hips tight to hers and she heard the sound of his breathing.

A few moments later he eased off of her. "I'm going to cut away the rest of the wrap."

She waited, her entire body relaxed, as he took care of the plastic. The air chilled her a little as the wrap fell away.

After being mummified, and after the incredible orgasm, she felt a bit light headed, but that faded a few moments later.

He pulled the rest of the wrap away from her face. "How was that?"

"Incredible." She smiled up at him. "I loved it."

He eased onto the couch beside her and brought her into his arms and held her.

Chapter 5

Kelley rested her head against Nate's shoulder. He had his arm around her as they watched sea lions off the pier and looked out on San Francisco Bay. The wind off the bay was biting and his embrace helped to warm her.

The past two months had gone by in a whirlwind. Nate had completely taken her in with his caring, his dominance, and how much he wanted to take care of her.

And that was nice. Nothing else in her life seemed to slow down enough to allow her to take a step back. Demands of the job and of her position of head nurse kept her beyond busy. She had to deal with the mess her ex had left her finances in and she had to solve squabbles between her adult siblings who often didn't act like adults.

But Nate was always there for her. He gave her advice when she needed it and helped her invest her money in the right places, which was already making it easier to pay off her ex's debt. She knew Nate would have paid off the debt for her, but she would never allow him to do that. It was her responsibility, and she always took care of her responsibilities.

He made her happy. She loved how he took control and took away having to make decisions when she was away from the other things in her life. He picked out what they ate, what they did, what he liked her to wear, and other things. If she had balked at anything, she knew he would have backed off, but he knew how much she loved it.

The sea lions' barking brought her attention back to them and she smiled. "Noisy, aren't they?" she said. "Love watching them."

He squeezed her shoulders. "Ready for dinner?"

"Mmmm." She nodded and looked up at him. "I could really go for some clam chowder and sourdough bread."

"We'll have crab, too." He started to guide her away from the pier.

"Sounds wonderful."

They took the trolley then headed to their hotel room at the St. Francis in Union Square to change into something nicer for dinner than the jeans and shirts they'd been wearing. For her he picked out her emerald green corset, garters, and panties, along with nude stockings to go under the black dress he'd selected.

They had a fantastic dinner along with a couple glasses of wine at a fabulous seafood restaurant on Polk Street.

After chocolate mousse for dessert, Nate covered her hand on the tabletop. "I don't know what it is about you, but you've captured me. I'm completely taken with you."

Kelley turned her hand up so that they were holding hands. "I feel the same way."

"I've never felt this way with anyone." His gaze was serious. "I enjoy our time together, our talks, our interests."

A pleasant warmth filled her belly. "It feels we've known each other forever."

"It was love at first sight." He searched her gaze. "Now it's love at the sixty-fifth sight."

Her whole body was now enveloped in heat. "It was and is for me, too."

He leaned close and kissed her. She didn't care if they were in the middle of a restaurant. She kissed him back with just as much intensity and passion as he gave.

When they parted, they held each other's gaze.

"You're better than what I dreamed about," she said softly.

He smiled. "Let's head home for some real live dreams."

Also by Cheyenne McCray

From St. Martin's Press:

"Night Tracker" Series
Demons Not Included
No Werewolves Allowed
Vampires Not Invited
Zombies Sold Separately
Vampires Dead Ahead

"Magic" Series
Forbidden Magic
Seduced by Magic
Wicked Magic
Shadow Magic
Dark Magic

Single Title
Moving Target
Chosen Prey

Anthologies
No Rest for the Witches
Real Men Last All Night
Legally Hot
Chicks Kick Butt
Hotter than Hell
Mammoth Book of Paranormal Romances
Mammoth Book of Special Ops Romances

Cheyenne writing as Jaymie Holland

Excerpt… *Roping your Heart*

Cheyenne McCray

"I guess that will have to do for today." Cat brushed her hair out of her eyes as she started to organize the papers on Blake's desk. "We can work on this more another day." She glanced from the papers to him. He was sitting in the chair beside her now, in front of the desk. "My schedule is still pretty open," she said. "When is a good time for us to get together again?"

He was studying her, his gaze so intense that she felt the heat of it on her skin. "Friday night at seven," he said.

"Friday night?" It took a moment to register that he was asking her out. "Oh." She hesitated and he kept looking at her with that same dark look. "I— sure."

She felt warning bells going off in her head, but too late. It wasn't good to spend so much time with the man. She was going to fall head over heels for him again.

If she hadn't already.

She looked away from the intensity of his gaze and got to her feet. From her peripheral vision she saw him stand, then felt the heat of his body when he moved closer to her.

"I think we made pretty good progress." Her heart pounded faster and she busied herself with making each stack on the desktop perfectly neat. "We might be able to get everything done in one more meeting." She rushed her words, feeling like she was babbling.

"KitCat." His voice was soft and she went still at the low, throbbing quality of it.

Slowly, she lifted her eyes to meet his. He was looking at her intently. Her lips parted, but she couldn't think of a thing to say.

He took her by the shoulders, bringing her face to face with him. "Damn, Cat. I don't know how much longer I can be around you without having you."

Her eyes widened and her lips parted. He wanted her?

He gripped her upper arms tighter, the pressure of his fingers almost hurting her. "Damn," he said again before he jerked her up against him and brought his mouth hard down on hers.

She gasped as he took control of her mouth, kissing her hard. It was more primal than the night before, almost wild. She didn't remember him kissing like this before. It was as if the man he had been before had matured, becoming more dominant and decisive. She knew he'd decided he was going to have her. If she said no, he'd let her go, but she didn't want to say no. She wanted him.

A groan rose up in him and she followed his lead, letting him take the kiss to a level of passion she'd never experienced before. He released her shoulders and slid his hands over her blouse to her waist then cupped her ass and pulled her up tight to him. The feel of his erection against her belly sent fire through her straight between her thighs.

She breathed in his clean, masculine scent and reveled in his taste and the feel of his hands on her. She moved her hands up his chest, feeling the soft cotton of his T-shirt beneath her palms, and then she wrapped her arms around his neck and pressed her breasts against him.

When he broke the kiss, he moved his lips along her jawline to her throat. His stubble felt rough against her skin but something about the sandpapery feel of it made her even more excited.

"I'm not going to be able to help myself with you." He groaned as he pulled her short skirt above her ass and felt the silky panties underneath. The heat of his palms burned through the thin material to her skin and it almost felt like she was wearing nothing at all. "Hell, you'd better tell me now if you want to stop."

"Don't stop." She moaned, as he trailed his lips and tongue from the hollow of her throat to the V in her blouse.

He whirled her so that she was backed up against the desk and she had to brace her hands on the stacks of papers to either side of her in order to balance herself. She arched her back as he moved his hands to the buttons on her blouse. His big fingers fumbled with the buttons and he gave a low growl and grasped the material.

Buttons flew and she gasped as he tore the blouse open. She heard the ping of buttons but was barely conscious of them as he pushed her blouse over her shoulders and down her arms before she shook it the rest of the way off.

Excerpt... *Branded for You*

Cheyenne McCray

The afternoon was cooling off as it turned to dusk and then darkness descended on them. They each grabbed a light sweat jacket from the camper and slipped them on.

Ryan took a couple of steaks out of the cooler to cook over the fire. Megan sliced the potatoes and wrapped them in foil with butter and seasonings and put them in the coals first. Ryan buttered, salted, and peppered the corn on the cob and wrapped them in foil, too. When it was time, they placed the corn along the edge of the fire. Ryan had cored out the onion and put butter in the center and wrapped it in foil and put it in the coals, as well. The steaks went on last, when everything else was just about finished cooking.

When it was ready, they sat on the camping chairs in front of the fire and ate dinner.

"This is unbelievable," Megan said with a smile.

Firelight flickered on her pretty features, casting shadows in the darkness as they ate. He thought about what he'd said to her earlier.

"I might be falling for you, Meg."

He didn't regret his words. He'd dated a lot of women in the past but there'd just been something missing. Something intangible that he hadn't been able to name.

He'd never been a love 'em and leave 'em kind of guy, but some thought so. He just wasn't going to hang in there with someone if he knew she wasn't the right one.

He'd never felt the same way with anyone that he did with Megan.

Last night he'd taken her hard and rough, and the memory caused his groin to ache. Damn she'd been amazing. But she needed to know that he wanted more from her than a night of good, hard sex.

When they finished dinner and had cleaned up, he brought a blanket from the camper and handed it to her before he put out the fire. After he extinguished the fire, he lit a candle within a glass and metal hurricane lantern.

He took her by the hand. "I've got something I want to show you." Her hand was warm in his.

She smiled up at him, her smile causing something deep inside him to stir. He led her into the forest, candlelight from the hurricane lantern lighting the way. The candlelight was much gentler than a regular camping lantern and the shadows from it bounced from tree to tree.

"I saw a place somewhere over here," he murmured as they walked through the forest then came to a stop. "Here we go."

A small clearing lay on the other side of a fallen tree, a bed of leaves at the center of the clearing. They stepped over the tree and then he found a sturdy place to set the hurricane before taking the blanket from Megan and spreading it out on the leaves.

He slipped out of his jacket and set it on the fallen tree. "I'll keep you warm," he said as he held out his hand.

She looked up at him, slid off her sweat jacket, handed it to him and he set it on top of his own.

He sat on the blanket and beckoned to her. She eased onto her knees beside him and he cupped her face in his hands and lowered his head and kissed her.

Her kiss was sweet and his desire for her kicked into full gear. He wanted to take her hard again, right now. But more importantly, he wanted to show her that it wasn't only about rough sex with him. It was all about her.

When he drew away from the kiss, her lips were parted, hunger in her pretty green eyes.

"You're an incredible woman." He brushed his thumb over her lips, which trembled beneath his touch. "I've loved every minute of this weekend."

"So have I," she said, her voice just above a whisper. "I wish it didn't have to end."

"It doesn't." He nuzzled her hair that was silky now that it had dried. "When we return, we just pick right back up where we left off."

She smiled and he kissed her again. She felt so soft and warm in his arms. He slid his hand under her T-shirt, pleased she didn't have her bra on as he cupped her bare breast and rubbed his thumb over her nipple. He watched her expression as her lips parted and her eyes grew dark with need.

He drew the T-shirt over her head and set it on the fallen tree. Candlelight flickered, gently touching her bare shoulders and chest.

"You know how much I love your body and how beautiful I think you are," he murmured before stroking her nipples with the back of his hand.

He cupped her breasts, feeling their weight in his hands before he lowered his head and sucked a nipple.

She gasped and leaned back so that her hands were braced behind her on the blanket, her back arched so that he had better access to her breasts. He pressed them together and moved his mouth from one to the other, sucking one nipple before moving his mouth to the other one. Her nipples were large and hard and he loved sucking on them.

"I want you on your back, looking at me." He adjusted her so that she was lying on the blanket. Her eyes glittered in the light, desire on her features.

He was surprised at how she made him want to go slow with her, to be gentle and show her how much he cared. She stirred things inside him he'd never felt with another woman.

Excerpt... *Lingerie and Lariats*

Cheyenne McCray

When they'd finished dinner and washed up the dishes, she walked with him to the living room. They paused and stood in the center of the room as he studied her and she met his eyes. Her belly flip-flopped at his intense gaze. He looked her as if she was a treasure he wanted to protect.

But at the same time he looked at her like a man who wanted a woman. A look of passion and need was in his gaze that couldn't be disguised.

He reached up and ran strands of her long hair through his fingers. "I want to kiss you, Renee."

She bit the inside of her lip as her own need expanded inside her. She slid her hands up his chest to his shoulders and offered him a smile. "I want you to."

His warm breath feathered across her lips as he lowered his mouth to hers. The intensity of the moment was filled with a kind of fire that made her burn inside.

Her eyelids fluttered closed as he brought his mouth to hers, and it was like magic sparked between them when their lips met. She felt as if her mind was spinning and stars glittered behind her eyes. She fell into the kiss, her head whirling, her heart pounding.

His taste made her want more of him and she made sounds of need and pleasure. He deepened the kiss and she gave a soft moan.

She reveled in his embrace, the feel of his hard chest against her breasts and the warmth and comfort of his arms around her. She strained to somehow get closer to him, to become a part of him.

A deep, rumbling groan rose up in him and he kissed her hard before drawing away. He still held her in his embrace and she loved the feeling of security she experienced in his arms.

She opened her eyes and stared up at him, her lips moist from his kiss, her breathing a little fast.

He gently brushed hair from her cheek as he looked down at her, and his expression turned serious. "I've wanted to kiss you from the moment I first saw you at the Cameron's place, but I shouldn't have done that. I don't want to take advantage of you in a vulnerable state."

For a long moment she looked up at him, studying the sea green of his eyes. "When I was a young girl, living with the Camerons, I had the biggest crush on you."

The corner of his mouth quirked into a smile. "Is that so?" he said in a lazy drawl.

She returned his smile. "When you saved my life, you became my hero as well as my crush."

"I thought you were pretty cute." He slid his fingers into her hair and cupped the back of her head. "And you've grown up to be one hell of a beautiful woman."

She placed her hands on his chest, reached up on her toes, and kissed him. His lips were firm and he returned her kiss, his kiss as hungry as hers. Searching, longing, and filled with desire. She gripped his shirt in her hands as she pressed her body tight to his. She didn't think she could get enough of him.

Judging by the hard ridge she felt against her belly, she knew he was as affected as she was by the moment.

He drew away again and she felt his rapid heartbeat against her palm and his chest rose and fell with the increased pace of his breathing.

"It was a mistake to kiss you because it only makes me want more. A lot more." He slid his fingers through her long, glossy hair. "I want so much more of you than that. But it's too soon."

She closed her eyes, letting her breathing slow. When she opened them again she found him watching her. Her voice seemed a little shaky. "You're right, it's too soon. All of this with Jerry has been so emotional. I'm feeling everything right now… Hate and anger for him, and strong feelings for you. But I shouldn't take things so fast no matter how right it feels with you." She brushed her fingers along his shirt collar. "And Dan, it feels so right."

"It feels unbelievably right." He lowered his head and gave her a firm, hard kiss then stepped back. Her palms slid down his chest and then he took her hands in his. "How about watching a movie and getting our minds off of certain things?"

"That sounds like a good idea." Not that she thought she could get her mind off of wanting to experience more with Dan. She gestured to the front door. "Why don't we watch the storm first?"

He took her small hand in his big one and they went outside onto the covered porch and closed the front door behind them. Patches of warm yellow light spilled from the house onto the porch.

The sky was dark, the occasional crack of lighting illuminating the trees and outbuildings for seconds before everything went dark again. The air smelled fresh and clean as wind pressed her clothing against her body and her hair rose up off her shoulders. A gust of wind sent a mist of wetness onto the porch and she smiled at the feel of warm summer rain on her skin.

As they watched the storm, he squeezed her hand and looked down at her. She met his gaze and smiled. They stood on the porch a while longer and she watched bolts of lightning slicing the sky as thunder rolled across the valley.

Meet Jaymie

Jaymie Holland is the romantic erotica alter-ego of New York Times and USA Today bestselling author Cheyenne McCray. Jaymie's work should always be handled with oven mitts!

Cheyenne's books have received multiple awards and nominations, including

*RT Book Reviews magazine's Reviewer's Choice awards for Best Erotic Romance of the year and Best Paranormal Action Adventure of the year

*Three "RT Book Reviews" nominations, including Best Erotic Romance, Best Romantic Suspense, and Best Paranormal Action Adventure.

*Golden Quill award for Best Erotic Romance

*The Road to Romance's Reviewer's Choice Award

*Gold Star Award from Just Erotic Romance Reviews

*CAPA award from The Romance Studio

Cheyenne grew up on a ranch in southeastern Arizona. She has been writing ever since she can remember, back to her kindergarten days when she penned her first poem. She always knew one day she would write novels, hoping her readers would get lost in the worlds she created, just as she experienced when she read some of her favorite books.

Chey has three sons, two dogs, and is an Arizona native who loves the desert, the sunshine, and the beautiful sunsets. Visit Chey's website and get all of the latest info at her website and meet up with her at Cheyenne McCray's Place on Facebook!

Manufactured by Amazon.ca
Bolton, ON

13597811R00168